THE SPIRIT
of a
RISING SUN

K. R. GALINDEZ

Authors 4 Authors Publishing
Mukilteo, WA, USA

Published by Authors 4 Authors Publishing
11700 Mukilteo Speedway Ste 201 PM 1044
Mukilteo, WA 98275
www.authors4authorspublishing.com

Library of Congress Control Number: 2021938497

E-book ISBN: 978-1-64477-070-2
Paperback ISBN: 978-1-64477-071-9
Audiobook ISBN: 978-1-64477-072-6

Edited by Renee Frey
Copyedited by Brandi Spencer

Cover design ©2021 Brandi Spencer. All rights reserved.
Interior design by Brandi Spencer

Authors 4 Authors Content Rating and copyright are set in Poppins. Titles and headings set in Cinzel. All other text is set in Garamond.

THE SPIRIT
of a
RISING SUN

K. R. GALINDEZ

Authors 4 Authors Content Rating

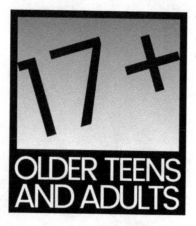

This title has been rated 17+, appropriate for older teens and adults, and contains:

- strong language
- graphic violence
- intense implied sex
- frequent alcohol use
- mild negative fantasy illicit drug use
- child trafficking

Please, keep the following in mind when using our rating system:

1. A content rating is not a measure of quality.

Great stories can be found for every audience. One book with many content warnings and another with none at all may be of equal depth and sophistication. Our ratings can work both ways: to avoid content or to find it.

2. Ratings are merely a tool.

For our young adult (YA) and children's titles, age ratings are generalized suggestions. For parents, our descriptive ratings can help you make informed decisions, but at the end of the day, only you know what kinds of content are appropriate for your individual child. This is why we provide details in addition to the general age rating.

For more information on our rating system, please, visit our Content Guide at:
www.authors4authorspublishing.com/books/ratings

DEDICATION

To my friend, Trey Gruber.
May your music play on and on.

TABLE OF CONTENTS

TABLE OF CONTENTS

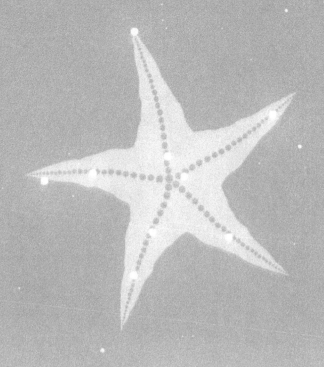

PROLOGUE

THE WASTES

The knight's face stung as the howling sandstorm behind the wagon came nearer. A pack of spectral Hellhounds chased close behind, their savage jaws dripping with blood and shadow.

"We've got to throw off more weight!" the driver screamed from the front of the wagon, his hands clinging to the reins of the frantic horses. Their hooves thundered on the cracked, arid land.

"We're not losing the mageware!" Yendra shouted. She clasped her arms as best as she could around the sides of the massive chest in the back of the wagon. Her raven-black hair fluttered in the wind as she wiped a sheet of gray dust from her eyes. She turned to the servant. "You—I order you to jump!" she commanded.

The servant's youthful eyes opened with disbelief. "Me? No. Are you crazy? Why not him? He's bigger!" he pointed his finger at the knight.

"You heard her." The knight lifted his hulking leg and kicked the servant's face.

Blood and teeth went flying. The young man tumbled into the Wastes amid plumes of dust. The Hellhounds butchered his soft flesh with glee. The gusts were so loud, no one heard his shrieks. No one cared. They got what they came for.

Yendra squinted and stared at the churning clouds tearing through the sky. "We need to go faster!" She wiped more dirt from her eyes and turned to the knight.

"We can open it and save the pieces," the knight said, his grisly voice buried by the howling gales. He opened the trunk's rusted latches.

"No." Yendra pulled back the chest. "It's too risky. We might lose a piece." She gazed into the chest at the broken sword. A large ruby shined on its hilt. With the whirlwind and the Hellhounds chasing them, they had no time to inspect it. If they were unlucky, it possessed no powers at all.

"We didn't come all the way to the Wastes for nothing," Yendra said. "We're not going to end up like all the *dead* magic hunters lying *dead* all over the desert. We're bringing the mageware back." She slammed the container shut and froze. "For years you've served our family well, and I thank you for that. But now, I order you to jump."

The knight narrowed his eyes. The wagon rocked against the ground.

"Go on then, jump!" Yendra said. "I order it!"

He turned his head and saw the Hellhounds were even closer than before. A crack of lightning swept through the storm. The knight took a deep breath, then reached for his ax.

Yendra fumed. She grabbed her dagger as the knight lunged at her. They wrestled and thrust their blades at one another as they desperately tried to keep the chest from sliding out. A sudden jolt sent them tumbling about the wagon. The trunk nearly fell from the back before the knight caught its handle. Yendra pounced on him again. The knight caught Yendra's wrist just before the dagger could pierce his throat. She shrieked and tried to drive the thin blade into his jugular.

"Sorry, Lady Yendra." A smirk crept up his stubbled face. "It's been my pleasure serving you." With a grunt, he threw Yendra from the wagon.

Her body tumbled into the dirt. The knight watched her crawl for a bare second on the cracked ground before the Hellhounds devoured her body. Her shriek pierced him louder than any dagger could have.

The knight grabbed the trunk and opened it. He picked up the broken pieces of the sword and began to slide the chest out the back when he noticed a small ragged scroll inside. He caught it just as the trunk fell and slammed into the sands. It burst into fragments of wood and metal. *What is this?*

"Xalos" was written at the top of the paper followed by several lines of script. There was a faded image of a winged, fiery demon who seemed to mock him. The wagon hit another bump as a gust of wind pulled the scroll from his hand. It disappeared into the Wastes forever. He leaned back.

"Yendra, what's going on back there?" the driver screamed.

The knight wiped beads of sweat from his brow. "She fell." *Gods help me.*

"What? What's going on?"

"They fell! Both of them, when we hit the bump!" The knight fixed his eyes on the cyclone as the storm fell into the distance.

"May the Gods forgive me," he whispered, eyeing the Hellhounds one last time as they disappeared behind the sandy winds. He closed his eyes and leaned back, clutching the fragments of the sword at his chest.

May the Gods forgive me.

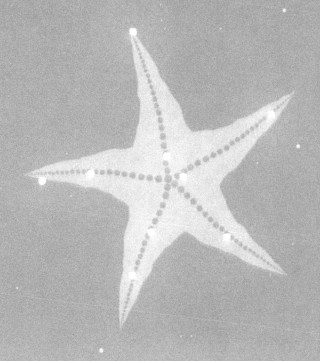

PART 1

GOLDFALL

CHAPTER 1

About to turn another page, Oyza started when a shout rang from the hallway. She rushed to tuck the book back in its hole in the wall, enclosed the crack with a loose brick, and zipped to the heap of straw in the middle of her cell. Plumes of dust hovered in pale rays of light.

She glimpsed down at her hands. Their sandy tone, their intricate rivers weaving and whirling about, their scrapes and scars—all of it was there, as it always had been. *Someday these hands will set me free.* She gave her fingers a stretch, thinking for a moment about all they used to do for her—writing scrolls, pouring wine, even wielding swords. That was long before she was thrown in the jails at the heart of the Parthassian Empire.

The groan of swollen wood forced from the door jamb stopped Oyza's thoughts. She wriggled to the edge of her chamber and pressed her face between rows of cool rusty bars. Sunlight shot through the darkness, obscuring her view of whoever strode down the corridor. *Probably the guards.*

"Mapa," she whispered across the hallway to another cell.

It was closed off by an iron door, but a window let air and whispers pass through. No response. Oyza shrank back, unsurprised. Mapa never spoke much after he'd been tortured.

"Quit crying and move," a tall guard with missing teeth snapped. He and a shorter guard with a grizzled beard led a man in chains behind them.

The short one thrust the blunt end of a dagger into the prisoner's belly. The man fell and let out a choked cry.

"Up!" the tall one fumed.

Oyza eyed the man. *He can't be more than twenty years old*, she thought. *Looks younger than me, and I'm always the youngest here.*

A torn cloth was wrapped around the prisoner's waist, and a blood-stained bandage covered his eyes. His bare feet were black from the dungeon's filthy floors.

And he's so thin, Oyza thought.

"I don't know why we don't just kill him now." The short guard placed his hand on his dagger's hilt.

"Watch it. We're to make an example out of this one later—gotta keep 'im alive. Orders from Emperor Edras," said the taller guard. "Looks like he 'asn't eaten in weeks. Fetch some food, whatever we got left down 'ere. If there isn't no food left, get some from the kennels."

Oyza yearned to do something for the new prisoner, but she had learned to keep her mouth shut when the guards were near.

The prisoner tripped and knocked over a barrel. A liquid spilled—rum, maybe? Glass jars shattered on the stone floor.

The taller man cursed and turned to the other. "Go get that food. And fetch a couple o' Moths to come fix up this mess while you're at it."

The short guard pouted and turned down the hall.

"In you go."

The man fell to his knees, curly hair flopping over his eyes.

The tall guard growled as he passed the liquid on the floor. He slammed the door and locked it behind him.

Oyza stared through the bars at the prisoner and wondered who he was. She saw his Starmark tattooed on the back of his neck—the sign of the Hound. Everyone in Vaaz had a Starmark tattooed on their neck, indicating which of the fourteen Origin constellations they had been born under. *Perhaps he was a squire? Or a herald? Or maybe a watchman? Whoever he was, he must've done something bad to end up here.*

The Moths, both young children, arrived with buckets and mops some time later to wipe up the spill and bring meals to the prisoners.

Oyza plopped down on her pile of straw. The servants left her a bowl of crusted white bread and a vine of half-rotted berries. They gave a small plate to the new prisoner, but he still didn't move, not even for the food. The ocean pounded on rocks below as soft red light poured through the window. Falling asleep, Oyza looked again at her hands. *Someday,* she thought. *Someday...*

❦

The next morning, Oyza rose and inspected the new prisoner as sunlight splashed onto his hair. Birds chirped, and the scent of sea salt wafted through the window.

The man coughed and lifted his head, rubbing his eyes with scarred hands. "Where am I?" he muttered.

"You're in Goldfall. The dungeons," Oyza said.

The prisoner sat up on a mound of straw. A swarm of flies droned. He coughed again and clutched his stomach, looking as if he might vomit. "I feel terrible." His voice shook.

Oyza flinched. "The guards were pretty rough with you."

"It's not that... It's nothing." He ran his fingers through his hair.

Oyza twisted her lips at the sight of his sunken eyes, pale skin, and thin arms. *He must be a witchdust addict.* She raised her chin. "There's some water. And a little food."

The man rested his back against the stone wall. He stared at Oyza. "I'm fine. I'll be all right. I'm just a little foggy-headed..." He groaned.

Oyza took a slow breath. *An addict...and a liar.* "What's your name? What're you here for?"

The man scanned her body cautiously. "Name's Yars. Yars Gadea. You?" He picked up the plate of wilted berries and flicked at them.

"Oyza Serazar."

"Nice to meet you, Oyza Serazar." He bit into a berry. His face contorted.

"Those guards last night, they said they wanted to make an example of you. What for? And do you have any news from out there? What's going on?" Oyza asked.

Yars swallowed some water and wiped his mouth with the back of his hand. He raised an eyebrow at Oyza and sighed. "What do you care?"

"I'm just asking." Oyza crossed her arms.

Yars looked away. "I stole. Was working in the mines at Judge's Pass, but I ran. Me and my crew ran for the Emerald Isles, just out there." He gestured toward the cracks of blue sky. "But we stayed in Goldfall when we heard about the fishermen disappearing off the coast, getting taken by the Men without Gods. We stole a bunch—easy work until they catch you. And then, well, I got caught up in...some things." He finished the last of the berries and reached for his stomach again.

He means witchdust, Oyza figured. "Minister Valador told me another ship disappeared three weeks ago."

A rat scurried into a crack. Yars wiped sweat from his brow. "And what about you? What're you here for?" He eyed the bread in her bowl.

Oyza dropped her eyes. "It's a long story. But I shouldn't be here."

Yars shrugged. "Yeah, what were you doing before you got here? What's your Starmark? You're a..." he squinted at her.

Oyza felt his eyes trace the strands of hair dangling over her shoulders, her thin arms, the small bump in her nose, and the coarse pieces of cloth covering her body. She saw him examine her hands—soft, but with a few scars—then inspect her bronze skin. They locked eyes. She saw his eyes were brown like hers, though darker, almost like the chocolate treats her master had sometimes given to her.

"Serpent?"

Oyza shook her head. "Wrong." She turned around, lifted her hair, and showed to Yars the Starmark tattooed on the back of her neck: a starfish, painted in black ink.

"Starfish. Ah, shoulda known."

"And why's that?"

"Your hands—too soft for real work."

Real work? "I was a servant for years, actually. That's *real* work. And I used to train as a scribe too. My father wanted me to work at the library of Oyvassa." *Home,* she thought.

"Oyvassa? Nothing there anymore," Yars said.

"I know. But that was before—"

Oyza and Yars stopped abruptly as the door down the hall scraped against the bumpy floor. Two guards wearing ripped leather jerkins and carrying daggers walked in and made their way to Mapa's cell. They opened the creaky door. "Come on, let's go."

Oyza and Yars watched as one guard entered and reached for Mapa inside. The old man's skin was pale, and his arms were skinny. A raggedy beard hung from his chin. Dull, hollow eyes stared bleakly into the distance, not even registering the guard.

Yars's eyes grew wide as the guard lifted the man. "He...has no legs."

The guards unchained Mapa and dragged him away, moving with a mechanical precision that always fascinated Oyza. She and Mapa locked eyes for a brief moment before the guards disappeared and slammed the door.

I hate it when they take him. Every time. It never gets easier.

"Who was that?" Yars asked. "And where are they taking him? What happened to his legs?" His face turned white.

Oyza wrinkled her nose. "That's Mapa. Every few months or so, the guards take him away. He used to talk much more—before the guards started torturing him more frequently. They've taken a lot out of him." She closed her eyes and slumped her shoulders. *It's horrible.*

"But...he's got no legs. What happened?" Yars gestured with his hands as if to pry answers from Oyza.

"Mapa told me he tried to assassinate Emperor Edras years ago," she said with some hesitation. "But instead of executing him, they keep him around to torture him."

Yars ran his fingers through his hair before burying his face in his hands. He peeked at Oyza from between his fingers. "And they've been doing this for...for years?"

Oyza nodded. "Yes."

"Gods, I'll kill myself before I let them do that to me," Yars said.

The morning sun's rays warmed the dungeon. A wave splashed against the rocks below.

Yars picked up a piece of straw and began tearing it. "So...you didn't tell me yet. What are *you* here for then?"

Oyza took a slow breath, not sure if she even wanted to tell the story she had repeated so many times to so many prisoners over the past few years. She stared into space. "I was—well, I *am*—a servant of Minister Valador." She scratched a flea on her ankle.

Yars sat up and tossed the straw.

"I was a servant—a scribe, mostly, in his library—and...later, his mistress. That's been almost my whole life. He's an advisor, you know, to Emperor Edras himself." Her voice was flat, like a river drifting without purpose. She tucked a long lock of hair behind her ear.

Yars pondered the story. "How did you end up there?"

Oyza took another deep breath. She fidgeted her arms and wiped away dust from her amber skin.

"If you don't want to talk about it, I get it." Yars leaned back and laced his fingers behind his head, his eyes tracing the zig-zagged cracks between the bricks in the ceiling. "So what do you do to pass the time here?"

"Minister Valador brings me things to read sometimes, but not as much recently. When I was his scribe in his library, I read all sorts of things. I got a little lucky, at least. Most Starfish never have a chance to work in libraries."

Yars's eyes kept following the lines in the ceiling. He looked at Oyza again. "Doesn't look like the worst place, at least. Clean. You read a lot?"

"I keep it as neat as I can. I guess when you've been a servant so long, you never lose the habit."

Yars laughed. He looked up again.

"Besides reading, there's not much to do. Mapa and I talk sometimes, but he's been quiet lately. The torturing...he gets worse every day." *I hope he's okay this time.*

Yars gulped. "So...Mapa. You guys are close?"

Oyza shrank bank, wrapping her arms around her knees. "He's the only one who's been down here as long as I have."

"The torturers, what do they do?" Yars asked.

She looked at Yars, taking a moment to survey his strong jaw, his friendly eyes, and the way his black curls dangled over his forehead.

11

"I'm sorry," she said. "Mapa's never told me. I just know he comes back in a lot of pain."

Yars grimaced.

"I didn't mean to scare you," Oyza said. *Poor guy, he doesn't know what he's in for.*

"Do they ever torture *you*?"

Oyza raised her eyebrows. *No one's ever asked me that before.* "I guess not." *This one's different.*

"You guess not? Either they do or they don't," Yars blurted.

"You wouldn't call this torture?" Ozya asked, raising her arms.

Yars shrugged. "Must be boring to be locked up all day." He flung a piece of shredded straw. "Safer than the streets, I guess."

Oyza's eyes widened. "At least you are free out there." She nodded at the window, her black hair bouncing slightly. "What did you steal anyway?"

"Free?" Yars asked. "Free to do what? Get roughed up all day? Chased by guards? Steal every meal just to survive?" He rubbed a bruised spot on his calf. "Doesn't look like you have it too bad in here."

Is he serious? Oyza squinted at him. "You've only been here one day, Yars Gadea. Give it time. Imagine eating it for years." She aimed a finger at a plate of old berries. "And you didn't say. What did you swipe to end up in a place like this?"

Yars frowned. "I'll tell you what, Oyza Serazar. You tell me what you did, and I'll tell you what I did. Only fair."

Oyza leaned back, avoiding Yars's eyes. "I didn't do anything."

Yars rolled his eyes. "Sure, sure."

Oyza felt the muscles in her neck tighten and turned away. *I don't have to tell him anything.*

A long moment passed, birds chirping outside the window and the late-morning sun illuminating specks of dust.

Oyza reclined on the pile of straw, then turned to her hidden bookshelf. *I guess I should be nice, though.* "You can borrow a book if you'd like," she offered. She pulled a withered one from the hiding place and leafed through its worn pages. It was *The Edible and Medicinal Plants of the Kingdom and Dominion of Oyvassa, Fourth Edition*, one she had read four or five times—or was it six now?

"Can't read, but thanks." Yars shrugged. "What's your favorite one?" he asked before letting out a nasty cough. He gripped at his waist with mangled fingers.

His withdrawal symptoms are bad, Oyza surmised, *and worse than he's letting on.* She thought about his question for a moment, crawled to the wall, then peeked at the door to make sure there were no guards. She pulled out the loose brick and removed the hidden book. "This one. But you can't tell anyone I have it." She held it, title up, to Yars.

He tucked a curl of hair behind his ear, eyes narrowing. "I told you, I can't read."

Oyza smiled as she opened the tome's withered pages. "This is *On the Frailty of Kings and the Illusions of Power, Notes of a Concerned Soul.*"

Yars shrugged flippantly, refusing to look at the book. "Never heard of it."

Oyza's mouth hung open. "Never? This book is illegal in every kingdom in Vaaz. The Celesterium outlawed it too. I found this old copy in Minister Valador's room. He doesn't know I have it." She pressed the book closer to Yars.

"If it's banned, then how would I know about it?" Yars still didn't look.

Oyza squinted, annoyed, and put the book back down. "It's famous. Everyone knows about this book."

"So why's it banned?"

"The book says we don't need rulers. It says that kings only have power because we say they do, not because the gods give it to them. And it says the people can rule themselves and should take control of everything—the fields, the harbors, the workshops—everything." She closed the book and stashed it away. "And it won't be easy—it'll take a revolution, a violent one, to get it. It's written in the laws of history."

Yars scratched his chin. "And then what?"

"What do you mean?"

"Who's going to, you know, be in charge of everything?"

"Well, *we* would."

Yars let out a low sigh then looked up at the window. A seagull sat against a cloudy sky on the ledge.

"I think this is what the Ungoverned have done," Oyza added.

Yars sneered. "Those demons-worshippers in the swamp?"

Oyza creased her brow. "I don't believe that. They're from Oyvassa, like my people. They're not demon-worshippers."

"I dunno, sounds like it'll never happen anyway. They're going to overthrow the empire? Give me a break."

"You don't think it's worth a try?" Oyza asked.

Yars scratched his chin. "Stealing a necklace is worth a try. So is nabbing a gold coin or two. 'Cause I know I can do these things. But I can't change the world, Oyza. I survive, every day and night, because I have to." He looked around for a moment, inspecting his plate for crumbs. "So, a scribe to Minister Valador? What's it like being around highborns? Got any good stories?"

Oyza's head tilted a little to one side. *He changed the subject quickly. I wonder what he really believes?* She played with the ends of her hair. "Well, Minister Valador's Starmark is a Moth. He never worked as a servant or worked the sewers. Nothing like that. A real highborn. His father trained him to be a lawyer for a Parthassian minister, but he was so good at administration that he's been an advisor to Emperor Edras for decades. He says this is right, though, with the gods because—get this—his duty is to 'clean up' the Empire, like a Moth."

Yars snorted. "The men back in the mines told me about lords born as Mammoths working as scribes, Hawks leaving the army, Frostpetals as sailors...no one cares anymore, do they? Whole world's gone to shit."

Oyza shook her head. "The Celesterium still cares. The priests say the Men without Gods, the Haf, are a curse brought here because we betray our Starmarks."

Yars coughed and grasped his gut, hiding a moan. "You think it's true? People from Hafrir really have no gods? How could there be no gods?"

Oyza shivered, trying to forget about the first—and last—time she had seen the strange invaders from across the sea, from somewhere called Hafrir, some fifteen years ago, and the terrifying sounds their weapons made.

"I don't know, but that's what they say. The man Emperor Edras captured didn't speak our language at all and refused his last rites before death. Said there were no gods...spit on a Celesterium priest too," she replied.

"I know the story," Yars snapped. "But I wonder if it's true."

The door opened. An older man approached. He was draped in a long black and violet tunic made of smooth silk. Oyza grimaced at the bald head, the short beard, and the leather sash bearing the Hawk-and-Tower sigil of the Parthassian Empire. It was Minister Valador.

He walked to Oyza, ignoring Yars. Oyza slouched and dropped her eyes. The muscles in her chest tightened.

"It's been such a long time, my sweet jewel—far too long." His voice was raspy like an old door scraping across a stone floor. He pulled a key off his belt and unlocked the door. "This smell..." he covered his face with a handkerchief. "I'll be sure to have some Moths sent down to tidy up a bit. Have the guards not been treating you well? These new recruits, they really are worthless. Idiot country bumpkins."

Oyza looked at Yars, who sat wide-eyed on his lump of straw, then stared up at her master with weary eyes.

"Come now, sweet jewel," Minister Valador extended his arm to her.

Oyza gulped and stood up, grabbed his hand, and let him lead her away.

"Troubled times, these are—the Men without Gods have been spotted off our coasts again. But you don't need to worry, Oyza. I will keep you safe. But first, let's get you a warm bath."

Oyza's stomach twisted. She threw Yars a last glance Yars as she left. *Someday. Someday, I'll be free.*

CHAPTER 2

Liviana sat at a table buried in scrolls and letters. Raven-black hair fell down her back, and her skin was a golden tan, much like the boundless fields of wheat that sprawled across the plains of the Parthassian Empire. The black leather tunic she wore had bronze trim around the edges, and a Hawk-and-Tower was embroidered on it in shining gold. She turned toward the door as her wrinkled advisor, Minister Woss, stepped in. He was clothed in silvery robes with a white silk sash hanging across his chest.

"I swear, if I'd have known how much mail poured into Judge's Pass, I'd never have conquered the damn city in the first place. Can you believe it? Took the whole city with hardly losing a single man, and now I can't even find one letter," Liviana said as she dug through the scattered papers. She paused to rub her temples.

Minister Woss raised a feeble hand to his mouth and cleared his throat. "The message we received from the Celesterium commands you to halt today's execution of the captured rebels. The priests say three are innocent. They want to execute five, not eight. I believe that's what the letter said." He wore a smug smile on his face as he recited the contents of the letter from memory.

Liviana leaned back in her chair and lifted an eyebrow.

"Unless you have other ideas for them..." the minister added hesitantly.

Liviana pursed her lips. "Let them go? We will proceed with hanging all eight of them today. The more insurgents we make an example of, the better. We can't afford to let the Ungoverned stir up rebellion and cause trouble. Certainly not as we prepare our invasion to deal with them for good."

Minister Woss lowered his eyes and fidgeted with his beard. "As you say."

"Am I not in charge of this city? The people listen to me—Blacklance—not Archvicar Uriss and the priests. We command the armies here, and we keep the city safe. Not the Celesterium."

Minister Woss grimaced at the name Blacklance. Liviana knew he hated the name—but she had earned it and earned it well. Every time she passed the rows of Parthassian lances dug into the ground, turned black with the dried blood of her impaled enemies, she smiled at the minister's shudders.

"True, Commander. But no one sits on the throne here. Uriss and the Celesterium will not permit you to ignore them," the minister said.

Liviana shook her head and rested her elbow on the table. Her eyes stumbled upon the letter.

"And with the famine, maybe it's best not to execute more than we need?" Minister Woss suggested.

Liviana grabbed the letter and stood up, her cape dangling down her back. "That the people starve is *their* fault. It's *their* fields in *their* monasteries that aren't producing, not ours."

She held the letter in a candle's flame.

"Well, the war was difficult on us all." Minister Woss's fingers fidgeted as he tried not to watch the official notice burn. "The Celesterium has always kept the right to grant clemency and halt executions in this city. This is the precedent."

Liviana sighed as her troubles turned to ash and a wisp of smoke coiled into the air. She walked to one of the bookshelves lining the wall and picked up a book, then flipped through the pages. It was a manual about siege strategy—just one in a fifteen-volume series. "When Uriss commands the armies, he can call the shots. He is a priest. I don't care if he's the Archvicar and the emperor's son, he does not command me. We will execute all of them." She snapped the book shut and put it back on the shelf.

Minister Woss bowed his head. "As you say, Commander."

They left the room and descended the winding steps of the citadel. Liviana stopped to look out a window. "Quite a crowd gathered. Certainly won't be wasted." A sea of weary eyes stared at an empty stage. Dim sunbeams shot through the thick clouds of ever-present dust hovering over the city.

"Not wasted at all, Commander. Half of them came out of fear, no doubt, and the other half just want a good show. We've learned that very few here support the insurgent activities of the Ungoverned—our lies seem to be working, somewhat." He straightened his back and wiped down his sash.

Liviana nodded and clasped her hands behind her back, her cape swaying behind her as the ruby-tipped handle of her massive sword, Xalos, gleamed in the sunlight. "Good. An execution a day keeps rebellion away, no?" she smirked. She eyed the mural along the twisting wall as they made their way down. It depicted the long blue arc of the Sword of Creation—the star whose tail tore across the night sky through the constellations that comprised the fourteen Origins.

In Vaaz, it was believed all life was created after the son and daughter of rival gods, who were forbidden to love, pierced their bodies together with a sword to die and live together for an eternity. The gods cast them from the heavens, but from the blood of their shared wound poured all the other creatures of the world, embodied by the Origins. Liviana didn't care much for Starmarks, but she still felt a little proud as she passed the constellation of the Hawk on her way down—the sign of courage, strength, symbol of the Parthassian Empire, and her own Starmark.

They reached the bottom of the steps and entered a broad hall. Polished stone pillars rose from the ground and a rust-colored carpet straddled the middle. Black and bronze streamers draped from the walls. Delicate rays of light poured through giant windows, illuminating thick dust before splashing onto the floor. At the front of the hall sat an empty throne—a small, plain chair made of solid rock. *For one entire year now, I have ruled this city, and still the emperor forbids me from sitting the throne. Soon,* Liviana reminded herself.

"Ah, Commander Liviana. The pleasure is mine," a man said to her. He was flanked by four Celesterium guards who wore heavy blue-gray plate mail. Over one shoulder they wore rumpled cloaks. Each carried a curved blade engraved with a star on its hilt.

The priest knelt and kissed Liviana's hand. Golden robes dangled down his sides. In one hand he held a frayed book, and in the other, a twisted oak staff with a sapphire orb at its top. He had small eyes, a thin nose, and an even thinner chin. Dark hair was slicked back atop his head.

Great, just great, Liviana thought. "How nice to see you, Archvicar. I assume you're here for today's execution?" she asked, an annoyance in her voice she didn't even try to hide. She had hoped to get this done before seeing the Celesterium priests at all, especially Uriss.

"Please, just Uriss. No titles needed between friends. But yes, my men informed me we captured *five* insurgents of the Ungoverned this time. I believe we sent a letter to you this morning. Three men are to be released on their innocence, I presume." His smile mocked her.

If it's a challenge he wants, it's a challenge he'll get, Liviana thought, angered but not surprised. She flashed a glance at the throne. *He hardly even tries to hide his lust for it.* She sighed, knowing she should have pretended she didn't receive the notice at all.

"I have ordered all eight to be executed. We can't risk letting these rebels slip from our fingers, and we have to make an example of them. If we cannot keep the peace at Judge's Pass, we will not be able to launch our invasion to the south where they hide. We have to strike now, while the northern front remains at a standstill." *They don't need to challenge me on this,* she thought. *Nobody cares about the lives of three fucking commoners.* She crossed her arms.

Uriss pinned his narrow eyes on Liviana. "Well, Commander, regarding the invasion of the Ungoverned, I have other news, from *my father* himself." He waited, half-grinning. "I was going to wait until after the executions, but since you bring it up now..."

Liviana turned to Minister Woss and raised an eyebrow.

He gave her a blank stare and a blanker shrug.

"Go on then, what is it?" Liviana asked.

"As you know, fishermen have been disappearing off the coasts of the Emerald Isles for some time now. My father received reports claiming ships bearing the sigil of Hafrir have been spotted. No raids yet, thank the gods, but my father fears they may be preparing an attack on Goldfall next. All the years he's spent wisely building the walls may finally pay off. There's just one small problem, though. My father hasn't got enough men to defend them." Uriss smirked.

Liviana winced. She knew what to expect next. *The emperor's such a fool.* Her hands tightened into fists. *His foolishness will be the utter end of our Empire.*

"So how many men does he want from me?" She cocked her head slightly to one side. Her heart started to race.

Uriss could barely contain the grin on his face. "My father needs ten thousand men, Commander. And he needs them now."

"Ten thousand? He's not serious." Liviana grabbed the handle of her sword and began to unsheathe it.

The Celesterium guards reached for their blades.

"Now, now, there's no need for this," Minister Woss interjected, waving his hands.

Liviana sheathed her anger. "Indeed. Uriss, you may give word to the emperor I will send his ten thousand men promptly. But let him know he is leaving us dangerously unmanned here. And let him know I insist we launch our assault south into the Shimmering Woods as soon as the Men without Gods leave. The Ungoverned are causing unrest in the city. We need to snuff them out. They grow like weeds down in their swamp."

Uriss smiled condescendingly. "With all due respect, Commander, although your capture of the city was doubtless one of the finest military victories in Parthassian history, you've had an entire year to bring peace, and from the looks of it, we are executing *five* more men today. My father loses patience each day. How many more must die before there is peace?"

Liviana tucked a strand of hair behind her ear. "*Eight* more must die, in fact. And I'd have already achieved peace in Judge's Pass if we had marched on the Ungoverned years ago. *And* if the emperor would supply the food we requested, on account of the bad harvests plaguing *your* lands. Until then, it's not possible." *We will execute eight men today, even if I have to cut off their heads myself.*

Uriss stared at Liviana. "With the gods, Commander, all things are possible. Perhaps you'd know if you bothered to see them once in a while. I must be off now." He bowed, turned, and walked away, his robes flowing like waves behind him. The Celesterium guards followed, armor clanking.

Liviana glared at their backs and let out a quick sigh. "Minister Woss, make preparations to deliver ten-thousand men to Goldfall. I won't challenge the emperor, not now. We'll have to postpone our invasion."

Minister Woss nodded.

"And prepare my things too," Liviana added.

"Commander?"

Liviana cracked her knuckles. "I'm going to Goldfall too. I'm not leaving my men. They're loyal to me, to Blacklance, not the emperor and his idiot sons. I won't let the emperor send them away anywhere—especially not Mélor. When the Men without Gods leave, they must return to Judge's Pass." She adjusted her gloves. "I trust the Celesterium less each day, if such a thing were possible. This city starves while Uriss tells me their harvests only become worse. Something has to change."

"I'm afraid we can't do much about the bad harvests on the Celesterium's lands, save pray to the gods for relief," Minister Woss said. He always seemed to state the obvious, which annoyed Liviana.

"Fourteen temples. They have fourteen temples—well, fifteen if you count the ruined temple in Oyvassa—across all Vaaz. They have the Basilica of One Thousand Stars here, and Uriss says he can't get the Celesterium to issue anything more to us. Lies, all lies. They're challenging me, minister. The Celesterium colludes against us. I know it." She wiped dust off of the Hawk-and-Tower on her chest. One thousand stars split into each of the fourteen Origin Constellations. Liviana gave thanks every day she was born under the sign of the Hawk. "Anyway, it's been too long since I've seen my father. I haven't been back to Goldfall since our victory parade a year ago, now that I think about it. He wrote me a message recently, and I've been meaning to get a delivery to him. I'll bring it myself. It's an important one, minister. The day we've anticipated for so long...may be sooner than we think." She concealed a grin.

The minister nodded.

"Tomorrow, I'll leave with two-thousand men on horseback. We'll ride hard and arrive in Goldfall within two weeks. See to it that the rest of my men arrive quickly. Be light on supplies. We'll have what we need in Goldfall. Better to leave what food we can to this city."

They proceeded down a long hallway that led outside. The dusty air smelled like chiseled stone. In a small courtyard outside the citadel, water poured from a statue of the Two as green vines tangled around smooth marble columns. Eleven Parthassian guards, heavily armored from head to toe and carrying broadswords and giant shields, followed as they passed through a gate. On each of their shields was painted a bronze tower. Liviana nodded at them. These were the men of her personal guard—her Iron Towers, her father had called them. *But where is Sir Yirig, my best Tower?* Liviana wondered.

She laced her fingers behind her back as a light wind tugged at her cape. "Can you believe he calls off our invasion? Ridiculous," she hissed. She rested her hand on the hilt of Xalos. "Sometimes, Minister Woss, I feel I'm the only person in Vaaz who hasn't lost their mind."

The minister smiled. "That's why it's best not to think at all sometimes. Just carry out orders, I say."

Liviana grinned. "That's why I like you, minister. It is good to know one's place."

Minister Woss nodded. "Indeed."

They reached the hefty iron gate to the city's streets. The ragged crowds of Judge's Pass stood on the other side, eager for a show to bring a brief moment of excitement interrupting their miserable lives of occupation under the Parthassian Empire.

"Let's go. The people are impatient. We have *eight* men to kill, after all," Liviana said.

And soon, it will be more.

They made their way to the city plaza and stepped onto a high deck surrounded by rows of Parthassian soldiers in black-and-bronze chainmail. Each held an enormous shield on their left side and a carried sharp black sword in their right. Others carried crossbows. Behind their backs fell bronze capes with towers embroidered on each. Liviana stood with her hands held behind her back, eyeing the soldiers. Her arms pushed her coat aside just enough to expose Xalos, its ruby hilt barely gleaming in the dim rays of the sun. The light struggled to penetrate through the thick layer of dust blanketing the city, owing to the Hollowed Mountains nearby where mining took place.

Before her stood eight men waiting to be hanged, muttering their final prayers. Liviana ordered their bodies be left there until the crows had picked them clean and only bones remained. The crowd murmured and shuffled when eight bells rang from a tower. Silence.

Liviana raised her chin and cleared her throat, her gloved hands wringing behind her back. "Let it be known," she shouted, "all those who oppose the Parthassian Empire will meet a swift and painful death. Let it be known that as the world falls to pieces and the Men without Gods terrorize our shores, only we have the strength to hold it together. Only the bravery of the Hawk and the fortitude of the Tower. Spies, insurgents, rebels—they will not be tolerated within our lands. They will not be tolerated behind our walls. They will not be tolerated in our Empire."

She dug her boots into the wood below. "These men before you were caught conspiring with the enemy—spies from the Ungoverned, the savages and devil-worshippers in the Shimmering Woods who have come here to take everything from us. Who seek to undermine our Empire. To kill our children while we sleep, to poison our waters and bring curses upon our lands. Men and women of Judge's Pass, I ask you, do we worship demons?" Her voice boomed.

The mob erupted. "No!" They booed and roared and hissed and jabbed their fists into the air.

"And what do we do with savages who threaten to destroy the very bedrock of the world?" Liviana bellowed.

The crowd erupted again as cries of "Hang them!" echoed through the cobblestone streets. Some threw rocks and rotten heads of lettuce. Liviana knew half of them were lying. Her men could only capture so many, and the reports of Ungoverned insurgents only kept growing. Today, she hoped, she would begin to end this.

The eight men stood frozen on the stage, nooses hanging just above them. Liviana could see the Starmarks on their necks as they stood before her: a Scarab, two Moths, an Ox, a Frostpetal... *It doesn't matter*, she thought. *They're all the same. In death, we are all the same.*

The people grew silent. Liviana nodded to Minister Woss. He raised his hand as soldiers covered the heads of the prisoners with hoods.

Liviana tilted her head back and stood perfectly straight. "On the orders of Emperor Edras, with the strength and might of the Parthassian Empire, and by the justice of the gods, you are accused of conspiring against the crown and the church and of plotting to terrorize the great people of Judge's Pass. I, Commander Liviana Valador of the Parthassian Empire, sentence you to die."

She looked around the swarm of pitiful faces for a brief moment. *Odd. Uriss is not here.* Another priest stood in his place, chanting last rites from a book. A man behind her began to turn an enormous wheel.

"For the darkness comes for every star, may the gods have mercy on your souls," Liviana announced.

The wooden floor collapsed from beneath the prisoners' feet. The crowd burst into cheers as the prisoners jerked and twitched.

"Death to the Ungoverned!" they screamed. "Death to the demon-lovers!"

The prisoners writhed before the last traces of life left their bodies. Then, stillness.

Liviana turned and began walking back toward the citadel as the cheers began to dissipate. Minister Woss and her Iron Towers followed, the guards surrounding them on all sides.

"Where is Sir Yirig?" Liviana said. "He was supposed to be here with the rest of my guard. When we leave the citadel, I want all twelve of my guards in my orbit at all times. What good is my guard without Yirig?"

Minister Woss shrugged. "I'm certain you'll be safe enough with eleven of your Iron Towers. They're the best trained guards in Vaaz. Your father has seen to that."

"Yes, but Sir Yirig is the best. If all eleven of my Towers fall, I know Sir Yirig will still stand." *It had better not be his nightmares again.*

They continued their walk back toward the citadel as its strong walls and thin towers grew larger, spiraling into the dust-filled sky like jagged mountain peaks.

A tall man wearing a shining black cuirass awaited them. His sleeves were made of bronze thread, and a layer of white stubble covered his jaw. Wavy gray hair sprinkled with milky streaks sat on his head. At his side dangled a massive ax, and on his back was a round black shield with gold trim around the edges bearing the Hawk-and-Tower.

"Sorry I'm late, Liviana," he said in a deep voice. His muscles seemed to bulge out of his armor.

Liviana ordered Minister Woss to leave and begin preparing the army for their march to Goldfall. "Where were you?" she fumed to Sir Yirig. "You missed the execution. Uriss wasn't there either. He sent some other stupid boy in his place." As they scaled the steps to the citadel, she began to remove her leather gloves.

"My apologies, Liviana. I made sure the rest of the guard was present," he said.

Liviana nodded. "You weren't late because...nightmares? I heard you were having them again." *Here we go.*

Sir Yirig shook his head, eyes looking away. "No."

"Good. Don't let the past haunt you, Yirig. Your time in the war is long past," Liviana said.

Sir Yirig cleared his throat, then took Liviana's side. He seemed to tower over her. "I was talking with Voy when we saw Uriss leaving the citadel earlier. He looked upset about something. We followed him back to the basilica. I kept a watch outside while Voy crawled into her ceiling space." He lowered his sunken eyes to Liviana. "Aye, she'll be meeting with you later." He grinned.

Liviana nodded, eager to learn what her most trusted spy had to share with her. *What is that priest up to?* "I need you to do something important for me," Liviana began, "but wait until we are upstairs."

"Aye," the hulking knight said.

They climbed the steps into the citadel as Liviana greeted Parthassian guards with thoughtless waves. An immense stone arch soared above them. They continued through the arch and down a hall to a small meeting room near the top. A wide table stretched to a window framed by dangling white curtains. A violet rug decorated the floor.

Liviana sat down, waving away the Moth following them into the room with a jug of wine and a plate of breads, cheeses, and grapes. Liviana leaned back in her chair and sighed, changing her mind about the wine. She snapped her fingers as the Moth ran back in and poured two glasses of red wine. Liviana took a sip. It was warm and floral, reminiscent of a late summer breeze blowing away the day's hot air.

She turned her eyes to Sir Yirig and handed him a small letter she kept in a locked drawer. "A rider arrived a few days ago carrying this scroll from my father. He's asked us to pick up some...things from the markets." She sipped more wine, then set her glass down next to a pile of scrolls. "He's requested we bring him crushed wyvern talons, snakeskin powder, shark's tooth extract, beetle shells... The list here goes on and on. But I believe I know what he has in mind."

Sir Yirig scanned the note. He rubbed his stubbled chin and squinted.

"We were to send these to Goldfall in separate shipments, but we can deliver them ourselves. You must go to the markets and acquire these as soon as you can. Tell no one." She gave him a deep stare.

She picked up the glass of wine and rose to her feet, turning toward the window and peering out at the sprawling city below. The city buzzed with life. Horses, wagons and multitudes of people navigated narrow zig-zag streets. The bronze dome of the Basilica of One Thousand Stars soared in the distance, buried in a haze of dust.

"Aye." Sir Yirig folded the letter and tucked it in his pocket.

Liviana looked away thoughtfully. "I haven't seen my father in a while...or visited my mother's grave."

The knight looked down. "I'm sure Nalus is doing well. And I still think about your mother every day."

Someone knocked on the door.

"Enter." Liviana turned away from the window.

A short woman with wavy hair falling down the sides of her face appeared. Her curved body was draped in leather fabric, and a delicate black cloak hung from her back. Rows of silver bracelets adorned her arms, while a sapphire pendant wrapped in sparkling brass hung from a necklace around her neck. Her long nails were impeccably trimmed and painted a dark green.

"Voy, great to see you." Liviana snapped her fingers again. "Please, sit down."

The Moth came into the room and served a third glass of wine.

"Thank you, Liviana." Voy bowed and took a seat at the table.

Liviana leaned forward. "Sir Yirig tells me you have new information on Uriss?"

Voy cast a gentle glance at Sir Yirig. The knight awkwardly shifted his eyes away from Voy's breasts.

Voy rolled her eyes then turned back to Liviana. "Yes. He plots against you. He and the Celesterium. I don't know what or how, but they are up to something different this time." Her words were marred with a slight lisp that was impossible to ignore. She pulled a strand of hair behind her ear then played with her necklace, stroking it between two nails.

Good. I can always count on Voy. Liviana slouched back in her seat and tapped her fingers on the table.

"And the harvests. We're working on finding out more, but we suspect the Celesterium is not being honest about their supposed crop failures."

Of course. I knew it. "Thank you, Voy," Liviana said. "As always, your services are much appreciated."

"Anytime." Voy played with one of her polished bejeweled bracelets.

"I am leaving for Goldfall tomorrow. While I am gone, I want you to keep an even closer watch on Uriss and the Celesterium. I hope to deliver more spies to you soon as well." Liviana opened a small trunk sitting on the desk. She tossed a bag of silver to Voy.

Voy glimpsed inside the bag with a wide smile, then tucked the silver into a pocket. "There is one last thing you need to know, Commander," Voy continued. "Uriss plans to go to Goldfall. He will arrive before you do. You should be careful while there."

Liviana squinted her eyes. She looked for a moment at Sir Yirig, who was listening closely. His eyes narrowed slightly.

"Thank you, Voy. I'll deal with Uriss in Goldfall then. In the meantime, I want you to find out more about what the Celesterium is doing when they think we aren't looking. Look everywhere you haven't already. I want nothing to slip past the monasteries without our eyes on it. Got it? That's all for now."

Voy stood, curtseyed, and exited the room. Her silk cloak rippled behind her as her boots echoed down the corridor.

THE SPIRIT OF A RISING SUN

Sir Yirig turned to watch her leave, eyes trailing to her hips.

"*Ahem*," Liviana coughed.

Sir Yirig turned back to her. "Men in the war would kill for a woman like Voy."

Liviana rolled her eyes. "Well, you're not in the war anymore, Yirig. And Voy is not a whore. She is my eyes in this city."

"Can you believe in one hand the gods bless her with a body like that and, in the other, curse her with that tongue?" he asked, regarding Voy's lisp.

Liviana pressed her lips together. "Yes, but she's learned to use her body well. The gods are not fair, Yirig. But the strongest among us—we don't play by the rules laid down by the gods. We make our own. And Voy is the best at what she does." Liviana sighed and began fingering a feather pen. "Uriss is going to Goldfall then, is he?" A sly smile crept up the side of her mouth. She walked to the window, staring at the Basilica of One Thousand Stars' dome in the distance. "When you go to the markets, get double of everything—no, triple."

"Aye." Sir Yirig grinned, gripping the handle of his ax.

Liviana gazed at the dull sky. "The emperor's days are numbered, Yirig. I hear he's sicker than ever before. With his oldest sons in the north and Uriss here, now is the time to act. Tomorrow, we make for Goldfall."

Goldfall. The word put a sourness in her stomach. *Where* she *is. My father's little jewel.*

CHAPTER 3

Oyza's skin felt warm and smooth, and her hair smelled like fresh flowers. Even the grime underneath her fingernails was gone. She sat on a soft bed in a dimly-lit room, naked except for a heavy towel around her body. She had been to Minister Valador's private room beneath the castle many times and always appreciated the softness of the bed. It reminded her of where she used to sleep each night before she was imprisoned—a servant's bed wasn't great, but it was better than straw. Her eyes flitted around the room, examining the same old things from all her other visits there: a desk covered in scrolls and dusty papers, a few burning candles, maps on the walls, shelves of old books. *And what's that?* A glimmer caught her eye. *He left a dagger on the table...*

"And how have you been, my jewel?" Minister Valador closed and locked the door behind him.

Oyza looked away from the blade and stared at her toes.

"I apologize for not visiting sooner," the minister continued. "It's been quite a stir in the outside world, I'm afraid. Everyone is panicking about another attack."

Oyza stared at the old map of Vaaz hanging on the stone wall. She had seen it so many times—there was the kingdom of Mélor in the north, frozen and cold and buried in the endless Stonewood Forest; the Parthassian Empire, which stretched from Goldfall to all its cities across the plains; the Emerald Isles outside Goldfall; Petrovskia, where wyverns stalked the mountains; the volcanic isles of tropical Chan-Chan-Tuul; and of course, there was The Wastes, a sprawling patch of desolation. All of the Celesterium's fourteen temples were marked too. Judge's Pass was not included in the Parthassian Empire, owing to the map's age.

Her eyes drifted south to the Indigo City, as it was often called, the city of Oyvassa. Memories of the city from her childhood flooded into her thoughts. She could feel the ways its cool salty water burned her eyes. She could smell the fresh seafood—clams, oysters, octopus, fishes—that filled the air in the city's markets. She could practically feel the smooth, gleaming white marble pillars of the Temple of the Starfish warm in the sun. She remembered the indigo wall that stretched across the whole beach from the mountain to the sea, ending at the Pearl Spire, the towering lighthouse rising from the ocean to light up every night like a fiery star. She felt the breeze sting her face with bits of sand.

She played with the end of a blanket as Minister Valador rattled on. He could talk to Oyza about anything, and it would never leave the dungeons.

"Oyza, I can tell something's on your mind. What is it?" He stood up and approached her.

Oyza waited a long moment before responding, her eyes still gazing at the map beside her. "Nothing. I'm just a little more tired today. The new rations...the food, it's worse than ever before. We've had nothing but lumps of stale bread and old berries for weeks now." *The dagger...don't look at it.* She jerked her gaze away.

"Oh, dear," Minister Valador said. "I should apologize. Times grow tougher each day. The front at Mélor hasn't budged, I'm afraid, and Liviana's invasion to the south has been called off. The emperor never intended to let it happen anyway, not with the situation in Judge's Pass still so uncertain. There are more important things to do than waste precious men on fighting devil-lovers in a swamp, after all."

You're lying, Oyza thought, finding the truth in his distant eyes. *You'll support your daughter, no matter what, like you always do.*

"It's a pity the Ungoverned still won't move back to Oyvassa." The minister gazed at the kingdom with Oyza. "But, then again, who knows where the Men without Gods will strike? Maybe they are right to hide in the swamp. We're safe here, though; the emperor has seen to that. They may raid our shores and burn our villages, but the new walls of Goldfall are unbreakable. I'll have to arrange for one of our little walks outside so you can see them with your own eyes. They're near completion and truly magnificent. Not even their guns will help them pierce our fortifications. They would need impossibly high ladders, and even then, our arrows will rain on them like a thunderstorm."

A brief lull hung in the room, punctuated by the flickering of candles.

"I know it's hard down here, Oyza, but this was the only way. You have to understand—you nearly killed my daughter. The law says you were to be put to death. I fought long and hard to let you live here instead. You know that."

Her eyes bounced back to the blade. *I...didn't.* The muscles in her throat tightened as the memories of that day came back to her: the vines curling up the sides of the courtyard, the clashing of swords, Liviana cackling through blood-soaked teeth.

"I can tell your mind is not in the right place. You're bored down here, but the guards will only let me do so much for you. But how about this? Before we leave, you can bring any book back with you." He gestured to the bookcase. "If they complain, I'll just slip them a few copper coins."

Oyza faked a smile. Minister Valador didn't keep his best books down here, not in his little room in the dungeon. Nevertheless, she scanned the shelf. They were all boring titles, their contents more likely to put her to sleep than be a reward. Her eyes jumped from the books again to the dagger on the table.

No, no, stop looking! Her fingers fidgeted.

Oyza's eyes swung to the map on the wall, back to Oyvassa. She thought about what the city must look like now, empty and in ruins after the Haf raided fifteen years ago and the people abandoned the kingdom. *Are you still out there, Mother? Father? And you, Brother and Sister? I'm so sorry.*

Minister Valador kissed her cheek. "I'd love to stay for one of our little chats, but unfortunately, my jewel, I must be off. There are important matters to discuss upstairs—sooner than later, I'm afraid. I just...wanted to see you. But I'm expecting an important delivery from Liviana. Go on then, pick out a book."

The tension in Oyza's chest melted. She walked over to the wall opposite the bed and skimmed the bookshelf. Minister Valador shuffled some paperwork on the desk and then attempted to unlock a small metal drawer underneath the desk. His key didn't seem to work.

"Damn thing," he moaned, trying all the keys around his belt.

Oyza eyed the dagger again. *I should take it. I could hide it in my shirt. Or I could just end this all now...* She reached for the dagger, slowly, patiently, cautiously. Her heart began to thump.

She eyed Minister Valador. His back was turned as he fiddled with a lock. The room was dim. It was remote. It was perfect.

If it's quick, maybe no one would hear him. Maybe I could escape...but then where? How?

"Ah ha!" the minister whispered as the drawer opened. He emptied its contents onto the desk. There was a small pile of torn letters, a couple of empty vials, and quill pens and ink.

Oyza flinched. She turned back to the shelf. *Not today.* Panicked, she chose the first book she saw. "This one is fine." She grabbed a dusty one with worn green binding. She handed it to Minister Valador.

He blew off the dust and wiped it with his sleeve. "Ah, let's see here. *Studies of the Path of The Sword of Creation: Inquiries into the Nature of the Movement of the Heavens, First Edition,* by Sir Drius Perho of Bezabahd, in the Year 33 of the Second Age of the Raven. Well, it's not your usual interest. Very well then."

He handed the book back to Oyza as they left the room and made their way back. Locking the door behind him, he led Oyza down the dark winding hallways and stairs back to her cell. The air became musty.

"I know you expressed some unhappiness with the food. I'm sorry, Oyza, but I don't think there's much I can do. The emperor has imposed strict rationing, and the war has cost us dearly, not to mention we have to feed my daughter's army soon. But when we send the armies away, there will be more than enough food to go around, I promise. Just as soon as the Men without Gods are dealt with. If the Haf attack, they'll break like water on the walls."

Oyza looked away and took a slow breath. *I should have taken the dagger.* She looked down, something stirring in her chest. "And if they don't?"

Minister Valador squinted his eyes. "And if they don't *what*?"

"And if they don't break like water? What if they win? What if they take everything from us like they did in Oyvassa?" Oyza thought about the first time she had ever seen men from Hafrir, or the Men without Gods—so average they seemed, so normal, so friendly, and yet capable of such cruelty. She clutched the book at her side as they walked through the cold stone hallway, but she wished she had the blade instead.

Minister Valador pondered for a moment. He let out a sigh and cleared this throat. "My sweet, sweet, jewel. You shouldn't trouble yourself with such thoughts. I assure you, we'll be fine. It is said, though, in times of great strife, when cities suffer under siege and the harvests have failed and famine has turned even the most virtuous of men into the lowest of criminals, when men have nothing to eat, they may eat the nothingness itself." He grinned smugly.

Oyza blinked. *What? Always talking like this...he thinks he's clever.* She had walked the path to Minister Valador's room a hundred times but still found herself getting lost. One path went upstairs to the gardens, where the minister took her for walks in the sunlight. Another path led to a room where nobles would sneak forbidden lovers in the light of the moons. Other rooms held torture instruments—metal hooks, screws, ropes and sharp blades.

They passed through the door and then came to an abrupt stop. Yars was yelling.

Oh no. Oyza's stomach sank.

"Get off me!" he screamed. "No, you can't take me!" Two guards had cornered him.

"Fine, have it your way!" one of them grunted. He launched his fist into Yars's face.

Yars screamed as he dropped to the ground, and his wrists were shackled. "Oyza! Oyza, help me! Mapa!" Yars cried out.

Oyza ran toward him, but Minister Valador grabbed her arm. "Make them stop! Make them stop!" she shouted.

Minister Valador shook his head and jerked her back, his fingers cutting off the blood to her arm. "You know I can't do that."

"You can! I know you can! Pay them!" Oyza pleaded. She gripped the book at her side. *If only I had that dagger...*

The guards beat Yars into submission, then dragged him down the hallway. His curls dangled over his face as his bare toes dragged along the floor. They were taking him to be tortured.

"He is a prisoner, Oyza, who broke the emperor's laws. He must be punished. Surely, you know this by now. We must have justice," Minister Valador said unequivocally.

Oyza stepped into her cell.

Minister Valador locked the cell. "Can you imagine how the world would be if the emperor's laws were not respected? A world where the wicked were not punished for their crimes? I don't know what that young man did, but surely, there must be justice. Now, I must be off." He turned to leave.

Oyza pressed her face into the bars. "And will there be justice for me?"

Minister Valador paused. "I beg your pardon?" He twisted the end of his gray beard.

"I *didn't* try to kill your daughter. Liviana's a liar. But you've left me down here to rot in this dungeon anyway." The bitterness of Oyza's voice rang off the cold walls of the empty hall.

Minister Valador whipped around. "I don't know what's gotten into you lately," he hissed, "but *don't* forget your place. I saved your life, and now you dare to call my daughter a liar? I'll never know what happened between you and Liviana that day—I don't care, really—but I do know that if you so much as snap at me ever again, you will never see the light of day again. If not for that pretty face of yours, you'd've been dead years ago. You are a *whore*, Oyza, without a soul in the world to care about you, save for *me*. Never forget that, my little jewel!" He glared at her and stormed off down the corridor, slamming and locking the door behind him.

Oyza shriveled on the pile of straw beneath her, tears in her eyes. *What good would a dagger do anyway...*

Red light poured through the window, and waves crashed below. The stench was nauseating, as always, and the air damp and moist. Fleas jumped in the straw. Oyza couldn't help but think about what the guards might be doing to Yars with all the awful tools she had seen in the dungeon. She sat in silence, her shoulders slumped.

It's not fair.

Mapa coughed across the hallway. "Oyza." His strained, weak voice was just barely audible through the small window in his door. "Good to have you back."

THE SPIRIT OF A RISING SUN

Oyza rested her hands on her cell's rusted iron bars. "Good to hear from you, Mapa."

The old man hacked and spit. "I spoke with our new friend, Yars... Seems like a good boy. A thief, but a good boy."

And a witchdust addict.

"Nalus again, eh? Sorry, Oyza..." Mapa used Minister Valador's first name.

Oyza tried not to think about him, but her mind raced back to the dagger. She hunched. *Forget it.*

"Something's on your mind this time, Oyza..." Mapa wheezed.

Oyza sighed. "Three years now, Mapa. I don't know how much more I can take."

Mapa cleared this throat. "Ah, try twenty." He laughed hoarsely.

Oyza grinned. "I know... I'm sorry." Oyza tapped her fingers on the cold floor. "I shouldn't have snapped at Minister Valador like that," Oyza finally said. "He'll probably cut my rations now."

"No," Mapa said. "You've got every right to be upset." He coughed and wheezed. "We all do. Don't ever forget that, for people like us...rebellion is always right."

Oyza slouched. "What good is being right if you can't do anything about it?" She leaned on her palms.

Mapa chuckled. "Always smart, you are. You'll get out of here, Oyza..." He spat and rattled his chains. "I know it."

"You sound worse, Mapa."

A rat twice the size of Oyza's hand scurried in the corner, pausing their conversation.

"I'm dying, Oyza."

Oyza closed her eyes. Somehow, she already knew. *I just wish he wouldn't say it.*

"I can feel it. Now, deep inside, I'm dying..."

Oyza took a deep breath. "Mapa..."

"It's all right," Mapa said. "For twenty years, I've waited to die."

Oyza shuddered.

"But listen closely, Oyza... I've got something I need to tell you..." He struggled to speak through his wheezes.

Oyza leaned in as close as she could get.

Mapa took a deep breath when the door opened at the end of the hall. He let out a loud sigh. "But perhaps some other time."

A Moth carrying a small plate of food accompanied the guard. The young boy slipped it into Oyza's cell without ever looking at her and just as swiftly turned away. The guard sat at a small table in the hallway, paying them no attention.

Oyza eyed the plate of stale bread and nearly gagged. She had spent three years waiting for Mapa's story about when he tried to kill the emperor. She cringed and pulled the bread close, picking off the moldy parts. Her belly growled.

After it became clear the guard was staying for the night and she'd have to wait for the rest of Mapa's story, she fell into her mound of straw. She finished off the bread. *At least I have this.* She lounged back again, staring at the ceiling and thinking about her conversation with Minister Valador earlier in which he insisted she be thankful to him for being alive.

No, I have every right to be upset. Rebellion is always right. She closed her eyes and dozed off to sleep.

CHAPTER 4

Liviana stood on her father's balcony in the castle of Goldfall, bathed in warm sunlight, legs still aching from two weeks of hard riding. Silky white curtains swung in the breeze, and flowery vines wrapped around marble pillars. The air smelled sweet, like jasmine and lavender. The streets of the city buzzed with life, radiating outward like veins in a leaf from a broad central road that stretched from the outer walls to the castle high on its peak overlooking the sea. Liviana lifted her eyes to the castle's throne room. She followed the edge of the building down to a statue of a hawk jutting out from the side of the ridge. It faced the sea with outstretched wings, but much of it had chipped away. Her eyes went lower still. *The dungeons. Where she is.*

"There you are—my daughter. How are you? It's been...a year?" Nalus entered the room. He gave Liviana a hug, then pulled away back toward a table. "You look fantastic—look at you! Just like your mother. And I'm sorry I'm late. Go on, sit down," Nalus said. "You must be exhausted."

"I'm fine," Liviana said. "A boring ride, but easy. And it's nice to have a break from Judge's Pass. The city is a nightmare to administer. You wouldn't believe what I have to put up with there."

"I'm sure. Such a dreary place, all the dust, the famine. But I hope Minister Woss has been helpful. And Yirig too. I'm sorry we can't do more to help you from here."

A couple of Moths finished setting up their breakfast—warm pastries, burnt bacon, a pile of plump berries—and a jug of mint tea. They'd have had ice too, but the war with Mélor had put a stop to the glacier trade long ago.

Liviana gazed out at the city, her eyes stopping at the sparkling bronze dome of the Temple of the Hawk. She turned to her father. "It's different here now. Worse. There were so many beggars when we came in. And the castle. It's barren. Why is it so empty?" She sat at the table across from her father.

Nalus picked up a knife and reached for the bacon. "Yes. Times are hard here. But we've finished the walls."

Liviana took a sip of tea. "Impressive. But worth all that gold?"

Nalus raised his glass. "They're the biggest walls ever built, going from both sides of the ridge under the castle all the way to the ends. Their guns won't help them. If they do attack, our fleet will come in from behind and trap them."

Liviana's brow creased. *Not with my men. I'll not have them slaughtered atop some wall.* "I haven't seen the emperor yet. Is he as sick as they say?"

"He's not good. Old, sick, losing his mind, I'm afraid. Commands that any wealth he can find is stored in the vaults, now that his defenses are complete. And I'm sure you saw the Celesterium guards everywhere."

"Yes. What happened to the palace guard?" *And where is Uriss?*

Nalus sighed. "The priests run the castle now...always whispering in the emperor's ears."

Liviana tucked strands of hair behind her ears and poked her fork into a pastry. "And Sir Yirig brought you our delivery? I heard from others that the court stands behind us and is ready."

"Yes, dropped it off last night, and I've stored it all below." He shoveled another bite of bacon into his mouth.

Liviana put down her fork and scowled. "Down where you keep your little whore?"

Nalus's eyes narrowed. "Liviana, I will not have you speak to me this way."

Liviana scoffed. "The bitch tried to murder me, and you let her live. I should go kill her myself. The emperor's men whisper behind your back, you know. Your plaything in the dungeon brings nothing but shame and embarrassment to our family."

Nalus took a bite of a buttered biscuit and chewed, staring at her with thin eyes. He swallowed. "This is not the time. What's done is done. I'll not hear about this again."

Liviana sipped more tea, gazing off the balcony into the city streets.

"Sir Yirig brought me much more than I asked for. Why?"

Liviana smirked. *Why do you think?* "Uriss came from Judge's Pass too. And he's a threat. The Celesterium is a threat. If we take him out too, we'll cut the head off the beast."

Minister Valador shook his head, crumbs on his chin. "We have your armies, Liviana. I've got enough support at court. We shouldn't meddle with the priests, not now."

"I'm fairly certain if we slay his father and usurp the throne, Uriss will not be friendly to us." *My father, always two steps behind.*

Nalus cleared his throat and took a sip of tea. A small yellow bird landed on a polished statue and chirped brightly. "Perhaps you're right." He observed the little bird as it sang. "But perhaps not."

Liviana took a deep breath, lips pressed thin. *Eventually, coward, you have to make a choice.* "Father, now's the time. You've said it yourself for years: the Edras line is over. They have no one backing them except for the Celesterium. His sons are fools. Everyone in the Empire clamors for someone new, someone strong, someone with vision. And no one has more approval than our family."

Nalus stared at his plate for a long moment. "We'll have to wait and see. In the meantime, let's be ready. The emperor wishes to order your men to the walls. Don't leave them," her father warned. "Your men look up to you, and *only* you. We can't jeopardize that."

My men? No. She took a bite of a fluffy biscuit. "Do you really think they will attack?"

Nalus stroked his chin. "We don't know. They're near the Emerald Isles, at least. More boats, bigger ships, the fishermen say. But if they see our fortifications, they'll turn around and search for somewhere easier. Hopefully, they turn north and head to Mélor."

"They've never gone to Mélor, not in the whole twenty years they've been here. Probably too cold for them," Liviana said. "Speaking of Mélor, what of the emperor's sons there? Their armies?"

Nalus downed another cup of tea. "You already know the war's not going well. The emperor's sons are mired in stalemate. The mammoths seem to breed even faster than our horses. Actually, look up there."

Liviana turned. A massive white tusk hung from the ceiling in the other room.

"Sent as a gift." Nalus grinned.

Liviana turned back with a smile. "Don't show Yirig. Still calls them 'mammoth-lovers' after all these years. You know, he's been having nightmares of the war again."

Nalus shrugged. "I can't do anything about that." He scarfed down a piece of black bacon. "Anyway, Cerras is holed up in a fortress somewhere near the coast, and Gré holds a string of villages in the Stonewoods, but only barely. This whole mess of a war is a waste. When I'm emperor, I'll push for peace immediately."

Liviana nodded. "Good. Then we can finish the Ungoverned and retake Oyvassa."

"Oyvassa, yes—but you're not really worried about those swamp people, are you?"

Liviana drank her tea. It tasted cool and fresh. "You haven't been to Judge's Pass. You don't know. We just caught and killed eight more of their insurgents. They're a threat, more each day. Not only that, but the last one we captured and tortured confirmed to us that three of King Liorus's children are still alive."

Nalus leaned back and sighed, popping a berry into his mouth. The juice trickled onto his beard. "Speaking of, the emperor is not happy about that. Uriss got him up in arms about defying the gods and spilling the blood of innocents. He's going to demand an explanation from you."

Liviana straightened her spine and pulled back her shoulders. "Then let him." She washed down the last of her breakfast with a gulp of water.

Nalus stared at her then smiled. "Just like your mother was...stubborn and brave."

A knock sounded on the door. "I beg your pardon, but the emperor requests your presence at noon," a young Moth said.

Nalus nodded and waved the Moth away. "Well, then." He grabbed one last red berry as he rose from the table. "I'll see you shortly. I have some things to take care of before the meeting. Do not be late." He gave Liviana a pat on her shoulder and turned to leave.

Liviana watched him go, stood up to look out of the window one last time at the Temple of the Hawk, and left.

"No one is taking my legs!" Yars woke with a start in his pile of straw. He looked around the dungeon, rubbing bruises on his limbs where the guards had beat him. *Oh... I'm back. Gods, everything hurts.* He inspected his legs: thankfully, everything was still there. In the cell next to him, Oyza slept, her head resting on an open book. She looked thinner and paler than usual. *She must be bored down here, but at least she can read. Guess I would if I could.* He crawled around the cell. *Nothing to eat?* He looked again in Oyza's cell. There was a plate of old bread and mushy apples.

Oyza yawned, stretched, and sat up, picking straw from her hair. "You're back? What happened? It's been over a week."

Yars massaged a black spot on his forearm. "I just woke up too. They must have brought me back last night."

"You don't remember?"

"No. I remember them hitting me, slapping me." He looked across the hall to Mapa's empty cell, the door hanging open. He gulped. "Not as bad as they do to him, at least." He placed his hands on his legs. *Gods, thank you. Not my legs—please anything but that.*

"I'm sorry," Oyza said. "They always do that to new prisoners they bring in."

Yars grunted. "I don't know why. Not like I could answer anything they wanted." The last week was little more than moments, blurs, flashes: wrists and ankles tied to a chair somewhere, questioned, hit. His stomach growled. "Hey, if you're not gonna eat that, can I have it?" *Shouldn't waste perfectly good food.*

Oyza cast him a flippant glance. "I'm going to eat eventually," she said. "I just don't feel like it now."

"You look like you haven't eaten in days. It's gonna go bad."

Oyza looked at the window. The morning rays burst in. "I'm worried about Mapa. They've kept him a long time this time."

Yars slumped back on his palms. "I'm sure he'll be back. You said he's been here twenty years, right? Can't imagine they'd kill him now." He shuffled in the straw, massaging a purple wound on the inside of his thigh near an image of a pickax burned into his skin.

"What's that?" Oyza asked.

"Got it in the mines. Everyone got branded." He kneaded the spot. *At least I'll never have to go back there. I hope...*

Oyza looked away. "How long were you down there?"

"I grew up in an orphanage, but I was sold off to the mines when I turned twelve."

"I'm sorry," Oyza said. "Did you...did you ever know your parents?"

"Nope. No family, nothing, no one. Just me and my crew."

"Your crew?"

"Me and three friends, like brothers. We got out of the mines."

"Until you got caught here."

Yars nodded.

"What happened to the others?"

Yars's stomach twisted. "I think one...might have been killed already. The other two, I don't know." He shrugged. *Gods be with you guys, wherever you are.*

"Maybe you'll find them again?" Oyza asked. "You never know."

"Maybe."

"Maybe they'll join the Ungoverned?"

Yars scoffed. "Doubt it."

"Why?" Oyza bent closer.

Yars eyed Oyza closely. A ray of sunlight lit up her face. *She is pretty, even with that bump in her nose. But she kinda acts like a noble.*

"No money in that."

Oyza's eyes opened wide. "Money? It's not about that. It's about what I told you in *The Frailty of Kings.*" She glanced at her secret crevice in the wall.

Not about the money, she says! She's never been poor, has she? "Don't bother," Yars waved his hand. "I don't wanna hear about all that again. It's a bunch of horse shit."

Oyza threw him a nasty glare. "Well, fine then. Go on and chase after money if that's all you want. Is that what you'd do if we were free, go stealing witchdust again?"

Yars folded his arms and frowned. "What do *you* know about that?"

"I know I would never try the stuff. I've seen what it does to people. Why don't you quit if you know it's going to kill you?"

Yars rolled his eyes. "Oh gee, why didn't I ever think of that? Why didn't I just quit smoking it?" *She doesn't know anything. Raised in a lord's house all her life. Another spoiled noble.* Yars looked away. *But I guess she's all I have now, isn't she? Her and Mapa.*

"Look, it's not that easy," Yars turned to Oyza after a long moment. "Something happens... It just takes you over. It's all you ever think about." *Gods, what I would do for some now. Just a little.*

Oyza nodded. "Still, I don't think I'd keep doing it if I knew it was so bad for me..."

Yars threw up his hands. He stood and peered at the window instead. A light gust blew in, carrying the scent of sea salt. *How did I get here? I gotta get out. I have to. Somehow, or I'm gonna die here.* He turned back to Oyza, deciding to change the topic. Being scolded about witchdust was the last thing he wanted right now. "Where would you go if you got out?"

Oyza tucked a strand of hair behind her ear. "South. Then east. I'd go to Oyvassa right away."

"Oyvassa? There's nothing there anymore."

"I know, but I miss it. It's my home. I just want to see it again—the beaches, my old house, the blue fireflies..." Her voice trailed off.

Home. The word pierced Yars like a cold dagger. *At least you had a home once. And then a lord's home after that.* He sat cross-legged. "Blue fireflies?"

"In the Shimmering Woods, blue fireflies come out at night. That's how they made Oyvassan thread. The priests would cast spells on captured fireflies—that's why the thread glows blue in the dark."

"I didn't know that." Yars thought about some of the cloaks and vests the nobles wore sewn with the glowing thread. *Almost stole some of that one time.*

"Why do you think they called it the Indigo City?"

Yars frowned. "Well, I knew *that*, but I didn't know it was fireflies."

"It's not just fireflies, though. Oyvassa traded indigo cloths to the world, dyed with the indigo flowers that grew everywhere."

Yars nodded. *She knows everything, huh?*

"And there's an old story about the indigo flowers. They say two goddesses once argued there about who was more beautiful. The other gods got sick of their fighting and crashed the sky down onto them, pulling their bodies and the sky itself deep into the dirt. So now, the sky itself grows from the ground in Oyvassa. That's why cloudstones can only be found in the mountains there. It's a useless rock, but it's pretty."

Yars let out a half-irritated chuckle. "All right, I get it. You're smart, and you've read a ton, and you're all proper now."

Oyza smiled. "I'm sorry. I just miss the city. It's my home. And I *am* a Starfish. They trained me to scribe."

"Well I'm a Hound, doesn't mean shit now, except to the priests. I do whatever I want."

"And that's how you ended up here." Oyza smirked. "And why you're an addict."

She better watch it. Yars tore at a piece of straw.

"Well, if you got out, where would you go?" Oyza asked.

Yars gazed up at the cracks in the ceiling. "I wouldn't keep running to the Emerald Isles, definitely not. I'd go back the other way. Make for Talazar City. Get away from all this as fast as I could. I'd steal some gold, buy a little land somewhere in the middle of the Talazar Plains. Fuck, I'd go to edge of The Wastes if I could." He rubbed a bruised spot on his arm.

Oyza shuffled on her mound of straw. "Talazar City? Why so far?"

"I wanna get as far away from all this as I can."

"What makes you think the Haf won't raid there too?"

Yars flicked a pebble. "Well, I'd wouldn't stay there. Get my gold and get out to The Wastes. Maybe I'd find a mageware."

"So you would just run from everything and hide?"

"You got a better idea? What're you gonna find in Oyvassa? Nothing? And where you gonna go after that?" he shot back. "Gonna pray to demons in a swamp?" *What's her deal?*

Oyza stared into space, playing with a loose thread in her tunic. "I guess I don't know yet. Anywhere but here, at least."

Yars looked around the grimy cell. "I can agree with that. Anywhere but here."

CHAPTER 5

Liviana made her way through the castle, weaving in and out of endless hallways. They were barren, without the usual displays of priceless paintings, jeweled swords and shields, or holy relics of saints and martyrs. She sneered at the thought of all the wealth in the vaults beneath the castle and how wasteful it was in times like these. *Soon*, she reminded herself, *that fool will be off the throne.* Near the top of the castle, she reached the emperor's council room. Huge opened windows overlooked the bay, while long plum-colored drapes swayed in a tender breeze. Maps adorned the wall, and silver trays of breads, cheeses, jugs of wine and teas covered the table. After bowing to Emperor Edras, she took a seat next to Sir Yirig.

The emperor was pale and slim, and his frosted hair hung like shriveled seaweed under a golden crown covered in rubies. On his hands, he displayed silver rings filled with shining gems of all colors. The only empty seat was one of the seats next to Liviana's, ostensibly saved for her father. Around the table sat priests, commanders, and advisors of all stripes.

Uriss rose to his feet as Liviana sat. "How good to see you, Commander Liviana. If I had known you were coming, perhaps we could have ridden together. The road from Judge's Pass is so long and dreary."

Liviana threw him a quick smile. *Gods, I can't stand him.* She scanned the room and saw a face she wasn't expecting: Gré Edras, second son of the emperor. She took a deep breath, wondering why he was there. It made her more nervous than she wanted to admit. She made quick eye contact with her father's friends and allies around the table.

"It seems your father is not here yet," an older man sitting next to the emperor said. He was donned with long golden robes and an enormous topaz ring on his finger. Liviana recognized him as Vicar Dolinast, head of the Temple of the Hawk.

She noticed there wasn't a single Parthassian guard present, but plenty of Celesterium men. She shared a cautious glance with Sir Yirig, who was dressed in his Hawk-and-Tower plate mail, ax dangling at his side.

"A pleasure to see you," Liviana said as a Moth poured her a glass of tea. It smelled like roses and honey. *Where is he?* "My father will be here shortly."

The emperor cleared his throat and spoke in a deep, booming voice belying his otherwise sickly appearance. "Vicars, ministers, commanders, my sons—thank you all for being here today." He flicked away a Moth carrying a jug of water toward him. "We have important matters to discuss. Fishermen from the Emerald Isles report that ships from Hafrir—the Men without Gods—have been spotted off our shores. Yet there has been no attack on the Emerald Isles. We believe they may be headed here instead." He looked at each person at the table in turn, stopping at Liviana. "Hence, Commander Liviana, we are relieving you of the soldiers you've brought. Half will stay here at Goldfall, and half will go with my son, Gré, back to the Stonewoods. The men you have left at Judge's Pass should be more than sufficient to keep the peace."

Silence hung in the room as all eyes froze on Liviana.

"I will *not* give up my men," she fumed. "And they will *not* abandon me. My lancers would charge with me to the ends of Vaaz. You think they'll march north to go die in the Stonewoods? I will not have it." She glanced sharply at Gré.

Gré glowered at Liviana. He had short coarse hair and a square jaw. His arms were strong, covered in gray silk sleeves adorned with the Hawk-and-Tower emblem embroidered in red. "It is not your place to address me—or my father—that way," he said. "You will do as you are told." His eyes did not move from Liviana.

Uriss grinned.

The sniveling bastard, hiding behind his father. Liviana took a deep breath. "If we don't send my men back to Judge's Pass, we will lose control of the city. The Ungoverned are stronger every day. We captured eight of their insurgents stirring rebellion and revolution."

Gré's eyebrows rose.

"We will speak no more of the Ungoverned, Liviana," Emperor Edras commanded. "You've had a year to get control of the city. And it is only by the grace of the gods Talazar has not sent its army to invade our lands, nor anyone else for that matter. The Ungoverned are not a serious threat."

Liviana tapped her fingers on the table. "Three of King Liorus's children survive among the Ungoverned, and every day we do not wipe them out, they grow stronger. Do you want them to reclaim their kingdom in Oyvassa?" *How can everyone here but me be so stupid and blind?*

The emperor grumbled while Uriss spoke up. "If I may, regarding these so-called insurgents, I do believe we have another matter to discuss." He turned to Liviana.

Emperor Edras sighed. "Liviana, you will cease your insistence on defying the gods immediately. Uriss says you spilled innocent blood at Judge's Pass—commoners or no, if justice is not carried out according to the gods, you will damn us all. You will not defy the Celesterium again, is that understood?"

The look on Uriss's face resembled a child torturing a small animal for pleasure.

Liviana leaned in. "If I may, it is my men who patrol the city. It was I who conquered it and have administered it for a year. I will not take orders from priests who know nothing of ruling."

Gré sneered. "Who do you think...?"

"And if I may, Liviana," Uriss added, "you have mocked the gods for far too long. The Empire suffers because of it. Goldfall suffers because of it. We all suffer because of your blasphemy."

The room fell to a hush as Minister Valador walked in and took the seat next to Liviana. He nodded at Sir Yirig. "Sorry I'm late. But I stand behind my daughter. She is the only force keeping Judge's Pass at peace.

Sending more soldiers from the city would be disastrous, and it does not please the gods to let criminals, thieves, and agitators run loose. Execution was the right decision."

Good.

And everyone allied with her father nodded. The emperor stroked his beard with frail fingers and stared at Nalus with thoughtful eyes.

Uriss grimaced. "Please—what does a Moth know of the gods, a Moth who betrays the gods with his very existence every single day, who spends his time playing with whores in dungeons?"

Liviana sprang from her seat as Gré beat his fists and rattled the table. Yirig reached for his ax. The room fell into argument.

"Enough!" the emperor bellowed.

Everyone lowered their eyes.

"This is not what we are here to discuss. Nalus, Liviana—I have made my decision. The armies will stay here and go north. And you will never defy my son in Judge's Pass again. Let's move on."

Liviana rolled her eyes and slouched back. *Utter foolishness.*

The meeting dragged on as Gré gave updates on the war with Mélor, arguing that an additional two-thousand lancers would be enough for them to hold the Stonewoods while his brother Cerras led forces up the coast. They had lost many soldiers to the cold but secured supplies from the Temple of the Frostpetal. The Celesterium supplied them with wheat, barley, beer, apples, cherries, and walnuts from their monastery lands, but more would be needed. Uriss insisted he would do more to pressure the priests at the Temple of the Mammoth, far north of Mélor, to side with the Parthassians, but could give no guarantees.

As the emperor bragged about his new fortifications, a messenger appeared at the door, panting and out of breath. He knelt and lowered his head, exposing the Hound tattoo on his neck. "Your excellencies, I bring urgent news. The Men without Gods—they are headed this way. Twenty vessels, bigger than ever before."

Silence fell over the room as everyone turned toward the emperor. Liviana's brow furrowed.

"And how long until they arrive?" the emperor asked.

"If they continue on their present course...they will be here tomorrow night," the messenger said.

The emperor stroked his beard as the giant rings around his fingers sparkled in the sunbeams. "We have an important gala tomorrow night..."

Liviana glanced at her father with sharp eyes. *A gala? Is he serious?*

43

The emperor continued to stroke his beard, lost in thought. "What do you think, Gré?"

His son thought for a moment, staring into his cup. "I say we hold the gala. We can defend the walls while the guests watch from the castle above. Many people mocked the gold we spent on the defenses. Well, let them see firsthand why it was such a wise decision." He took a drink.

Liviana scoffed. "This is madness. We should evacuate the castle, not hold a dinner party. And send our warships, now, filled with archers, to block off the bay before they arrive."

Nalus and Yirig agreed.

Uriss whispered in his father's ear.

The emperor lifted his hand. "My son tells me the Sword of Creation moved last night into the Crab, a most auspicious sign for us. We will defend the city, and we will hold the gala as planned. And once the Men without Gods are in the bay, our warships will come from behind and trap them. This is the moment we've all waited for."

He rose. "Son," he said, turning toward Gré, "you will lead the defenses. Prepare our archers and trebuchets. And get the new lancers ready, in case they manage to land. Notify the commanders and the city watch. I will not have chaos in our streets. Nobody is to leave unless we say so."

Liviana clenched her jaw. "And what about me? Shouldn't I lead my men?"

The emperor smiled. "You will join us for dinner and watch from above. The merchants and bankers want to hear about your progress at Judge's Pass. Lots of money to be made there once the trade gets up and running again."

Unbelievable.

Everyone else exited the room as Liviana, Nalus, and Sir Yirig exchanged subtle glances.

⁂

"I'm worried about Mapa." Oyza straightened the books on her shelf and blew away dust.

"I know, but can't do nothin' about it," Yars said, lying shirtless in his cell with his hands under his head. "It's too hot today."

Oyza wiped away sweat from her forehead. The dungeon did feel especially warm and moist. She stole a quick glance at Yars—he was terribly thin, but there were still some muscles in his arms and chest. *He reminds me of my brother, a little.*

"You know, the last thing Mapa said to me was, 'rebellion is always right.'"

Yars rubbed a bruise on his side. "So?"

So? "What do you think about that?"

Yars twisted a piece of straw. "Doesn't matter if you can't win. Right now, I don't see anybody winning."

"Well, won't know if you don't try," Oyza said.

"Why do you care about all that anyway? The Ungoverned and that book you like?" He gave a flippant nod toward the secret hole in the wall.

"Yars, I've been a servant my whole life. I lost my family, everything. And the Empire is corrupt. Someone has to stand up to it, don't you think?" She extended a hand, demanding a response.

"You think a few people in a swamp are gonna bring down the Empire?"

Why is he so difficult?

The door creaked open. A tall sentry with a mangled beard walked in. "You, Oyza, better clean up. Minister Valador's coming to see you later." He turned and left.

Oyza slouched. *I don't want to see him ever again. Should have taken that dagger when I had the chance.*

Yars sat up on the hay and inspected crumbs on a plate. He turned to Oyza. "I'm sorry, Oyza. Sounds like a real pain."

A real pain? "I'm sure the mines were hard, Yars, but you wouldn't know anything about being a mistress."

Yars laughed. "Yeah, must be hard living in a fancy lord's home all the time, eating nice food and all that."

Oyza pursed her lips. "It wasn't fancy for me. And I didn't eat well. I had to stand and wait on his family and his daughter all day long."

"I thought you were his scribe?"

"Scribe and servant. And later, mistress." Oyza resumed straightening her books—they were already very neatly organized, but there was always room for refinement.

"Well, I'd rather be a mistress than slogging in the mines all day. It's hot and dangerous, and the food is shit."

Forget it.

"You still haven't told me. What'd you do to get locked up down here? Must not have been too bad, since your master didn't have you killed."

Oyza took a slow breath, leaving behind her books and crawling to sit by Yars. "Do you know the one they call Blacklance?"

45

Yars shrugged.

He really knows nothing. Oyza shook her head with surprise. "Commander Liviana, the one who took Judge's Pass, you know, the city you lived in?"

Yars scratched a flea bite on his foot. "The war didn't really get to the mines. We mined for the merchant kings; then we mined for the Parthassians. Made no difference."

Oyza's eyes grew wide. "Well, she's Minister Valador's daughter. I grew up alongside her, having to wait on her, all that. She hated me."

"Why? What'd you do?"

Oyza scowled. "It wasn't my fault. She always seemed...jealous of me. I think she hated the attention her father gave to me. But also, he let me train with a sparring sword sometimes."

Yars's eyebrows rose. "You? But why?"

"He wanted Liviana to practice without the emperor or his sons knowing. Figured I would be easy for her to take."

"So what happened?"

Oyza piled up some straw under her. "Well, I did all right sometimes. I wasn't good, but I could hold my own. Liviana would get so angry if I defended myself well. She would get reckless. And she often drank too much wine."

"And you tried to kill her?"

"No! I didn't. One time, I brought her a tray of fruits and wine to the courtyard. She screamed at me, 'Pick up a sword!' I refused. Her father had told me I was forbidden from fighting without him. But Liviana threatened me. Knocked the tray out of my hands with her sword. And so, we fought."

Yars tilted his head.

"It happened like always—I dodged a lot of her blows while she got more and more angry. Then, at one point, with her back against the wall, I knocked her sword out of her hand—disarmed her. But then she grabbed my blade with both her hands and gashed her own face with it. There was blood everywhere. I tried to run, but Sir Yirig—this knight who watches over Liviana—caught me at the gates. Liviana told everyone I tried to kill her."

"And that's why your master said you should be thankful? You tried to kill a highborn and should have been executed." Yars laughed.

Oyza squinted. "You don't believe me? You think I did it?"

Yars shrugged. "It does sound a little fishy. Why would Liviana do that?"

Oyza furrowed her brow. " She must have wanted me killed."

"Well, whatever really happened, it sucks you had to go through that." Yars flung his curls from his eyes.

Oyza sat up, her hair shining in warm sunlight. "So, you see, like Mapa said, rebellion is always right."

Yars laughed. "We'll see, Oyza. We'll see. First, we gotta get outta here."

✴✲✷

Liviana sipped a glass of wine from a golden goblet and peered from the colossal windows of the throne room. She scanned the horizon with thin eyes, gazing where the evening sun sank toward the water. There was still no sign of the Men without Gods. Highborn guests clamored at the windows around her, dressed in festive silks adorned with all the latest fashions of the capital: flowery patterns of ivy and thorns, lavender cloaks that dragged on the floor, gold-embroidered dresses covered in zig-zagging black stripes, opal necklaces and emerald rings. They fought one another to glimpse at the emperor's new walls as commanders ordered archers into formation and loaded the catapults. Candles and incense filled the room with the aroma of orange, vanilla, and sandalwood.

Liviana saw Gré on the wall, and her muscles tightened. *I should be there with my men.* She touched the ruby-tipped handle of Xalos as it dangled at her side. With a sigh, she turned to Sir Yirig. "At least they aren't talking to me." She gestured to the crowds of nobles gathered in the room.

"Aye." At the insistence of Nalus, Yirig had shaved his stubble for the party.

Liviana looked around the throne room. Golden chandeliers adorned with diamonds glimmered, black and bronze streamers hung from the walls, and vases bursting with dazzling flowers covered a long table buried with food. Moths fluttered about back and forth to the table, hands full as they brought tray after tray of decadent dishes: roasted pigs, piles of plump berries, stacks of savory cheeses, bottles of sweet wines, barrels filled with beer and rum. In one corner of the room, a small band played lutes and drums while a tall woman, wearing a glittering black dress that spilled far across the floor, sang traditional Parthassian songs: songs of victory, triumph, and courage. On her head sat a tremendous golden wig shaped like a crane with outstretched wings and a long coiled neck. It was meant to depict the Crane Starmark, ruler of music and art, pleasantries, and love.

"It's all horse shit if you ask me. This is a party, not a war room," Sir Yirig munched from a small plate of fruits and cheeses.

"And have you noticed...?" Liviana gestured with her eyes to the doorways.

"Aye." Sir Yirig scratched his chin with giant fingers.

"Celesterium guards everywhere." Liviana took another sip of wine. Her Iron Towers were scattered about, keeping a quiet watch while her father spoke with the emperor near the table. They wore black plate and mail with silk sleeves underneath and carried swords at their sides. Shields adorned with the Hawk-and-Tower in bronze marking rested on their backs.

Uriss strolled over to Liviana. He was flanked by two highborn women. They flaunted silver feathers in their hair and onyx jewels around their necks. Each held a glass of wine and ate lush berries and smooth chocolates from a sparkling tray Uriss held.

Liviana greeted them with a tortured smile. *Gods, I hate this man.*

"Not enjoying the party?" Uriss donned his oily grin. The band seemed to play louder as more nobles streamed into the room, arms full of gifts for the emperor and his family.

"There's an invasion coming, Uriss. It's unwise for anyone to be here now," she said.

Uriss rolled his eyes. "Oh, don't be so sullen. Look, there." He eyed the walls below. "Do you think ladders can reach us? We're fine, Liviana. Have another drink, and relax."

One of the women at his side giggled.

"You see," Uriss said to the woman, showing her with one of his hands, "when the heathens come in and see our walls, it'll be too late. Around the corner, our warships wait. We'll capture them all, and we'll finally get their weapons after all these years."

Liviana and Sir Yirig exchanged weary glances.

"Have you ever seen war, Uriss?" Sir Yirig asked.

Uriss gave a tight-lipped smile.

"Ever know what it's like for blades to pierce your body and think you'll die in a second? Ever drown a man in his own blood?"

Uriss grimaced. "No need for this now, Yirig."

Liviana looked down into her wine to hide a smile.

"In any case," Uriss said, "my brother has the situation under control. And with his new lancers, we'll be unstoppable."

"Those are *my* lancers," Liviana interjected.

Uriss jeered, "It's over, Blacklance. They are not your men anymore. When we get back to Judge's Pass, let's put all this behind us, eh?"

Good thing you'll be dead before we get back to Judge's Pass. Liviana squinted and turned back to the window. She took another sip of wine and eyed the horizon. "And if we don't?"

"And if we don't what?"

"If we don't put this all behind us?"

Uriss scoffed. "Know your place, Commander. You speak to the Archvicar and the son of the emperor."

"I'm sorry, Uriss," she said. "You're right. Judge's Pass will be fine without the extra men. My father has some ideas for how to make sure things run smoothly from now on."

Sir Yirig tried his best not to laugh.

"Very well then," Uriss said.

Liviana gazed out of the window. The sun hovered just above the horizon and would set behind the sea soon. A cool salty breeze blew through some of the opened windows. She looked down at Gré and her men. "Are there any plans for evacuation?"

Uriss chuckled. "So nervous, aren't you? It's only twenty boats, Liviana. It would take hundreds, thousands maybe, to storm the city."

"They usually raid with four or five. Never twenty," Liviana said.

Uriss sighed and stole a sip of wine from a glass one of the women next to him held. "There are no plans for retreat. The Hawk doesn't back down, Liviana. You of all people know that."

Liviana was staring at the setting sun when suddenly she saw them: rows of white sails climbing over the horizon. Her heart froze. "Let's hope you're right," she said, "because it looks as if they've arrived."

Uriss scrambled to the window. "By the gods..."

Murmurs and gasps swept through the room as everyone ran to the edge of the room.

"Out of my way," the emperor said, his bronze cape flowing behind him. Celestrium guards escorted him through the crowd.

Nalus and Liviana exchanged quiet glances. Nalus disappeared.

The music stopped for a brief moment until one of the emperor's assistants ordered them to keep going. The guests gawked at the strangers as they advanced, mouths open as nervous whispers spread through the room. Liviana felt her muscles tense. She placed her hand, sweaty inside its glove, on the hilt of the Xalos.

The fleet sailed closer as the sun fell toward the horizon and turned the sea a dark red. The ships were larger than any the Men without Gods had ever brought to Vaaz. Liviana scanned the walls. Gré rallied soldiers to their posts as they prepared the catapults. Archers climbed atop towers and crouched behind turrets. Some carried torches.

"Prepare yourselves," the emperor shouted, a mug of beer in his hand, "to witness the destructive power of the Parthassian Empire! Today, we will bring ruin upon our enemies from across the world should they dare attack us. Then, onward to Mélor to finish what we have begun: our conquest of Vaaz!"

The nobles cheered and clapped, gaping in awe as the ships drew near and the troops below scurried.

Sir Yirig grimaced. "Exciting, war is, when you've never seen one..." he said to Liviana.

She didn't take her eyes off the fleet.

"Uriss, what do the gods say of us today?" Emperor Edras asked.

"The gods have assured our victory. Just yesterday, the Sword moved into the sign of the Crab, a sure sign of a victorious defense."

"Indeed, the gods smile on all of us today and offer their aid as we destroy the godless heathens," Vicar Dolinast said.

The emperor beamed, watching as the Haf drew nearer to his walls. Parthassian battle songs thundered through the hall as drumbeats echoed. The vocalist, with her arms outstretched as she balanced the great crane wig on her head, channeled the voices of powerful gods with the mighty melodies she bellowed out.

Liviana fidgeted with her glass of wine. She surveyed her men, unable to bear the thought of Gré earning their respect should he score a stunning victory.

The ships were close. They split off into two lines, one pulling closer toward the city at an angle while the other row stayed back, wooden hulls facing the walls. Sailors scurried on their decks like bees. They lowered their sails as they slowed and came to a halt, rocking gently in the dark green waters of the Emerald Sea.

"I've never seen them before," Uriss muttered, his eyes wide.

The emperor cleared his throat and tried to speak, staring at the ships in the bay as Parthassian war songs echoed through the hall. His eyes flickered for a brief second to the walls where his son stood ready atop a tower, golden cape flapping in the salty wind sweeping over the bay. The catapults were ready. Archers clad in gleaming black-and-bronze chainmail stood in tight ranks, quivers full of sharp arrows.

The emperor sipped his beer as the Haf sat still. "You see, they recognize the folly of their ways. We will not burn down like Oyvassa did—we, the Parthassian Empire, will conquer all our foes."

Highborn guests smiled nervously as they watched the invasion.

Liviana gripped Xalos harder. *This is complete foolishness!* "Yirig, gather my Towers. I want all twelve of you near me, now. My father will be back from the dungeons shortly," she whispered.

"Aye."

"Give our captains the signal," the emperor commanded. "Tell them they may strike when ready."

A Celestrium administrator nodded and ran off.

Uriss pulled his shoulders back and downed a glass of wine. "Congratulations, father—the walls paid off."

The emperor was beginning to speak when the ships moved. Wooden flaps on their sides flipped open. Long metal rods appeared in the windows.

Liviana gripped her sword. *What's this?*

Loud booms interrupted her thoughts. Guns on the largest boat—bigger guns than anyone in Vaaz had ever seen—fired three shots into the city walls. The throne room drowned in gasps as chunks of the wall tumbled on the beach.

"By the gods..." Uriss whispered.

The rest of the fleet fired. The blasts echoed through the bay as plumes of smoke snaked into the air.

Liviana stared out of the window, heart pounding. "My men," she said to herself, watching as bursts rocketed into the walls and sent stone, flame, flesh, and guts into the ocean. The booms were so strong, they shook the room. Dust fell from above.

The emperor took another sip of beer.

The Haf fired another round. All four towers holding catapults came crashing down onto the Parthassian soldiers in a storm of dust and blood.

The emperor's eyes darted down as archers and soldiers scrambled atop the walls. The men were buried in smoke that glowed black and red in the light of the setting sun. Flashes of fire burst through the smoke as more bangs jolted the ridge under the castle. The highborn guests began to panic and flee. The music played on.

"My son," the emperor cried. "Where is my son?"

51

A blast exploded near the castle, sending a dangling chandelier crashing onto the table below. Sparks and flames erupted in all directions as scattering guests shrieked, tripping over chairs and tables and each other to escape the room.

Liviana stormed to the emperor, surrounded by Sir Yirig and the rest of her Iron Towers. "Call my men back, now. We must evacuate!"

Seeing her, Uriss ran to find more Celesterium guards.

More blasts fired.

"No!" the emperor boomed. "Our ships can stop them!"

Archers fled as fires engulfed the walls. Stone crumbled.

"My son! Get my son out of there now!"

Liviana fumed. "Get *my men* out of there, now."

More shots rocked the throne room. A blast shattered a window to a thousand pieces, glass falling like glittering shards of rubies. The war song roared on—good Cranes *never* stop playing until told to do so. The vocalist did not even notice the wig on her head had caught fire, burning like a torch and sending more flames into the air.

Liviana scanned the room for her father. There was no sight of him.

An advisor ran to the emperor. "Your Majesty, should we call off the attack?"

"No! No retreat. The Hawk hunts; it does not retreat. Signal the full assault now."

The advisor ran.

Liviana, Sir Yirig, and the Iron Towers stood in his way. "You will not," she commanded. "You will order a full evacuation of the city and the retreat of our warships, now."

The advisor puffed up his chest and tried to squeeze past them.

Liviana withdrew her sword. "You will tell our men to evacuate now, or I will have your head."

Uriss arrived with a contingent of Celesterium soldiers. "How dare you, Liviana. You do not defy my father's orders. Guards, arrest them at once! Arrest *her!*" he hissed, pointing at Liviana.

A flaming stone fell from the ceiling.

Liviana looked for her father one last time. There was still no sight of him. She lifted Xalos and aimed its tip at the emperor. "You always were a fool."

"Seize them!" Uriss roared as Celesterium guards lunged. The emperor retreated, escorted by guards.

Sir Yirig sneered and hoisted his ax, rushing to defend Liviana.

The Celesterium guards charged, swords drawn, and crashed into Sir Yirig's ax and the blades that Liviana's Iron Towers wielded. Clashes of metal echoed against the walls of the flaming room.

Sir Yirig swung his ax into the chest of one of the guards and sent the guard's body flying. The man squealed as his lungs crunched inside his chest and blood leaked from his cuirass.

Two Celesterium soldiers sprang at Liviana as her Towers stepped between them, raising their shields to block the attack. One wielding a long pike jabbed toward Sir Yirig. The knight evaded the attack, yanked the end of the spear, pulled the man close, and hurled his head into the man's skull as a loud crack turned to blood that gushed on the floor.

Uriss drew a twisted dagger from his cloak and charged at Liviana. He lunged at her throat. Liviana parried the attack with ease, Xalos clashing into the dagger and nearly knocking it from his hand. Thick smoke burned her eyes as flaming streamers fell from the wall. *I will kill you now!*

Uriss launched himself at Liviana, his dagger thrusting for her neck repeatedly, gleaming and flashing in the lights of the fiery blaze burning around them. One slash tore into her cloak. Liviana stumbled backward, slipping on a tablecloth. Uriss made a swipe at her chest as Liviana fell backward again, her sword slashing at his stomach but missing. She swung her leg low and flung it into Uriss's ankle. He tumbled as Liviana fell into a Celesterium guard. The fires made her skin sweat.

Liviana rolled to the ground as a flaming chandelier dropped onto the man next to her. His body was buried in chains, fire, and glass as he howled in pain and thrashed around the room.

"We have to leave. Now!" Sir Yirig gestured at the Iron Towers to follow him.

Liviana agreed, wiping a stream of blood from her chin. She turned and saw Uriss crawling on his knees behind a wall of fire. "Fine. Let's go. We'll deal with Uriss later."

Fires engulfed the hall as more windows shattered and rattled on the stone floor. Beyond the windows, the city burned like a fiery inferno. A blast landed into the dome of the Temple of the Hawk. It crumbled to pieces as a dust cloud engulfed the capital. Liviana and her men had almost reached the exit when a stream of Celestrium guards appeared in the doorway, swords drawn. *Great.*

Sir Yirig and the Iron Towers surrounded Liviana like an impenetrable wall. "If you want to live, you will do as I say, and you will follow me out of here," Liviana commanded. Xalos gleamed in the blaze as a flaming beam fell and exploded in a burst of sparks.

"You heard her." Sir Yirig lifted his ax and dug in his heel.

Parthassian guards poured into the room, armed with long halberds.

"There they are!" one of the guards said, pointing at Liviana. He was young, with short, brown hair and pleasant eyes. His breastplate glistened.

Liviana and Sir Yirig exchanged nervous glances as Liviana gripped her sword tightly. They were greatly outnumbered.

The Celesterium soldiers began to close in when the young Parthassian sentry gave a command. Halberds plunged into the Celesterium guards. They howled, blood spewing from the cracks of their armor and staining the wavy blue capes they wore over their shoulders.

Sir Yirig smiled as he and Liviana charged the Celesterium guards. Sir Yirig's ax ripped through one while Liviana drove her sword through the throat of another. The Empire's guards butchered the rest.

Liviana straightened.

The castle guards knelt. One spoke to Liviana but kept his head bowed. "Glad to see you're safe, Blacklance. My name is Plinn Hales. I'm with the castle guard. We'll escort you out of here."

Liviana slid Xalos back into its sheath. *Gods, that was close.*

"Come," Plinn said, "your men await you at the city gates."

Liviana turned to look at the throne one last time. She could hear the Haf firing. The fires roared as she wiped sweat from her forehead.

One of her Iron Towers ran up to her. "Commander, I followed Uriss and Vicar Dolinast. They went separate ways, but I heard Uriss shout to him, 'Empty the vault! Drain it!' I don't know what he means. Should we pursue him?"

"No, no." Liviana shook her head. "We need to go now. Sir Yirig, take our men with Plinn to the city gates. And send word to the captains, have our fleet set sail for the harbor at Parthas immediately."

"Aye," the knight replied, sweat pouring down his cheeks.

"And evacuate our men from the city and prepare to march to Judge's Pass. Take as many from the city as you can. If anyone tries to escape, kill them. Plinn, see to it that nobody escapes. Understood?"

The young sentry nodded.

Liviana started down the hallway. "I will not leave without my father." They parted ways and ran into the halls, flames blazing around them.

CHAPTER 6

"What do you think it is?" Oyza asked, staring up at the ceiling. The dungeon rattled, and dust fell into her hair. She shook it out with her hands.

"I don't know." Yars shrugged.

A sudden blast shook the walls so much that Oyza and Yars were nearly thrown to their feet. A large crack appeared in the ceiling above Oyza as a rock the size of her head tumbled to the floor.

"Look," Yars said, pointing above Oyza's cell. The crack stretched from the outer edge all the way to the iron bars.

Another blast roiled the room. The crack widened as Oyza bounced out of the way of the debris. *Gods!* She ran to the iron bars and began to pull. "If I can...just pull...hard enough..." she said, gritting her teeth and pulling on a single bar with both hands as hard as she could. Her heart raced.

"Come on!" Yars said.

Another blast threw them off balance as a giant stone fell behind Oyza. "Come...on....!" Oyza grunted. She looked up and saw the top of the bar was more exposed as another piece of rock fell. An explosion sent her tumbling as the bar flew completely out of place. Her skin scraped against the rough floor.

"You got it!" Yars shouted.

Oyza rose to her feet, rubbed dust from her eyes, and gave the bar one last pull. It ripped from the floor. "Yes!" *Gods, we can get out of here!*

"You did it!"

She turned her body sideways, exhaled as much air as she could, and squeezed through the bars.

"Now, keys! Keys, keys, keys!" Yars jumped in his cell.

"I know!" Oyza's heart pounded. She ran to the end of the hallway and found a ring of keys.

"Come on, come on, come on!" Yars hopped as Oyza tried every key on the ring at his cell. Her fingers shook and fumbled with a combination of fear and excitement—she wasn't sure which. *We're really getting out of here!*

The lock clicked.

Yars flung the door open and hugged and kissed Oyza. "You did it! You did it!"

They embraced for a quick moment before running toward the door.

Yars stopped, grabbed a bottle of rum from the table near the door, and drank. "Ah!" He smiled as he handed the bottle to Oyza.

She smiled back and took a drink. The alcohol burned. She took another swallow, then passed the bottle to Yars. "Come on." Oyza wiped her lips with her sleeve.

They ran to the door.

"We have to be quiet, or else they might hear us," Oyza said, crouching a little. She tucked her hair behind her ears.

Yars nodded, his giant wily smile consuming his entire face. He brushed aside a pile of curly hair from his eyes.

They opened the door and crept around the hallway, hiding in the shadows and making as little noise as they could. More bangs jerked the dungeon. Torches on the wall quivered. They tiptoed around a corner, Oyza poking her head on the other side to make sure no one was there.

"Where are the guards?" Yars said. "There's nobody here." He looked back and forth both ways down the hallway.

"I don't know," Oyza replied.

They snuck down the hall and reached another corner.

"I don't know the way out. I know how to get to the gardens upstairs, but we don't want to go that way."

Yars nodded.

Oyza creased her forehead. *Mapa! We can't forget him.* "I'm not leaving without Mapa."

Yars took a deep breath and bit his lip. "He could be anywhere. It's been weeks. He's probably being flogged in the town square right now!" A trickle of sweat poured from his brow.

Oyza shook her head. *No, absolutely not.* "We can find him. Come on, this way." She took off running.

Yars hesitated but followed.. They twisted and turned through empty halls, at one point climbing up a flight of steps. Nothing but darkness and empty rooms. Not even guards.

"This is crazy, Oyza," Yars grumbled some time later. "We gotta go. Now! We're just running around in circles, and the guards could show up at any minute."

Oyza frowned. "I'm not leaving without Mapa." She ran down another path. *Where are you?*

Yars shrugged and followed.

Oyza ran past a hallway, then froze. She knew where she was. She turned to Yars, horror on her face. "Go! Go find Mapa, please!" She waved her hands at Yars to leave. "Find Mapa. I'll come find you later."

Yars threw up his arms in confusion and turned back. "Fine!" He balled his hands into fists and stormed down another hall. A flurry of bangs rattled the walls.

Minister Valador's eyes widened when he saw Oyza as he exited his private room around the corner. He fidgeted nervously with a bottle in his hands before hiding it in his cloak. "Oyza, what are you doing here? How did you get out?" He grabbed her arm. "I didn't tell the guards to release you."

"Let me go!" She pulled away from him.

Minister Valador tossed Oyza into the room. Her body tumbled on the floor. "Stay here, Oyza."

Oyza jumped to her feet and dashed forward, blocking the doorway as Valador closed the door on her. She snagged a thick book sitting near the door and smashed it into the minister's knees. *No! I am not getting trapped now.*

Minister Valador wailed and keeled over. He slapped Oyza's face and twisted her arm. Her skin burned. She cried out in pain as she pulled the minister into the room. His hand left a sting on her cheek as it turned red and began to throb.

They wrestled on the floor, knocking over a table as burning candles and stacks of dusty scrolls crashed to the ground. Minister Valador grabbed the dagger on the table and lunged at Oyza.

She grunted and stopped his wrist just before it could pierce her throat. "No!"

Minister Valador seized her neck with his other hand and began to strangle her. Oyza pounded her forehead into his eyes as the minister recoiled in pain. The dagger went flying. Oyza desperately reached for it.

"You bitch!" Minister Valador snatched her ankle as they fought on the ground. Flames began to leap around them.

Oyza picked up the dagger and stabbed the minister's arm. "Get off me!"

He pulled his arm back. Blood soaked through his clothing. "You bitch! You filthy bitch!"

Oyza sprang to her feet. She managed to run two steps before the minister stretched out his leg and tripped her. She fell, her skin scraping against the coarse floor and drawing blood. Oyza went in to stab him again. Minister Valador grabbed her body and pulled her close. He grabbed her wrist, keeping the knife she plunged at his face from breaking flesh, then lifted his knee and slammed it into Oyza's chest.

The dagger catapulted across the room. The minister wrapped his hands around her neck.

Flailing, Oyza noticed the leather belt around his waist was loose. She stole it and looped it around his neck. Papers on the desk and shelves burned as Oyza's skin grew hot. She tightened the belt.

"Why you..." Minister Valador's voice was strained and bitter.

His grip on her throat grew weaker as Oyza pulled on the belt, gritting her teeth. Tears welled in her eyes.

He gasped for breath. "My...my jewel! Please," he pleaded. "I was good to you! I was...good to you!"

Oyza pulled harder, flames spiraling around her. "I'm sorry..." she said through her teeth as Minister Valador's body jerked. "But you were not good to me!"

The minister's face turned blue. His hands twitched. "My jewel...!" he begged.

Oyza stared into his dying eyes through tears. "My name is *not* little jewel! My name is Oyza Serazar. I am from Oyvassa. I will find my family, I will bring an end to your empire, I will free my friends, and no one is going to stop me! Rebellion...is always right!"

The minister gagged one last time before his body fell flat.

Oyza sat back, palms leaning on the floor as tears streamed down her face. *What have I done? I killed him!* She licked a trickle of blood from her arm, breathing heavily and staring at her master's still body as flames engulfed the room. Her heart pulsed.

She felt fear. She felt joy. She felt excitement. She felt horror. She fled.

❦

"I'm going to escape. I'm going to head east. I'm going to find a fat sack of gold. I'm going to Talazar City." Yars's heart pounded as he ran through the corridors. *Witchdust and gold, that's all I need.* He looked left. He looked right. There was nothing but empty rooms and doors leading nowhere. He took a torch from the wall and darted into a dark hallway.

Prisoners around him hollered. Yars ignored them. He turned another corner and peeked inside an opened room.

Found him: a frail old man with no legs, hanging by his wrists on a wooden board.

Fuck. Yars's grip on the torch tremored. *Fuck, fuck, fuck.* He took a deep breath. *No. No, no, no.* He turned and ran. *Not my problem.*

He tried to run, to sneak and bolt down the hall and disappear into the shadows forever, but his legs felt like giant stone pillars weighing him down and growing heavier with each step. He stopped.

"Oh, fuck me!" He turned back. *I can't believe I'm doing this.*

More blasts jolted the dungeon, and flakes of dust fell.

"Mapa, it's me! It's Yars!" He ran into the room.

The old man coughed. "Yars... Where is Oyza? What's going on out there?"

Yars sat the torch down and worked to undo Mapa's chains. "I don't know. But let's go, now." He lifted Mapa onto his back as Mapa wrapped his skeletal arms around Yars's neck. *This is stupid! I should just run.*

Yars lifted the torch and turned, ready to leave.

"Stop!" a warden boomed from the doorway. "How did you get out? Put him down!"

The warden lifted his sword and approached Yars. He was a foot taller than Yars, with a slitted black hood over his face. His blade gleamed.

Yars lowered Mapa to the ground then lurched right, dodging the sword. The sound of metal scraping against the floor made Yars shudder. Yars darted to the other side of the room. There was a rack of torture devices. He chose the biggest one—a long, curved hook with a wooden handle.

The warden lunged at Yars. Yars deflected the blow as he rolled across the floor. He knocked over the rack of torture devices. They rattled across the ground, echoing down the halls. *I should have just run! See what happens when you try to do the right thing?*

Yars jumped to his feet and swiped at the hair falling into his face. With gritted teeth, he stared right into the warden's eyes. Yars thrust his makeshift weapon at the warden in a swift blow. The warden sidestepped, and Yars lost his balance, falling into the wall.

The warden swung his sword high above his head.

Yars's eyes grew wide. He dodged one more time. The blade scratched the side of his arm and drew a trickle of blood. Yars was cornered. He called out to Mapa, but the old man's body lay on the floor, blood seeping out of cuts on his skin.

"Yars!" a voice called from the doorway.

Oyza charged into the room with a sword aimed at the warden. The warden turned to face her, his blade swinging. Oyza plunged her sword into his stomach. The man shrieked as he keeled over. Yars drove the hook into the warden's back. The warden yelped as blood spewed on the floor.

"Oyza!" Yars embraced her. "You found us! Come on."

"Mapa, are you all right?" Oyza sat at the old man's side.

"There's no time." Yars picked up the torch and a sword. "Get him up."

"I got it," Oyza said.

Mapa wrapped his arms around Oyza's neck, and they fled the room.

Oyza breathed heavily, sweat trickling from her forehead onto her face. Carrying Mapa was harder than she'd anticipated. Her muscles ached.

"Which way?" Yars shouted, running ahead with his torch.

Mapa coughed. "Oyza...not this way! Go back down, follow...the path toward our cells and turn left instead. I'll point the way to an exit. It will take you...to a path the guards use sometimes, to get outside... You'll find a ladder leading down to the water... There may be a small boat down there..."

Oyza nodded, and they dashed into the hallway. They followed Mapa's instructions. It was barely more than a minute before they heard someone shouting from behind.

"Guards," Yars said.

Oyza gulped. They winded through the halls, up and down, left and right, until they reached another room full of prisoners.

Oyza stopped. "Yars, we have to help them! We can't just leave them." The weight of Mapa on her shoulders began to crush her. *We can't just leave all these people here.*

"There's no time, Oyza. We have to go!" Yars said, the torch illuminating his face.

"Keys! Where are the keys?" Oyza frantically searched the room. The men behind the iron bars—gaunt, scared, toothless and filthy—begged for them to help.

The sounds of footsteps grew louder.

"Oyza if we don't leave now, we're going to die!"

"I'm not leaving anyone behind again, not again!"

Yars stopped Oyza and held her head with his hands. "Oyza, forget it! We have to run!" He knocked over two barrels and a rack of rusted spears to slow the guards.

Oyza took a deep breath and wiped away sweat. The weight of Mapa on her back was too much. "I'm so sorry," she said to the prisoners. "I'm sorry."

They dashed out of the hall and turned a dark corner as booms continued to shake the ground. After some turns, they found the door. It was old and rusty but ajar. Yars slammed his shoulder into it. The door swung open. On the other side was a cliff over the sea. A winding path hugged the side of the ridge.

Oyza ran to the edge of the cliff as Yars shut the door behind them. Oyza gawked at the attack for a moment and sat Mapa down. A salty wind blew through her hair. Rows of ships were buried in smoke as the last light of day glowed on the horizon. Gold coins and jewels rained from the sky and splashed into the ocean. It glimmered, an endless waterfall of treasures.

"What's going on?" Yars frantically piled rocks and whatever else he could find in front of the door. "Is that...gold?"

Mapa coughed as blood trickled from his mouth and onto his beard. "Come here, Oyza," he gestured with his hand.

Oyza knelt next to him and held his hand.

"You must, Oyza, you must go without me... Around the corner, the ladder will take you down. There's a small cave beyond the beach just behind the ridge here. The guards use it. Find a boat there..."

Oyza panicked. *No. I won't leave him.* Tears formed in her eyes. "Not without you, Mapa, no..."

Mapa coughed up blood.

"They're coming!" Yars had piled up everything he could in front of the door and pressed his back into it.

"Listen to me closely, Oyza... I have something to tell you..."

Oyza leaned in closer. *This is it. Mapa's story.*

"Oyza...I am not the man I said I was. I never tried to assassinate the emperor... No...I was an engineer for King Liorus... When Oyvassa fell, I fled...but I found one of their guns... I took it, and I learned how it worked..." He paused, wheezing and hacking up more blood.

Oyza gripped his hand. His skin felt like warm leather.

"But the Empire found me... I burned everything before they could get it...but they knew...and they've tortured me for years to find out...but they don't know, I hid copies of everything... Buried in the Crypts of Oyvassa,

THE SPIRIT OF A RISING SUN

my wife's tomb, the Yillip family...down the hall of the Frostpetal, there, Oyza, there, you'll find the hidden schematics..." Blood spilled from his lips.

Oyza nodded. She squeezed Mapa's hands and fought back tears. *Gods, no...*

"We have to go!" Yars urged. Someone was pounding the door from the other side.

"Go," Mapa said. "But first...please...don't let them take me again..." He pointed at her blade.

Oyza fought back tears as she shook her head. "Mapa, I can't—I can't."

The Haf fired into the city. Gleaming treasures and gold coins fell from the sky.

"Please, Oyza..."

Oyza closed her eyes. Tears streaked down her cheeks, splashing on Mapa's chest. She looked back at Yars one more time. He still held the door shut. She looked ahead at the sea, the sun setting behind the fleet firing into the city as all the wealth of Goldfall plunged into the depths below. She looked down at Mapa, her eyes burning with tears as her hands trembled. *I can't.*

He begged her with a desperate plea in his eyes one more time.

But I have to. Oyza gritted her teeth and picked up her blade. She inhaled a salty breath and looked away.

"Thank you, Oyza..."

"Thank you, Mapa, for all these years together... I wouldn't have made it without you..."

Gods! Please tell me this is the right thing to do.

Oyza slit his throat and exploded into tears. She threw the blade and laid her head on Mapa's torso. He released his last breath as a fountain of blood soaked Oyza's hair.

"Here they come!" Yars said.

The door burst open and knocked him to the ground. He jumped to his feet and picked up his sword, clasping it with both hands. The barricade shattered as a woman emerged in the dust. In her right hand she held a massive sword.

"You!" Liviana hissed at Oyza. "You murdered my father!" She swung Xalos at Yars.

He ducked and staggered backward toward the cliff. He deflected another blow with his sword as the clash of metal rang into the air.

"I should have killed you!" Liviana swung again at Yars. She pushed him back toward the cliff. Liviana lifted up her sword for the killing blow as Yars tripped and fell over.

He rolled to his side as the blade collided into the ground. He scooped a pile of sand and slung it into Liviana's eyes. She cursed and flung her sword, lunging at Yars as he sprang to his feet.

"No!" Oyza flew at Liviana with her blade.

More shots rocked the city as gold and silver coins still fell from the sky.

"Run, Yars!" Oyza parried a blow from Liviana. "Liviana, just let us go!" The two circled each other, swords drawn and ready. Their eyes locked. Oyza wiped a trickle of blood from her jaw.

"Here we are again, Oyza. My father's *jewel*."

"Liviana, I'm warning you, just let us go!"

Two loud booms fired into the rocks near them. The roof collapsed, sending fragments of rock to crash into the ground as they all lost their balance. Liviana fell and dropped her sword.

Yars ran down the path on the cliff's edge. "The ladder! It's gone!" he shouted, staring at two ropes dangling and flapping in the wind.

"We'll have to jump!" Oyza and Yars ran down the path.

Liviana followed, swinging reckless blows at Oyza. Oyza dodged, the blade grazing the hairs on her arm.

"You bitch... I should have killed you when I had the chance!"

The ground rocked. A gargantuan stone fell in front of Liviana. Oyza and Yars slipped beyond her reach, hugging the precipice. The waves roared as salty winds stung their faces.

"You can run, Oyza, but I will find you! Wherever you go, wherever you think you're safe, I will find you, and I will make you pay for what you've done!" Liviana yelled.

They reached the end of the cliff, wind whipping and howling around them.

"This is it." Oyza gripped Yars's hand as they looked into each other's eyes.

His palm was warm and soaked in sweat. The gold still fell before them, glimmering in the sunset. After taking deep breaths, they jumped into the sea, splashing in the waves and sinking beneath the surface. The cold water sent shocks through their bodies.

Oyza was the first one up. She took a huge gulp of air and scrubbed the saltwater from her eyes. "Yars! Yars, where are you?" She splashed against the waves.

"Here!" Yars wiped his eyes as he popped out of the water. "I can't...I can't swim!"

Oyza swam to him and grasped his arm. "I need you to kick!"

A hefty wave pummeled their heads.

"This way! I think it's over here." She pulled them toward the bottom of the stone ridge.

They wrapped around the corner, fighting against the strong waves.

There! Just a few strokes away was the small beach Mapa had told them about. With a final kick, they swam ashore and crawled onto the sand, gasping for air on their knees. There was a small dark cave with a few rowboats sitting on the bank.

"Here, we can stay here. We're out of sight." Oyza rose to her feet. Water dripped from her hair and clothing.

Yars lay on the beach taking slow breaths. His wet body glistened. "They'll find us here." Yars crawled, fingers digging into the sand. "We should leave now."

"No. If we leave now, they'll catch us." Oyza's hands trembled, but she felt some relief. Liviana was gone. "Let's wait and see if the fog rolls in tonight. It'll be our only chance."

Oyza crouched beside one of the boats. "This will do. Let's wait here until dark." *Gods, what's going on? Mapa...*

Yars stared out at the sea. The firing seemed to stop as night fell over the waters. He started to laugh uncontrollably.

Oyza looked at him, confused.

"We did it, Oyza, we really did it! We're free!" Yars dropped to his knees and sat in the sand as a wave toppled into his waist.

Oyza looked down at her hands. *He's right. We did it. We're free...*

She wanted to think about Minister Valador. *Did I really kill him?* She wanted to think about Mapa. *Schematics? The Crypts of Oyvassa?* She wanted to think about the prisoners they left behind. She even wanted to think about Liviana. *She'll come after me forever.* But she couldn't think of these things now. For the first time in over fifteen years, she could think about only one thing: her freedom.

CHAPTER 7

An iron chain dug into the ship's hull as a row of sailors on deck tugged at the end. They grunted as they pulled, ragged clothing dangling from their frail arms. Greasy blond hair fell down their backs.

Alden stood near, his jaw tense. He wore a tight leather tunic emblazoned with the sigil of Hafrir on it: three green diamonds and a silver crown at the center. He watched the chain rise from the sea behind a thick layer of fog. "We staked everything on this mission, Svend. A whole fleet, new cannons. All to get the gold in Goldfall. Now every bit of it is gone—at the bottom of the *fucking* sea." Alden leaned over the ship's edge and rubbed his eyes. His black hair, normally well-kept, fell in messy strands. A splash of black ink covered the back of his neck.

Svend walked to the edge of the ship, a scowl on his shriveled white face. He was a stocky man, and he wore a heavy wool tunic with a pattern of green diamonds sewn into the sleeves. A gray cloak was thrown over his shoulders. "We'll have to find another way to please Dron Eerika, I'm afraid."

Alden would have choked if he had had the energy. *This was my first test, my one true chance to prove myself, to prove I'm better than these people, and now what? I have nothing!*

A wooden box splashed from the water at the end of the chain and scraped up the side of the ship, water and stringy seaweed dripping from its cracks. The sailors gave a mighty pull, and the box toppled onto the deck. It split open as water spilled in all directions. A lone fish flopped.

"It's nothing! " Alden fumed "Forget it. The damn harbor is too deep." *I'm going to be killed for this.* "Svend, what do you think we should do? Tell me. We can't return to Hafrir empty handed." *And they need me, my family.*

Svend stared at the coast of Vaaz. "They may yet recover some gold from the city."

"Enough to fill twenty ships? It's gone, Svend. You saw it as well as I did." *I can't go back to Hafrir.* He eyed the shore. It was blanketed in mist. *Can't go back there either.*

"We need to go elsewhere. Why not go north to Mélor?" Svend asked.

Alden scowled. " It's too cold in the north this time of year and too far. No, the men would never accept that plan—they're angry at me enough as it is." They paced the deck as a flock of gulls circled overhead. "What of the Parthassian fleet?"

"A handful headed north, toward Parthas. Fled from the harbor. Cannons must have scared them off."

Alden stopped, placed his hands on the ship's railing, and inspected the castle above him. "We have to do *something*. Let's make camp. But not here in the city—too much is smoldering, and for all we know, they may come back. We'll anchor south of here, find a defensible position, and stay as hidden as we can." He imagined the gold and treasure sunk deep beneath the abyss. The hawk statue jutting out from the ridge seemed to mock him.

Svend grumbled. "Are you sure?"

Alden took a deep breath. "Yes. We'll make camp tonight and look for food. In the meantime, we'll figure something else out."

Svend acquiesced and made his way inside the ship to pass along the orders, leaving Alden alone in the mist, picking his nails. He took a deep breath as memories of his childhood in Vaaz came back to him. He never forgot anything about Vaaz, no matter how much he tried to throw it out of his mind. He thought again about the Scarab tattoo buried under black ink on his neck.

I wonder if they're here, somewhere...

He gazed at the plumes of smoke rising from the city.

Just like Oyvassa. Burning and ruined. Just like home. He turned away from the shore. *No. Hafrir is my home now.* He made his way back inside the ship and poured himself a glass of mead in an iron cup. Maps adorned the walls, and a fine green rug ran down the middle of the room. A brass telescope sat by a window. In one corner hung a green Haf flag decorated in diamonds and crowns.

Svend stepped in and took off his cloak.

"Mead?" Alden asked.

"Not now. Too early." Svend placed a pistol on the table.

Alden rubbed his eyes. "I was supposed to prove myself to the Dron with this raid."

Svend stared. "Yes, and getting the men to stay here much longer...it's going to be hard. They're already upset about, well, you know."

The words stung. For a Vaazian to be in command of a Haf fleet did not sit well with most back in Hafrir nor with the men on his own boats. But the Dron had come to love her captured foreign Vaazian over the last fifteen years, and when Alden convinced her he could fill twenty vessels with gold, she insisted he be put in charge of the mission. Alden knew little of warfare, but he was the only one who really knew Vaaz. And his family back in Hafrir needed him too.

"Is it hard? Being back here?" Svend spun his pistol on the table.

Of course it is. Alden tried to stop memories of his birth family and home. *I can't show weakness.* He raised his chin. "Of course not. I'm Haf now. I have been most of my life. These people...they're superstitious, they're stuck in old ways, they don't know what's best for them."

Svend ended up pouring himself a drink. "Barbarians, if you ask me."

"And they worship the comet." Alden thought again about his own Starmark. It always embarrassed him. "Can you believe they still call us the Men without Gods?" He laughed.

Svend chuckled. "Many gods, one god, no gods, what does it matter? We've got guns and cannons, and they don't. That's what matters."

"I'll drink to that." Alden raised his glass with Svend.

They spent the day figuring out a plan for the future and pondering ways to keep the men pleased in the meantime. By evening, Svend left to take a tour of the city. The men had already recovered food, horses, and some gold and silver, but perhaps there was more.

At nightfall, Alden downed another bottle of mead and examined the map. His eyes traced the coastline from Goldfall all the way south and east to Oyvassa, past the swamps. They stuck on Oyvassa longer than he would have liked. He shook his head and looked away before memories of that day came rushing back to him. He eyed Hafrir on the map, thinking about his life these past fifteen years: how scary it had been when he'd first arrived, how the air smelled like smoke and how the buildings were so tall. He remembered how the scholars in the Dron's court had examined him so thoroughly, their eyes and fingers prying his naked body like a strange beast from the far side of the world. He remembered how he would have done anything to go home, to see his family. All the nights he'd cried, the nights he was alone in a foreign world. But the Dron had taken him in. She was the only one who cared, the only one who saw a frightened little boy, rather than a lost animal. *And I owe it to her. I promised her all this gold. And she did it, against the wishes of her own generals and advisors.*

And yet, somehow, I still miss them. I still...I don't want to see them die.

He sighed. *It doesn't matter. Death and destruction like they can't possibly imagine come here.* He took another sip of mead and wiped his lips with his sleeve.

But it doesn't have to be that way if they just submit. If I find them, I will make them understand.

THE SPIRIT OF A RISING SUN

Alden woke to a pounding on his door and scrambled to throw on a shirt and pants. "Enter!"

Svend stepped in. "Caught one already. Hjan, that old drunk. Tried to run."

Alden moaned. "Already? Already one is running?" He opened the curtains as silver light from both moons poured in.

"What do you want us to do? The punishment for desertion is death."

Alden sat, rubbing his temples. "No, no, Hjan is popular with the men. If we kill him, it will only make things worse. Throw him in the brig. We'll let the Dron deal with him later."

"As you say." Svend left.

Alden returned to bed but couldn't sleep. *Running back to Vaaz. It could be so easy... No, I could never. If the Dron caught me, I'd be burned at the stake or disemboweled or worse. And would they even take me?* He rubbed the back of his neck, remembering how painful it was when they'd tattooed his Starmark. A Scarab. His father had wanted him to go into the priesthood and spend his life helping lost souls to find their way to the afterlife. Now, there was nothing there but a smudge of black ink. *How would I explain this to them, even if I did run? The priests would never allow it. And what would they think, Mother and Father, if they were still out there?* Alden tossed, unable to sleep.

The sun crept above the horizon, and Alden made his way to the deck to greet the morning over warm tea and roasted fish.

Svend approached him. "Morning. What plans for today?"

A cool wind shot through the fog. "I did some thinking after you told me about Hjan. The men came here not just for gold, but for glory. We need to give them something. Once we're settled, we'll launch a raiding party."

Svend smiled on one side of his wrinkled mouth.

"South of here, a quarter of the way or so toward Oyvassa, there is a trading city on a delta. Groshe, the Vaazians call it. Some of our men raided the coasts north of the city years ago. We can't take the city, but we might catch a few ships on their way in or out. We'll send three ships, and only three. You will be in command. You are not to raid the coasts, only intercept trading ships, taking everything you can of any value, understand? Kill everyone on board, take no prisoners, and sink the ships when you're done. If we find gold this way, we'll try more later. Stay clear of the harbor—there will no doubt be Parthassian warships there." *Kill everyone on board...* It nagged at him, but he dared not show it.

Svend nodded. "A sensible plan. The men are restless, and they want to see..." He stopped.

"To see what?"

"They are still...distrustful of you, Alden. Rumors are spreading that you knew about the trick at the castle, that the gold would fall. That you sent them here to die, that you'll run back to Vaaz.."

Alden slammed his fists on the table. "They're saying *what*? This is nonsense, Svend. You know that. I'll address the men later myself. Anyone spreading these lies will be put to death. The Dron put her trust in *me* to do this, Svend. They need to understand that." He glared at Goldfall. "Look at this city—it's ashes, burning, the people dead and scattered. Do they think I would do this if I still cared about Vaaz?"

Svend gave a hesitant nod.

Alden waved him off and stared through the fog at the drab waters. His heart began to pound. *But still...* He closed his eyes, then spoke without turning from the water. "Wait."

Alden said nothing for a moment, his eyes tracing the path of a peach-colored fish swimming near the surface. He exhaled. "Kill everyone except...for any young women with a Starfish tattooed on their neck. If you find any, bring them to me. They are not to be harmed. Is that clear? A reward—a bottle of our best mead and a fat sack of silver to whoever finds her first."

A puzzled look fell onto Svend's tired face. "This will not make the men happy."

"Then lie. Tell them it's the Dron's orders, not mine. I don't care."

Alden leaned over the vessel's edge, wringing his hands together. *If you're still out there, Sister, I will find you. I will make you understand. I will make you all understand.*

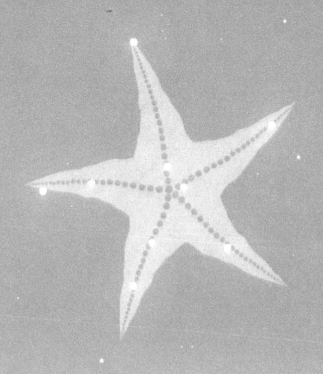

PART 2

GROSHE

CHAPTER 8

Liviana rose from the table, concluding the morning meeting with the gathered commanders. Her father's allies at court were there too. But the report was no good: thousands of refugees and little food. Hundreds of Parthassian soldiers dead. Goldfall in ruins. *At least the priests aren't here.* Liviana made her way through the encampment. Her Iron Towers followed in a tight orbit around her. Except for one. *Yirig. Where are you now?*

Livana rubbed her temples, then stood and raised her chin. Lancers and soldiers, huddled outside makeshift tents and warming their hands around pots of boiling stew, bowed as she passed. Livana kept a calm demeanor, determination in her eyes. That was all she had now. That, and her armies. She tried not to think about her father or about all the gold that had plunged to the bottom of the sea. But above all else, she tried to not to think about *her.*

Heavy boots splashing into the damp grass, Liviana noticed Sir Yirig's squire standing guard. She waved him away, then paused outside Yirig's tent.

"...may the Gods forgive me..." the knight mumbled in his sleep. "...forgive me..."

Liviana scrunched her lips. *Gods, again.* "Yirig! Up! It's time to go."

Sir Yirig jumped from his bed.

Liviana stepped outside, folding her arms and rolling her eyes at her Iron Towers. "You're late. You missed our meeting. Come on, get dressed, and meet me at the front of the line."

The eleven men shared weary smiles.

She told Yirig's squire to prepare the knight's horse, then returned to her black mare. She stuck a foot in the stirrup, swung onto the horse, and trotted to the front of the long column. Black and bronze streamers and rows of lancers followed.

After some time, Sir Yirig rode up next to her. "My apologies..." he said, embarrassed.

"It's all right, but do try to be on time. You're the leader of my Iron Towers, Yirig."

"It won't happen again. I think the news of Nalus's death was too much to bear. Liviana, I am sworn to defend you. With your father gone, I'll double my efforts."

Liviana stared at the horizon, wondering how many days or weeks away Judge's Pass was. "His body was so burnt, giving him to the ocean was the only appropriate thing to do." *Now I truly am alone. But I will carry on the Valador name.*

"Aye. And what of Uriss?" Sir Yirig said.

"Scouts say he's far ahead with a contingent of Celesterium soldiers. The rest of the Parthassian men in the city are with us too, as are what remains of my father's allies at court." She made sure to hold her chin up. Everyone was watching her, after all. What would she do, now that her father was gone?

Sir Yirig turned his head and spat. "Let the priests run, the chickenshits."

Liviana chuckled. "We laugh, but we'll have to contend with them until Cerras arrives. They say he is not going to make it from the North in time for his father's funeral. His coronation will not come for months."

"Funeral?"

Liviana nodded. "The emperor is dead. His son, Gré, is dead too. Died on the walls."

Sir Yirig lowered his head. "How?"

"He didn't make it out of the castle alive, apparently."

Sir Yirig's eyes widened. "Well, this seems good for us, right?"

Liviana snorted. "Indeed. But these new troops from Goldfall, we'll have to make sure we win their loyalty, and fast. It will be a long time before Cerras can arrive from Mélor."

"Aye."

"Plinn Hales, that boy—the guard who led us out of the castle—when I return, I'll make him a knight."

Sir Yirig furrowed his brow, a determined look in his eyes. "A good idea. But a bit young, don't you think?"

Liviana shrugged. "We have to win them now, certainly before the priests or Cerras do. And, Yirig, I want you to train Plinn personally." *I need allies, as many as I can get.*

"Aye." Sir Yirig squinted at the hills on the horizon.

Four Parthassian lancers galloped toward them, bronze streamers waving in the fog. They were armed with sharp black pikes. One of them removed his helm as they stopped. He bowed his head, brown hair flopping out. It was Plinn.

"Commander Liviana," he began, his head so low, it might break his neck. "We've captured six men, as you requested, who fled their lords, but some have slipped through." His tone reminded Liviana of one a man takes when he's desperate to please his superiors. She liked the tone.

"Excellent work. And where are they headed?" Liviana said.

"We believe they're headed south, maybe toward the swamps and the Ungoverned, Commander," Plinn said, the graveness of his voice belying his youth.

Liviana glanced over her shoulder at Sir Yirig. The knight gave a genuine smile—and few things made the old knight smile anymore.

"And what do you think of this?" Liviana turned toward Plinn.

She could see sweat forming on the boy's brow. His hands shook slightly. "I don't... I don't think much of the Ungoverned at all, Commander. Demon-worshippers, hiding in the swamps...all I know."

Liviana tilted her head. "Did you know, Plinn, at least three children of King Liorus survived when they fled Oyvassa fifteen years ago?"

"I did not, Commander, you'll have to excuse me. The emperor never spoke about the Ungoverned or the Shimmering Woods or anything happening there. Only ever spoke of his walls and the war with Mélor and the Celesterium."

"Three children survived, but the monarchy is no more, or so they say. The Liorus line is gone. Instead, they hope to spread rebellion across Vaaz, turning peasants against lords, low-borns against high-borns, commoners against we who are fit to rule." Liviana settled her shoulders. "But we cannot have that here, can we?" *The Celesterium, the famine, the Haf—this is enough to deal with as it is. And now without my father too.*

"No, Commander, we cannot." Plinn shook his head.

Liviana paused. "What did you think of Emperor Edras?"

Her eyes met Sir Yirig's as the boy fumbled for an answer. She saw the corners of the older knight's mouth twisting this way and that as the stoic knight fought to keep a smirk from crossing his face.

"I think he was an old fool, Commander." Plinn hesitated, eyes darting. "Emperors should be strong, should lead their men into battle, should know how to manage the empire's finances. Edras did none of these things."

Sir Yirig's brows rose.

"He has a son, Cerras, fighting way off in frozen tundras, who by law will succeed the throne. What do you think of him?"

Plinn choked and then cleared his throat. "He's a fool too, Commander. The Edras family has not served the Empire well. I think it's time for a change."

"And what of the law? If the law says Cerras is to be emperor but another wants the crown, what do we do? Do we respect the law? Do you—Plinn—do you respect the law?"

"I...well...I mean, the law is..." he stammered, looking like his heart might leap out of his chest.

Sir Yirig laughed.

Liviana interrupted him. "Plinn, let me teach you a lesson about the law. The Celesterium says the law is there to keep the peace with the Gods. But that's a lie. The law is there to protect the strong from commoners who could rise up against us at any moment. But look behind you. See all these men, women, children—sick, dying, sad—all of them following us to Judge's Pass? Why do they follow the law? If the law protects the strong, who protects the law?"

Plinn sighed and shrugged.

"It's whoever has the most swords, Plinn. And *we* have the largest army now in all Vaaz. The most powerful army anywhere. Never forget this, Plinn."

Plinn let out an exasperated huff.

A hawk circled overhead in puffy white clouds. A calm fell over Liviana. The hawk was with her, as was the army. This was what she'd trained for, waited for. "Cerras will wear a crown on his head. Uriss will have his Gods and his scepter. But only we will have swords, Plinn."

Plinn saluted. "Yes, Commander."

"Now, go on. Send out more riders. Capture anyone who tries to run. Kill them if you wish. We are the law now, Plinn," Liviana said.

"Yes, Commander." Plinn bowed his head and was preparing to leave when Liviana stopped him.

"One more thing, Plinn. What's your Starmark?"

"I was born under the Mammoth, Commander, a natural soldier."

Liviana tapped her chin with a finger thoughtfully. "Ah, the Mammoth. I never did visit the Temple of the Mammoth, you know. It's even farther north than the Temple of the Frostpetal in Mélor. Have you been to the Basilica of One Thousand Stars in Judge's Pass, to worship all of the Fourteen at once, Plinn?"

"Never been, Commander. I grew up in the fields of Groshe, only ever went to the Temple of the Hawk in Goldfall. Never even been to Judge's Pass."

Liviana eyed the road ahead. "Good, then your first time there will be quite memorable. Plinn, when we arrive at Judge's Pass, I will make you a knight. You will someday charge with my lancers and help me to put an end to the enemies of the Empire."

Plinn choked. "Commander, I...I don't know what to say..."

"I reward courage, Plinn, courage and loyalty," Liviana said, "and you displayed these in Goldfall. Now go on, keep this rabble from running away. We'll figure out what to do with them in Judge's Pass."

"Yes, Commander." Plinn bowed his head and galloped away. The other men followed him.

Sir Yirig's horse trotted up next to her. He leaned back, pulling the horse to a halt. "A wise move," he said. "I still remember when the emperor knighted me for my service in the war."

Liviana swatted a fly buzzing around her horse. "Yes. We need to make sure we win the hearts of every last soldier who came with us from Goldfall. There may be sympathizers to Cerras among them still."

"Aye, and Cerras, how are we gonna deal with him?"

Liviana nudged her horse onward. "We have only to contain his ambitions. And we'll find some way to deal with Uriss."

"Aye, the little shit. Should've killed him when I had the chance." Sir Yirig followed.

"The Celesterium will do as he commands, but I don't think he'll move on me. He's not so bold, and the other priests would never let him. The Gods forbid it." Liviana raised her head toward the foggy horizon. She removed a leather glove and ran her fingers through her hair. "Do you ever grow weary of the Gods, Sir Yirig? Spouting orders at us about how we ought to live?" *But perhaps we can outsmart even them, if we can make this new opportunity work in our favor.*

"Aye."

Liviana's lips curled into a sly grin. "Never mind. Anyway, I've also got a special task for you." She looked to make sure no one was listening. "After I found my father in the dungeons, I followed two escaped prisoners. I didn't tell anyone, but believe it or not, it was Oyza who murdered my father. The little whore he fought so hard to save ended up murdering him."

Sir Yirig tensed. "Oyza? But she wouldn't hurt a moth."

Liviana glared. "She tried to murder me, Yirig. Did you forget? You were the one who stopped her." *Just like him to take her side. Men...always with heads half-buried in the sand.*

Sir Yirig laughed. "My apologies."

"And before they ran, she was talking to Mapa—that old fool Edras tortured in the dungeon all those years. He died there on the cliffside. But I believe he told her something, something about guns."

Sir Yirig leaned a little closer.

"I want you to find her, Sir Yirig. As soon as we reach Judge's Pass, you and a handful of riders will make for Oyvassa. She'll no doubt head that direction to try and find her family. Stay clear of the Shimmering Woods and the Ungoverned. The patrols already there will be sufficient, and I know she knows that too. She will have to go by the mountains or by sea. I want you to find her and bring her to me, alive. She'll pay for what she did." She lifted her chin. "And bring Plinn with you too. I want him to know what it means to lead. Show him our ways, Sir Yirig. And make sure he wins the men's respect. Not every day a commoner becomes a knight."

"Aye," Sir Yirig said. "And the other prisoner?"

"If you find him, kill him. The bastard threw sand in my eyes when I found them on the cliff. Kill him however you like—slowly, painfully, whatever pleases you—but see to it Oyza watches." She scanned the horizon. "Oyza's forgotten her place. We'll make sure she never forgets again. We'll make sure everyone knows what happens to those who dare to cross Liviana Valador."

CHAPTER 9

Late morning rays crept over the horizon as the last wisps of the fog unraveled in the winds above the sea. Oyza gazed at the distant mountains on her left. *How far away is Oyvassa?* She looked across the boat to Yars. He had fallen asleep and folded himself into a ball. The water was calm, with small waves gently pushing them south. Oyza and Yars had managed to find two small oars, a loaf of stale bread, a small jug of water, and a bottle of rum. They had slept under the boat before leaving at dawn.

Oyza took a slow, deep breath. The cool air carried hints of seaweed and salt.

Yars yawned and lifted his head, his eyes squinting from behind the mess of black curls falling into his face. "How long... Where are we?" He stretched his arms.

Oyza kept rowing, staring into space.

"You didn't sleep?" Yars sat up and cracked his neck.

"No. Too much on my mind. Plus, if we both fell asleep, who knows where we'd end up."

Yars smiled. "Well, at least we made it out." He reached for the crusty loaf of bread, ripped off a chunk, and handed the other half to Oyza. "Where to now?"

Oyza straightened. "Well, we're low on food and water. We'll have to head to shore and figure something out."

Yars chomped on the grub and took a sip of water. "Sorry I slept all night. That cave was cozy. And the rum was good. I don't even remember getting in the boat this morning." He searched for the liquor. "Any of the rum left?"

Oyza twisted her lips. *He really is an addict.* "It's all gone."

"Oh." Yars slumped back. He splashed some water on his hair and beamed. "We're free, Oyza. Do you feel that? Freedom!"

Oyza couldn't help but grin. *His smile* is *cute, I guess. His eyes...they really shine out here.* "We are. We really are. You know, most of my life, I thought I'd never get out of there."

"Here, let me row." Yars reached forward.

Oyza handed him the oars, then stretched her arms.

Yars splashed the paddles into the waves a few times, then turned back to Oyza. "I wanted to ask you, when you wanted to free those prisoners, you said, 'Not again!' What did you mean by that?"

Sourness filled Oyza's gut. *We should have freed those people. What happens to them now?* She tidied up the things in the boat, then gazed out at the glimmering sea. A school of orange fishes swam underneath them. "You know how I mentioned I was taken by Minister Valador when I was young? Well, it started when Oyvassa was attacked by the Haf. My brother, sister, and I were playing this game: knight, princess, and dragon. We always played it with these little toys my father bought at the market. My mother would paint them too. My brother was the dragon; me, the knight; and Rosina, the princess. I always wanted to be the dragon, but my brother never let me."

She hesitated, remembering the toys vividly. "But we heard a Haf ship was near, so we snuck out of the house to go look. My mother warned us not to go near it, but people said there was only one ship, so we weren't scared. No one knew a whole fleet was coming to raid the city. I watched them—their horses, their guns, their torches—just bursting into the city, their green flags waving. We tried to run home, but the city was on fire.

They grabbed all three of us, but I squeezed away." She choked as she relived the painful story. "And I ran. I was scared. I didn't know where to go. I just remember the way my little sister screamed, the way the burning air smelled that day."

"What happened next?"

"I don't remember all of it. People ran into the swamps, there was fire and smoke. I remember sleeping under the roots of an old tree, remember how slimy the roots felt against my skin and the way it smelled like mud. I was hungry, cold—I just remember thinking I was going to die, was going to freeze to death in the cold swamp water. Then a Parthassian scout found me. They threw me in a wagon with other refugees, sent me to Goldfall, and Minister Valador eventually took me in. He insisted my parents were dead. And I'd been there ever since."

But you've gotta be out there somewhere, right? She peered toward the mountains. The sun was rising above their peaks. Warm rays melted through mist.

Yars squinted. "Fucked up, isn't it? People from who-knows-where show up with their guns, act like they own the place."

Gentle waves lapped onto the boat. Dolphins popped in and out of the water, greeting the dawn. Oyza rested her elbow on her knees as the clouds rolled by. "You know, that was brave of you, fighting Liviana like that."

Yars perked up. "Ah, it was nothing." He lowered his eyes as he paddled. "Hey, by the way, you didn't tell me. Back on the cliff, what all did Mapa say to you?"

Oyza shuffled a little in her seat. She cast her eyes into the distance. *Can I trust him?* A gull squawked. "If I tell you, you can't tell anyone else." Who else did she have anyway?

Yars's lips tightened. "I won't, I swear."

Oyza squinted. "Seriously—no one." *I hope this is right, trusting a thief and an addict...*

Yars rolled his eyes and gave a heavy nod.

Oyza edged closer to him, lowered her voice to a whisper, then burst into laughter—as if someone could hear them on their little boat in the middle of nowhere. "I thought Mapa was there for trying to assassinate the emperor." She told him what Mapa had revealed to her. "He told me to go find them." She bit her lip, praying she hadn't just made a terrible mistake.

"What would you do afterward?" Yars asked, eyes wide.

Oyza put a finger to her chin. She hadn't considered the question. "I guess I would go find the Ungoverned."

80

Yars grimaced. "I dunno about that. Demon-lovers, they say..."

"You already know I don't believe that. I'm from Oyvassa. They're not like that, not my family." She took a sip of water.

Yars stroked his jaw and beamed. "You know, you could sell those plans for a fortune. Oyza, you—*we*—could be rich. We could buy land, a castle...anything we wanted."

Oyza hadn't considered that either. *I shouldn't have trusted him after all. He is a thief. And an addict. All he'll care about is gold.*

Yars leaned forward. "Seriously, those Ungoverned—I've heard nothing good. What do you say, Oyza, let's find these weapons and get filthy rich? You don't really think some revolution in a swamp is gonna happen?"

Oyza's chest grew heavy. "I just... Look, even if we did, I'd be running from Liviana and the Parthassians forever. Where would we go? You can't hide from them. You heard Liviana... She says she'll find me anywhere."

Yars slouched. "So you don't want money? What is it then? Revenge? For locking you up?"

"No."

"Then what?"

What does he know? Oyza stared at him. "I'm sorry. It's the right thing to do. It's what Mapa wanted. And I don't have anywhere else to go anyway." *And I have to find my family. Then I'll know what to do.*

"But why?" Yars probed.

Oyza glared at him with thin eyes. "I spent my life around prisoners. Servants. Inside the Empire. I'm not leaving them behind like I did my brother and sister that day. If you don't want to help me, then don't."

A dolphin breached the surface nearby. A cool mist splashed on Oyza's skin.

"Liviana said you murdered her father."

Murder? Am I a murderer now? "Well, I did. He was trying to keep us from escaping the dungeon. I didn't have a choice." Oyza squirmed. There was a lull, the cawing gulls the only sound filling the silence.

"Yeah, fuck him. Fuck all the lords and kings and emperors. Fuck the Parthassians, the Men without Gods, all of them." Yars rowed, splashing the oars.

Oyza perked up. "So if not the Ungoverned, where will you go then? Talazar City?"

Yars blinked. "I don't know. I don't have anyone. I can't go back to Judge's Pass. Lost all my friends. Don't know if they're alive or dead or what. But yeah, I could go to Talazar City, maybe try my luck at the Wastes."

"I thought you were going to steal some gold and buy a little land somewhere?"

"Gotta take it day by day, you know?" He grinned, but only after a split second of sorrow crossed his brown eyes.

Who is this guy? Oyza wondered. *There's a sadness in his eyes, but he covers it up.* He seemed to Oyza like the kind of guy you could trust—even if he was a thief and an addict without any family. There was a kind of loyalty in his voice, almost like he really cared about her. When you have nothing, the few things you do have matter more than anything in the world. Oyza knew this feeling. And she could see it in him. "Why don't you just come with me? At least until we find the schematics?"

"Yeah?" Yars's eyes lit up.

"Let's do it. Let's never become slaves again. Let's see if we can find Mapa's schematics and take it from there," Oyza said.

"Never again!" Yars smiled as he lifted up the oars. It was a wily smile, the kind that could drive someone mad, a smile you could never truly be angry with, a smile that was carved into your memory forever.

"All right, but we're not selling them. Understood?"

Yars rolled his eyes. "We'll see what happens when we get there. I'm not going to those Ungoverned."

Disappointing. Oyza pretended not to hear the last part.

Hours passed as they sailed down the coast. The current pulled them, and they took turns rowing as the hot sun crawled across the sky.

Later in the afternoon, Oyza turned to study the beach. Her arms ached. "We have to get to shore now. Those woods over there, we should land there. They might be the edge of the Shimmering Woods. We're out of water and food. I don't know how we'll get them."

Yars stretched and grinned. "Leave that to me." He winked. He grabbed the oars back and rowed toward the shore as a salty breeze blew into their faces.

The sun burned in the sky as flocks of white gulls circled over their heads. Oyza peered into the green waters at bright fishes swimming in the depths, weaving in and out of a thicket of brown kelp. She dipped her hand into the water and trailed her fingers through the waves. The ocean chilled her skin.

They landed on the beach and hopped out of the boat, dragging it into the sand in case they needed it again. Soft waves soaked their legs as they made their way across the beach. White seabirds poked at piles of dried seaweed as the smell of dead fish and kelp drifted in the air. The trees just beyond the beach stood in thick rows. They were skinny and covered in a chipped white bark with few branches or leaves. A flock of hazel-colored birds sat on their limbs, chirping and singing warmly. Oyza and Yars darted into the woods as fast as they could, hiding among the verdure from whomever might be watching.

Oyza rubbed her eyes. "I don't think this is the Shimmering Woods, not yet."

"How do you know?" Yars picked up a damp twig and began snapping it with his fingers.

"I didn't think it would be anyway. The Shimmering Woods are surrounded by swampland. We're a lot farther north, I guess." *Plus, no palm trees, no vines, no glowing mushrooms. It doesn't look like home, not yet.*

They trudged through the forest as the sound of crashing waves faded away. The underbrush sprawled across the ground, crimson and periwinkle-colored flowers blooming everywhere. Dragonflies and bees buzzed about. It was a tranquil walk, one Oyza appreciated very much after spending years in the noxious prisons of Goldfall. After perhaps two or three hours, a pleasant beam of sunlight kissed their warm skin.

"I've been wondering," Oyza said. "All that gold falling at Goldfall. What was that?"

Yars shrugged. "No idea. What a waste, though. Should've jumped into the water after it."

Oyza pondered it some more as they trekked. *Does this mean the empire is bankrupt now? I wonder what Liviana will do next.*

"So...where are we headed?" Yars started snapping another twig.

"I'm not sure." Oyza tried her best to remember the maps she had seen, but nothing much came to mind between Goldfall and Groshe along the coast. "There are some villages around here, I think..."

Yars groaned. "We gotta find food. I'm starving." He placed his hands on his abdomen.

Oyza stared at a birch tree covered in lichen. "Me too. We'll probably find a town soon..."

"And then what? You heard Liviana—she says she'll find you. Probably has soldiers already looking for you."

Oyza shuddered. "I don't know. We'll have to figure out something. Maybe, if we're lucky, we can find some work somewhere in exchange for food."

Yars continued ripping away at the twig in his hands.

As dusk approached, they came to a clearing in the woods. A narrow, dirt road extended from left to right with nothing else in sight. Ahead, there were only more trees.

"Any idea where it leads?" Yars walked to the center of the road and glanced both ways.

Oyza followed. "No, but I imagine that way leads toward Goldfall." She pointed north. "And that way must head toward Groshe."

"So you think Groshe is our best bet?"

"It *is* a trading town on the coast. Minister Valador said they pay tribute to the Parthassians now. The empire's taken everything from here to the swamps. But it sits on a huge delta, and ships from all over dock there."

"Maybe we should head that way?"

"We could try. There will be Parthassians, but we can probably slip through if we're careful."

They hiked until nightfall. The Sword of Creation appeared in the sky, its long blue streak crisscrossing the darkness amid the Origins and a multitude of twinkling stars. Moonlight from both moons cascaded on the underbrush. They made camp in a small fold in the hillside covered by a giant fallen trunk draped in sticky moss. They slept close, quickly falling asleep as distant wolves howled at the moons.

CHAPTER 10

Birds crooned as the morning sky started to glow. Oyza rose to her feet and stretched, muscles sore from a night of sleeping on the hard ground. She pulled a few petals from her hair and wiped dirt off her face, then straightened up her torn clothing as best as she could.

There was no sight of Yars. *Gone already?*

She crouched beside a creek and rinsed her hands. The chilly water trickled between moss-covered round stones. The air was moist but nippy.

Where could he be? She walked back to the road, but there was still no trace of Yars. A lone bird cawed in the branches. She stood for a long moment, wondering if it would be wise to wander too far away without him. A worried thought raced through her mind: *What if he robbed me and ran?* She patted her pockets before realizing she had nothing worth stealing to begin with.

84

A deep rumble interrupted her thoughts. She turned, squinting and trying to make out what the sound was beyond the trees. The rumbling came closer, closer, closer...

Yars crashed toward her, driving a wagon pulled by a muscular brown horse. He flew at Oyza as she jumped into the forest. Thorns scraped her skin. The stallion reared its legs as Yars struggled to control it.

"Hurry, get on!" he shouted, reaching out his arm.

"Are you crazy?" Oyza jumped to her feet. Her heart raced as she picked thorns from her hair. "Where did you get this?"

An arrow flew past Oyza's face and slammed into a tree behind her with a loud *twang*! A man in the distance cursed.

"Just listen to me! Get up here, now!"

Another arrow came flying in their direction before slicing through leaves. A burly man ran down the road. He stopped and prepared another shot. Oyza's eyes bulged. She climbed into the carriage just behind Yars.

"Let's go!"

Another arrow zipped past them as they sped off down the road. The wagon clanked, its wooden wheels slamming into the rocky road.

"That way...I think!" Yars pulled on the reins in all directions.

"No! That just goes back to the sea!"

An arrow flew past the horse's side. The horse panicked and jerked as hard as it could, the wagon tumbling behind it.

"What about that way?" Yars pointed toward a split in the road. One of the pathways went deeper into the woods. He pulled the reins, and the beast veered to the right, heading toward the trail with a violent jolt as they both nearly fell off.

"Look!" Yars pointed at an old stone bridge crossing the river. Large pieces of rock were missing, and green vines coiled into its cracks.

"We can't cross this fast!" Oyza shouted, her tangled hair whipping in the wind.

"We don't have a choice!" Yars screamed.

The horse galloped in a frenzy. Oyza and Yars braced themselves as the horse dashed across the bridge. A wheel cracked loudly as it shattered on a raised tree root. The stallion pulled the carriage across the bridge and came to a halt. It reared its legs again and whinnied, then broke loose and ran into the woods.

Yars jumped down. "Whew, we made it. I think we lost him too."

Oyza climbed out. "Are you completely crazy?"

Yars raised his chin. "What?"

Oyza shook her head. "You can't just go around stealing people's horses!" *Where are we now?* She panted with her hands on her knees.

"We'll be fine." Yars caught his breath, then walked to the back of the wagon. "Well, look what we have here!" He slid a wooden box from the back. It was full of green apples. "Here, take one!" he said, throwing one at Oyza.

She hesitated a moment, then gnawed into it. The apple was fresh and sour, and it made her mouth tingle. Yars dug deeper, looking for whatever else he could find. Oyza bit into the apple again and savored each bite. She stared down the road, looking for the man who was chasing after them. She figured they had taken so many twists and turns, they'd lost him. She sat down and rested her legs, watching Yars rifle through boxes and crates.

"Look at this," Yars said as the lid burst off the crate. "Oyza, check it out! Jars of...something. What is it? I don't know, but I bet we can eat it." He pried one open, stuck his finger in and tried it. He scrunched his face and stuck out his tongue. "The fuck *is* this?"

Oyza laughed, not daring to give the strange substance a try either. She finished the apple, then climbed into the wagon. "Let's hurry. That man is probably still chasing us."

Yars paid her no attention. He gave the baffling substance in the jar one more chance. "Nope, definitely still not food." He tossed it aside and snagged an apple.

What's this? Oyza found a rusty lockbox and pulled it out. "Look at this, Yars. It's open." Inside was a small pouch filled with silver coins, a dagger, and a necklace. The blade was sharp, with a handle made of two twisting snakes eating an apple at the end. On the necklace hung a glimmering spiral seashell.

Yars yanked the bag and peered into it. "We can eat with this!"

Oyza reached for the dagger and inspected it. "Look at this, Yars. This is no normal dagger. I think this is a mageware."

Yars scoffed. "How would you know?"

"I've seen a mageware before. Liviana's sword, the Xalos. This is old, Yars."

"Well, what do you think it does?"

"I don't know. Let's hold onto it for now. Maybe in Groshe we can find someone to help us find if it's still enchanted."

"If it's a mageware, probably worth a lot of money?"

Money! Is that all he cares about? "Probably. But if it's a mageware, we're not selling it. We might need it." She tucked it into her pockets.

"And what about this?" Yars asked, picking up the necklace. "I bet this would fetch a gold coin—or a hundred." He held the necklace in a beam of sunlight. The seashell glimmered. "Oyza, check this out."

Oyza leaned in. The top of the seashell was sealed with some kind of wax attached to the chain. *Gods!* "Don't open it. I read about magewares like this. This is ancient, Yars. There could be anything in there."

Yars pulled the necklace back. "Another mageware?"

Oyza scanned the cart, but this was the only lockbox. There was a little food, water, some small swords, a crossbow, and a pair of old boots. "Yars, I think this wagon belonged to a magic hunter. We have to go now. If he finds us, we're dead. Hold on to the necklace and the gold. I'll take the dagger."

"Why do you get to keep the dagger?"

Oyza frowned. "Come on, we have to go before he finds us. Why don't you take those boots? You still don't have any shoes." She glimpsed down at Yars's muddy toes and chuckled.

Yars wiped away dried soil from the soles of his feet and graciously put on the boots, then dug some more in the wagon. "Here, a cloak. You should take this, Oyza."

She threw it over her shoulders. It was far too big, but it would provide some protection at night.

They found a bag and packed it with apples, a half loaf of bread, a pouch of salted beef, and even a little lump of savory cheese. They took the swords but left the crossbow—neither had the strength to cock it anyway.

"Which way?" Yars asked.

"I don't know," Oyza said. "We just have to keep going south until we reach Groshe." *I wish I'd taken that map.*

They made their way down the winding dirt trail.

Yars stopped. "Wait. Do you think it's safe to take the main roads?"

Oyza halted. "No, probably not. Let's go back in the woods." She pushed aside a low-hanging branch, her legs brushing up against thorny bushes. "Keep a watch for bandits or Parthassians or whomever might be out here."

"Right." Yars followed her into the woods.

They trekked for the rest of the day. Songbirds filled the air with music as sweet as the lush red berries they harvested along the way. A family of deer greeted them for a brief moment before diving into the maze of trees. Oyza's legs were sore, but she appreciated the scent of the ruby-colored flowers dotting the ground and the way the dead twigs snapped beneath her feet. She gazed at the cracks of blue splitting through the tops of the forest. For years, she wasted in the jails dreaming of this moment: of being free, of searching for her family, of being anywhere but Goldfall.

A few hours later, they agreed to take a break near a creeping river. Smooth stones draped in slimy moss poked out of the water. The stream shimmered as it twisted among tall thin reeds. Oyza took a slow breath, her nostrils filling with the scents of lush leaves, fresh water, and mud.

Yars sat next to her on the riverbank, dipping his feet into the water. "I've been thinking about something I remembered. My friend Pete, he told me once about a place in Groshe, a tavern called The Wayward Oyster. I think he said captains hang out there. A real nice place by the harbor."

Oyza cupped her hands with water and drenched her wrists. "The Wayward Oyster? Worth a try, I suppose."

A bumpy frog hopped onto a stone. It seemed to almost greet them before splashing back into the rushing waters.

Yars ruffled in the bag and pulled out two apples, handing one to Oyza. "Yeah," he said, mouth full, "I bet we could get on a ship. But we don't have enough gold, I think. Gotta find a captain who will give us work to do for a ride."

Oyza nodded. "I bet we can find someone. Ships don't go to Oyvassa anymore, but we could find one heading to Talazar. They could drop us off on the way."

Yars ran some water through his hair. "You really think we're gonna find those schematics there?"

Oyza wanted to scowl but didn't. *What else can we do?* "Yes. Mapa wouldn't have lied. And I doubt anyone has gotten there first. We'd have known about it already if they did."

Yars leaned back, palms digging into mud. "Twenty years. He really was tortured for twenty years?"

Oyza's stomach turned. The dungeons of Goldfall was the last place she wanted to think about. "It's hard to believe. But that's why we have to keep going."

Yars laughed. "You're funny, Oyza. You got free after all these years, and all you wanna do is go dig up some old papers somewhere."

A grin crept up the side of her face. He was right, in a way, but where else could she go? And besides, Mapa had died for this secret. It was the last thing he'd told her, after all those years together. It would be wrong to let that go to waste.

"Come on." Oyza stood up and wiped sweat from her forehead. "We gotta keep moving. That man could still be behind us. Or Liviana." She shuddered.

They marched through the woods, and the sounds of the trickling water became a distant memory. As the sun approached the horizon, they shared stories to pass the time. Yars recounted episodes from the mines at Judges's Pass: one time, an older mineworker told him about a mageware ring a lord had paid a handsome sum for because the ring gave him the strength of ten men—unfortunately, the enchantment wore off just as he was lifting a heavy boulder above his head. Oyza commented on some of the different plants they passed, remembering a few here and there from the books she had read while imprisoned. The Frostpetal plant didn't grow this far south, but one could chew on the bark of willow trees to relieve pain.

The sky turned a dark blue as the sun disappeared, and the Sword of Creation appeared in the sky, its blue tail arcing between the treetops against a dazzling blanket of stars. Ozya crossed her arms and buried them in her cloak, warming them against her body.

Yars rubbed his hands together. He reached in the bag, finding there were only two apples and a scrap of bread left. His belly growled. "We should stop, Oyza. It's getting dark."

Oyza paused by a shrub. "You're right. We can make camp here." She pushed away some decayed branches and sat.

"Should we start a fire?" Yars asked. "It's gonna get colder tonight."

"Sure." She cleared away some more brush as Yars collected a few dry logs.

A moment later, he tossed them down. "All right. I got some logs. So, now what?"

Oyza looked up. "Oh, I thought you knew."

Yars's eyebrows rose. "No, never really knew. My friend Gaspar always started the fires."

Oyza drooped. "Well, I don't know either."

"But you...you read all those books. They didn't teach you how to start a fire?"

Oyza laughed. "Books don't usually teach that sort of thing. But you never learned? Thought you would know after spending all that time on the run."

Yars shrugged, then sat down cross-legged in the dirt, thinking. He stared at the pile of logs. "Gaspar used to take a stick like this," he started, grabbing a thinner one, "and put it between his hands like this."

Oyza watched closely. She picked up a branch and mimicked Yars.

"Actually, wait. First, he took a knife and hollowed out a wider log. Maybe we can use this sword." Yars chipped away at a log with the end of the blade, then picked up the stick again. "Then, you just take the stick and rub it into the log."

Oyza did the same. And then they stopped, out of breath.

Yars gave up. There was no fire, no smoke, no nothing. "It's not working."

"Not for me either." Oyza panted. *Gods, this is exhausting.* She set the stick down.

"Maybe we can try again tomorrow. I'm too tired," Yars said. "I just want to sleep."

Insects hummed in the chilly evening air around them. Oyza took a deep breath, then picked up her stick again. "I'm gonna try again."

"Good luck," Yars said, yawning.

Oyza pressed with all her might, rubbing the stick into the hollowed-out log. But her arms quickly tired. Her muscles burned. She breathed heavily. And then she quit. "I don't know why it's not working." *How could this be so hard?*

Yars shrugged. "Let's just rest. We don't need it tonight anyway."

He gives up so easily. Oyza glanced at the sky, disappointed in herself, and held her cloak tight. *Fine then.* "You know, I haven't seen the stars like this in so long."

Yars raised his head but didn't say anything.

Oyza looked at her hands. "It feels weird, being free."

"Yeah? Nice, isn't it?"

"I haven't been free in fifteen years."

"That's a long time."

Oyza ran her fingers through her hair, picking out a small leaf. "I dreamed of it all the time. About running away and finding my family. Sometimes, Minister Valador would send me on his horse to run errands. Said if I ran and they found me, I'd be killed."

Yars massaged his legs.

A moment later, Oyza added, "Sometimes I wondered if that would have been better. I hated being a servant, you know? 'Oyza, get this. Oyza, get that.' It never got easier." She thought again about the moment she'd killed her master. Her stomach roiled. *Did I really do that? With these hands?*

"Have you ever killed someone, Yars?"

"No, I don't think so."

"Would you ever?"

"If I had to, I guess."

Oyza looked away.

"You shouldn't feel bad. He was gonna kill you, Oyza. Or throw you in a dungeon again. You had to do it."

"I know. But still..." She stretched her fingers. "I didn't think I had it in me." She yawned. *And Mapa too. That's two people I've killed.*

"I wouldn't worry about it," Yars said. "Hey, how far do you think Groshe is?"

Oyza couldn't keep her eyes open anymore. She laid her head atop her folded arm. "I don't know. Could be three weeks walking. I think if we stay on this route, we'll hit the meadows outside the city soon." She remembered something Minister Valador had told her. "The Haf raided there, I think. It should be abandoned."

Crickets, a hooting owl, and snores. Yars was fast asleep.

Oyza looked at the stars again for a last moment, then dozed off. Sleeping on the cold dirt ground was far from ideal, but anything was better than the crummy dungeons of Goldfall.

CHAPTER 11

Drab, slim spires rose from Judge's Pass against the snowy peaks of the Hollowed Mountains. Throngs of tired troops, weary lancers, and anxious refugees trailed behind as black and bronze streamers waved in a solemn breeze. Plinn turned for a moment to face them, then raised his chin forward. *No. I am better than them now. I am to become a knight!* The words sent a thrill up his spine.

"We should send a scout. Uriss may have set a trap." Sir Yirig rubbed stubble on his jaw. Plinn felt unworthy riding so close behind the giant knight, who rode an equally large brown-spotted horse.

Liviana's eyebrow rose. "No. No scouts—I will meet them myself at the gates. We must not show weakness." She lifted her eyes toward the mighty city as they approached. A dense haze hung over it.

Plinn perked up as the Basilica of One Thousand Stars's dome came into view. He could already see the rows of bloodied black lances that stood outside the gateway, the spikes that had earned Liviana the name

Blacklance. Vultures pried at mangled skeletons and scraps of flesh. Flies buzzed.

"Stay behind me, Plinn," Liviana said. Crews of lesser commanders followed, raising Hawk and Tower flags as they advanced toward the city. "Shields up, crossbows out, lances raised."

Plinn beamed and took his position. He almost sheathed his sword but then decided to keep it out. Perhaps the blood that clung to the blade would intimidate the priests.

As they reached the city, its immense gates shrouding all but the tops of the castle spires, townspeople scampered into the roads to steal a glimpse of Blacklance. They sank to their knees, begging the commander for copper coins. She ignored them.

"Look." Sir Yirig said, gestured at the main gate. "Uriss." He rested his hand on his ax.

Plinn's heart beat faster. Uriss stood at the gate surrounded by a coterie of Celesterium guards dressed in brilliant blue plate and mail, blue cloaks dangling over their left shoulders, armed with pikes and crossbows.

"Whatever it is he wants, I'm prepared to make offers. I'm a reasonable person, aren't I?" Liviana asked.

"Aye, of course."

They dismounted at the gate. Plinn and the other commanders followed, flanked by columns of armored Parthassian lancers on horseback.

Liviana stepped back for a moment to talk to Plinn. "See that man there? That's Uriss Edras, Archvicar of the Celesterium, youngest son of the emperor. Watch him closely."

Plinn nodded, clenching his jaw and holding his sword with sweaty hands. His eyes targeted Uriss like a hawk's on its prey. Celesterium guards armed with crossbows stood atop the walls. Black and bronze emblems hung, but so did blue Celesterium flags. An elderly administrator stood behind Uriss with hands folded, a few bunches of Parthassian soldiers waiting with him like statues holding halberds.

Plinn wanted to glance at Sir Yirig but dared not appear afraid. *I am to be a knight. Knights do not know fear.* His blood pulsed.

"Commander Liviana," Uriss said as they approached, his voice gentle and warm. He bowed, his golden cloak ruffling about his sides. As always, he carried a book and his scepter.

Liviana returned a half smile. "Uriss. What brings you, and all these others, to the gates?"

Uriss stared at Liviana with a mocking glance. A long moment passed.

Should I...should I do something? Yes, I should! I have to. He stepped forward, the tip of his sword aimed at Uriss. "The Commander asked you a question." He glared at the priest.

The Archvicar's forehead wrinkled. "Oh, and who might you be, boy?"

Sir Yirig jerked Plinn back by the shoulder. Plinn put his sword back in its sheath but kept his eyes aimed at Uriss. *Was that stupid of me? Yirig looks unhappy...*

Liviana took a step and clasped her hands behind her back. Her arms pushed her cape behind her, exposing the ruby-tipped hilt of Xalos. "Uriss, I hope you don't mean to block my entry to the city. Until your brother arrives from the North, I am the highest ranking Parthassian here."

"You defied my father, the emperor. You ought to be arrested for treason, Commander."

Plinn wanted to look away.

Livana motioned to the swarms of lancers behind her. "Do you see these men? They would follow me to the bottom of the underworld." She stepped toward the soldiers. "Lancers of the Parthassian army, are you with me?" she shouted, raising her arms in the air.

The lancers roared. Plinn felt a surge in his chest. Their shouts echoed against the walls of the city like thunder.

Liviana drew Xalos from its sheath and raised it. It gleamed like fire in the rays of the sun. "Will you forge a new empire with me? Will you finish off the Ungoverned, take back Goldfall, take Oyvassa and worlds beyond? Destroy the Men without Gods? Get back at all those who have wronged us? Men of the Parthassian Empire, the day comes when we shall rule West Vaaz!"

Plinn's eyes welled with tears as he pounded his fist toward the sky and cheered. Bronze banners fluttered amid howls and applause. The ground shook as the men pounded their lances and pikes into it. Liviana put away her sword and stepped back to Uriss.

Uriss's gaze darted to the lancers, to Sir Yirig, and then to Plinn. He took a slow breath and sighed. "You may enter, Liviana, but on one condition: you will not defy me or the Celesterium while you are here. Is that understood? When my brother arrives, I am sure you will be relieved of service."

Liviana agreed. Plinn observed the way she walked—chin up, shoulders back, steps graceful but confident. *By the Gods, me, a knight to Blacklance!*

Uriss's eyes again bounced around to those before him. "A good sailor knows when he can't fight the wind. My concerns are spiritual in matter, not of this world. I just want to be left alone in my temple now until my brother arrives. I must be off to finish our plans for the funeral," he replied, his voice soft and flowery.

Liviana extended her hand to Uriss. He reluctantly shook it.

"Good. You've made a wise decision, Uriss. We must begin to house these refugees right away. And we must talk about gold later. As I'm sure you heard, all the gold of Goldfall sits at the bottom of the sea now, and the Haf ships remain."

Uriss forced a half smile, bowed, and turned away. He raised his hand, and the Celesterium guards followed.

She's so strong. She can do anything. Gods, grant me this power!

Liviana climbed atop her black mare and made her way under the city gate, greeted by mobs of Parthassian soldiers and hollering townspeople.

"Blacklance!" they shouted. "The heroes of Goldfall!"

Liviana instructed Minister Woss to begin housing the refugees and to figure out a plan for rationing. He promptly got to work, sending a flurry of administrators away.

As they made their way down the wide cobblestone streets, Liviana slowed her ride and gestured at Plinn. "Plinn, do you remember what I told you before we came into the city?" Her eyes were fixed on the towering citadel's gray spires in the distance.

Plinn cleared his throat and gripped his reins. "Yes. You said to keep a close watch on Uriss." He tried his best to hide his nervousness.

"And did you?"

"Yes, I did, but I thought you meant...to make sure he didn't attack you." A frail tremor tinted his voice.

"But what else did you see? Do you think he was telling the truth?"

Plinn's palms grew sweaty beneath his leather gloves. "I...I don't know."

Liviana leaned in. "He was not. I could see it in his eyes. He'll never support me. He and the Celesterium conspire against me, no doubt. I suppose it's to be expected."

Plinn nodded, avoiding direct eye contact.

"You must learn to read people if you are to be a knight, Plinn. Sir Yirig will teach you, won't you, Yirig?"

"Aye. Gotta get better with that sword too," he said to Plinn.

"Indeed," Liviana said.

Plinn clutched his sword, unsure of how to respond.

"But Uriss is nothing we can't handle. The Celesterium has lost favor with the people. They're scared, scared of the Men without Gods, and the Celesterium has brought them nothing but bad harvests. Plinn, what do you think we ought to do?"

Plinn chewed on the inside of his lip. *Gods help me.* "We...we have to destroy the Celestrium?"

Liviana laughed. "I like the way you think, but destroying is too much. The Celesterium would rise up against us should we push too hard. Uriss says a smart sailor knows when he can't fight the wind. Nonsense. The better sailor knows how to fight whatever wind blows his way."

Plinn studied the crowd rather than respond. Beggars lined the gutters around them, half of them cheering and the other half desperate for a copper or two. The scent of dried piss and sour meat hung in the air. Plinn was careful to pay them no special attention. He fixed his gaze instead at the citadel ahead, feigning self-confidence as best as he could. It was unbecoming of a future knight to mingle with the filthy poor, after all.

Liviana scaled the steps of the citadel back to her private room. She glanced at a stack of letters and scrolls atop her desk and grumbled. A gentle draft blew through an opened window, bringing the sweet smell of roses from the vase on a smooth mahogany table.

A Moth entered. "Wine, Commander?"

Liviana gestured, and the servant poured her a glass. The Moth bowed and scurried out of the room. Liviana walked to the window and sipped the drink. It was tart, filling her chest with warmth. She observed the city below, its shoddy rooftops and meandering avenues buried under a dense haze. After finishing the drink, she retired to the bed that sat in the corner, her weary muscles appreciating the rest.

She groaned when a knock interrupted her nap.

"Come in." She walked to the desk and opened a letter. It was a harvest report from the Celesterium's fields outside the city. The recent harvests were even worse than before.

Minister Woss appeared at the door.

"Back already?" Liviana set the letter down.

The minister entered the room; dark bags hung under his eyes, and the white sash he wore across his chest was dusty and wrinkled. "Yes, Commander. There's a lot to discuss. You should know that some commanders loyal to Cerras fled after the attack, though others have stayed with Uriss." He gestured with his wrinkled hands at the stacks on her desk. "I've organized all the letters in order of priority. You'll want to start on this side and make your way across."

Liviana massaged her temples. "Minister Woss, see to it that we double our number of administrators as soon as possible."

The minister nodded.

Liviana stared at the window. "My father is dead. I'm sure you heard."

"We heard everything from Uriss. He arrived only a few days before you."

Liviana squinted. "Did you hear who killed him?"

"No, I assumed he died during the raid."

Liviana pursed her lips. "It was Oyza. The bitch who tried to kill me years ago. She escaped somehow and strangled him. But this is for another time."

Minister Woss shrugged and turned to the door. "I'm sorry to hear about Nalus. I always thought it was unfortunate he let his...plaything live. If you'll excuse me, then, I'll see that we carry out your orders." He bowed and closed the door behind him.

Liviana had begun rummaging through the letters on the table when another knock sounded. "Come in," she said, somewhat annoyed.

Voy entered.

"Ah, Voy, good to see you see again." Liviana straightened up in her chair. She pushed a stack of letters and scrolls aside as a Moth fluttered in and poured them wine.

"Commander Liviana." Voy bowed, then took a seat at the desk. Her nails were painted a radiant green, and her lips were covered in a lush red lipstick. Polished silver bracelets adorned her thin wrists.

"What news? What have my spies seen?"

Voy stared at Liviana and took a sip. "We haven't seen much. He's grown more secretive. But we know he's plotting against you, hoping his brother will return from the north with his knights and save him," she said, trying to cover up her lisp as best as she could.

"I suspected as much. Thank you, Voy. As always, your work is much appreciated." She tossed a small sack of coins at Voy.

Voy caught it, peeked inside, grinned, then buried the sack in a pocket inside her cloak.

"What else?"

K. R. GALINDEZ

She twisted a strand of hair around her finger. "We caught another insurgent from the Ungoverned. This one was making trouble in the mill district. They want to start a rebellion in Judge's Pass."

Liviana weaved her fingers together on the desk. "I don't think we'll have to worry about them much longer. Soon, we'll be going forward with our plans to launch our invasion south."

"Through the swamp? Do you have the men? And what about Cerras?"

"With our armies pulled from Goldfall, we command the largest force Vaaz has seen in hundreds of years. Cerras cannot stand in our way." A sly smile crept up her face. "Besides, I don't think he'll abandon the front, even with his father dead."

Voy sipped her wine. Her eyes darted around the room before turning back to Liviana.

"But before we launch our invasion, I have a special mission for you. It will be dangerous, but you're the one for the task."

Voy's eyes were cool and empty. She crossed her legs and folded her hands on her knees. Her smooth bronze skin glowed.

"After my coronation, I want you to go to the Shimmering Woods and find the Ungoverned. We've never sent a spy before, but I trust you can do it. You'll pretend to be a refugee from Goldfall. I want you to learn everything you can about them. You are to tell no one of this, understood? And get as close to the Liorus's children as you can."

Voy cocked her head with a lopsided grin. "How long?"

"As long as it takes."

Voy pressed her lips together and teased the ends of her hair between two nails. "And the reward?"

"What do you want?" Liviana asked. Voy always wanted more gold—for silk dresses, silver jewelry, extravagant rugs from Mezzer, chocolates, or chalices.

"I want a regular allowance. And, should something happen between you and Cerras, I want to know I'll be safe."

"Deal." Liviana leaned back in her chair and said nothing for a few moments. She picked up an hourglass on the desk. It was made of four black towers holding the glass in place. She flipped it. Its white sands began to fall. "I'm working on some...big plans. With my father gone, the emperor gone, Gré gone, the world belongs to me now." Liviana watched the sand fall.

Voy stroked a smooth silver bracelet on her wrist.

"The world stirs, Voy, and all of us are stirring with it. Like ants in a whirlpool, we flail and scream, trying to stop it with all our might." Liviana shifted her gaze to meet Voy's eyes. "Tell me, what happens when one gives up? When one decides to let the force of history and destiny overtake them?"

Voy's forehead creased.

"They drown, crushed by the weight of the cosmos, by their own inability to do anything about it." The last of the sand fell. "The world stirs, but it will not stir us."

The silk curtains hanging from the window tugged in the wind.

"This insurgent you captured, where is he?"

"In the dungeon, Commander." Voy shuffled in her seat.

"Good. I'll take care of this. For now, I want you to make plans to keep a watch on Uriss. On everyone in the Celesterium. They don't so much as sneeze without us knowing it, understood?"

Voy nodded.

"First thing tomorrow morning, let's go see this prisoner of ours." Liviana stood up. "I also want you to meet Plinn, a young soldier from Goldfall I plan to knight."

"A knight? For what?"

"He's young, weak, and stupid, but there's something I like about the boy. He saved us, if you can believe it, when we fled from Goldfall. I've asked Sir Yirig to take him under his wing. I figured it ought to please him. The boy is no older than Yirig's son was before the Haf killed him."

Voy agreed. "Maybe it will help his nightmares."

"Let's hope so." Liviana gestured at Voy to follow her to the door. "Tomorrow, we'll bring Plinn to the prisoner and find what our new boy is really made of. I will show him how the Hawk makes its prey squeal."

🜚

At dawn the next morning, Plinn began his sword lessons with Sir Yirig. The courtyard, draped in gnarled vines that fell from the balconies like waterfalls, seemed to swirl around him as sunbeams shot through the dusty air. It smelled like dry bricks mixed with sweet roses.

"Who taught you how to fight?" Sir Yirig asked, his sparring sword raised as he circled Plinn.

"My father, Sir." Plinn held his blade with as firm a grip as he could, but it kept slipping in his clammy hands.

"He did a shit job, didn't he? You fight like a street kid. Is this how they taught you how to fight in the castle guard?"

Plinn's throat was in knots. Sir Yirig lunged. Plinn parried in a whirlwind, metal scraping against metal. Sir Yirig seemed to be as fast as he was tall. Plinn was thrown off balance but sprang back to his feet.

Fuck!

"Tell me, boy, what do you want?" Sir Yirig asked.

"I...I don't know," Plinn replied.

Sir Yirig launched again. Plinn gave a pathetic defense, then dropped to the ground as his sword rattled against the stone floor, sending echoes through the courtyard.

"I'll tell you what you want," Sir Yirig said. "From now on, you want whatever your commander wants, got it?"

Plinn crawled to his feet and grasped his sword. It weighed down his arm. "Yes...I got it." He squinted his eyes and puffed up his chest.

Sir Yirig jabbed at Plinn in quick succession. Plinn parried twice before the blunt end slammed into his ribs.

"Now you're dead." Sir Yirig smiled.

Plinn frowned.

"Try to be faster. Keep a clear mind. Keep your eyes on me." Sir Yirig pointed to his own eyes.

Plinn gulped as the two circled around each other.

"What do you think makes the Empire strong?"

"Courage," Plinn said.

"No." Sir Yirig thrusted his sword again.

Plinn deflected twice before the blade smacked into his side. He whimpered.

"It's knowing your place, Plinn. Discipline. Parthassian lancers train for their entire lives. They take orders without question. They are trained to target and to kill. And they respect Liviana because she's stronger than anyone else. If you want her respect, Plinn, you'll do as she says."

Plinn gave as confident a nod as he could muster. "Yes, Sir."

"Who are you, boy?" Sir Yirig swung the sword.

Plinn wobbled backward on his feet.

"I asked, who are you?" Yirig aimed low and landed a blow on Plinn's shin.

"My name is Plinn." He recoiled from the attack. Plinn lunged desperately at Sir Yirig.

The knight dodged the swipe with grace. "I didn't hear you. Who are you?"

"My name is Plinn! Plinn Hales of Groshe!" He flew at Sir Yirig in a flurry of thrashes.

"And who are you, Plinn Hales of Groshe?" Sir Yirig whacked Plinn's side yet again.

Plinn cried out. He gritted his teeth and cursed. *I hate this!*

"I asked you a question, boy! Are you a knight? Or are you a peasant?"

"I am a knight! A knight of the Parthassian Empire!" Plinn leaped at Sir Yirig but failed to strike a blow.

Sir Yirig dodged with an unbelievable ease. "No, you're not, boy. You are scum. You're less than a peasant. What is your name, scum?"

Plinn balled his fist as his face turned red. "I am a knight! I am Sir Plinn, Sir Plinn Hales of the Parthassian Empire!" he screamed, lunging and thrusting and diving at Sir Yirig. Sweat gushed from his forehead. "I...am...Sir...Plinn!" Tears welled in his eyes. He swung and swung at the knight, whose smile seemed to mock him. "I am Sir Plinn!"

Then, with a single, perfectly timed thrust, Sir Yirig lifted his sword high and thwacked it into Plinn's side, knocking him off his feet.

All of Plinn's ambition went flying against the cobblestone ground.

Sir Yirig aimed his sword at Plinn's neck and grinned. "Not yet, boy. Not yet you're not. Don't ever forget your place."

Tears streamed from Plinn's eyes as the anger in his face gave way to frustration.

Sir Yirig reached out his hand. "Not bad, boy. We'll start real practice soon. You've got to learn to fight like a knight." He helped Plinn to his feet.

Plinn wiped the tears from his eyes as soon as Sir Yirig wasn't looking.

"Go on and take a break," Sir Yirig said.

Plinn nodded and threw the sparring sword back into a pile of rusted blades. He waved goodbye at Sir Yirig, then made his way through the courtyard doors and down a broad hallway. He breathed heavily, eager to remove his stinking leather tunic and lie down in a soft bed. His whole body still ached from the long ride, and his legs didn't seem to want to move in the right direction. If he was lucky, he might get a warm bath and a mug of ale. He was going to be a knight, after all, and didn't knights deserve fine things?

He turned down another hallway, passing by a large mural that depicted ore, coal, and all sorts of precious metals pouring from the depths of the Hollowed Mountains. It had faded and worn with time, emblematic of the city's shifting fortunes under Parthassian rule. He saw a row of judges standing on the edge of a crevasse and remembered a history lesson about how Judge's Pass got its name: since the city controlled the only safe land passage linking East and West Vaaz, its rulers forced traders to stop for more inspections and tolls than anyone could count, effectively tripling the cost of goods shipped across the continent. There was something that made him proud of Commander Liviana's triumph over the powerful merchant city. He thought of leading his own triumphs someday, of leading the Parthassian Empire to glory.

Plinn halted when he saw Liviana approaching him.

"There you are. Come with me," she said, a bronze-trimmed cloak trailing behind her.

"Yes, Commander," Plinn said, annoyed he couldn't rest but grateful for any time with Blacklance.

He followed her down a dizzying labyrinth of stairwells. They reached a cobwebbed hallway deep under the castle and entered a room lit by candles. A man lay face up, chained to a wooden table. His naked body reeked—a mixture of piss, shit, sweat, and blood—and Plinn turned away. There was terror on the man's face, a kind of terror that Plinn had only ever seen when the Men without Gods raided his village and murdered his family years ago. The man whispered to himself.

"Watch, Plinn." Liviana walked to the man. A plate of glowing coals sat on a stool. On top of the coals sat a dagger. The blade was red and hot.

"I am Ungoverned..." the man muttered between gritted teeth. His scared round eyes gawked at the ceiling. He refused to look at Liviana.

Liviana placed the end of her finger on the man's ankle and dragged it across his skin.

The man's body gave a violent shake. He let out a whimper. "I take no masters... I take no lords..." he whispered, his eyes shut.

Liviana slid her nail past his knee. Plinn stood at the end of the table.

"I shall bow to no one...and none shall bow to me." He tried to burst from his restraints, the veins in his arms nearly popping out.

Liviana's finger slid up his side. Plinn's heart raced.

"As equals, we share in all... We share in labor and in wealth..." he sputtered.

Liviana moved past his chest, her nail gliding against his skin like a shark through water.

"We share in joy. We share in sorrow..."

Liviana towered over him, sliding her nail past his elbow up to his hand with a grace that blurred the lines between pain and pleasure.

"We share in strength. We share in love..." He paused and swallowed.

Liviana dragged her nail to the tip of the man's index finger and left it there. With her other hand, she pulled a blade from her waist.

Plinn limbs went numb. *Whatever my commander wants is what I want.* He took a slow breath and tried to loosen the tangles in his throat.

"Together, we shall live. And together, we shall...die..."

Liviana lifted her nail from his finger and with a swift jab, drove the dagger into it. The man let out a terrifying howl that echoed through the halls. Plinn jolted, his heart pounding. The man wept as blood spilled onto the table.

"What's wrong? Aren't you going to finish your oath?" Liviana gave him a mocking smile. The ends of her hair dangled above his face. "Tell me, what is your name?"

The man squirmed. "I will tell you nothing!"

Liviana didn't lift her gaze from his eyes. "Plinn, go to the corner and pick up that dagger."

Plinn nodded. He picked up the blade, feeling the warmth that radiated from the glowing metal. His heart pounded.

"Listen closely, Plinn. Any time he doesn't answer my question, I want you to press the dagger into his skin. If it cools, warm it up again. Understand?" Her eyes almost seemed to look past the man, as if he were an object, a mere obstacle that stood in her way.

Plinn gulped.

Liviana walked around the table, fingers laced behind her back. "Again, shall we? What is your name?"

The man didn't answer, keeping his eyes shut. His muscles quivered. Liviana looked at Plinn.

Plinn froze for a half second.

Liviana frowned at him.

He balled his fist. He gritted his teeth. He lifted his chin and thinned his eyes. *Whatever my commander wants, I want.* He gazed at the man's body—skin covered in dirt and sweat, its bloody feet dotted with blisters, its hair in its groin soaked with dried piss, its muscles twitching. *This isn't a man. This is a body, a body that doesn't matter.* Plinn's eyes turned to stone. He seized the top of the man's foot with one hand and held it in place, then thrust the glowing metal into the bottom of the foot just underneath its toes.

The man howled in pain as he writhed and twitched.

Plinn's eyes bulged with fascination, with awe, with a twisted enjoyment. He pushed even harder. *I have to. My commander wills it.*

The smell of searing flesh filled the room as the man screamed and his limbs shook. Plinn nearly gagged at the scent.

"Vimoy! My name is Vimoy! Please...please just kill me!" He moaned as he desperately tried to break his arms and legs from their straps.

Liviana's hair glimmered in the torchlight. "Listen, Vimoy. I promise to let you go and run back to the swamps, but first, you must do as I say. Is that understood? Simple as that."

Vimoy sobbed.

Liviana glanced again at Plinn, who had sat the dagger's blade back on the coals. Plinn nodded. He took up the dagger, then pressed it into Vimoy's knee.

"Yes! Yes!" His limbs squirmed. "I understand!"

Liviana shoved her finger into the prisoner's skin. "I've heard that three of King Liorus's children are alive in the Shimmering Woods. Why have they not retaken their throne? Why have none returned to Oyvassa?"

Vimoy cried as the smell of his own melting flesh filled the air.

Liviana motioned to Plinn.

"No! No! I'll tell you! But please...please have mercy after I tell you... Please just kill me," he begged. "The children are alive. Yes—but they do not rule... We have no rulers anymore... Now please, I'm begging you, please just kill me!"

Liviana stared down at Vimoy. "I've heard there may be as many as fifty-thousand souls living in the Shimmering Woods. How can fifty-thousand survive with no rulers?"

"I-I don't know... Please, we just do..."

Liviana's face contorted. "Where in those god-forsaken swamps do the Ungoverned hide?" She dug her fingernails into his abdomen.

He flinched.

Liviana snapped with her other hand.

Plinn cut into Vimoy's skin. Blood spilled onto the table as he shrieked.

"Where? Tell me, and you can go free!" Liviana's voice was as shrill as knives scraping against rock.

"I will tell you nothing!" Vimoy closed his eyes and began whispering to himself. "We are Ungoverned."

Liviana tightened her fist. "Forget it." She yanked the dagger from Plinn's hand and slit Vimoy's throat in a flash of fury. Blood spewed onto the table and gurgled from Vimoy's mouth. His arms and legs jerked as the life drained from his body.

The room fell silent.

Plinn took a slow, shuddering breath. His heart still raced, and his palms were drenched with sweat.

"Come, Plinn. We have much to do tomorrow. Go fetch a Moth to clean up this mess," Liviana ordered. Plinn had begun to follow her when Liviana stopped. "No—fetch anyone. I don't care who. Actually, fetch anyone *except* Moths. The Ungoverned, the Celesterium, the Men without Gods, and the Gods themselves—nothing will stand in our way." She left.

Plinn stiffened. His eyes turned back again to the lifeless body that lay on the table, soaked in its own blood. *It's just a body. Nothing more.*

That night, Plinn retreated to his room, where a comfortable bed of soft linen awaited him. *Whatever my commander wants is what I want.* Plinn blew out his candle and lay down to sleep. *Whatever my commander wants is what I want.*

CHAPTER 12

Oyza was glad to breathe the crisp air, see the green vines wrapping around the trees, and feel the damp patches of soft mushrooms beneath her shoes. How long had they been walking? She wasn't sure, but it felt like days, if not weeks. She and Yars had survived the trek by scavenging some berries to eat. But they were always running out of food. Hopefully, Groshe, and a ship to Oyvassa in its harbor, was near.

Beads of sweat formed on her forehead as they climbed a hill that seemed to extend forever. At the top, Oyza rested her hands on her knees.

Yars pointed to the distance at endless rolling meadows. He panted and wiped sweat from his forehead. "This looks like the end of the forest, right? Nothing but fields out there."

Far on the horizon to their right was the coast, a sliver of shining blue. To their left were dense thickets of trees clustered in the distance. Ahead, rows of empty pastures, dotted with burned windmills, stretching to the horizon. Where farmers had once grown crops, there were now endless fields of red, gold, and white wildflowers. A warm gust carried a pleasant fragrance through the air.

"The windmills." Oyza scanned the fields. "It's true. This area was raided by the Haf. But I think it's safe now."

Yars shrugged. "If you say so."

They left the forest and descended the hilltop, wading through a tangled sea of stems and petals that rose to their shoulders. Green dragonflies, black-and-yellow-striped bees, and orange butterflies peppered with chocolate spots buzzed among slim stalks swaying in the wind. At one point on their way down, a hummingbird hovered near a ruby flower, its wings a blur. The muscles in Oyza's legs loosened as they descended, and the sun warmed her skin.

They marched through the wildflowers and found their way to an old cobblestone road. Weeds poked through the cracks between the rocks like prickly fingers grasping for the sky.

"Looks like no one's been here in years," Oyza said.

Yars flicked a jade dragonfly buzzing near his eyes. After just a few moments of walking, they missed the forest's dirt-covered ground. Their feet ached.

The field gave them some cover, at least. The sea had long disappeared from view, as did the mountains in the distance. They couldn't see much of anything, save for stalks of golden and white flowers. Ahead was a handful of charred windmills draped in vines. An eerie feeling filled Oyza's gut.

They made their way onto an abandoned farm, passing through a creaky wooden fence caked with squishy mushrooms. The farm was empty, except for a meager house long abandoned. The roof had collapsed and left a gaping hole in its place.

"Keep a close watch," Oyza said as they scampered past the abandoned farm. She covered her head with her hood. "You never know where bandits could be hiding."

They walked with a slight crouch through the field, trying to stay below the walls of blossoms surrounding them. They came to the remains of another windmill—little more than a skeleton of black wood—and hopped over a stiff gate with rusted hinges that refused to open.

"I remember more now. Minister Valador said the Parthassians were ready to attack this place when the Men without Gods showed up and raided. Burned everything. The Parthassians pressed on to Groshe anyway. Now Groshe pays a big tax to the Empire."

Yars shuddered as they left behind another burned windmill. Crows perched on one side of it.

"And like Oyvassa, no one wants to come back here anymore. It's a cursed land, they say." Oyza brushed aside a sunflower standing in her way.

"Sure does feel cursed," Yars said.

They passed a row of empty houses scarred with black burns. Where shutters once enclosed windows, there were only holes. A chimney on one had collapsed, now little more than a pile of busted bricks. Oyza read the family names carved into the stones: Theron, Biraz, Hales.

"Should we check one out?" Yars gazed up at the hollow remains of a windmill.

Oyza shook her head. "No, we should keep moving. There's nothing left inside."

They pressed on, eyeing the remains of a withering scarecrow nearby. It seemed to watch them as they passed, haunting them with its empty stare.

The road went on, a straight line between endless multitudes of flowers. They walked through the fields for the entire day, stopping for a night's rest inside one of the empty windmills. Oyza insisted they only sleep a few hours and press on toward Groshe as soon as the sun's morning rays broke the dawn.

At dawn, they ate a quick breakfast of apples, walnuts, and a few handfuls of grapes. The Sword of Creation dipped below the horizon as the sun rose. Swarms of butterflies drifted in the morning breeze as songbirds filled the air with music. They walked throughout the day and, by nightfall, found themselves camping in a small grove of trees.

"We're gonna starve, Oyza." Yars laid on his back with his hands over his waist.

Oyza frowned. "It's not that far to Groshe."

"How do you know? You keep saying that, but we never get there."

He's right. It's much farther than I expected. She had hoped they'd have been able to hitch a ride on a wagon with the coins they found.

"What do we have left?" Yars asked.

Oyza opened her bag. "Nothing."

Yars grumbled and turned over. "It's cold."

"I know." Oyza slouched. "But we have to keep going." She looked up at the dimming sky. "Why don't we try to start a fire again? There are some sticks and logs here."

"Every time we try, we fail. Just give it up."

Oyza scratched her chin, thinking. She rolled up her cloak's sleeves. "Wait, I have an idea; I can't believe we didn't think of this before." With her blade, she dug into the side of a log, then sharpened a stick. "I'll start it, and when I get tired, you pick up. Yars, this can work."

Yars perked up. "Why...why didn't we just think of that before?"

Oyza laughed. "Too tired, maybe?" She started but was quickly out of breath. "Here, you take it."

Yars seized the stick and began rubbing it into the log immediately.

"Is it hot?" Oyza asked, resting her arms.

"I can't tell," Yars said, panting. He started to sweat. "Here, take it!"

Oyza grabbed the stick. "Hurry, get a pile of dried leaves." She kept pressing, muscles burning. "Yars, look! Smoke! And, it looks like ashes here."

Yars piled up leaves underneath twigs. "Yes! Dump those ashes on the leaves here."

Oyza grunted, then hurled the ashes onto the leaves.A moment later, smoke. Oyza's heart raced. *Did it work?*

Another moment later, flames.

"We did it!" Yars said, hugging Oyza. "Fire!"

Oyza leaned back, exhausted but excited. "I knew we could do it."

She and Yars piled up some twigs, some smaller logs, and soon, a fire crackled and roared, filling the darkness with light and sending embers into the air.

Oyza held her palms to the fire, her cloak wrapped around her shoulders. "It feels great." Her stomach growled.

Yars nodded, also holding his hands to it. "Yeah."

They sat in silence for a long moment, listening to the fire pop and burn. Smoke coiled into the air.

"Wish we had food," Yars said, his shadow flickering behind him.

"Me too." Oyza pulled back her hood.

Yars sat back in the dirt. He sighed and pulled out the bag of silver and the seashell necklace from his pockets. "What good is this if we can't eat it?"

Oyza laughed. She pulled out the blade from her pocket and inspected it in the fire. It shone. "I still think this is a mageware." The twisted snakes biting the apple at the end were intricately woven.

Yars held the jewelry in the light. "It's pretty." The seashell sparkled. "Why don't you wear it?" He held it out to Oyza.

Oyza reached out for the pendant. "I don't know. If it's a mageware, maybe it's not safe?"

Yars scoffed. "I'm sure it's fine. What harm could a necklace be?"

Oyza spun it around. The spiral seashell gleamed like a sliver of moonlight. Oyza dared not take the wooden cap off—who knew what was inside. She held it up to her neck and put it on. "All right."

"It's beautiful," Yars said. "Just like you."

Oyza wanted to roll her eyes, but she didn't. She looked up at Yars and smiled. "You're right, though. Too bad we can't eat it."

Yars laughed, then put another log on the fire. "Good. We can sell it."

Something about the necklace *did* feel comforting. *I don't think I'll let him sell this. And not you either,* she thought, picking up the dagger. *A mageware! Can you imagine?*

She yawned, watching the fire burn away. Her stomach ached, but she figured they would reach Groshe tomorrow—which was what she told herself every night. At the very least, maybe they'd find some more berries.

"Can I see the dagger?" Yars asked, poking at the coals.

"Sure."

Yars examined it closely, then started twirling it with his hands. He clutched his waist. "What do you think this would sell for? Five-hundred gold? A thousand?"

Oyza frowned. "We're not selling it." *Certainly not so you can buy witchdust.* "Besides, we might need to trade it for a ride to Oyvassa."

Yars lay down in the grass, looking up at the stars. "We'll see. We don't even really know if it's a mageware. I get that you've read a lot of books, Oyza, but you don't know everything, you know? Dagger's probably worthless." He slammed the blade into the dirt.

Oyza squinted. Was that green light? "Yars."

"I've seen a thousand weapons, Oyza. I've learned a lot out here on the streets. And just 'cause a dagger is pretty doesn't mean it's a mageware."

"Yars...get up." Oyza's mouth hung open. She sprang to her feet. *Gods!*

"I'll tell you what. If this thing's a mageware, I will personally use it to hunt down Liviana myself and shove it right up her—"

"Yars!" Oyza yanked his hand and pulled him up. "Look!"

Yars stumbled to his feet.

A crack of green light burst from where the dagger pierced the ground. It spread like veins in a leaf.

"What's happening?" Yars reached out to grab Oyza's hand.

"I don't know. Stay back." She looked down at their combined hands. Yars's hand felt nice—warm, strong, and safe.

Vines leaped out of the cracks and shot toward the sky, growing as high as the trees. It swelled higher still, a tangled, dense mess of stalks wrapping and coiling in a frenzy around each other. Leaves burst from its sides. A green shine shot in all directions, so bright it lit up the undersides of the treetops.

Oyza's eyes grew wide. She turned to Yars, her mouth hanging open. His eyes glowed like emeralds in the sun. Clusters of small green pods popped from the stalk and then exploded into a hodgepodge of fruits and vegetables.

Then, as suddenly as it started, it stopped.

Oyza's chest pounded. "Is it...is it safe to eat?"

Yars wasted no time. He lunged at the stalk and sank to his knees. "We're saved, Oyza! Oh, thank the Gods!" He plucked a carrot and bit into it, then scooped a handful of grapes.

Oyza followed him. Why not? She picked a strawberry and bit. It was sweeter than anything she had ever tasted. "We *are* saved." She filled her arms with more food. "See? I told you. I know a mageware when I see it."

Yars snagged some potatoes, onions, and peppers and sat them at the edge of the fire. "I thought we were going to starve, Oyza!"

Oyza laughed. She hurried behind him to put garlic and more potatoes on the fire. "Let's eat as much as we can. We can fill the bags for tomorrow. There will be enough to last until we reach Groshe."

They spent the night filling their bellies with vegetables and fruits of all kinds. Exhausted, they fell asleep without even putting out the fire.

When dawn came, they wrapped up the mageware dagger and made sure to keep it safe—it was worth a fortune, Yars figured. Or, as Oyza suggested, it might come in handy on their way to Oyvassa. Either way, they both agreed Yars was now indebted to Oyza and that she would hold him to his promise the night before.

As they left their camp, Yars nibbled on berries and turned to Oyza. "So how did you know it was a mageware?"

Oyza stepped over a rotten piece of wood spattered with ants. She thought for a moment about the mageware sword her father had carried—a blade that could turn into an ax. He had won it by gambling with sailors, and it was the most precious thing in their family. *No, I'd better not mention it. Maybe it's still in Oyvassa.* "That sword that Liviana fought you with—it's a mageware. The dagger reminded me of it. The handle is old, intricate."

Yars nodded. "Where'd she get it?"

"From the Wastes. There's this knight her father hired to be her personal guard. Sir Yirig. He went there with Liviana's mother and two servants. But only two of them came back." She paused for a moment. "I was close with one of them. He was one of the only other servants in the household I confided in."

"I'm sorry." Yars leaned forward.

"Yendra died in The Wastes. Yirig said they fell out of the wagon during a storm. Nalus was never really the same after that. Neither was Liviana. But they found a sword there called Xalos. That's what Liviana fights with. It's a mageware, but it doesn't do anything."

"Huh," Yars said. "I still think I'd like to try my hand at the Wastes some day."

Oyza shook her head, lowering her hood. The morning sun was growing hot. "No. It's too dangerous. At Ten Orchards, there's a temple where the Celesterium gives magic hunters a blessing, but after that, you wander through a desert for days. The maps aren't very good, there's no water, and Hellhounds come after you. Yirig was chased out by a storm too." Yirig had only told the story once, then never again.

Yars perked up. "Hellhounds?"

"Yes. They say the Hellhounds are like mad dogs, spirits out to kill anyone who goes too far."

Yars sneered. "Yeah, but if you find a mageware, just think Oyza, gold for life. Mountains of silver. I think it's worth it."

"Suit yourself."

In truth, Oyza badly wanted to visit the Wastes someday too—if only just to see it. Entire cities turned to dust, forests where the trees were made of stone, magic older than time. *Maybe someday.*

"Xalos, does it do anything? Any enchantment?"

Oyza shook her head. "No. When they got back, it was in pieces. Minister Valador had Goldfall's best blacksmith put it back together again. But it never did anything special."

"Maybe it's not a mageware then?"

"No, it is. You can just tell."

As they made their way, Oyza found herself staring at her seashell necklace. What did it do, if anything? She would have to find out somehow.

At midday, they reached the bottom of a monstrous hill. "Here we are," Oyza said, pausing for a moment to rest. "On the other side is Groshe, I think. It has to be. Can't you smell the rivers?"

110

Yars plopped down and sprawled out on the grass, bees buzzing around his head. "I can't smell anything. My body is done," he said. "I'm done."

Oyza smiled. She sat down too, resting her hands on her knees as her messy hair dangled over her back. "Come on. Let's go."

As they climbed, a cool draft from the sea carried whiffs of salt and dried kelp through the wildflowers. Swarms of dragonflies droned behind them. The slope was deceptively steep, with its slow rolling climb taking nearly an hour for them to ascend.

They rested again at the top, out of breath and legs like jelly.

"It's beautiful." Oyza peered at the sprawling town below. It was surrounded by sturdy walls on each side and seated at the mouth of an immense delta. Parthassian banners drooped from the walls, and plumes of smoke billowed from chimneys. Two coiling streams met before emptying into the ocean, their brown waters mixing with the dark green of the Emerald Sea. Sprawling roads, dotted with horses and oxen pulling wagons, led to the gates. Ships of all sizes sat in the bay, bearing sails of all different colors: the vibrant yellows of Chan-Chan-Tuul, the dull grays of Petrovskia, the deep violets of traders from Talazar City. There were plenty she didn't recognize. But others, she knew all too well: the black and bronze sails of Parthassian warships. They were much longer than the others, and on the front of each was fixed a long rod with a hawk statue at the end used for ramming enemy boats.

"It looks like there's an entire fleet here." She raised a hand to block the sun from her eyes as her hair blew in the wind.

Yars placed his hands on his hips. "The Empire's ships are everywhere. Doesn't surprise me."

Oyza scanned the town some more, squinting her eyes. She gazed at the Parthassian warships in the harbor, then at the city's gates.

"You gonna go or what?" Yars asked.

Oyza didn't reply. Her eyes were fixed on the Parthassian fleet.

"Oyza?" Yars asked again, leaning toward her.

"Yes," she replied. "I'm just...trying to remember something."

"Let's go. I wanna check out the tavern—The Wayward Oyster."

"Yars, wait. Let me see that dagger."

Yars pulled the blade from his bag and handed it over.

Oyza grabbed it, pulled her hair tight, and chopped off half its length. After tossing the strands away, she pulled up what remained and tied it behind her head. A few strands dangled loosely. "We should try to disguise ourselves." She tucked the seashell pendant beneath her cloak.

Yars rubbed his hands together. "If we get caught, we'll just make up names. Come on!" He darted down the hillside.

"Yars!" Oyza followed, trampling through a thicket of white, saffron, and plum-colored flowers.

The ocean receded from view, and colorful pastures gave way to a broad dirt road speckled with gangly shrubs and smooth stones. Oyza and Yars covered their heads with hoods and tried their best to blend in with the crowds filtering into the town. Carts with food of all types lined the roads as merchants shouted at passers by. There were wyvern talons and barrels of coal from Petrovskia. Another man sold idols of the Origins carved out of the thick oak trees that flourished only in the Stonewoods. One merchant even claimed to sell fine rugs from Mezzer at half their usual price—surely, they were fakes, though the golden thread weaving together their mosaics of squares and triangles seemed convincing enough. Nearer the entrance to the town, Ozya walked past a cart full of caged animals: jet-black cats with mischievous yellow eyes, spiny lizards in rusty cages that were much too small, and beautiful birds of brilliant reds and radiant blues, no doubt shipped from Chan-Chan-Tuul. *Gwugi! Gwugi!* one of the birds cried out. She pitied the thing, trapped in its little cage.

Beggars clustered in the streets, their bony hands reaching out for a copper piece. Their putrid scent reminded Oyza of Goldfall. She had nothing to give them. She looked away. Guilt ate at her heart. A ring of unkempt children sang a familiar song:

> *Here they come*
> *Across the sea,*
> *The godless men*
> *For you and me.*
> *Round we go,*
> *Who will it be?*
> *The darkness comes*
> *For every star!*

The kids scattered in all directions as the one in the middle chased after them. A chill swept up Oyza's spine. *Gods, to hear children singing a song like that...*

"Oyza, look." Yars pointed at a tottering wagon driving beneath the entrance. Men and women sat crouched inside on beds of straw, skeletal wrists bound with heavy chains. On their necks, smudges of black ink coated their Starmarks.

"Starless..." Oyza whispered. "I wonder what they did."

"Must've been bad. I remember, in the deepest parts of the mines, they sent Starless down there, where the worst was. They didn't survive long." He grimaced.

Oyza led him to the gate, trying her best to blend in with the crowds of people streaming in. "Yars, look." A throng of Parthassian guards inspected incoming travelers, each dressed in black-and-bronze chainmail and wielding halberds. But they didn't seem to be stopping anyone. "Just keep your head down. Don't look suspicious."

Yars huddled close to Oyza. "My name is Yig. You'll be..."

"Lendrix."

"Right, Yig and Lendrix, traveling from Judge's Pass." Yars gulped. "Nothing suspicious here."

Oyza's heart raced as they approached the gateway. They funneled in, avoiding eye contact with the sentries. *Just stay calm.*

"Wait," one of the guards called out. He was a tall older man missing several teeth. "You two, come here." He grabbed Oyza's arm with a gloved hand.

Yars followed.

"Names. And state your business in Groshe."

Oyza tried to settle herself. "My name is Lendrix. This is my guide, Yig, from Judge's Pass. We're picking up some things in the markets to bring back to my father in Judge's Pass." Oyza did her best to put on her "noble" voice. She tried to read the man, his age, his rank in the army, his knowledge of the Empire. *Surely, he'll know.*

"Bullshit," the guard said. "Look at you, you're filthy. And no horse?" He whistled and signaled at more men behind him. "Seize them."

"Wait!" Oyza cried out. The guards held her arms.

Yars resisted, but a burly sentry punched his abdomen and clinched his wrists behind his back.

"You're bandits. Been robbing wagons, have we? Take these rats to the dungeons. I'll deal with them later."

"Wait! Which way did the morning hawk fly?"

The guard froze. "What did you say?"

"Which way," Oyza began, wriggling, "did the morning hawk fly?"

The man glanced at the others. He gave a slight nod, and they loosened their grip. "Toward the tower on the mountain. North, south, east, or west?"

"East," Oyza said without hesitation. *Gods, I hope this works.*

The guard spat. "Who do you work for?"

"Commander Liviana. I am on a mission. I cannot say to where or for what purposes, but you must let us pass as quickly as possible."

The guard grunted. "Knew the code, I suppose. But we're looking for criminals just like you."

"Bandits? You think us common thieves? If you delay our mission any longer, you know Liviana will send Sir Yirig after you. Or worse, Xalos."

The guard glared. "Yirig, eh? How's the old man doing?"

Oyza straightened her cloak. "We've been traveling some time. But last I heard, he was in Goldfall with Liviana."

The guard shook his head. "Goldfall... The Gods spit on us, eh? Whole city gone up in smoke." He glanced at the rest of the guards, then back at Oyza. "Go on then, be on your way. For the glory of the Empire." He bowed.

Oyza returned the bow, then grabbed Yars's wrist. They bolted away from the wall and disappeared into the city, collapsing underneath an ornate statue of the Two Lovers and the Sword of Creation. A curved blue sword pierced their marble bodies.

"Oyza, that was amazing!" Yars wrapped his arms around her.

Oyza's heart still pounded. "I know! I was worried he wouldn't remember the code."

"Code?"

"Yes. That question, it's an old Parthassian code. Minister Valador told me about it one night when he was drunk."

Yars lay down on a flat rock. "Gods, Oyza, I thought we were goners."

Oyza took a few seconds to calm herself, then burst into laughter. "Lendrix and Yig!" They shared an ebullient laugh, then prayed to the statue for good fortune.

After resting, they strolled into the city. The muddy scent of the rivers mixed in the breeze, a smell like wet grass and rotting wood. At the center of town, Parthassian flags hung from a keep behind castle walls. Houses lined the streets, sometimes with three or more stacked on top of each other like piles of thrown-away junk. After twisting through a handful of busy roads, they found themselves at a vast square packed full of people laughing and drinking to music.

"I think the Sword just moved into the Crab—must be the faire," Oyza said.

They pushed through colorful festival-goers and stumbled upon a theater troupe putting on a show but kept moving through the town. They had turned down another road, walking through zig-zagging alleyways when Oyza stopped. She pulled a small branch out of her matted hair, then noticed her clothes were caked in dried mud. It hadn't really sunk in yet how dirty they were.

"Do you know if there are any baths we can use here?" she asked.

Yars stroked his chin. "I think so." He looked down at the torn shoes on his feet. "And we need some new clothes."

Oyza frowned. "We do...but we should keep the silver in case we need to buy a spot on a ship."

A smile crept up his face as he turned to Oyza. "Well...I wouldn't be so sure about that." He pulled not one, but two leather bags out of his pocket.

Oyza's lips twisted, barely concealing a smile. "You're going to get us thrown back in prison."

Yars winked at her and threw her the bag. Inside were eight copper pieces, three silver, and even one gold coin.

"Where did you...?" Oyza began to ask, her mouth open. But part of her didn't want to know.

"*Pssh*, don't worry about it." Yars put the bag back in his pocket and brushed his curls from his eyes. "Told you, I'm good at this."

🦋

Oyza and Yars appreciated the baths: their skin was clean and soft, perfect for the new clothing they wore. They weren't able to afford anything too nice, but fresh pairs of linen pants, new shirts and cloaks, and old but comfortable leather boots made a world of difference to them. They made their way through the winding town, criss-crossing over bridges above narrow canals, and found the tavern. It was near the waterfront. The air smelled like seaweed, dead fish, and garbage.

"This is it," Yars exclaimed with his arms outstretched. "The Wayward Oyster."

It was a small rickety building with drab shutters and a thin line of black smoke rising from the chimney. A wooden sign swung on the porch. It depicted a moth encircled by a windy cyclone.

"My friend said this is the finest pub in all of West Vaaz. You won't find finer folks anywhere else," Yars insisted. Just as he reached for the doorknob, the door burst open, and a man fell backward on the steps, knocking Yars off his feet before Oyza grabbed his arm and pulled him up.

"And don't come back around here again, you hear?" a woman bellowed from inside the tavern.

The doors slammed shut. The man stumbled to his feet, let out a belch and bumbled away. Oyza and Yars laughed, but then something by the door caught Oyza's eye.

"Look." A board was pinned beside the door, bestrewn with scribbled notes. "Maybe we can find something about a ship here. Help me look."

Yars leaned on the railing with folded arms. "Can't read."

"Oh, that's right. I'm sorry." She scanned the jottings, reading aloud for Yars: "Oxen or similar Starmarks needed for brush clearance. Lady seeks personal astrologer: Serpents or Starfish only." Her eyes darted around the board. "Celesterium seeks Serpents for monastery orchard, proceed to Temple of the Crab. Lord seeks palace guardians. Hounds, Mammoths, and Hawks encouraged." Oyzas's eyes glanced at another. "Parthassian Empire recruiting medics: Frostpetals only."

She read silently for a moment, then pointed. "Look at this one! Travel to Talazar City by boat, looking for Starfish, men or women, for scribing purposes. Inquiries inside; attractive applicants only, signed, 'Captain Seralus of the *Chandelier Lover*, Queen of the Five-and-a-Half Seas of Vaaz.'"

They looked at each other, puzzled, and shrugged. Attractive applicants only?

They stepped in the tavern, and the scent of ale, tobacco, and roasting meats crashed into them like a tidal wave. A band played music in the corner, barely audible over the roar of the crowd. Everyone from Vaaz and beyond seemed to be at The Wayward Oyster. Froth dripped from mugs as huddles of grizzled men flung dice and played cards. A slender red-headed woman dressed in sultry robes danced on a Celesterium priest's lap. In the center of the room, a fire burned inside a gigantic clamshell. Oyza and Yars squeezed through and found a table in the corner.

"This is my kind of place!" Yars tapped his fingers on the table to the beat of the music. He looked over at the men throwing dice at a table near them. His eyes grew full.

"Don't even think about gambling our money away." *And you'd better not spend it on witchdust either.*

"I know! I know," Yars said, happier than Oyza had ever seen him yet. "I won't, trust me." A grin lit up his face as he pointed to his cloak where the stolen coins were stashed away.

A waitress came over to the table, short with curled hair pulled back and ears full of brass piercings. Yars pulled out four copper coins from his pocket and ordered two tall ales, two cups of beef stew, and a full loaf of rye bread served with butter. He plucked another coin and added dessert too: two bowls of strawberry pudding, cream, and a side of honey cakes. As the server walked away, Oyza saw her Starmark. She was a Turtle, the sign most associated with money. It was believed turtles hid wealth in their shells. Most households kept a turtle shell full of coins in their houses for good luck.

"Wait," Oyza said.

The waitress turned back.

"We're looking for a Captain Seralus. Is he here?"

The server rolled her eyes with a half smile. "Captain Seralus? Yeah, around that corner. He's an odd one, watch out." She flicked her chin.

"Thanks." Oyza eyed the hallway, then turned back to Yars. "I guess we'll see what he's about."

A few moments later, the waitress returned with two pints of beer.

"Cheers," Yars said as he and Oyza picked up their drinks.

"Cheers to our freedom!" They clanked their mugs together and drank.

"Did you ever think you'd be here? Drinking at The Wayward Oyster? Chasing after—well, you know what?" Yars said.

Oyza shook her head. "Never in a thousand years." She drank. "Feels good to be free." She paused for a moment. "You know, this is the first time I've *ever* been served by someone else. Usually, I'm the one running to the kitchens for teas, wine, whatever."

Yars laughed.

Oyza slouched a little. "But I wish Mapa were here with us."

Yars wiped froth from his lips, then set down his mug. "I wish my friends were here too."

"A toast to Mapa?" Oyza raised her glass with Yars again.

As Oyza took another gulp, she noticed two men arguing across the aisle. She winked at Yars, and they decided to eavesdrop.

"That's not how the story goes, you idiot!" One of them slammed his flagon into the table. He was a giant of a man with a ragged wool belt strapped around his middle so tightly, he looked as if he might pop. Across the table from him sat another man so skinny, you'd think he hadn't eaten in weeks.

"Please, and what do you know? Have you ever been to the Wastes?" The thin man tossed up his hands.

"Doesn't matter—and don't act like you've ever been!" The beefy man took a drink of ale, froth running down his beard.

"I have so!" The slim man picked up his mug and chugged.

The bigger man shook his head. "Anyone who's actually been to the Wastes should know how the story goes! And clearly, you've never been!"

The other folded his arms. "I know what I saw. I saw the Hellhounds! Ran before they could catch me, ran for my life, I swear. Almost didn't make it back, save for my horse—faster than lightning." He snapped his fingers at a host.

"Then you would know—damn you—you would know that Soralir was a wizard, the most strongest wizard ever—who was fed up with all the war in Vaaz. Turned seven armies to stone with his staff, was never seen again. Turned the whole region into dust, haunted it with Hellhounds that'll kill you as fast as you look at 'em. And the dust storms too! So don't you bloody lie to me again, you ain't never seen no staff or no Hellhounds!" He snapped at a waiter and was promptly ignored.

"Everyone knows the story of Soralir! I'm not saying I saw the staff. What I'm saying is that there's more to the Wastes than anyone knows. Whole villages haven't been found yet—villages and woods turned to stone. I went to where the maps don't go—got my own map, I did!" He jutted his chin out.

The burly man slammed his mug so hard, it sounded like it might shatter. His face turned red. "A map of the Wastes is worth more than your weight in gold! You ain't got no map!"

"Oh yeah? If I ain't never been to the Wastes, then how do you explain this?" He pulled a red candlestick from a pocket and sat it on the table.

"It's a stupid candle, so what? And how do we get more drinks in this place?"

"Just watch!" He edged forward and blew on the candle.

Oyza and Yars exchanged curious glances.

The candle wick sparked into flame. A red fire, bright as a ruby, flickered.

The burly man rolled his eyes. "That's no mageware, you damn idiot. That's a gods-damned parlor trick!"

"Is not! I got deep into the Wastes, truly did. Found this candle in a house and ran! A pretty little lord's lady in Talazar City'll give me a fortune for a mageware like this!"

"You did not! You're full of shit, you know that? You really are!"

Oyza and Yars decided to turn back toward each other.

"You think anyone'll ever find it? The Staff of Soralir?" Yars sipped his beer.

"I don't know. Either way, both of them are wrong. I read lots about Soralir. Everyone's got different stories. Some say he purposefully preserved magic in the magewares thousands of years ago. Others say they only became enchanted after Soralir. No one knows for sure. But everyone knows the prophecy: one day, someone will find the staff when Vaaz is in trouble, and well, there are different prophecies. Some say the staff grants you a wish. Some say it can bring back the dead. Others say it...allows you to command dragons."

"Dragons?" Yars asked.

"Yes. Back in those days, men fought with dragons. Not like wyverns in the North—dragons, bigger, and they breathe fire."

"Sounds like we need it now." Yars said. "What with the Men without Gods and everything."

"That's also why the merchant kings of Judge's Pass venerated Soralir so much. It was always a neutral city, never taking sides in war, until Liviana took over. It's the same reason why the Basilica of One Thousand Stars is at Judge's Pass where the Archvicar lives."

A half-puzzled look swept over Yars's face. "'Venerate?'"

Oyza looked down and tapped her fingers on the table. "Venerate means...well, it means you idolize something, you almost worship it. You love it very deeply."

"Ah," Yars said, staring back at her. His eyes lowered to her lips. They shared a long smile.

The waitress returned with their dinners, and a long silence elapsed as they ate. Each focused intently on their food, enjoying every last savory detail. It felt great to eat meat too. They had had nothing for days, except for the fruits and vegetables from the mageware dagger's stalk.

After finishing their meals, they made their way to the back of the alehouse, where they found the captain sitting on pillows with three others at a round table, wisps of smoke coiling around them. The captain was a tall lanky man with long legs dressed in violet pants. His boots were spotless. On his head sat a huge velvet hat with a tremendous white feather in it. The feather was so heavy, it dangled halfway down the side of his face. On his chest, he wore a faded violet jacket adorned with round golden buttons. His eyes, painted with dark make-up, looked up as they approached the table. "Excuse me. Can we help you?"

Oyza and Yars exchanged a quick glance, then Oyza spoke. "We saw the ad outside. I'm a Starfish, and I served a lord scribing for most of my life. We'd like to inquire about passage to Talazar City aboard your ship."

The captain stood up, inspecting them both with thin lips. "*Mm-hm, mm-hmm*, yes, yes, I think you will do." He didn't even look into Oyza's eyes. He inspected her hair, her face, and her chest. He turned to Yars, his eyes stumbling all over his body, then turned back to Oyza. "My name is Captain Seralus." He gave a dramatic bow and a flourish at his fingertips. The white feather in his hat bobbed and bounced. "And you are?"

Oyza crossed her arms. "My name is Oyza."

"*Uh huh, uh huh.*" Captain Seralus began to pace around them. "And this one is?" He whirled to Yars.

"My name is Yars."

"Oyza and Yars. Wonderful!" Captain Seralus clasped his hands together. "Now, both of you. I need you to turn around." He rotated his finger.

Oyza raised her eyebrows. "What? You think we would lie about our Starmarks?"

"No, no, love, of course not. Don't be so obtuse! You see, I am an arts trader. Captain Seralus, Queen of the Five-and-a-Half Seas of Vaaz, and I can only take the magnificently beautiful—like myself, of course," he said, rolling his eyes back in his head and grinning, "on board my ship, the *Chandelier Lover*, the most beautiful vessel in all Vaaz."

Oyza and Yars glanced at each other with wide eyes. They reluctantly spun around.

"Yes, yes, yes, wonderful—all very beautiful! But there's one small problem." He stared at Oyza. "I only need you, love. I only need a Starfish. I've got a hull full of scrolls I need organized. Can you read, love? I've got a mess of old paintings that need organizing too. My last Starfish was awful, truly awful! I mean, you wouldn't *believe* the things I had to put up with! That princess, prancing around *my* ship like she—" He shook his head. "My apologies, love. I don't want to talk about *her*. Not worth my breath. And you have been trained as a scribe?"

"I have." Oyza provided a slow but assured nod. "But I can't leave without my friend."

Captain Seralus rumpled his lips and stroked his chin. His white feather fell in front of his face. He flicked it out of his eyes. "Hmm. A Hound. Let me think. Let me think..." He eyed them up and down as he paced. "*Hmm... Mm-hmm...* Yes..." His eyes traced Yars's body from the top of the of his head to his feet. "Ah! I can find work for you. Yars, you can help clean the deck, give my men a break—we'll just say you're watching the deck for them, and helping to wash too, like a good watchman would."

They paused, unsure if they could accept work against their Starmarks. It was certainly a common practice, but one never wanted to risk being caught by the Celesterium, at least not without enough money to bribe the priest.

"Yes, yes, I know what you're thinking—but I don't see any priests around here, do you?" He pretended to scan the tavern. "We'll just keep this between ourselves, loves. I'm on a deadline." He lowered his voice. "Between you and me, I get sick of all those Celesterium priests anyway, tellin' the rest of us how to live our lives. Real sticks up their asses, no?"

Oyza and Yars shared another awkward smile.

"There's also one more thing," Oyza said. "I can do whatever you need me to do on your boat, but only until we reach Oyvassa. We need to be let off there, as close to Oyvassa as we can get."

Captain Seralus's lips narrowed. "Love, no one goes to Oyvassa anymore. What business could you possibly have in that dismal place?"

"Our business is our own. You don't need to take us right to the city, only near it. We'll find the rest of the way ourselves," Oyza replied. "If we don't finish all the work before Oyvassa, we can pay the difference in silver."

Captain Seralus pondered the request, playing with the end of the white feather as it brushed against his cheek. He sighed. "Well, I suppose we can do that. The journey from Oyvassa to Talazar City is long, though, and if you're getting off near Oyvassa, you won't be able to do all the work I need in time. So, yes, I'll need whatever coins you can pay."

"Of course," Oyza said.

A brief pause passed between them as Captain Seralus pondered some more. The band roared as travelers laughed, and the sounds of clanking glasses rang throughout the tavern. The paper moths hanging from the ceiling swayed.

Captain Seralus clasped his hands together. "Well, then, it is done! Loves, meet me at the third dock in the harbor at sunrise. You shouldn't have any problem finding my ship. The beauty of the *Chandelier Lover* is unparalleled." He turned his head up and stretched out his arms.

Two drunken sailors stumbled by their table, staring at Captain Seralus and snickering. "The *Chandelier Lover*, eh?" one asked with a laugh.

"You guys better watch out for this one," the other sailor sneered, nodding toward Captain Seralus with raised eyebrows.

"Especially *you*." He winked at Yars and slapped the other man on his bottom. The men snorted as they left the tavern.

Oyza concealed a grin while Yars looked away, mouth hanging open. His face turned red.

Captain Seralus crossed his arms. "Don't listen to them, loves." He cast an angry glare across the room. "Go get some rest. The *Chandelier Lover* departs first thing in the morning!"

CHAPTER 13

Liviana sat with Sir Yirig in her private chamber atop the citadel at Judge's Pass. A Moth fluttered in the room and poured them both glasses of wine. It was a cool night, and a fire crackled in the hearth. Livana told the servant to leave and closed the door behind the Moth.

"You're really not going tomorrow?" Sir Yirig asked after the door shut.

Liviana pursed her lips. "No. I don't care what Uriss wants."

"Then I'm not going either."

Liviana smiled. "Good. My Iron Towers, the other commanders, the boy Plinn—none of us are going. If the emperor and his son's funeral are poorly attended, perhaps they'll think twice about challenging us."

Sir Yirig took a sip of wine and rubbed his neck. "When do you want Plinn and me to go? Oyza's probably made it pretty far by now."

Liviana looked away, tapping her nails on the table. "I know. I meant to send you off earlier." She stepped to the window. The bronze dome of the Basilica of One Thousand Stars gleamed in pale moonlight. "Instead of going to the funeral, tomorrow I will knight Plinn. You'll ride right after."

"Aye. And what will you do in the meantime?"

Liviana wrinkled her nose. "I must deal with Uriss. We're fortunate Cerras will not be attending his father's funeral and was crowned in the North. It's bought us some time. I haven't told you yet, but Voy believes

Uriss is funneling food from Celesterium monasteries to Mélor. That's why we have so little food here."

Sir Yirig's eyes narrowed. "But why? That doesn't make any sense."

Liviana sat down across from Yirig, reaching for a lump of cheese. "Think about it. He's starved the people here, where I rule, causing unrest. He's aided Mélor against his brothers, causing more unrest there. I think Uriss meant to gain his father's favor; perhaps he wanted to make a claim to the throne."

"But betray his own family?"

Liviana bit into a grape and feigned a look of shock. "You think he cares about his family?"

"So what will you do?"

"I'm not sure. Minister Woss and I will inspect the monasteries, but we haven't announced it yet."

"Aye."

Liviana stiffened for a moment, looking into the flames with hard eyes. Xalos rested by the fire, its blade gleaming. "My father should be here. Politics was his game. War is mine."

Sir Yirig closed his eyes and nodded. "It's hard to believe Nalus is gone."

"And my mother too. It's just me now, Yirig." She stared at the blade, watching reflections of the flame twist.

"Yes. I miss them both dearly."

Liviana removed her gloves and rolled up her sleeves. "How is Plinn?"

"He's learning quickly; I think he'll be a fine addition to the mission. He's naive, but that just means we can mold him how we like."

"Excellent." Liviana reclined and sipped wine. "You know, when you leave for Oyvassa, I'm sending Voy to the Shimmering Woods."

"Voy? For what?"

"She is to pose as a refugee from Goldfall. We need eyes on the Ungoverned. We need to find where they're hiding in the swamp, and we need to find a passage there. And with Goldfall burned, I'm sure they're plotting something."

"Of course," the knight replied.

Liviana rose and stretched her neck. She eyed the Hawk and Tower flag on the wall, then stepped toward the window and peered at the mountains on the horizon.

"The world's changing, Yirig. And I don't mean to get left behind."

Plinn sat alone in the castle's chapel room, kneeling before a stained-glass window. A rainbow of colors, full of warm golds and tender shades of rose, splashed onto his head and the smooth floor. The window depicted Soralir. The wizard shoved his staff into the ground as beams of white light shot out at soldiers and turned their bodies to stone. Above him, the World Scar blazed through the Origins as drops of blood rained from the sky. It was a familiar scene in Judge's Pass, the ever-neutral city, which had long taken up the wizard as an icon. Plinn pondered the legend and prayed quietly.

The sound of soft footsteps interrupted his thoughts. A woman approached. She had bright red lips and short black hair cascading in waves down to her chin. There was something enchanting about the way she walked, a kind of haunting allure in every step.

"You must be Plinn," she said with a slight lisp.

"Yes." Plinn tried to ignore the lisp. He cleared his throat and straightened his back. "Plinn Hales of Groshe." He bowed.

Voy crossed her arms, then raised a hand to play with the ends of her hair. Her silver bracelets sparkled. "My name is Voy. I came to give you a message from Commander Liviana."

Plinn perked up. *My knighting? Any day now.*

"You are not to attend the funeral tomorrow. Instead, at dawn, you will meet here to be knighted. Then you and Sir Yirig will leave the city."

Skip the funeral? He wrinkled his brow. *I would be hanged!*

"Won't Cerras be upset with me? And the Celesterium?"

Voy tilted her head and pursed her red lips. "Cerras? I don't see him here. You answer to Commander Liviana now, remember? Whatever your commander wants, you want. That's what makes a Parthassian knight strong: duty, honor—all that blah, blah, blah."

Plinn fidgeted with his sleeve. "If you say so."

Voy took a seat in the pew, her hair sparkling in the colored light like a bouquet of spring flowers. "So you're from Groshe then? You're young. What brought you to Goldfall?"

Plinn wasn't sure if he wanted to relive the painful memories. "Well, the fields outside Groshe were raided by the Men without Gods." He paused, remembering the last moments he had seen his family. His father had spent years painstakingly saving money from their successes through long-distance trade to Talazar. They were going to be rich, his father had said, never like all those filthy beggars in the streets of Groshe. Plinn's neck muscles tightened at the memory of their farm burning to the ground. "And I lost everything that night. Had nowhere to go. Wandered around some, then ended up getting taken into the army and sent to the palace guard at Goldfall. We heard Blacklance was going to be there. When I heard she was in trouble, we went to find her."

Voy listened, tapping her fingernails on the bench. "A poor farm boy, now become a knight. Not too different from my own story. When Liviana took Judge's Pass and impaled my old master, she took me in because, well, let's just say I knew things about this city—things nobody else knew."

She's a spy, then?

Voy stood and lifted her eyes to Soralir. "Listen close, Plinn. We all died when Liviana chose us, but we're reborn, Plinn, reborn for the Empire." She stared at Plinn with bewitching eyes. "Why do you fight for the Empire? For Liviana?"

Plinn gathered his thoughts for a brief moment. *Always these tricks!* "Because, well, there's no one better to lead the Empire. And she's the only one who can stand up to Hafrir."

Voy smiled. "Cute. You're cute, Plinn. But tell me, what do you want?"

Plinn blushed and scratched his arm. "I...well..." *What do I say? I want to be rich? I want to be a knight? I want only the glory of the Empire?*

"Listen to me closely, Plinn. Stay on Liviana's good side, and she will reward you. But cross her even a little, and she will cut you down. Remember, whatever your commander wants, you want. That's what it means to serve under the Parthassian banner. Don't forget it." She ran her fingers through her hair. "I must be off now. Best wishes to you and Sir Yirig on your journey south." She bowed and turned to leave, her long cloak dangling behind her.

Plinn barely acknowledged her. Instead, his eyes wandered to Voy's hips as she left. *Is this another game?* He took a deep breath. *Is it my place to ask questions?* He raised his chin. *I am going to be a knight, a knight of the Parthassian Empire.* "Wait."

Voy stopped.

"What is it *you* want?" Plinn asked.

Voy studied him over her shoulder. Her delicate, black cloak whirled at her sides.

Plinn held his breath.

"Whatever the commander wants, of course," she responded with a radiant smile. She left the chapel.

Plinn turned back to the stained-glass window. Voy was an odd character, but he knew she mattered to Liviana, and so it would be in his best interest to get to know her. *She was beautiful too.*

He knelt before the window again, but rather than pray to the Origins or to Soralir, he closed his eyes and repeated a phrase over and over: *Whatever my commander wants, I want.*

CHAPTER 14

Oyza woke to neighing horses, rickety wheels, and early morning chatter. She sat up and stretched, her muscles relaxed after sleeping in a comfortable bed in an inn. The sun wasn't up, and the horizon glowed a dim blue. But where was Yars?

Did he run off? We're going to miss the ship!

She sprang from bed, dressed, and ran downstairs.

The innkeeper, an older man with a huge belly and bushy mustache, washed a table. The aroma of bacon drifted from the kitchen.

"Excuse me." Oyza tucked her seashell necklace under her cloak. "Did you see my friend, Yars, this morning? He's not in the room."

The innkeeper scrubbed dust from his hands. "Yeah, I saw him. Left about an hour ago, I think. Didn't say anything, just took off." He shrugged and started wiping another table.

Oyza crossed her arms. *I knew it. He's selling the dagger. I should have never trusted him.*

Or maybe he went to the docks already. But why go without me?

"Do you know which way he went?"

"He turned left out the door, I think."

Great. Away from the harbor. "Thank you."

She decided to skip breakfast and dashed into the streets to find Yars.

At least the sun had not risen. But the city was waking; already, horses and shepherds and wagons full of oats and beans and barley came and went. Roosters crowed, mixing with the sounds of flimsy wheels turning on cobblestone streets and morning prayers. *Gods, should I just go without him?*

Four Parthassian guards walked in her direction; she ducked into an alleyway, crisscrossing through the town.

I should have known. She clenched her jaw as she ran, nearly stumbling into a cart brimming with jugs of milk.

She checked everywhere she could: by the fountains, next to houses, behind the armory, even near the castle in the center of town. There was no sight of him. She passed the Temple of the Crab and saw two Scarabs carrying a cart with the body of a dead man lying in the back. Oyza felt jitters. Her older brother was a Scarab.

She paused, out of breath. "This is ridiculous." The sun was rising too. She had to make for the docks before it was too late.

I guess that's the end of us, then. She felt an emptiness in her stomach. Had their time together meant nothing to him?

She sighed and turned down a narrow alley toward the bay when a voice called out to her, "Oyza!"

Clenching her jaw, she turned. "There you are. Yars, we have to go. We're going to miss the ship. And tell me you still have it. You didn't sell the dagger, did you?" *And please tell me you didn't run after witchdust.*

Yars walked up. His eyes seemed droopy, and the ends of lips curled into a half smile. "Hey... I was just... coming to find you."

Oyza fumed. *Oh no...* She stared into his eyes. His pupils were small. "You've been...you've been smoking witchdust..."

Yars looked away, but the smile on his face remained. "It's not a big deal..."

"I can't believe you would do this." She stormed away toward the harbor.

"Wait," Yars cried. "I'm fine. I just needed a little, that's all. I swear." He ran after her. "I didn't buy more! It was just this last time. I promise!"

Oyza folded her arms. *I'm going. I don't need this.*

As they reached the harbor, the scent of the river mixed with the salty breeze of the ocean and the smell of rotting fish. Sailors on the piers lifted crates on and off of the many ships.

"Wait," Yars pleaded. "Oyza, just talk to me. Please don't leave me!"

"You sold it, didn't you? The mageware blade?" Oyza said through gritted teeth.

"What? No, Oyza, it's right here. I just used a little of the silver I stole."

Oyza shook her head, taking hard steps toward the harbor. "So that's how you live then? Just stealing and buying witchdust?"

Yars followed Oyza, begging her to stop.

They passed ships from all across Vaaz, but there was only one vessel whose sails were decorated with purple and white streamers, that seemed to gleam and sparkle like a diamond in the first rays of the sun. In all the Five-and-a-Half Seas of Vaaz, there was only one *Chandelier Lover*.

Captain Seralus greeted them on the dock. "Ah, there is my Starfish! Come, come, hurry—you are late!"

"I'm sorry, Captain." Oyza bowed her head. Yars stood behind her. "We got held up." She glared at Yars. *Why did you follow?*

Yars gulped and avoided her eyes.

The captain shook his head. "Not good, not good. You barely made it. But it's in the past now. Come, I must show you my boat." He gestured to the *Chandelier Lover* behind him. Its hull was smooth and polished, almost as if it had never set sail before. Captain Seralus led them to the deck. "You, the Hound, go talk to those men over there. They'll tell you what to do."

Yars nodded and made his way to the other side of the ship, avoiding eye contact with Oyza.

"But, you, come with me. We've got lots of work to do down below," Captain Seralus said.

The crew buzzed around them, moving trunks, crates, and barrels full of goods to send back to Talazar City. A man walked past Oyza, carrying a stack of paintings wrapped in thick cloth and tied together with heavy rope. Part of the wrapping had ripped, and Oyza saw a part of a painting depicting a lord and his family standing near a fireplace.

The captain led Oyza down two flights of steps to a small door. The door was painted white, and around its border was a ring of vines covered in violet flowers and rose-colored butterflies. The captain clutched onto the edge of his opulent velvet hat, bending it inward so it fit through the door. The room was small, packed with wooden caskets of scrolls and stacks of paintings rising from the floor to the ceiling. The air was thick and musty, and it stank like mold and old rags. *Beautiful on the outside, at least.*

"Take a seat, love," the captain said. "This is one of our storage rooms. You'll notice it's a bit...unpolished, shall we say. The place became a real mess after my last scribe, whom I mentioned yesterday—this prissy little Starfish from Mezzer, really acted like she ran the place—you know how they are in Mezzer, what with their golden pyramids and emerald jewels and all that. I mean you would *not* believe the way she acted, it was *just*— Oh, I'm sorry, let's forget I mentioned her."

He sat down on the opposite side of the desk in the middle of the room. "Here's what I need you to do. These boxes are full of past orders. I need these to be arranged first into kingdom and then according to date."

Oyza's stomach growled; she could have eaten something if it hadn't been for Yars. There must have been two decades of orders in the room, and Oyza felt an urge to organize all of it. Something about the clutter irked her. *Years of being a servant, I guess.* And yet, part of her felt excited too, to see what kinds of things were here.

The captain lifted a box and pulled out a torn sheet. He sat it on the table and pointed to an unsigned line at the bottom. "And you'll notice some of them are unfulfilled. I need you to match those with the piles of works in the next room. Basically, everything down here needs to be reorganized. Do you think you can do this?" He gestured at the jungle of scrolls and papers around him.

Oyza nodded. "Of course, captain."

"Good. I'm gonna poke around up top for a moment and check up on your friend. We set sail now. There will be a short break for lunch at midday and dinner just before nightfall. I'll give you a moment to get acclimated, but come back up before we launch, and my men will show you to your quarters." He turned back toward the door.

"One question, Captain. How long is the passage to Talazar City? And how long to Oyvassa?"

The captain brushed the feather from his face. "It's about a month by sea to Talazar City. We'll be making a few stops along the way. We'll get to Oyvassa in under a week with good weather. We can drop you off about a day's walk from the city, but no closer than that. Don't want to get mixed up with the Ungoverned or whatever else is there now."

Oyza nodded. "Thank you, Captain."

The captain clasped his hands together. "Excellent! I'll be upstairs." With a twist of his hat's white feather, he turned and left the room.

Back on the deck, the crew showed Yars the work he needed to do on the voyage. Yars stood with his arms crossed. He tried to mask the fact that he had been smoking witchdust only two hours earlier. *What was I thinking? Just a little? Oyza hates me now. Fuck, fuck. Why did I do it?* The strongest effects had worn off by now, but he still felt relaxed, like his body was wrapped in a warm cloud. He nervously tapped his fingers together.

"Clean out these buckets, scrub underneath these railings, rinse and dry these barrels of sheets—oh, and we'll also need you to help us untangle these nets. Watch out—could be sharp scales all over, you'll need some gloves," one the sailors said. He was a handsome man, with almond-shaped eyes and a pearly-white smile. The muscles in his arms bulged from underneath his tunic.

A woman with braided hair and a dazzling silver piercing in her nose nudged Yars's shoulder from behind. "And once you've done that, we'll need lots of help down below. Got potatoes to skin."

Yars took it all in and tried his best to feign an eager smile. He kicked a pebble. *Oyza needs me. I fucked up. I shouldn't have. She's mad at me now. Why, why, why do I always ruin things?*

Another shipmate higher on the deck yelled, "Oh, and we'll also need help cleaning out all these boxes of junk."

Yars scaled the stairs, trying his best to stay focused. At the top, there was a massive crate filled with scraps of metal. There were fragments of furniture, a rusted shield bearing a symbol of a bear, a collection of half-shattered plates decorated with blue flowers, and an old lute.

Yars's eyes grew wide. He pulled the instrument out. "Whose is this?" He held it in both his hands and examined its strings. Nine of the thirteen strings were still there. Two pink roses were painted on the front.

"You play?" the sailor asked.

"Yeah, a bit." Yars strummed the strings. "It's really out of tune, though." He examined the instrument. It was made of a fine chestnut wood and had probably belonged to a noble before being tossed away.

"I'll tell you what," the sailor said, "get all your work done today, and maybe I'll let you sing us a song tonight."

The crew laughed.

Yars grinned and placed the fragile lute back in the crate. *I have to make this up to Oyza now...* He felt for the mageware dagger under his tunic. *At least I didn't sell this. Gods, she would have never spoken to me again.*

Captain Seralus emerged. "All right everyone. No more dillydallying. Let's set sail!"

The sailors buzzed around the deck, loosening ropes and dropping sails and doing all sorts of things Yars didn't understand. He watched them carefully and awaited orders, standing with folded arms.

Oyza climbed back onto the deck. He noticed she refused to make eye contact with him. He straightened his back and raised his chin. *Whatever, it's just a little witchdust. If I want to use it, that's my business.* A breeze blew through his curly hair. He inspected Oyza from afar: the strands of her hair, her shining hair, her smile. He remembered the way her hand felt so soft in his that night. Her weird determination.

No, she's right. I shouldn't have done that. He slouched and started at his boots. *Oyza's all I got in this world now. I can't fuck up again. I hope she forgives me.*

The ship drifted away from the dock, cutting through a low fog hovering over the bay. The air smelled like mud and seaweed.

A few observers on the dock waved farewell and shouted blessings as sailors on board blew kisses. The docks faded from view, and the rooftops of the city receded into the distance. A pack of gulls followed them, cawing as they circled overhead.

I should go say sorry. Maybe she'll listen. Yars swallowed, then inched his way toward Oyza.

She stood with her back turned to him, facing the ocean. Her cloak billowed in the wind.

Yars cleared his throat. "Oyza, listen, I'm really sorry..."

Oyza crossed her arms, still facing the ocean. "They almost left without us. You didn't bring witchdust with you, did you?"

Yars waved his hands. "No. It was just that one last time. I'm sorry, Oyza, I'm just so stressed..."

Oyza was silent for a long moment as she stared at the waves. "This is important to me, Yars. That we get to Oyvassa. You almost ruined the whole thing."

Yars kicked at the deck. "I...I'm sorry, Oyza. Look, we still have some silver. And the dagger. And I swear, I won't look for witchdust again."

Oyza turned around. Her eyes were thin. "Do you even care, Yars? About Oyvassa? Mapa?"

Yars swallowed. "Of course. I coulda just ran a long time ago."

"Why? You already said you don't care about the Ungoverned. You just want to sell the schematics. Why not just run then? I can do this alone, Yars."

Ouch. The words stung him harder than any knife ever could have.

The boat swayed in the water where the river gave way to the ocean. The towers of Groshe slowly disappeared.

Yars rubbed his arm. "Because I care about *you*, Oyza. And because you *can't* do it alone."

Oyza tapped her lips on the railing.

"I'm sorry, Oyza. No more witchdust. Let's just get to Oyvassa and figure it out from there."

Oyza crossed her arms and took a slow breath. "Fine. But you have to promise you didn't bring more witchdust. It ruins people, Yars. I can't risk that right now. You know, I don't...I don't exactly have anyone else either."

After a long moment, she reached out to hug him.

A wave of relief washed over Yars. He embraced Oyza, burying his nose in her neck. She smelled wonderful. "I don't have any witchdust, Oyza. I won't use any more." *Thank the Gods.*

Captain Seralus walked up to them.

Oyza pulled away. "What are these warships doing?" She eyed a huge row of Parthassian ships bobbing in the water. Black and bronze sails dangled from their masts. Menacing hawk statues sitting on the front of each vessel sent shivers up Yars's spine.

"Sometimes inspections, but we got clearance this morning. Bastards, all of them."

Yars brushed some curls from his eyes. He bent over the edge and looked down at the water. The ship glided through the calm green waters as a school of fish swam nearby.

"Why do you ask? Hiding from the Empire, are we?"

Yars turned to Oyza.

"No, no," she said. "Just wondering."

The captain laughed and turned away. "I don't know what you hope to do in Oyvassa, but better I don't know, I suppose. Come on, plenty of work to do."

Yars smiled. The mountains behind Groshe disappeared over the green horizon of the sea as strong gusts blew into the ship's white sails. Dolphins bounced in the waves beneath them. Yars squinted into the morning light and wondered how far away Oyvassa was. He couldn't help but wonder how he ended up here. He examined Oyza again. The loose strands of her onyx-black hair fluttered in the wind. *I'd better be careful from here on out.* He caught up with the sailors and busied himself with work.

✿❊✿

Oyza went inside, trying to put Yars out of her mind for the moment. *It must be hard being an addict. But I can't let him risk everything.* She tried to start but kept thinking about Yars: his cheery smile, his big eyes, how the muscles in his arms already seemed bigger than when they had fled the dungeons. They both seemed so much better than the first day they had met. *How fast things can change in just a few weeks.*

No, no. Get to work.

She began to sort through stacks of scrolls and notes on the desk. Clouds of dust leaped into the air and hung in pale sunbeams as she shuffled around. As her hands fingered through the reams of dry and faded papers, she shuddered to think about what would have happened if those Parthassian warships had stopped them. How many times would that old code actually work? Her mind wandered to thoughts of Liviana. *She's out there, somewhere. Coming for me...*

The work was mind-numbing, but Oyza was glad for the chance to read again. Learning about art dealers and traders and all their misfortunes wasn't the most exciting reading, but it was something to pass the time. Oyza learned about a Lord Barnabith of Cla, who demanded payment from Captain Seralus for a collection of ivory carvings of the Origins that never arrived. Ivory was expensive, she learned, and it only came from Mezzer. Another letter revealed a wealthy widow named Lady Lelna, in a town called Strathorm, was awaiting the shipment of a portrait she had commissioned of her late husband when she suddenly died. The portrait sat buried deep in the *Chandelier Lover*, never to be delivered—apparently, it was quite ugly, and not even the artist nor any relatives wanted it back. One report was especially interesting to Oyza: it referenced a mageware necklace made of ruby found in an ice cave in the tundras near the Temple of the Mammoth. It had once radiated heat when pressed against one's body—until the enchantment ran out, which was quite unfortunate for the young woman on whose frozen body the amulet was discovered. It was now merely a piece of jewelry. The letter revealed Captain Seralus had lost the amulet along the route to Chan-Chan-Tuul, and he was to pay a thousand pieces of gold to a lord in Degras. Oyza lost track of how many hours went by, as there was something soothing about the feeling of riffling old papers in her hands again—frayed, rough, and gritty. The musty odor reminded her of Minister Valador's library, which, to her surprise, brought her some comfort. *No matter where you are, a room of books smells exactly the same.*

Her mind, however, kept drifting back to thoughts of Liviana. *Liviana, Parthassian commander.* It was crazy—that spoiled, angry, petulant psychopath was now the most powerful commander in the world? Oyza thought about that day all those years ago in the vine-covered courtyard. She thought it would have been the last day she would ever see Liviana. She remembered the way Liviana laughed, blood trickling between her teeth. Oyza shuddered and got back to work.

At lunch, a shipmate brought to Oyza a small bowl of beef soup served with a side of crusty rye bread and a cup of mint tea. She worked some more, and the hours passed by until the sun sank to the horizon and the room darkened. Dinner would be soon, she figured, but she wanted to keep working until given orders to stop.

Something upstairs caught Oyza's attention. She set down a half-torn scroll and squinted at the door. *Is that... music?*

She ascended the stairs to investigate. Captain Seralus and the crew gathered around someone sitting. It was Yars. He was playing a lute, strumming an otherworldly tune full of graceful notes and chords that seemed to spring from a dream itself.

Oyza crept onto the deck, careful not to interrupt, her ears fixed on the dazzling song flowing from the instrument. A delicate wind caressed the ends of her hair. The setting sun was little more than a glimmer of scarlet sinking toward the depths of the sea. Oyza gently pushed her way through the edge of the gathering, mesmerized by the intoxicating melody leaping from Yars's fingers.

He looked up at Oyza. A melancholy smile swept across his face. Then, he sang:

> *We ran from the mines, but where are we to go?*
> *We're poor and broke and homeless now*
> *And flying with the crows.*
>
> *We're running for our lives, to the desert or the snow?*
> *The Emerald Isles call us now.*
> *Come on, come on, let's go.*
>
> *Through the marsh and through the wood,*
> *The roads went on and on.*
> *We stole everything we could*
> *Until the morning dawn.*
>
> *The Tower casts a shadow,*
> *And the Hawk, it stalks the sky,*
> *And we just keep on runnin',*
> *Runnin', runnin,' 'til we die.*

The Gods, they have abandoned us,
And kings, they never cared.
We're the fallen of the world,
The fallen and the scared.

Through darkness and through shadow,
Through sorrow and through night,
The fallen cry out to the Gods
To make the world right.

The fallen cry out to the Gods
To make the world right.

CHAPTER 15

Plinn waited in the chapel, bathed in tranquil warmth under the stained-glass window of Soralir. He was dressed in full Parthassian plate mail that was black, shiny, and decorated with bronze trim around the edges. A striped cape fell over his back. On his chest, the Hawk and Tower sigil glistened. He looked at his gloves. *I've never been so well-dressed in my life. I wish Father and Mother were here. Imagine their faces! Me, a knight!*

He worried for a moment about skipping the emperor's funeral, just down the street at the Basilica of One Thousand Stars. No. He raised his chin. *Whatever my commander wants, I want.*

Tall candles filled the room with a solemn glow. He thought again about his father, about how they were so close to a life of riches before the Haf took everything from them. *I'll never be poor again. I won't be like those people anymore.*

He closed his eyes and recited his knight's vows one last time. Minister Voss had taught the words to him only the night before. He took a deep breath as he heard footsteps.

Liviana and Sir Yirig appeared at the door. Liviana carried Xalos, its ruby-tipped hilt glimmering in the delicate light, while Sir Yirig held a sword and a shield. The blade was slightly curved, and it sparkled like a polished ring. The round shield was thick, sturdy, and decorated with bronze towers.

Plinn knelt and lowered his head. His heart pounded, but he tried to stay calm. *Show no weakness.*

After a long silence, Liviana lifted Xalos. Plinn could feel its tip just above his mop of brown hair. "Plinn Hales of Groshe, for your courage and your loyalty and for your dedication to the Parthassian Empire, we gather here to proclaim your ascension to the rank of knight. May you be strong like the Tower and brave as the Hawk, as you serve the Empire in life and beyond. Plinn Hales, you may now recite your knightly vows."

She skipped some words. It caught him off guard a little. All the words about the Origins, the Gods, the Celesterium: she left out all of it.

Plinn's palms were moist. *I should skip the lines about the Gods too if that's what my commander wants.* "Today, in the presence of the Commander Liviana Valador, I do swear my allegiance to the Parthassian Empire. I swear to defend its people with strength and courage, to uphold its decrees with honor and determination, and to represent the might of the Hawk and the Tower wherever I may go, for now, and all time to come."

There was a pause. *The priests usually perform a ceremony here,* he remembered. Instead, Liviana tapped the end of the Xalos on the top of his head. "Rise, Sir Plinn Hales of Groshe, Knight of the Parthassian Empire."

Sir Plinn! I am a knight! He lifted his eyes, suppressing a grin.

Sir Yirig smiled and gave him a slight nod. He stepped toward *Sir* Plinn, bowed, and handed him the sword and shield. Sir Plinn grabbed the blade, its weight pulling down his arm. It glimmered in the faint light spilling through the stained-glass window. Next, he picked up the shield. It was heavy, but Sir Plinn was sure to hold it with pride.

He turned back to Liviana and knelt again, pointing the sword into the ground and setting his forehead over its hilt. "Commander Liviana Valador, I pledge my life, my heart, my soul to you and to the Parthassian Empire."

He felt a weight pour onto his shoulders, as if the burdens of reigning became his burdens too. He looked down and marveled at his sword's deadly edge. His mind surged with thoughts of battle and valor, of victories to be won for the Empire, of rewards and accolades.

I'll never be poor again. I'll never be like those people. I am a knight, a knight of the Parthassian Empire.

❀❦❀

Liviana stood in her chambers and scanned the city. Somewhere below, Sir Yirig, Sir Plinn, and twenty of her fastest riders raced toward

136

Oyvassa. The neighborhoods of Judge's Pass sprawled toward the horizon, shrouded in a cloak of dust. Beeswax candles burned, and a musky aroma infused the air. A Moth popped into the room and poured a glass of lavender tea.

Liviana sat at the table, which was covered in more scrolls and letters than ever before. She rubbed her temples, then rested Xalos on the floor as Minister Woss knocked. "Come in."

"Commander, you should know, the entire city is talking about your absence at the funeral." Dark bags hung under his eyes.

Liviana didn't look at him. "Good. Let Uriss talk. That's all priests do, talk."

"Really, Commander, you must be more careful. And do you think it's prudent to send Sir Yirig away right now?"

Liviana pursed her lips. "I want Oyza brought to justice, and there's no one better at tracking than Yirig. If anyone can find Oyza, it's him."

Minister Woss fingered through the stacks of papers on the desk.

"Besides, I think it would be good for him to get out again. And Plinn too. I think Yirig will enjoy teaching the boy."

"That may be so, but you must understand, Liviana, the priests conspire against you. And you've sent Voy away too? I implore you to just make peace with the Celesterium. And there is still Cerras to contend with."

"Nonsense." Liviana flicked her hand. "What can the Celesterium do? Raise an army? I am done taking orders from priests. On Parthassian lands, the priests will take orders from us."

Minister Woss shrugged. "I served your father for many years, Liviana. Would he behave so cavalierly?"

Liviana leaned back and ran her fingers through her hair. "We can't make the same mistakes my father did. Do you know what his weakness was?"

Minister Woss wrinkled his nose.

"He was scared. Too gripped with fear to act on his power. Ever since my mother passed, he was so cautious, making his littles allies in court and raising me to one day lead the armies he could not. And he was a hypocrite too." She walked back toward the window and peered at the Sword of Creation. "Always acted like his little jewel in the dungeon should be so grateful for what he did, for saving her life from the Haf. He was a weak man, deep down."

"Be kind, Liviana. Your father was a great man. The Empire would be in much, much worse shape if not for him. He was the only one who spoke sense to the emperor."

"I can't believe she's free out there, after murdering him." She thought for a moment about the last time she had seen her, all those years ago in the vine-draped courtyard. Then she thought about her father. *This is all his fault. He should never have let her live. He should have had her killed. She runs free, and I'm all alone. It's just me now. Me, Yirig, my armies.*

She took a sip of tea then set down the cup. "Minister, I have an idea. Our scouts tell us the Haf have made camp south of Goldfall. Once things are under control here, I will ride out to meet them myself."

Minister Woss choked. "Commander, I don't think that's a wise move. It's not safe. It's—"

A smirk crept up her face. "We will obtain their arms, Minister, one way or another. And there's no guarantee Yirig's mission will succeed. If we cannot buy them with gold, then with something else."

"But what? What can we give to them? Their cannons will destroy you. The wealth of Goldfall was lost. Liviana, you cannot solve every problem with force alone."

We'll see about that. My whole life, they've told me I can't do things. That I'd never be a commander. That I couldn't take Judge's Pass. That I'd always depend on my father's name. "You'll see soon enough."

CHAPTER 16

Pale moonlight splashed through a circular window. The ship bobbed in the waves, creaking gently. Oyza woke and saw Yars was gone. *Again? Gods. Does he never sleep a full night?* She rubbed her eyes, threw on her clothes, and crept up the steps.

The night air felt chilly, and the Sword of Creation tore through the center of the sky against a multitude of stars. Yars stood at the back of the boat, looking out at sea, not wearing a shirt.

"Aren't you cold?" Oyza said.

He turned around, curly hair glistening. "Oyza. You should be asleep…"

"And so should you. What are you doing here?"

Yars looked down. "Nothing. I just was having trouble sleeping." He turned to face the water. Calm waves sparkled in the moonlight.

"You didn't come here for...witchdust, did you?"

Yars shook his head. "I didn't bring any, Oyza. I told you that."

Oyza sighed. *Thank the Gods.* She stood next to him and stared at the ocean and the stars. "I'm still thinking about the music you played. It was beautiful."

Yars shrugged. "It's nothing. Just something I picked up over the years."

"Where?"

"When I was at the orphanage, the nuns made us all pick music, art, or sports. Don't know why I picked up the lute. I just did."

Oyza smiled. She rested her hands on the wooden railing and lifted her chin toward the darkness. "The fallen of the world," she said, remembering his song.

Yars laughed. "Yeah. I played a little for money here and there." He sat his hand next to hers.

Oyza's heart started pounding. She glanced over and peeked at his eyes. They were beautiful in the starlight, but she detected in them a sadness. She placed her hand atop his. It felt cold. She opened her cloak and wrapped it around both of them. Yars flashed her a smile and rested his arm around her shoulder. The way his strong fingers gripped her arm sent tingles through her.

"I'm sorry that I was so hard on you. About the witchdust."

"No, you were right. We could have missed our ride."

She snuggled closer together.

Yars smiled and looked up. "Can you believe it? Here we are, on a ship to Oyvassa. Doesn't even feel like that long ago we were just sitting in that dungeon."

Oyza looked up too. The Sword of Creation glimmered. "Mapa is up there, somewhere."

Yars nodded. A moment of quiet passed, the water below gently lapping against the hull. "Do you think they care? The Gods...do they care about us at all?"

"I don't know." Oyza paused for a long moment without saying anything. The stars twinkled. "Does it matter if they care?"

Yars weaved his fingers into hers. "I guess not. So long as we have each other. I'm glad I found you, Oyza." He leaned his shoulder against hers.

"I'm glad I found you too, Yars."

They stood for a few moments in the darkness.

"Let's go, we'd better get some sleep," Oyza said.

Yars nodded. They returned to their beds.

✾❀

"Oyza!" Yars said. "Oyza, wake up!" He scrambled for his clothing.

Oyza sat up and rubbed her eyes. "What's going on?"

The room was dark, save for the dim blue light sneaking through the window. Oyza climbed from her bed and saw the sun would rise soon, its rays barely illuminating the black sea. The sounds of footsteps and muffled shouts came from above.

"Come on, let's go!" Yars said.

They bolted up the stairs to the deck, where a light breeze tugged at the sails. The crew raced around the ship, loosening ropes and donning chainmail armor.

Captain Seralus turned the wheel as fast as he could. "Swords! Spears! Crossbows! Now!"

Sailors emerged from the stairs with arms full of weapons. "Here," one of them said to Oyza, handing her a sword. Another one handed a spear to Yars. Others loaded crossbows.

"Captain, what's going on?" Her hair whipped about her face in a gust. She reached for the seashell necklace around her neck, nervous.

"There, look!" The captain pointed.

Oyza and Yars ran to the edge. Three ships approached from the horizon, barely visible in the darkness.

"They're coming toward us." The white feather in his hat jerked in the wind.

"Who?" Oyza squinted. *It's Liviana, it has to be. Those Parthassian warships, I knew it.*

"Those ships belong to the Men without Gods—to Hafrir! But it's not too late to outrun them! The morning winds are picking up. The *Chandelier Lover* has never been captured. Faster, faster, faster! Get the smoke ready!" the captain said.

The crew cheered. They placed small vials on the perimeter and prepared to light them with torches.

"You two—you should get inside if you hope to make it to Oyvassa," Captain Seralus said. "If they board, we're going to light those lamps and fill the air with smoke. It's the only chance we've got against their guns. If we can take enough of them out, we might just make it out alive. Now, onward!" The captain swung the steering wheel.

Oyza shook her head, gripping the blade. "No, we can help."

Yars gulped.

A look of confusion crossed Captain Seralus's face. "Suit yourselves, loves—but I suggest you hide!"

Oyza strained to see the vessels. "They look just like the boats that were at Goldfall."

Yars tapped his fingers on the barrier. "Or maybe there's more of them—maybe they came from somewhere else?"

Oyza ran to the other side, boots thumping on the wood. She scanned the horizon. "Are there any other ships nearby?" The water was flat like black glass. She would have even called for help from a Parthassian warship if it were near.

"I don't see anyone," Yars said. "We're all alone." He gripped his spear and turned away.

A loud boom and a splash of water rocked the ship. A second blast followed, sending a jet of water high into the air.

"They're firing on us!" Oyza ran to Captain Seralus. A third boom rocked through the air as another jet of water splashed out of the sea. "They're part of the fleet that attacked Goldfall," Oyza said. "We have to go faster!"

Captain Seralus shook his head and flicked the feather out of his eyes. "This is as fast as we can go." The sails flapped in the wind as purple streams fluttered. "Get down below!"

Oyza and Yars grasped the ship's railing, desperate to watch as long as they could. Another burst sent water flying onto the boat as deckhands took defensive positions behind barrels, crates, and piles of coiled rope. One of the ships pulled ahead of the others, roaring through the sea. The sun rose, revealing green diamonds and silver crowns on the sails. It fired a blast, and this time, it landed into the side of the *Chandelier Lover*.

Oyza stumbled as the floor shook. She squinted at the approaching ship. Gathered soldiers in iron plate mail armed with pistols, swords, and crossbows were ready to attack. It was the first time she had seen them this close since she was young. Oyza's throat tightened.

"We have to take cover!" She fled from the ship's edge and dodged behind a stack of barrels.

Yars knelt beside Oyza, curls flopping over his eyes. Sailors ran to the side of the ship carrying torches. They lit the bottles, threw the torches into the sea, then darted back. Smoke erupted and drenched the air with black clouds.

Oyza's heart raced. She tried to stay calm, leaning her back against the wooden barrels, clutching her sword. She glanced at Yars. *This can't be the end already.* The air smelled bitter.

A hail of bullets zipped into the boxes and barrels around them, sending flayed bits of shrapnel into the air. Oyza covered her neck with her hands. A sailor who was too slow to hide wailed as shots tore through his body. He clutched his waist; blood spilled through his tunic. The man collapsed as another round of blasts knocked him over and sent his body toppling.

Oyza and Yars panicked, grabbing each other's hands.

"Here they come!" someone said.

Captain Seralus dashed into the clouds of charcoal-colored smoke. He hid behind a barrel near Oyza and unsheathed a long thin saber that hung around his waist. Bright blue dolphins were carved into its silver hilt. Oyza tried her best not to cough, but her eyes stung.

The firing stopped. Silence gripped the deck. The immense ship pulled up alongside the *Chandelier Lover* and slammed against it. It towered above the smaller Vaazian ship.

"Fuck it," Yars whispered. He squatted on the balls of his feet and peeked around the barrel. "I can't see a lot. Too much smoke. Wait. They're dropping planks."

Oyza heard the planks land. She clenched her sword in both hands, fingers weaved into each other. She closed her eyes and slowed her breathing once more, just like she used to do before fighting with Liviana.

"Here they come!" Yars said.

The sounds of footsteps and battle cries rang through the dark as the Men without Gods boarded.

"Now!" a sailor cried.

The crew of the *Chandelier Lover* charged, swords and spears drawn. Bolts, arrows, and musketfire shot through the air.

Captain Seralus sat behind the mast. A bullet zinged past his face, drawing a trickle of blood. "Not my ship, not the *Chandelier Lover!*"

Oyza and Yars stared at each other. "What do we do?" Yars asked.

"We should fight." Oyza gulped and held her sword up straight, eyeing its edge closely.

More blasts from the other two ships punctuated the clash of metal. The crew shrieked, shots cutting through their leather jerkins. Oyza looked over at the captain.

"For the *Chandelier Lover!*" He charged into the battle with his saber. Four heavily-armored sailors hoisting spears sprinted beside him.

We don't have a choice. Oyza looked back at Yars. *We have to fight.* "Let's go!" She rose to her feet. Yars flew after her.

Oyza's sword crashed into a musket. She saw the eyes of the man from Hafrir—blue, weary, and swelling with rage—as Yars stabbed the Haf man in his gut. He keeled over, grasping for his stomach as blood poured. The stench of metal and flesh mixed in the air. Oyza and Yars shared a quick glance as they moved toward the captain through the smoke. Another Haf, carrying a short sword and an iron buckler, leaped at Yars. He wore gray plate mail decorated in a pattern of green diamonds.

"Yars!" Oyza ran toward Yars as more soldiers lunged at them, but got held back.

One fired a gun at Yars but missed. The bullet grazed the side of his arm, and a streak of blood leaked through his skin. Yars ducked and dashed, his boots thudding. He butted his head into the soldier's iron-covered middle, knocking him into the railing. Yars stuck the end of his spear in the Haf's side. It slid into his flesh like a knife through bread. The man yelped; then Yars drove his fist into his chin and, with both his hands, knocked him from the ship and into the sea.

Ozya rushed to Captain Seralus. The captain grunted as his saber banged into another blade, sweat and blood splashing.

"Captain!" Oyza held her sword high and her head low, trying to stay under the cover of the smoke. The vials were almost empty.

"Oyza!" the captain yelled. He parried a blow and inched forward. The white feather in his hat hung down the side of his face.

"Watch out!" Oyza lunged forward, driving the end of her sword into a sailor's abdomen. She pulled it out just as quick. Syrupy blood spewed like a geyser onto the deck. The sailor fell with a loud thud and screamed. The fear in his eyes reminded Oyza of when Minister Valador died—panicked, scared, unable to accept that death was so close.

"Ha *ha!*" the captain shouted, flicking the white feather from his eyes. He pushed a man over the edge and into the sea.

Oyza clutched her sword with sweaty fingers, ready for whatever emerged from the blackness next. *Where is Yars?*

"Get down!" the captain said.

A crack of bullets ripped through the air. Oyza covered her neck and ducked. Sailors cried out and fell backward as more Haf rushed into the brawl. Men and women from inside the *Chandelier Lover* jumped out with long spears.

Oyza found Yars. He struggled near the edge of the boat where the last vial still burned. He sprang at a soldier. The man blocked Yars and laughed, wiped sweat from his blond beard. He swung a spiked mace like a miner striking impenetrable stone. Yars ducked like lightning and charged at the man, sliding his knees on the deck and tumbling between his legs. The mace crashed into the floor, and splinters of wood exploded in all directions. He grunted and fell backward, wrestling with Yars.

"Yars!" Oyza jabbed at a man who stood in her way.

"Get off me!" Yars grunted.

The burly beast wrapped his arms around Yars, then slammed his fist into Yars's chin. He pulled back then smashed into Yars a second time. A third time. Yars gasped as blood spewed from his jaw.

"Yars!" Oyza gritted her teeth at the man who blocked her way.

The soldier was laughing at Yars when a bolt shot into the soldier's side. He howled as Yars knocked him off. But just as Yars rose to his feet, the man rolled over, seized his mace, and flung it into Yars's stomach. Yars stumbled backward, his hands clutched at his waist.

Oyza shouted again. Yars looked down at bloody fingers. He looked up one last time, his eyes wide with horror. Falling against the railing, he mouthed something at Oyza, then tripped off the edge and tumbled into the water.

"Yars!"

The Haf man lying on the ground turned over and laughed at Oyza. His eyes were filled with twisted delight. Oyza groaned and swung her sword at him. She plunged the tip into his throat. The man gurgled blood, then turned white.

Yars, where are you? She was running toward the edge of the ship when someone jerked her from behind and pulled her down. Burning pain pulsed through her muscles. She kicked and rolled over.

Haf soldiers encircled the captain. The crew of the *Chandelier Lover* lay dead.

The soldiers laughed at Oyza with mocking blue eyes. Sweat dripped from their blond hair. Oyza tasted blood on her lips.

The captain glanced at her. "I'm sorry, love." He shut his eyes.

One of the soldiers—an older, stocky man with a painful scowl on his face and white hair—stepped forward and pressed a pistol into the captain's head. Without hesitation, he pulled the trigger.

"No!" Oyza screamed. Her heart leaped out of her chest.

The captain tumbled with a thud. Oyza jumped to her feet, but a Haf seized her arm and slapped her face. She fell again and landed facedown, her cheek scraping against the wood.

The Haf gasped and pointed at her neck. *"Krafla! Krafla eeri!"* one of them said.

Oyza climbed to her feet again, but an officer rushed toward her. He raised her up by her neck and grinned at her with rotten yellow teeth and breath stinking of alcohol.

With a blow to the head, Oyza passed out.

CHAPTER 17

Oyza's head throbbed. Yars? The captain? Where was she? Had they captured her and brought her to Liviana? She remembered very little of the past few days: thrown in a brig, someone bringing her water and hard bread, men speaking in Haf.

She sat up on the scratchy wood when the door opened. A Haf man, tall with blond hair, entered. He wore an iron breastplate with gray sleeves underneath. The man opened the lock and grabbed her. Oyza wanted to fight back but was too tired—where would she go anyway? The guard led her up to the deck.

The sun was so bright, Oyza shielded her eyes with her hands. Around her sat a fleet of Haf ships. On the shore were tents, fires, horses, men, and Haf streamers waving in a salty wind. The sailor led her to a small rowboat, then took her to another ship. A man stepped out of a door. A gray cape hung from his shoulders, a pistol sat at his waist, and on his chest, he wore a pattern of green diamonds and silver crowns. His hair was black instead of blond. He had brown eyes too and dark brown skin. And the shape of his jaw—

There's something about him, his eyes... Oyza's throat tightened. *He looks so much like... It can't be, it just can't be...* She tried to stand, but her muscles ached.

The man stopped in front of her and waved away the others. *"Rikka kjon, Svend."*

The sailor left.

Oyza's heart raced as she inspected the dark-haired man. *It can't be... It just can't be...but he looks just like him...*

The dark-haired man stroked his clean-shaven chin as he inspected Oyza.

It is. It really is.

"Come." The dark-haired man led her to the bow of the ship. There was no one else around.

Oyza followed but couldn't keep her questions any longer. "Séna...? Brother, is it...is it really you?"

A smile crept onto the man's face. "Séna." His eyes trailed into the sky. "Haven't heard that name in years." He spoke Vaazian, albeit with a slight Haf accent. "Sister." He embraced her, tears welling in his eyes.

Oyza wrapped her arms around him, too stunned to know what to think or how to feel. *Is it really him...? After all these years...?* "Brother... I can't believe... I just can't..."

"It's all right," Séna said.

They hugged for what seemed like an eternity. Oyza silently thanked the Gods.

"My name is Alden now," he added.

Oyza scrunched her eyebrows. "Alden? Séna, what happened to you? What happened to our sister?"

Séna smiled. "Oyza, there's a lot to discuss. I've been to the other side of the world, you know, for fifteen years now, living in Hafrir."

"I don't believe it," Oyza said. "Turn around. Your Starmark—a scarab."

Séna—no, Alden—smirked, then turned and pulled up his hair. Only a black smudge. "It's gone, Oyza. I am Haf now."

"You live with the Men without Gods?"

Alden nodded. "It's true, many say there are no gods. But not all."

Oyza wiped away tears. A salty breeze tugged at the ends of her hair. "And what about our sister? Is Rosina in Hafrir too?" She edged closer to him, then backed away. She wanted to cry, wanted to fall, wanted to scream—but her body was tense.

Alden scanned the Emerald Sea, fingers fidgeting. He lowered his eyes. "I'm sorry, Oyza. Rosina didn't make it on the journey over. The voyage to Hafrir is many months at sea. She fell sick on the boat and..."

146

Emptiness crushed Oyza's chest. She stumbled backward, prompting Alden to step forward and catch her. Oyza waved him off, catching herself. "I'm fine." She took a slow breath. "I just... I've been looking for you—for you both. I was a prisoner of the Empire. And I always thought when I got out... What about mother and father?"

Alden shook his head. "I haven't seen them since that day, the day Oyvassa was attacked."

Oyza's heart raced. She lifted her eyes to Alden's. *Is this truly my brother? He sides now with them?* She felt a bubbling in her chest. Was it rage, despair, confusion? How could he? How could he do this? She balled her hand into a fist, but then couldn't hold it inside anymore. "Attacked by *you*," she hissed. "By Hafrir, just as you attacked us again. Why? Why did your men kill my friends, the captain, all of them? Why, Séna? Is this why you've come back here? You killed everyone I knew, everyone I loved."

Alden's lips tightened. "Oyza, I had no choice. For fifteen years, I lived in Hafrir. The Dron—Dron Eerika, she's like a queen—she took me in. And I was just fourteen years old when they took us away. And you were only, what, seven? What would you have done?"

Oyza shook her head and backed away from him. "You had no choice? No choice but to murder everyone I knew? Do you know what happened to me, Séna? For fifteen years I was a slave to the Parthassians. I dreamt every day of returning to our family, and now you—" Tears leaked down her chin.

"And you helped the Parthassians? You're no better than me."

"I didn't *help* them. I was a servant. And then I spent years rotting in a dungeon. But you—you took ships from Hafrir and raided Goldfall. And then you murdered my friends. Why, Séna? How can you support these people—the people who burned our home?"

Alden frowned. "Oyza, what happened in Oyvassa was a mistake. They never meant to burn the city. Hafrir meant to make a show of force. They ransacked the city and burned everything they could. And the city panicked and fled like fools into the woods."

"The *fools*? You mean our family! You mean mother and father!" Oyza yelled. "How could you, Séna? How could you betray all of us?" Her hands tightened.

Alden gritted his teeth. "I had nothing to do with Oyvassa! I was still just a child."

"And *now*? What are you doing *now*? Burning and pillaging and murdering everyone in Vaaz? Is that what you are now? Yars, the captain—all of them, everyone I knew, everyone I knew in the entire world, you and your men killed!"

Alden took a half step forward, then stopped. He rubbed the back of his neck and straightened his spine. "Oyza, you must understand. There's another world out there, a world across the sea. And the Haf mean to rule it all."

Oyza stared at him icily. She glared at the green diamonds and silver crown on his chest. She wanted to tear them up, spit at them, watch them melt.

"Listen to me, Oyza. Hafrir will send more. More and more and more, more than anyone here can possibly understand." He gestured toward the horizon. "You need to realize something, Oyza. You cannot win. Not Parthass, not Talazar, not Mélor, no one. Oyvassa was simply the first to go. They will send more ships, more soldiers, more cannons—you can't possibly fathom this, Oyza. They are even planning to bring legions of armies and their families to live here—permanently." There was a hint of desperation in his voice. He ran his fingers through his hair. "The sooner you understand this, the better. Don't fight us, Oyza. You don't understand the kind of power we have. What happened to Goldfall is only a taste of what's coming to Vaaz. You *must* realize this. Stand up to those with more power, and you'll only be destroyed. That's just how the world works."

"But we *do* have power," she insisted. "We have armies, we have fleets, we have magewares—"

"Magewares!" Alden scoffed, mocking Oyza with a twisted smile. He placed his hand on her cheek, rubbing with his thumb. "Little sister, you *must* listen to me. If you do not submit, everyone here is going to die, just like in Oyvassa," he said in a tender voice.

Oyza threw his hand off her and pulled back. "Only because you betrayed us!"

"Oyza, you don't understand, I had no choice—"

"Lies! You *chose* to come here. You *chose* to attack Goldfall, to murder my friends—"

"Oyza, listen to me!"

"Listen to you? The one who betrayed his family, his people, his sisters—Rosina!"

Alden struck Oyza's face. She slammed onto the deck and landed with a thud. Her skin scraped against the rough wood as blood trickled from her shoulder.

Oyza didn't move.

A moment later, Alden looked down at Oyza. "Oyza, I'm sorry." His voice was stern.

Oyza turned over and crawled to her feet, wiping away blood from her arm. *He doesn't mean this. He can't. My brother! Mother, Father, help me!*

Alden shouted something in Haf. Svend and two officers grabbed Oyza's wrists and pulled her to the stairs. Oyza cast a last, sorrowful glance at Alden.

He stared back at her with cold eyes. "I'm sorry, Oyza," he said again, "but this is for the best. Give it time, and you'll understand. I promise. I will make you understand."

CHAPTER 18

A candle burned on a table, dripping hot wax and casting shadows on the walls. Flies buzzed, and the smell of piss and mold made Oyza want to choke. She lifted her eyes to a round window, peering at silver beams of moonlight leaking through. The brig was filled with partially illuminated junk: broken barrels, torn fishnets, a few rusty spears, and a small spherical object rolling on the floor. Oyza couldn't quite make out what it was.

She didn't want to move. She didn't want to think. She didn't want to eat, drink, or pray. She lowered her head, gazing at her knees. *I'm a prisoner again.* She slouched against the wall and massaged the back of her head. It still throbbed, and her cheek stung. *Yars, Liviana, Mapa, Captain Seralus*—so many people and thoughts swirled in her head. *How could you, Brother?* After all these years of waiting, searching, hoping—and now this? And Rosina—dead? She felt shriveled like an old apple, empty and hollow.

In another cell, a man with frail arms slept curled in a ball on a pile of straw. His blond hair was full of knots and fell like a waterfall. He was barefoot, and his toenails were black. A bottle sat nearby. He groaned, spun over, turned toward Oyza and revealed blue eyes. Behind a bushy blond beard, a wrinkled face smiled. But it was a youthful smile, belying his scraped and scarred skin. He sat up, stretched, and drank from a cup of water.

Oyza rubbed her eyes. *A Haf? Imprisoned?*

The man stared at her without saying a word, the flicker of the candlelight barely illuminating his pale face. Oyza fidgeted a little on her stack of straw, not sure what to say either. The man cleared his throat, cracked his neck, and sat up.

A few moments later, he spoke. "My name...Hjan," he said in a thick accent.

Oyza perked up. "Hjan...you speak Vaazian?" *Fascinating.* She crawled forward, trying to keep her mind off of her brother, Yars, and everything else.

He wriggled to the edge of the cell. "Yes. Alden, he teached us."

Oyza slid to the bars. "My name is Oyza," she said, speaking slowly. She pointed toward her chest with both hands.

Hjan grinned. His teeth were yellow, and there was a large gap between his top two teeth. "Oy...*zuh.*"

Oyza smiled. Having someone—anyone—to talk to brightened her mood a little. "Where are you from, Hjan?" She made sure to articulate the words as clearly as she could.

Hjan paused. A look of uncertainty swept over his eyes as he shook his head. He didn't understand all of it.

Oyza took a slow breath. "Where? You? Where is your home?" She lifted her arms above her head and held them in a point like a roof.

Hjan pondered the question for a moment, eyeing her carefully and stroking his beard. "Ah! I from farm...farm. Kjundastir, farm by Hafrir. Hafrir is big, big, *uhh*, city. I from Hafrir." He moved his hands in the air and made shapes with his fingers. He pulled his arms far apart.

Oyza smiled again. She froze for a moment, wondering what she should say next. "I am from Oyvassa. City by the ocean, in a swamp, south of here—big city, old city." She also drew her arms wide apart.

"Oy...*vah-suh*... Yes, yes. I know city. Alden teached us, Oyvassa."

Oyza crinkled her nose. "Why are you here? Why are you in jail?" She wrapped her fingers around the iron bars. They were cold and rusty, just like the ones back in Goldfall.

Hjan thought about the question. "I run," he said. "I run. Alden kill—want kill me."

Oyza's eyebrows rose. "Where? Where run?"

Hjan scratched the back of his head, then flicked away a gnat hopping on his ankle. "Run...to you," he said, stretching out his hand and pointing a feeble finger at Oyza. "I run to...Vaazians."

Oyza leaned back, her head tilted with surprise. *He's not so different from us.* She thought about all the prisoners she had met over the years back in Goldfall. All she had ever dreamed about was running too. "Why?" But she suspected she already knew the answer.

Hjan took a sip of water from his wooden cup. "Alden...telled us, we have gold here, he told us, very small sailing and many, many gold, but small sailing," Hjan said, holding his hands close together. "But we *uhh...* We here, we in Vaaz, long time—no food, no gold, no nothing."

Oyza clasped the barrier. A black rat scurried into the room, crawling in and out of dim rays of moonlight. The spherical object on the floor lightly rolled as the ship swayed. It caught Oyza's eye. "What is that?"

"Ah, that is globe. That is, *uhh*, world." He made a circle with his hands.

The candle flickered as Oyza struggled to make out the markings on the sphere. "Globe..." she repeated.

"World is, uhh, this," he said, emphasizing to Oyza the sphere he made with his hands. "Hafrir there." He pointed at it.

Oyza strained her eyes and pressed her face between the cool bars. She could just barely make out continents on the object she didn't recognize. There were three massive islands she had never seen before, and a fourth in the very center of them. That one was marked with a silver crown. It suddenly turned to the other side. Oyza saw Vaaz.

"It's a map. A map of the world." *Fascinating!* She rested her palms on the rough wood. "Alden said Hafrir wants all the...globe." She pretended to hold a blade and strike with it.

Hjan twirled the blond hairs at the end of his beard. "War... Hafrir is...war on everyone, Dron Eerika, always war ..." He stared at the globe as it rocked back and forth. "I no like war," he said with a shake of his head. "I come...Vaaz, for gold."

Oyza understood perfectly well. *None of us want war. Even on the far side of the world, kings and queens send us off to die in their wars.* "What do you think of Alden?"

Hjan's face wrinkled up. It was clear to Oyza he didn't quite understand the question. She asked again, slower, carefully choosing her words.

Hjan nodded. "I no like, no, do not like Alden. He, *uhh*, lie to us. We want to, *uhh*, go back Hafrir, or Vaaz, for farm, for land."

Oyza clutched the metal bars with both hands. "I don't think I like Alden either. He...killed my friends." She hunched over.

"Friend," he repeated, pointing at himself.

Oyza shook her head. He clearly didn't understand the word.

"What is...friend?" Hjan asked, pointing at himself. "You are friend?"

"Friend is...a person you trust. Trust?" Oyza asked.

Hjan blinked. They shared a brief laugh. He didn't understand at all.

Finally, Oyza pointed at Hjan. "Friend is *you*," she said. She aimed a finger at herself. "Friend is *me*." She extended her hands at both of them at the same time. "*We* are friends."

Hjan smiled and bared his yellow teeth. "Yes, friends." Hjan drooped his head. "I am sorry. Sorry Alden and Hafrir war on friends."

Tears welled in Oyza's eyes. Somehow, the words of this man, this stranger, this poor prisoner from across the sea made her cry. He felt her pain, and she felt his. They were friends. *Incredible how quickly we understand each other.*

A guard appeared some time later and blew out the candle. Oyza tried to sleep, but her thoughts tormented her. *Séna, how could he? How could he really betray all of us? And yet, somewhere inside, I can still sense my brother from all those years ago... I know he is still in there.*

⁂

Days went by, and Alden never came to visit Oyza. Sailors brought her rainwater and bits of stale food, but she struggled to eat. Her body felt hollow. She passed the time by talking with Hjan. At least she wasn't alone.

The fallen of the world. Oyza recited the lyrics of Yars's song in her head. The light of both moons poured through the window. She figured she probably wouldn't sleep at all again tonight. Somehow, she kept hearing the sound of Liviana screaming, blood spilling onto her teeth. And Yars: his laugh, his curly hair, the way his eyes glistened in the starlight and how warm his hand felt. *Are you out there, Yars?*

She dozed in and out of a half slumber, waking when she heard footsteps above. Someone fumbled with keys before the door opened. A dark figure approached her, covered in a cloak from head to toe. A glowing lantern cast flickering shadows on the walls. Oyza squinted her eyes but couldn't make out who it was.

"Shh," Alden whispered. He opened the lock, lifted the lantern up to his face, and placed his fingers up to his lips. "Come."

Oyza's eyes widened. "Brother," she wanted to whisper. Before Alden led her out of the room, she took one last glance at the snoring Hjan. *Friends.*

Alden grabbed her arm and pulled her away. They crept up the stairs to the deck.

The Sword of Creation blazed across the sky through a blanket of stars. Alden led Oyza to the side of the vessel and directed her to a rope ladder hanging down the side. "Down." He gestured to a small row boat floating next to the ship.

Oyza climbed down, Alden following. Alden began to row. When she tried to ask him a question, he glared at her. Oyza bit her lip rather than ask anything after that.

They didn't head for the beach, but turned south. Oyza wrinkled her nose but said nothing. She took a deep breath of the chilly air and eyed the waters below. The smooth surface gleamed. *Is he doing it? Is he leaving Hafrir and coming with me?*

Alden's rowing slowed. He bent forward but did not remove his hood. "Oyza, I'm letting you go."

Oyza tugged at her sleeve. "Why?"

Alden shook his head. "You're my sister, Oyza, and I won't hold you here. And I know you wouldn't want to stay."

Oyza's lips curled into a half smile. *I knew he was still Séna, still my older brother. There is still good in him.* She ignored the part of her insisting that, if he were still good, he'd come with her, return to Oyvassa, and forget the Haf.

They headed for a rocky spot where giant trees covered the coastline, their roots tangled over stones and dangling in the waves.

Oyza inched forward and stared into her brother's eyes. "Come with me," she said. "Come with me, come home—it's not too late, Séna, you can come with me and—"

"And go *where*, Oyza?" he hissed. He glowered at her. "Oyza, I can't. I am on a mission for Dron Eerika. I'm Alden now."

"Your mission for gold? All the riches you promised your men?"

Alden rolled his eyes. "You were talking with the drunk, I see."

"Hjan is a good man. You should let him go too."

Alden gave her a deathly stare. "Listen, Oyza, this is my life now. I am letting you go so you can tell others, tell everyone here. You must tell everyone here what I've told you. Everyone in Vaaz is going to die if they do not submit to Hafrir. Dron Eerika will not stop. They are coming, Oyza—coming to invade Vaaz, to stay here forever. You must understand, Oyza."

Oyza gazed into the water at the reflection of the moons. "No, Brother, *you* must understand. The people of Vaaz will fight. We will never submit."

"What you do is up to you, Oyza, but you *must* make them understand Hafrir is coming, and others will come soon too." His voice had a hint of desperation.

He really means this. Oyza kept peering into the black abyss, wondering if there might be a tentacled critter floating beneath them now. "You know, the way you lecture me, it reminds me of Father."

Alden rolled his eyes.

"Really. You have his eyes exactly. Do you ever think about them? Our parents?" Oyza asked.

Alden squinted at the shore. "Yes, sometimes. You don't...you don't know if they're alive?"

Oyza shook her head. "I don't. I've been trapped for years, never had a chance to even look until now."

"Are you going to look for them?" Alden asked.

"Yes."

"Where?"

Oyza looked down. "I don't know. I'll look everywhere." Her eyes darted to the pistol at his hip. She dared not tell him about Mapa and the secret buried beneath Oyvassa. "Do you think Mother and Father would be proud of you?"

Alden glared at her. "Oyza, stop before I throw you in the sea."

"But I don't understand. You could just run away with me. Right now. Let's go, once we hit the shore."

Alden shook his head. "Oyza, for fifteen years the Dron has taken care of me."

"You mean held you captive?"

"She's practically treated me like a son."

"Why? Why would they take you in?"

Alden sighed. "I don't know. The Dron has a taste for...curiosities, odd things from the world. They seemed to think I was exotic."

"I don't believe that. They took you in to learn from you, to learn the secrets of Vaaz. They groomed you so they could use you against us."

Alden rowed especially hard, angry. "You don't know what you're talking about."

Oyza said nothing.

"Besides, if I ran and they caught me, do you know what'd they do to me? I'd be tortured, Oyza. Plus, there's..."

Oyza leaned forward. "There's what?"

"There's, well...I have children, Oyza, living in Hafrir. Two sons, two daughters. And a wife. And for this mission, I was promised land, an estate, if I truly did come back with twenty ships of gold."

Oyza's heart sank. *So that's what this is about, then.* "So you threw away your old family for a new one? A new family of rapers and pillagers?"

Alden frowned. "I will not have you talking about my family that way."

"Couldn't you bring them all here? Come home, Brother."

Alden shook his head. "I cannot, Oyza. There's no chance."

Oyza shuffled in her seat, glancing at the shore. She searched her memories. "Do you remember how Father used to play tricks with his mageware sword?"

Alden's eyes drooped.. "Oyza, please..." He lifted the oars out of the sea again. They were near the coast.

Oyza smiled. "Do you remember the time the neighbor came over, wanting to borrow an ax? Father told him the ax was outside, stuck in a log. And the man went to go look for it but came back and said he only saw a sword, no ax, so father went out and—"

"Yes, yes, I remember." Alden hid a smile. "Father walked out, picked up the sword and turned it to an ax behind the man's back. The poor guy was so confused."

They shared a laugh as they neared the beach.

"Do they have magewares in Hafrir?" Oyza asked.

Alden shook his head with a smirk. "No, no magewares. No staff or dead wizards named Soralir. Magic, though—at least, some say there was. There are sorcerers. The Dron keeps them around but loses patience with sorcery—it's all guns now. Guns, cannons, ships, iron, gold. You should see Hafrir, Oyza. It's nothing like the cities here. Big machines, burning coal night and day."

Oyza twisted her lips, pondering the thought of what Hafrir must be like—a land without Gods or magic... "Do you remember playing knight, princess, and dragon: you, me, and Rosina?" she asked.

The corner of Alden's mouth lifted. "Yes, I do. Those little figurines Father bought and mother painted. You always wanted to be the dragon, but I wouldn't let you."

"I suppose the knight suits me better anyway." She looked up at the stars.

"I remember the time you dropped the dragon in the well, but we told father Rosina did it. Do you remember? She was so mad, she didn't speak to us for days." Oyza laughed.

Alden chuckled too. "Yes, yes, I remember."

Oyza moved closer. *Gods, Rosina.* A sudden hole formed in her chest. "What was it like...when Rosina passed?"

Alden rowed, looking down. "I'd rather not talk about this, Oyza."

Oyza didn't prod. The rowboat slid into the sand. Tiny waves lapped onto the shore as Oyza and Alden climbed out, their boots splashing and filling with saltwater. Alden grabbed a backpack sitting in the boat. They made their way into a thicket of trees humming with insects and frogs. After a few moments of walking, they came to a gray horse who was much too skinny. The saddle on top was torn. Oyza gave it a gentle pat, caressing its fuzzy, warm fur with the back of her hand. Its eyes seemed to thank her.

Alden handed Oyza the bag and knelt to untie the horse. "Take this. It's not much, but it's enough. There's a cloak inside, and some food." He fumbled with the rope. "My men recovered this horse from Goldfall. He's not the best one, but he'll do."

Oyza wrapped the cloak around her shoulders. It was itchy and thin, but it would shield her from the wind. "Thank you, Brother."

Alden stood up. "Do you remember how to ride? I remember...Father and I were teaching you."

Oyza nodded. "Not well, but well enough. My master sent me on errands sometimes."

Alden placed a hand on Oyza's shoulder and pulled his face close to hers. The stench of some kind of alcohol hung on his breath. "Sister, I'm so sorry it has to be this way. I don't know where you plan to go, but take all this as a gift from me. Ride far and warn everyone here. You *must* submit to Hafrir."

Oyza looked at the moons. "Why not come with me, Brother? It's not too late." *And I know you're still good.*

Alden stepped back. A breeze tousled his hair. "Oyza, I can't. Hafrir is my home, not Vaaz."

Oyza scanned the sky and saw the Sword of Creation dipping below the horizon. The sun would rise in a few hours. She wanted to say more, to beg him, but she held her tongue. With dawn approaching, she needed to get as far as she could. "I will ride to Oyvassa to find Mother and Father," she said.

Alden lowered his eyes. "And one more thing, Oyza. Do not come back. My men cannot see me here with a Vaazian, not when we already have so little food. Do you understand?" His eyebrows rose.

Oyza looked away. "I understand, Séna." *If that's how it must be, then so be it.* And yet something nagged at her heart.

Alden's face contorted. "From this point on, Oyza, we're on opposite sides. Is that clear? Unless you are willing to pledge yourself completely to Hafrir, we are enemies."

She embraced her brother a final time. She mounted the steed and trotted away, turning her head back more than once to watch her brother paddle back to his fleet. The mighty ships towered over the horizon. She didn't want to look back, but she couldn't help it. *But I'll see you again, Brother. I know it.*

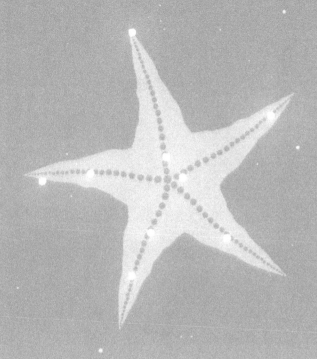

PART 3

SHIMWOOD

CHAPTER 19

Oyza breathed in, filling her lungs with crisp air that smelled like fresh leaves, damp bark, and wet dirt. The sounds of the hoofbeats thumped beneath her against the road that seemed to go on forever, weaving and winding between trees. Oyza's mind wandered, thinking more about Liviana than she wanted to. *She could be right behind me. Or Yars. Is he out there? Gods, he can't be dead. He just can't be.* She thought about their last conversation aboard the *Chandelier Lover*, about the feeling of his hand in hers...

As the forest thinned and the trees grew sparse, the sun's hot rays poured between the rustling limbs overhead and burst onto white and purple flowers below. Oyza slowed down to conserve her horse's strength and breathed in the scent of petals, sugar, and honey. Her legs ached. She decided to stop for a few bites of a mushy pear and some bitter dried cranberries. Her horse drank from a stream, and Oyza petted his gray mane.

"You have green eyes," she noticed. "Never seen a horse with green eyes."

The beast paid her no attention, determined to rip up and eat as much grass as he could.

"Did my brother give you a name? I know. I'll call you Olive." She wasn't sure if it was the best name, but it would do.

She pressed on, trying to stay attentive to the road ahead. She turned east toward the Shimmering Woods, where she might find a road to cut the corner and land at the Oyvassan coast. There, she could ride to Oyvassa on the Coral Trail—the road built out of crushed coral by King Liorus years ago.

The road split. One path wrapped around a village through a smattering of trees. The other ran straight through it.

"Let's go." They plodded down the road toward the branch circling the town, kicking up clouds of dust. She covered her head. The itchy cloth clung to the back of her sweaty neck.

The smell of roasting meat and charcoal wafted in the air. Her stomach growled. She wanted to stop at the tavern. A Celesterium monastery sat just outside the village, its gray spires soaring into the sky. Oyza considered stopping to see if a priest might give her something to eat.

No, it's too risky. She sighed and moved on, following the path beyond the village's edge. *I wish I still had that mageware dagger.*

She cut through a thicket of trees lining the road, keeping her head buried under her hood. The sky began to turn a dark purple. A stocky man pulling a cart turned a corner in front of her. Oyza came to a halt but nearly knocked into him.

"Watch it!" he screamed in a gravely voice.

The horse whinnied as Oyza struggled to get him under control. "Whoa, whoa, whoa..." The beast rested. "I'm sorry—"

"You almost hit me!" He dropped his cart. It was full of baskets of what looked like seeds, oats, and barley.

She nodded. "I'm sorry."

The man grunted. "Where you goin' that you have to cut through the woods anyways?"

"I'm riding...this way." She wasn't sure what to say.

"Aye, I can see that," the man quipped, squinting his tough eyes at Oyza. "But there ain't nothin' down that way. I wouldn't go there if I was you." He lifted up the cart and said goodbye to Oyza with his chin.

"Why not?"

"Ungoverned that way, they say. Bandits, killers, rapists. Parthassians here keep 'em out of town. Why you goin' south?"

Oyza scanned her surroundings to look for Parthassian scouts. She turned back carefully, considered her words, not wanting to reveal too much to the stranger. "My business is my own, but thank you." But she tilted her head a little and leaned in. "Parthassians? Where?"

The farmer snorted. "All up and down here—whole border, all the way south, by the Shimmering Woods. Ain't on the road much—keep toward the woods, mostly." He stepped back. "Wait. You're...you're one of those...?" He stepped backward a little more and reached for a switchblade.

"No, no—I'm just a traveler." Oyza waved her hands. "Do you know where I might find a bite to eat without going into town?"

The man scratched his chin with chubby fingers but kept his knife out. "Keep headin' south like you're doin'. There's an old monastery. Celesterium gave it up years ago—too many bandits. Might find some old food there if the Two are smilin' on ya." He picked up his cart and nodded farewell to Oyza.

She replied with a wave and took off. The village's thatched roofs disappeared behind the horizon as Oyza rode faster. Crickets filled the air with a soft tune. She raised her eyes toward the setting sun, pressing her horse faster as she tried to beat the night. "I'm sorry. We'll get you to bed soon."

Her shadow stretched along the road. Oyza had all but lost hope when the outline of a towering building appeared, rising above a dense grove of trees. She could make out the curved edge of the hill only by the stars it blocked. "That's it! Come on!" She saw the ruins of the abandoned monastery. It was a giant building, much bigger than she had assumed. An overgrown orchard sprawled in all directions. Coiled vines crawled up the cracked stone walls, wrapping their thorny fingers in and out of holes and crevices.

Too tired to think about food, Oyza tied up her horse and crept inside the building. Part of the roof had caved in, and pieces of brick and rock littered the floor and the tops of rotted wooden benches. A fresco of the Sword of Creation was painted on one of the walls, chipped and faded with time. The stained glass windows that had once decorated the chapel were shattered. Oyza gazed at the stars shining through the empty spaces and the silver moonbeams kissing the dusty ground. The air was brisk, but the smell of stone and moldy wood hung in the air. There, beside an old bench, she wrapped herself in her cloak and slept.

The next morning, Oyza packed her satchel with figs, almonds, lemons, and grapes before leaving. As she entered the forest, she twisted her head over her shoulder to watch the monastery fade away.

Ozya moved at a slower pace than she would have liked, but the horse could only go so fast. The trunks of the trees seemed to reach higher, and the leaves grew larger. The horse trotted down the dirt road, stepping over twisted roots and avoiding pools of water forming in shallow trenches left behind by recent rainstorms.

She tried her best to focus on reaching Oyvassa, suppressing all the memories flooding her thoughts, save for one: the old map that had hung on the wall in Minister Valador's private room in the dungeons at Goldfall. *I wish I remembered more of it.* Days elapsed, with Oyza stopping at rivers to let her horse graze. Her whole body ached, and by the time the sun was going down on the fifth day, Oyza started to worry. *What if I misread the map and I'm nowhere near the Shimmering Woods?* There were still no blue fireflies at night.

She came to a crossroads and stopped at two signs wrapped in spiderwebs. One arrow pointed east, and another pointed south, but there were no markings on either. The wood was old, and oozing moss draped down its sides. Oyza frowned. She decided to head farther south, still wary of the farmer's words about Parthassians patrolling to the east.

She pressed on as hard as she could, using every last moment of daylight. Just as she was about to stop and make camp, she saw a palm tree ahead. Her heart fluttered. She dismounted and walked up to it. She slid her hand across its giant smooth palms. Oyza realized she hadn't seen a palm tree since the day the Men without Gods took her away. A smile overtook her face.

"Come on. Just a little more. And then we can rest."

They passed more palms as darkness fell. The other trees seemed to grow bigger too, and their branches rose high into the night sky. Oyza could see the Sword of Creation between the cracks of the canopy stretching across a sea of stars. Some of the trees had fat green vines curling around their trunks. Pools of water appeared on each side of the road, punctuated with fallen logs and mossy stones. The air turned wet and moist.

Oyza slowed the horse, moving with care down the unkept road. A thousand insects hummed as frogs splashed into water.

This has to be it. "We did it," Oyza whispered, leaning her head toward the horse's ears. "The Shimmering Woods." *I'm almost home.*

Just as Oyza turned from the road to make camp, something else caught her eye: two faint flickers of blue light. There was another and then another. A few moments later, the entire forest was infused with flashes of blue light swirling around her and reflecting into ponds of water. Oyza dismounted, enchanted by the bright bursts around her. She took off her boots, feeling the squishy soil beneath her soles.

The fireflies. It's been fifteen years. A cautious smile conquered her weary face. Memories of her childhood came rushing back to her. She remembered the way she, Séna, and Rosina had captured the fireflies for fun, locking them away into little glass bottles and jars. Their mother always told them not to, so they never kept them for very long.

"Fireflies are gifts from the Gods," her mother would say, "sent here to share their light. It's not right to lock them up when they should be free. You can try, but the more you imprison, the brighter they shine. And eventually, the light breaks through."

Oyza slept under a tree, her heart warm with the knowledge she would be home soon.

CHAPTER 20

Liviana marched through the orchard, boots crunching on dry twigs. She wiped a trickle of sweat from her forehead. A flustered Minister Woss and eleven of her Iron Towers kept a close watch. Liviana didn't expect trouble at the monastery but agreed to bring her guards after Minister Woss complained.

"Commander." The farmhands bowed as Liviana walked by. She eyed their Starmarks as she passed: all Serpents, as was expected on Celesterium lands. She grimaced. *Anyone can do this kind of work. What madness.*

"I still find it hard to believe they shipped so much food to Mélor without us noticing. We'd better find something today." Her hands were clasped behind her back, pushing aside her cloak and exposing the hilt of Xalos. It sparkled in the sun.

Minister Woss nodded. "Indeed. And quite surprising it took Voy so long to find out. She's a smart one, that girl, cunning and pretty. In truth, I fear Voy. I fear most around these parts."

"I've trusted Voy ever since I found her," Liviana said, "and so does Yirig. Voy's good at what she does, but somehow they evaded her. Evaded us." Liviana looked up and saw the gray spires of Judge's Pass piercing the dusty sky. She had never visited the Celesterium fields beyond the city walls. She plucked an apple from a tree and inspected it—crisp and ripe.

A young boy bowed before her, his body falling on the dirt.

Liviana squatted down and handed the boy the apple. "This is a good one, wouldn't you say?"

The boy stared at the dirt, quivering.

"It's all right. You can answer," Liviana said, her voice gentle.

The boy reached out and accepted the apple but didn't lift his head to look up. "Yes, Commander."

"What is your name, young man?"

The boy kept his eyes down. "My name is Nidis, Your Highness—I mean, your Excellency, err, Your Grace—Nidis Gorn of Biria."

"Nidis Gorn, what is your Starmark?" Liviana asked, even though she could see it.

"The Serpent, my lady, trueborn for the Celesterium."

"A Serpent." Liviana said. "But tell me, Nidis, if you could do anything, what would you do? Pretend there are no Gods for a moment."

The boy froze. "I—I don't know," he stammered. "I'll do what my father tells me. He says I'm to work for the Celesterium, says I'm born for it."

"But if you could do *anything*, Nidis—whatever in the world you wanted—what would it be?" she asked as sweetly as she could feign. *Gods, kill me. Just speak, boy.*

Nidis trembled. "I think...I'd like to be a fisherman, maybe... Or, no, a soldier!"

"A soldier, hmm? I can make that happen."

The boy's eyes widened. "But how?" he asked. "The Celesterium, and my father, they won't..."

"I am a commander of the Parthassian Empire, Nidis, and the leader of this city. I tell the Celesterium what to do here, not the other way around. Do you see the Gods anywhere?" She pretended to look around. Birds chirped on a flowery branch.

"I-I don't...your ladyship..."

Liviana rose. "Minister Woss, take note. Nidis Gorn of Biria is to join the infantry as soon as he's old enough. Show him the barracks tomorrow."

Minister Woss nodded nervously.

Liviana crouched again and stared into the boy's eyes. "Now Nidis, I need you to tell me something, something very important. If you're going to be a soldier, you've got to learn to be honest, right? A Parthassian soldier always does what he's told—that's why we're the most powerful army in all Vaaz. It takes years of training, of duty, of honor."

Nidis nodded, his hands fidgeting.

Liviana edged closer. "The priests of the Celesterium, they may be doing some very, very bad things here. They may have lied to me—to the whole Empire. They may have sent food to our enemies while the great people of this city—like you and your family—go hungry. What do you know about that? You can tell me the truth. I won't tell the priests that you told."

"I...well..." the boy stuttered. "Well...I don't know nothin' about that, Your Majesty." A cold expression fell on his face.

Liviana forced an exaggerated look of disappointment.

"Wait!" Nidis exclaimed. "Vicar Miln...started havin' us put the harvests in trunks, 'steada the baskets we always used...told us Judge's Pass was starvin' 'cuz...well, 'cuz you brought too many people here, too many soldiers. He said it was all your fault." A scared but hopeful expression overtook his face.

"And what happened to these trunks?"

"Went on the wagons, like always."

Liviana thought for a moment. "Thank you, Nidis. Your honesty will be rewarded."

She and Minister Woss continued through the farm as Nidis led out a great sigh of relief.

"So we're onto something here." Minister Woss stroked his chin, gazing at the monastery's brick spires ahead.

"Corruption all the way up and all the way down," Liviana said, "all the way to Uriss himself."

"Uriss," Minister Woss began. "He has not been around lately."

Liviana twisted her lips. "No, he hasn't. I'm not worried, minister. He has no real power here."

Minister Woss scrubbed sweat from his eyebrows with a handkerchief. "Well, what are we to do then?"

Liviana glared. "No more wagons leave without Parthassian inspection first. Should have done this years ago. We will intercept their shipments, find out what's going on, and expose Uriss for what he is. I want our men stationed at every Celesterium field first thing tomorrow. Make it known that anyone who resists or bypasses inspection will answer to me."

Minister Woss coughed, flustered. "Are you sure it's wise to antagonize Uriss so much?"

"We must be strong, Minister. And two steps ahead."

"Glad I don't do politics, Commander. Administration, bureaucracy, rules—this I know well. But politics will forever be a mystery to me."

Liviana reflected for a moment. She folded her hands behind her back, rubbing her leathered fingers together. "It's all politics, Minister. From the grandest vision to the smallest, most insignificant rule, it's all politics."

They reached the steps of the monastery where a marble statue of Soralir stood, his robes painted blue as his staff dug into the ground. There was a serious look on his face as if he were contemplating something profound. Liviana stared into its eyes. It had worn with time, showing cracks in the stone and bits of flaked off paint.

"They venerated him here for so long. The Eternal City, the ever-neutral Judge's Pass. Lies, Minister. There is no neutrality. There is only taking sides." A breeze tugged at her black hair. "I remember the way my mother would chastise my father for his wavering. Never taking a side, always waiting for the right moment. We should have killed the emperor years ago. But he waited and waited until the perfect opportunity arose."

She left the statue behind and continued up the steps. "And now he is dead. I learned much from my mother before she passed. She was bold, unafraid, always pushing my father to do more. I learned a simple but important truth: one must always pick a side. And fight for it until the bitter end. When I chose to lay siege to this city, my father implored me not to. But I knew what I was doing. Our spies told me the merchant council was hungry for new leadership. That morale was low and their armies weak. And so I did the unthinkable. I conquered the Eternal City."

Minister Woss raised a finger. "But don't you think it prudent to search for a middle ground? Compromise keeps everyone happy. I like to hear the whole story, you know, before picking a side. I like to weigh the options. I like to hear from our lawyers and priests, from our tax collectors, sheriffs, the generals..."

They stood before massive doors decorated with carved stars and flowers. She turned again to Minister Woss. "At some point, Minister, you must take a side. Those who do not take sides will have sides take them. I will tell the people which side they ought to take. I will lead the Empire against the Gods themselves if I have to."

Minister Woss adjusted his sash, avoiding her piercing eyes.

"Make a note. I want that statue of Soralir replaced with a Hawk and Tower as soon as possible. There is no room for neutrality in the world, not anymore," Liviana said.

Minister Woss scribbled a note.

Liviana cracked open the door, then stopped. "And one more thing. After we leave here today, I want you to load twenty wagons with food and prepare our fastest riders. Tomorrow, I ride for Goldfall."

CHAPTER 21

After breakfast, Oyza and Olive walked through the swamp at a slow pace, owing to the poor condition of the road. It was blanketed with decaying logs, thorny rocks, and slick patches of algae. After a week or more of riding deep into the forest, there was hardly any road left. Swarms of flies buzzed.

She scanned as far ahead as she could, keeping a close watch for Parthassian scouts. It was dark, save for a few beams of sunlight piercing through the tangled canopy. The trees stretched taller, soaring high into the sky—so high and so buried behind vines and coats of moss, she could hardly see the tops. Glistening spiderwebs occupied the gaps between leaves.

Unable to cross a splintered bridge with a collapsed center, Oyza decided to wade across the water. Frogs dashed into the water, splashing near the roots of the sturdy reeds springing from the stream. Oyza held her boots, feeling the cool mud squish between her toes. After reaching the other side and turning the corner back toward the road, she paused as something caught her eye: a mushroom as tall as Olive, with a trunk as wide as the palm trees surrounding it. At night, Oyza knew, it would glow blue.

The Shimmering Woods. We really made it.

"Come on." She tapped Olive with her boots. "We're almost to the coast, I think." *At least I hope so.*

The next day, the trees were thinner. There were fewer giant mushrooms, and it seemed a little brighter. She looked up at the canopy and noticed it was thinner, with wide swathes of blue sky bursting from gaps between the branches. The humming of insects and chirping of birds soon gave way to total silence. The air was fresher, and there was even a hint of sea salt in it.

Oyza's heart raced. After another night of camping and eating berries, she came to a paved road, and far in the distance, Oyza saw a bright light shining from between the last row of trees. "I think we made it," she said to Olive, nudging him into a canter.

Oyza reached the light and found herself soaring toward a clear blue sky and a hot sun. The rays pummeled her, warming her skin. A gust knocked her hood from her head, unleashing black hair to blow wildly in the wind. Her lungs swelled with crisp air.

The dirt road that had carried her for so far through the swamp came to an end. In its place was a broad white road. It was partially buried in specks of sand, but Oyza still recognized it. It was the Coral Trail, the one King Liorus had built years ago. She looked up and down the coast, following the road with her eyes. First, she wanted to see the Oyvassan Sea: to hear its roar, to taste its water, to feel its cool waves crashing against her skin.

"Let's go." She gave Olive a gentle kick. The beast whinnied, and they made their way toward the beach, stopping at the foot of an immense mound of sand. Tall grasses sprinkled its surface as tiny white birds hopped about. It blocked Oyza's view of the water.

"Wait here." A cautious smile sprang on her face as she dismounted. She climbed the mound, slipping and sliding up the loose sand, then paused at the peak. Her heart fluttered. Before her sat the Oyvassan Sea, sparkling like a turquoise gem. A sandy wind stung her cheeks. The scent—raw, salty, and crisp—reminded her of her childhood. For a moment, she simply stood, doing nothing more than breathing. Memories came rushing back to her like waves on the shore.

She slid down and stepped toward the water, treading over piles of white and orange seashells littering the sands. They crunched beneath her feet. At the water's edge, she removed her boots and walked into the waves. They soaked her ankles. It was warmer than the chilly currents outside Goldfall but still a little cool. She stepped farther, wading into the water until the ocean was up to her waist. The cloth trousers she wore were drenched, as was the bottom of her cloak, but she didn't care.

She dipped her head under the water and felt the current tug at her hair. It was calm and quiet under the water. Nothing seemed to matter. She was frozen in time, suspended in a kind of ethereal bliss that made all other concerns melt away.

Soaking wet, she walked back to Olive—who chomped on a patch of coarse grasses—and climbed atop the saddle. Salt water dripped all over the horse, but he didn't seem to mind. They headed east on the Coral Trail. Oyza knew there was a string of abandoned settlements between Groshe and Oyvassa. Compared with traveling in the swamp, riding on the shoreline was easy. They kept a swift pace.

The sun continued its slow march across the cloudless sky as Oyza passed through deserted hamlets. Empty piers crawled out to the ocean like bony fingers. Rotting wooden buildings filled the towns, lonely and quiet. There was an occasional crane or heron, and Oyza was sure she saw dolphins too, but it was puzzling how so much could be forgotten for so long. But with a raid by Hafrir possible at any moment, perhaps they were right to never return.

After passing through more derelict fishing villages, Oyza stopped to make camp, sleeping in the soggy ruins of an old tavern. There was nothing inside, and the walls were damp and half-rotted after years of neglect and the sea's relentless winds. Before sleeping, she foraged in some bushes sprawling outside the town, packing her bag with sweet berries. Olive gobbled down an overgrown patch of grass.

Dawn came, and Oyza and Olive trotted off.

Oyza decided to rest one night in an old church. She made a bed by a dull mural of a Starfish. She brought Olive in with her through a collapsed wall. Olive stared at the Starfish on the wall.

Oyza smirked. "You like that?"

The horse didn't react.

"Funny, isn't it? The Starfish. Supposed to be the smartest sign—mathematics, writing, astronomy—but a real starfish, they don't seem too smart, do they? Do you know why that is?" Ozya grinned. "Course you don't. But I'll tell you. They say Starfish are stars that fell from the heavens and landed in the sea. They know the secrets of the Gods, the sacred patterns underlying everything in the universe. What do you think about that?"

Olive snorted.

Oyza smiled. She wanted to believe Olive had understood her. She lay down her head and was fast asleep.

When the sun rose again and a chorus of loud gulls filled the air with cawing, Oyza took off. After a few more days of trekking along the seaside, she saw something rise over the horizon she hadn't seen in fifteen years: the Pearl Spire of Oyvassa.

Her heart leaped. "There it is!" She tugged at the reins. The hot sun beat down on her as chilly ocean mist sprinkled her face. She wiped a trickle of sweat from her brow. "Come on!"

The Pearl Spire ascended from the waves, a shining white pillar, but its base was connected to an indigo wall stretching from the waters all the way across the beach to the hills. Years ago, the top of the tower would have gleamed—it guided ships to shore. During the day, it sparkled like a diamond. At night, Oyvassan watchmen would have burned a fire inside, and the top of the spire would have lit up like a burning ball of coal.

The rest of the city soon came into view. The wall was in ruins, with chunks having fallen out and tumbled onto the beach. Oyza remembered the wall was once covered with polished indigo tiles. Skinny palm trees rose near the wall as the tops of white buildings appeared. In the center of the city, the palace's ivory towers soared into the sky, its immense indigo dome glimmering in the sun. The four blue towers of the Temple of the Starfish also rose above the wall. Creeping vines covered every brick.

"We're home," she whispered to Olive. An unbelieving smile took over her face.

They followed the Coral Trail to the front gate. Where a massive iron barrier once stood, there was instead a vast hole.

171

She recalled the way cheerful Oyvassan guards would greet her family when they entered. Only ghosts manned the gate today. On both sides stood the remains of massive statues of tridents—the sigil of the Liorus house—carved into the wall. They, too, had crumbled. Flakes of green paint lay scattered in the sands. *Not like I remembered it.* Oyza put her hood back on.

A ghastly silence hung over the city's lifeless streets and desolate homes. At the center of a large square, a statue of the Two had toppled over, broken into a thousand shards of stone. Oyza could still make out parts of the statue in the lichen-covered pieces: a slab of a hand, a bit of a sword, a pair of gloomy eyes peering into the sky. Shrubs and weeds proliferated where gardens once flourished. Spiny lizards slithered in the ruins, the only signs of life, save for the tangled vines wrapping around everything. The still air smelled like salt, dried seaweed, and rock.

She passed the Temple of the Starfish and stopped to have a look inside. The rows of gleaming marble pillars she envisaged from her childhood were gray. Chunks of pebbles littered the ground. Roots cracked through the foundation, overtaking wooden benches. At the front of the room, a Starfish fresco was hardly recognizable, its orange paint chipping away.

So empty. So quiet.

She decided to head home, speeding through the streets and passing more abandoned houses. Palm trees stretched through torn roofs. After more turns through the city—past the University of Oyvassa, whose once-shining marble columns were draped in blooming white flowers—Oyza followed a long road leading to the edge of the city, making her way past the outer walls and toward the fields between the mountains.

This is it. Home. Her old house sat under clusters of palm and oak trees. There was a single door that opened to a garden out front and two windows with gray shutters over each. Strings of ivy crawled up the walls. As Oyza stepped in, she fought back tears. A cloud of dust hung in the musty air, and the walls were bare. The furniture was gone. She remembered the house perfectly: the small doors, the red brick chimney in the corner her mother used to roast fish over—all of it was just like her memories.

But would it *still be there?* She scaled the steps, brushing cobwebs out of her face. At the top, a sour feeling settled in her stomach. *It's my fault*, she found herself thinking. *My fault they're gone. My fault they got captured.* A stinging overtook her chest. Her heart stirred with contradictory emotions: joy, sadness, grief, guilt.

She made her way to a closet and knelt. Underneath a thick layer of dust was a wooden panel. Oyza lifted it up and reached her arm inside. At first, she felt nothing, but she lifted her hand up along the inside and reached as far as she could, right where her father used to hide his mageware sword.

Oyza's heart leaped. *It's really here!* She pulled the blade out and held it close to her eyes, blowing away dust. It gave off a pale glimmer in the faint light creeping through the windows. It was shorter than she remembered, but perhaps it had only seemed longer when she was a child. Its edge was still sharp, and at the end of its hilt was the same silver pearl. She polished it with her cloak, then swung it a few times in the air. She tried to turn it into an ax, like her father had always done with it. Nothing. She never really knew how her father made it work. *The enchantment's probably run out anyway.*

Oyza left the house and returned to Olive and packed the sword in her bag. The handle stuck out just behind her head. With a light kick at her steed's sides, Oyza left for the Crypts of Oyvassa.

CHAPTER 22

Oyza rode swiftly through the city, toward the feet of the sloping mountains hugging the far side of Oyvassa. Abandoned houses and soggy wooden huts were scattered in the hills. She passed underneath an arched gate draped in sheets of moss. Oyza slowed Olive as they rode into the cemetery. She tied Olive to a wooden post. "You wait here. I'll be quick, I promise." After a careful glance at the trees around her, Oyza stepped into the catacombs.

For the darkness comes for every star. She passed through the doorway. She plunged into shadow and wished she'd had a torch, but at least rows of sunbeams burst from small holes overhead. The steps were moist and coated in slime. Drops of water fell from above, and her lungs swelled with humid air. She wasn't sure if it was out of fear of the darkness or that someone may be following her, but Oyza pulled the sword from her bag and set her hood over her head. *My father's mageware. I'm holding it, but I can hardly believe it.* She polished the milky pearl on the hilt with her sleeve.

The sound of splashing water grew louder as Oyza descended the steps. The crypts were built over one end of an underground river that directed swamp water from the Shimmering Woods to the sea. Some of the water was let in to pass through a network of channels and corridors, and Oyza remembered her parents said the water carried the souls of the dead to the ocean. The labyrinthine vaults were criss-crossed with waterfalls, rivers, and even statues that shot streams of water into the air. As Oyza slogged deeper, the light faded. Thin rays of light leaked through cracks so high up, they barely reached the ground.

Oyza relived how the descent felt as a child—how scary and dark it was in those days when she was so small. But she didn't forget the ways blue light permeated the darkness. For centuries, her mother explained to her, the rulers and priests of Oyvassa maintained a network of glowing Oyvassan thread throughout the crypts in a crystal casing. As a result, the water flowing through the underground tomb glowed a brilliant indigo. Near the bottom of the stairs sat a massive stone wheel. Once turned all the way, two ends of the thread deep inside the rock would connect and illuminate the entire crypt.

Well, here we go. Oyza cracked her knuckles and felt her way through the dark for the handles on the wheel, if it had any. She started to turn it, but it was stuck. Her muscles burned as the monstrosity began to rotate, sending a horrendous grinding noise down the corridors. The wheel clicked and came to a stop. Oyza took a moment to catch her breath, then turned around. *Not as bad as I thought, at least.*

The entire crypt erupted with blue light. Oyza inched toward the light, weapon in hand. Her heart fluttered. The crypts were far larger than she remembered, and the streams seemed to wind endlessly in all directions. Pale blue light reflected onto the rounded ceilings of the halls above. Oyza passed over a long narrow walkway flanked by shining water on both sides. Her steps echoed against the walls, mixing with the sounds of trickling water. A giant sculpture of a mermaid sat at the center, tail full of stony scales. Glimmering water gushed from its mouth and drizzled down its sides.

Oyza stopped next to the statue and looked in all directions. Above her, the inside of a huge dome was illuminated. Fourteen pathways radiated outward like spokes on a tire.

Down the hall of the Frostpetal, Oyza recalled. *The Yillip family tomb.*

She spun around and found a Frostpetal carved above one of the halls, then followed the narrow pathway toward it. At the end, she turned down another hallway decorated with a faded mural on top of ships casting nets into the Oyvassan sea. At the end of the walkway, Oyza found herself surrounded by four more passageways. *Yillip... If these are organized alphabetically, perhaps it's near the end?* Without a better plan, she took off to the farthest right side. It was silent, save for the echoes of her boots patting the damp floor.

At the end of the hall was a frayed fresco of a Liorus king, his white crown resting on black hair. His eyes were full of determination, yet there seemed to be a thoughtfulness in them. She came to a room filled with rows of sarcophagi. Most of them were plain slabs with little ornamentation. Others were adorned with statues of the Origins or the Oyvassan Trident.

Oyza stretched her arms. Her chest felt tight, and she was more nervous than she wanted to admit. She inspected the closest sarcophagus, kneeling by its side and wiping dust away to reveal a family name. "Yenrett." Oyza shook her head and moved on to the next. She stumbled through the dark, careful not to fall in the streams around her, and made her way toward the other end of the room.

"Zartius, Zerra, Zoffe."

Too far, she thought as she pulled a cobweb out of her hair. She turned back again in the other direction and knelt by another sarcophagus. This one had three small whales painted on its side. She blew away a sheet of dust. "Yonrius." She let out a heavy sigh and moved to the next one. Again, no luck. She tried another, but again, it was the wrong name.

Her knees began to ache from being shoved into the cold hard floor. *Mapa, couldn't you have made this easier?* Something crawled onto her hand. Oyza sprang to her feet, heart racing, as she flung a hairy spider to the ground.

All right, all right, stay calm. She headed toward the darkest corner of the room. A single dull ray of light burst through a hole overhead and splashed onto a sarcophagus. Oyza rushed to it and fell to her knees. At its base, a few blocks looked out of place, as if they had been removed and lazily put back. Oyza wiped away dust with her sleeve. "Yillip" was inscribed in silver letters.

Oyza's heart bounced. *This is it!* She grinned, closed her eyes, and thanked Mapa and the Gods. She tore away at the bricks, then reached her hand inside the hole, hoping there wouldn't be any more spiders. Finding nothing, she knelt next to the ground and slid her arm in up to her elbow.

Nothing but dry piles of disappointment. Oyza tried to remove more pieces, but nothing would budge.

There has to be something here. She pulled her arm out and slouched. *Maybe I had the name wrong?* She checked. Same name. She ran her hands all over the stone coffin, but there were no more loose spots. She scoured the back side next, scratching and pulling and poking at bricks. *Perhaps there are more Yillips?* She stumbled over to the next one and scraped away grime concealing the inscription. "Yurladi," it read. *Damn.* She ran to another. Again, it was just another name. She returned to the one with the loose bricks, feeling around inside one more time.

Damn, damn, damn. She sighed, sat down, and leaned her head against the cold rock. *No. No, no, no.* She shut her eyes and gripped the hilt of her blade. *Was this all a waste?* After all those years, Mapa waited until the last moment to tell his secret. And was it all truly for nothing?

Oyza took another slow, deep breath of the rank, humid air before opening her eyes and peering into the gleaming blue rivers swirling around her. Her chest felt empty.

Her head snapped to one side as the sound of footsteps echoed into the room. The walls began to glow orange and red. Someone approached carrying a torch. Oyza's heart jumped. She retreated to the shadows and squatted behind the sarcophagus. Her sweaty fingers slipped around her sword's hilt. The footsteps came closer, closer, closer...

A man stood in the doorway. Oyza peeked around the corner and saw black plate mail lined with bronze. The man unsheathed a black sword. Oyza could see a golden Hawk and Tower on his armor. She held her breath.

"I know you're in here," a boyish voice called out into the abyss. He edged forward.

Oyza considered lunging at him. Her chest pounded. *Stay calm. Don't give yourself away.*

"There's no use running, Oyza." His voice rang, "In here! She's in here!"

Oyza gulped and pulled her satchel's leather straps around her, preparing to run if he walked too far and passed her. *He's right there.* Her heart thumped. *Calm, stay calm...*

The man stood just on the other side. His flame cast quivering shadows on the walls.

This is it. I have to go NOW. Oyza fled.

"Stop!" the knight yelled as he chased her. His mail rattled.

Oyza ran through the winding corridors back in the direction she had come from. *Gods, help me! Is this the right way?* The blue light marked her path—the only path out, as far as she knew. After turning a last corner, she found herself back where she began, running toward the exit as her cloak fluttered behind her.

But more Parthassians stood in her way. Some waited near the mermaid statue, clasped in chain mail from head to toe. They held torches and short blades. "Here she is!" one of them shouted. The soldiers drew their swords and marched toward Oyza.

Damn. She turned back around. But the one who chased her blocked her way forward. Oyza was surrounded, trapped on a pathway.

"Stop!" the knight said, raising his weapon.

Oyza readied her blade. "Stay back!" She pointed her sword straight at the man. The pearl shimmered.

The soldiers behind her laughed.

"It's useless," the man said as he approached. He stepped into a pale ray of sunlight, revealing youthful eyes that were much too young for a knight. "Oyza Serazar," he said with his blade's tip aimed at her neck, "you are under arrest for the murder of Minister Nalus Valador and for fleeing the dungeons of Goldfall. On behalf of Commander Liviana Valador, you are to be brought back to Judge's Pass to face the justice of the Empire."

Oyza lifted her weapon. "And who are you?"

He scoffed. "I am Sir Plinn Hales of the Parthassian Empire." He moved closer again, holding the torch to his side.

Oyza turned, her cloak whirling as she faced the men behind her. She glanced down at the rivers. *I could jump... Their armor, they couldn't follow me...but where does the water go?*

More soldiers entered the room, armor clanking. They stopped in the center.

One of them, taller than the others, stepped forward. He brandished a huge ax. Gray stubble peppered his jaw. "Oyza," he said in a deep and cold voice.

Oyza recognized the voice immediately. "Yirig," she said with a slight tremble.

Sir Yirig laughed. "Oyza, we knew we'd find you back in Oyvassa. Back with your family." He paused. "They're dead, aren't they?"

The words sliced her chest like hot daggers. She grimaced but said nothing. *Yirig. You haven't changed.*

"Why here? Why the crypts?" Sir Yirig asked. He gestured to Sir Plinn to back off.

Oyza held her blade tight.

"The last time Liviana saw you, you were talking to Mapa, the old fool in the dungeons, right?" Sir Yirig said.

Oyza said nothing, heart racing. *Mapa...I need your help, now.* She *glanced again at the water.*

"And he told you something, didn't he? Something about guns?" Sir Yirig lifted his ax.

Oyza swallowed. A bead of sweat trickled down her cheek. *I don't have to tell you anything.*

Sir Yirig and Sir Plinn closed in.

I have an idea. Oyza pulled her leather bag off of her back and held it over the water with a straightened arm. "You know what's in here," she said with a defiant voice.

The hulking knight paused.

"These are the schematics the emperor wanted for twenty years. Mapa hid them here, hid them from *you.*"

Sir Yirig froze, turning his ax away. "You wouldn't. I know you, Oyza. Everyone in Vaaz needs those papers. You know that."

Oyza straightened her back and raised her chin. "Then, let me go. Tell your men to let me through and the papers are yours." Her voice was sharp and confident. "Or else they go in the water. What will you tell Liviana?"

"If you throw those schematics," Sir Plinn said, "Liviana will do more with you than let you rot in prison. Hand them over, now! I order it!" He inched forward, blade aimed right at her throat.

He's young. I wonder what Liviana's told him. "Liviana," Oyza said to Sir Plinn, "is only using you for her own gain. That's all she knows." *Gods, help me!*

Sir Plinn took a step and laughed. Sir Yirig closed in on the other side.

"Hand it over, Oyza," Sir Plinn said. "And maybe Liviana will go easy on you."

What now? Oyza held the satchel over the water. In her other hand, she raised her sword toward Sir Yirig. She dug in her heels and swallowed. *I wish Yars were here.*

Suddenly, the rivers turned dark. The only light came from the torches and the slim sunbeams cascading through the dome above. Oyza turned to Sir Plinn, her arm still dangling over the water. *What happened?*

"Go back," Sir Yirig said to the men behind him. "Go now! Turn that back on!"

Before they could turn around, an arrow pierced one's throat. He howled and clutched the wound, then tumbled into the water. A loud splash bounced through the halls. A second arrow came at Sir Plinn, only to bounce off the shield on his back. He ducked.

"Run!" Sir Yirig cried. "Out, now! Get those papers!" He covered his neck with his hands and dashed toward Oyza, slamming into her body. He reached for her backpack but missed, then kept running.

Oyza fell to the ground and dropped the satchel. Another shot landed just near Sir Plinn's chest.

Sir Yirig disappeared into a hallway. "Run, Plinn!"

Metal crashed, and wood splintered. Men screamed. Arrows hit the pavement, splashed into the water, and tore through flesh. Oyza scrambled to her feet and seized the bag just as Sir Plinn grabbed it.

"Give it to me!" he said.

Oyza pulled back with all her might when another idea hit her. She let go.

Sir Plinn tumbled backward and slipped into the water. He thrashed and screamed, reaching for the edge just before his plate mail could drown him.

A man sprang from the shadow behind Oyza. He wielded a long pole with two blades attached to each end. Oyza recognized it as an Oyvassan glaive, the double-bladed weapon only Oyvassan warriors knew how to fight with. Three more Oyvassans came with him. They pulled Sir Plinn from the water.

"Get off me!"

"Stop resisting, and maybe I'll let you live!" the man said, his voice firm.

They tossed Sir Plinn onto the pathway and held their blades at his neck. The waters glowed blue again. Oyza got a better look at the warrior. He seemed to be about the same age as herself, with a bob of black hair atop his head. His face was smooth, and his firm eyebrows radiated a certain confidence.

Oyza spun around as she heard more footsteps. The hall filled with rangers, each wearing leather jerkins and wielding swords, glaives, or long bows. One of them carried a small sword and a wooden buckler. He walked up to her. His face glowed blue.

Can it really be...?

CHAPTER 23

Oyza threw her arms around Yars. "You're alive!"

"Oyza!" Yars dropped his weapons and wrapped his arms around her. The sword and shield sent rattles through the halls.

"I knew you were alive." Oyza snuggled her face in his neck.

Yars kissed Oyza's forehead. "Yeah. And I knew you'd be here."

The rangers dragged Sir Plinn away, his mouth, hands, and feet bound with coarse rope.

"Who are all these people?" Oyza asked Yars.

"Well...the Ungoverned."

Oyza's jaw dropped. She turned to the man wielding the glaive.

"Come," he said. "We should leave now. There may be more Parthassians nearby. We'll have lots of time to talk on the way back to the Shimwood." He signaled the rangers to follow him. "Teresa, take the vanguard with the others. I'll talk with Yars and Oyza by the wagon, where we can tie up this knight."

"That's Jarus," Yars said. "He's the leader of the rangers. And that's his twin sister, Teresa."

Teresa nodded. Her dark hair was woven atop her head behind a gray headband. She carried a sword, shield, and longbow. "Let's be quick. One got out, it looks like." She nodded toward the tunnel where Sir Yirig fled.

The Ungoverned. Oyza scanned the flurry of rangers around her. *It's really them...*

They ascended to the surface as fast as possible, moving with silence. Each had a patch on their chest depicting weaving strands of blue leafy vines. At the surface, Teresa took off with several rangers on horses, riding into the drooping willow trees ahead, while Yars, Oyza, and Jarus carried Sir Plinn to a small wagon. Jarus and the rangers lifted Sir Plinn into the back of it.

Oyza embraced Yars again. "I was worried I lost you."

Yars massaged her shoulder. "I was worried I lost you too."

"So you are Oyza Serazar." Jarus bowed slightly and kissed Oyza's hand. "My name is Jarus Liorus."

Oyza froze. *Liorus? The King's son...?* "Liorus...Your majesty, I—"

Yars laughed. "It's not like that, Oyza."

Jarus rolled his eyes, then turned his head to spew black juice. Netiss nut, Oyza surmised—as addicting as witchdust. In the sunlight, she could make him out more clearly: his almond-shaped eyes, his muscular arms and chest, his broad shoulders. He was handsome but a little shorter than the princes in the books Oyza had read about.

He smirked and shook his head. "No formalities. We are Ungoverned. We are equals—no royalty or rank here. Isn't that right, Yars?" He reached out to pat Yars's shoulder.

Oyza turned to Yars with scrunched eyebrows, then back to Jarus. *What do you possibly say in a moment like this?*

"We'll have plenty of time to talk later." Jarus walked them to the horses. "I'll drive the wagon. Yars has a horse, and it looks like you've got your own, Oyza. Anyway, I'm sure you two want time to catch up. But before we leave, I want to say thanks, Oyza. Yars told us about you, about the schematics, about all of it. You'll be pleased to know the papers are back in Shimwood in my sister's archive, being studied now by our engineers. When you get back, I'll make sure Teresa shows them to you." With a wink and a hearty thump on Oyza's shoulder, he climbed aboard the wagon.

Oyza's heart leaped. *The schematics? Thank the Gods. Thank you, Mapa.* She turned to Yars with a smile. "So you didn't sell them, then?"

"Course not. After all we have been through? *Psh*, I wouldn't sell those for all the gold in Goldfall."

Oyza grabbed his hand. "I knew you wouldn't do it."

"You'll love 'em when you see 'em, Oyza. Really cool stuff that Mapa drew."

They mounted their horses and followed Jarus, hooves sticking in the wet grasses and muddy tracks below. Blue-tinted vines dangled like curtains.

"Didn't know you could ride," Oyza said.

Yars fumbled with the reins. "Jarus is teaching me how to ride. I've never ridden a horse before." The poor beast seemed confused.

"You'll get the hang of it."

Oyza watched the canopy as they trekked through the forest, peering at slithers of twilight between the branches. Sapphire sparks of firefly flashes lit up the trees and shrubs. "I told you they were blue, didn't I?"

Yars smiled, then struggled with his steed before turning back to Oyza. "So, how did you get here then? What happened after the boat was attacked?"

Oyza tapped her fingers. Could she tell him about her brother? Maybe she had better not tell anyone about that. Not even Yars, not yet. "After you fell, they knocked me out. I woke up on a beach later, no idea what day it was. An older fisherman took me in. I tried to find you, but I couldn't." *Maybe not the most believable story, but it'll do.*

Yars stroked his chin.

There was something odd about seeing Yars atop a horse in his clean leather jerkin, sword and shield on his back. He looked older, more mature. It made her smile.

"That's what happened to me too. I can't really swim. Woke up on a beach by a ranger, and then I met Jarus. They were out on patrol."

"We're both lucky, then," Oyza said.

"Yup. Well, I'm glad you're back, Oyza," he said. "You'll love Shimwood. They built a whole city way out in the Shimmering Woods. I didn't think anything was there at all. Colder here than I thought, though."

"People always think the swamps would be hot, but it's always cold here at night."

"Your home was in Oyvassa, right? Are you gonna go back?"

Oyza tugged at her sleeve. "Yes. I'd like to, sometime." She adjusted her bag, then realized the end of her blade was sticking out of it. She might have to explain where she got the sword from.

"So where you'd get the horse?"

Oyza blushed but tried to hide it. "I...I stole it."

Yars howled. "Wow! Learned a thing or two from me, then? Look at you, stealing horses now."

"Let's not get carried away."

"So, the captain...did he?"

"He...he didn't make it. I don't think anyone from the *Chandelier Lover* did."

Yars's eyes fell.

They trudged deeper into the forest. The gigantic mushrooms began to glow, and above, the Sword of Creation appeared through the branches. Crickets chirped. Ahead, a fire burned, lighting up the undersides of giant leaves.

"We're about to stop," Jarus shouted.

Oyza and Yars followed him to a clearing where Teresa and the other rangers gathered. After dismounting their horses, they sat in patches of moist grass beside the flames. Rabbits roasted beside skewered potatoes, carrots, and onions. Jarus took the wagon holding Sir Plinn off to the side. A ranger guarded it. Someone played a flute, infusing the air with sweet sounds. They passed around bags packed with salted beef, satchels of dried fruits and jars of ale.

"Sit with my sister," Jarus said to Oyza and Yars before disappearing inside a tent.

Oyza and Yars plopped down next to Teresa and hoisted their palms toward the heat, warming the muscles in their aching hands.

Teresa pressed her nose into a leather-bound notebook and a feather quill pen. She seemed to be drawing something. On her knee sat a dead moth with violet wings folded out. "Glad to see you made it." She didn't look up from her work. "Excuse me, just a few more seconds."

Oyza and Yars exchanged brief smiles. Oyza tried to get a glimpse of the winged insect.

Teresa finally set down her pen and closed her notebook, folding the creature inside of it. She handed a small sack of dried cherries and walnuts to Oyza. The cherries were tart, and the walnuts rich and crunchy. Teresa gave her a bottle of ale next. Oyza drank—a little too much, probably—and wiped a trickle from her lips before passing the drink to Yars. She took a long look at Teresa, whose sharp eyes sparkled in the campfire's flames. There was no doubt she was Jarus's twin—the strong jawline, prominent cheekbones, shapely eyes, all of it was there. *And...Princess Liorus?*

"Oyza. Nice to meet you. Yars tells us you're the one who knew where the schematics were." Teresa untangled the gray headband holding her black hair. It fell in waves above her shoulders. As she leaned back to place her headband away from the fire, Oyza saw her Starmark: the Crab.

"That's right," Oyza said. "And you're...Teresa Liorus, daughter of the king?"

Teresa smiled at the ranger sitting to her right.

He laughed, then hunched closer to the fire and stared at Oyza. "We have no kings or queens anymore, and no lords for that matter either." The man's voice was deep and calm, and his jaw was overrun with a bushy black beard. He smiled with crinkling eyes. "My name is Quorig." He extended a grizzly hand to Oyza. "I serve on the Assembly of the Ungoverned. I wanted to extend my thanks to you and Yars. Oyza, you may have saved us—all of us, not just the Ungoverned. Maybe all of Vaaz. The Gods smile on us." He bowed his head.

A knot formed in Oyza's neck. It was all so much to take in. "Well, I didn't really do much. There was a friend of mine in the dungeons of Goldfall. Mapa was his name. He was the one who hid the scrolls there. And Yars found them."

Glimmers of crimson shined in Yars's curls. He beamed at Oyza and shrugged. "Nah, not true, Oyza. We both did this."

Teresa handed the bottle of ale to another ranger, not taking a drink herself. "You've caused quite the stir here. And the rest of the Assembly wants to see you. In fact, I think all of Shimwood wants to meet you. My brother already told you about initiation? Only if you want it, of course." She seemed to speak with much more warmth than Jarus did.

"Initiation?" Oyza asked.

"Yes. If you want it, we'd like you to join us. Become one of the Ungoverned."

Oyza stared into the crackling fire. The roasting rabbits were almost done, and Oyza's stomach grumbled as the aroma saturated the night air. She was so tired and hungry, it was hard to even imagine what being initiated into the Ungoverned might mean. Teresa watched her with a kind of intensity behind her eyes.

"Did you get initiated yet?" Oyza asked Yars.

"No," he said. "I was waiting for you."

Oyza tossed a twig into the fire, then yawned. She looked around at the gathering of rangers, their faces flickering in the light. *What am I thinking? Of course I want to be initiated!*

"You're tired," Teresa said bluntly, "which is understandable. Tomorrow, when when we arrive at Shimwood, we'll get you a place to stay. But tonight, I want to hear from you, Oyza. I've heard a little from Yars, but tell me, who are you? Where are you from? Who was Mapa, and how did he get the schematics from the Haf?"

A lot of questions, but Teresa has a kind way of asking them.

After a few moments of shuffling in the dirt and warming her hands by the fire, Oyza told her story—but not the parts about her brother and her time on the Haf ships. Not about Hjan either. If they knew her brother was one of the Men without Gods, let alone the commander who had led the attack on Goldfall, she might lose their trust. The story dragged on so long, Yars began to play soft, sweet music on a lute one of the rangers gave him.

"Incredible," Teresa said. "You've been through so much."

Oyza flinched a little. Teresa was right. Oyza realized she had hardly even had the time to really process everything.

She took a sip of a musty beer and dug her heel in some mud. The rangers shared lumps of juicy rabbit meat and sizzling vegetables. Oyza happily filled her stomach—the rich meat and crisp veggies were just what she wanted.

Jarus emerged from his tent, ready to partake in the meal, and sat down next to Oyza cross-legged in a patch of dry dirt. He spat out a black glob of netiss nut juice, then stretched for a piece of rabbit, revealing his Starmark: a Crab too. He grinned at his sister and glanced at her notebook. "What'd you find this time, Teresa? A newt with six legs, a flying frog, a talking bird?"

Teresa twisted her lips a little, then smiled. "A moth, actually, down in the crypts. One I've never seen before." She opened the pad of paper to show Jarus, but he raised a hand and pushed it away.

"So little paper in Shimwood, and you waste it drawing pictures of bugs!" He burst into laughter, then took a gulp of ale. Some of the rangers chuckled with him.

Oyza and Yars traded smiles.

Teresa frowned. "It's not a waste. It's for my encyclopedia. It's important."

Encyclopedia? Oyza eyed Teresa's little notebook and decided she would ask Teresa about it later. She glanced at Yars, but he shrugged.

Jarus chuckled. "Whatever you say." He tore into a chunk of meat and drank more beer.

"He likes to drink more than I do," Yars whispered to Oyza, leaning over his lute.

They talked over dinner, sharing stories and histories, but a question irked Oyza. Ever since reading *On the Frailty of Kings and the Illusions of Power*, she had been dying to know how the Ungoverned really functioned. Jarus had said something about sharing everything and there being no poverty or hunger either. But how could this be?

"Jarus, I have a question," she began. "With no masters, no lords, how does...well, how does everyone know what to do? Is there enough food for all? How do you make decisions?"

Jarus rubbed his neck. "Well, it's...complicated, but it all works out. When our people fled into the swamps—and I was just a child, but I remember it all—there was chaos. But my father, well, there was this old philosopher friend of his who had insisted for years, I learned later, that the crown is a kind of lie. If you think about it, why do the peoples across Vaaz submit to rulers who mistreat them? It's just because they are forced to. Kings rule because they have more power than anyone else, not because

185

they come from the Gods or something, and not because they earned it. You can't see it, but power is like gold coins: there's only so many of them. You either let one person take all the coins, or you give a coin to everyone."

Oyza nodded, listening closely. *Fascinating...*

Yars listened too while he strummed.

"But in the chaos after Oyvassa fell, and after my father and mother were killed, the people decided they didn't want another king to hold all the coins. And my father's friend—he passed some years ago—gave them a vision. A vision of a world held in common, run by equals, without rank or title. The land, the fields, the workshops—we hold it all in common," Jarus said. There was an element of courage in his voice, or perhaps inspiration. Either way, Oyza was engrossed with his words.

"Every few months, everyone gathers from the districts of Shimwood. We meet to decide who is going to do what and who is going to get what. It was a messy system for years, but eventually, it worked out. The Assembly makes other sorts of decisions in the meantime. By now, actually, most things stay the same. The younger ones are brought into a trade when they come of age. Many enlist in the rangers, who also work the fields from time to time. Everyone learns to defend themselves. But it's really up to their family to decide," he said.

"But what about the Celesterium? What about Starmarks?"

Jarus bent over and spat. "The Ungoverned do not force anyone to take on work they do not wish to do. Many of us still honor Starmarks. Many do not. But the Celesterium pays us no attention. In fact, only the Parthassians do, sending scouts into our lands to keep an eye on us. Our spies have told us for years Blacklance was planning an invasion, but she never did, not with the war with Mélor still going. And certainly not now after Goldfall."

"I remember hearing a lot about the spies—insurgents, my master called them—of the Ungoverned infiltrating Goldfall and Judge's Pass. I remember when they were executed too. Minister Valador would compare them to cockroaches. He didn't think you were a real threat." Oyza turned to avoid Jarus's gaze, embarrassed.

"Yeah," Jarus said, "we've been sending our spies and revolutionaries across Western Vaaz for years now—to Judge's Pass, Groshe and Mélor—to reach out to the common people about the Ungoverned. Some of us here believe this is the only way we can persist into the future—by ending the Empire and provoking revolution everywhere."

186

He slouched a little. "And, yes, sometimes they don't make it. In Judge's Pass, we lost eight good men recently. And another, my friend Vimoy, we haven't heard from in a while, but I hope he's all right. You'll see in time. Among the Ungoverned, there are those of us who want to expand, to incite uprisings in other lands. To spread the rebellion. Constant movement, constant growth—this is the lifeblood of revolutions."

He tossed a bone into the bonfire and shared a concerned look with Teresa. "And then there are those who want us to hole up here, alone, and defend the Shimmering Woods until we die. It's nonsense. Refugees stream in from Goldfall that we can hardly take care of. Food runs low. And with each passing day, the threat we pose to the kings and lords of Vaaz grows," Jarus said.

Oyza crinkled her nose, nibbling a hot onion. "But why not return to Oyvassa? It's empty, they say..." She flashed a puzzled look at Yars.

He shrugged, his fingers dancing on the lute's strings.

Jarus shook his head. "The people will not return. Not yet. It's a cursed land, Oyza. And look at what just happened to Goldfall. They came with bigger guns than ever before—guns that burn entire cities. No, we'll never go back to the coast."

Oyza paused. It was all so much to take in, and her body ached. Her knees hurt. She glanced over at Yars. She kept thinking of him on his stallion dressed in leather armor with a shield on his back—he looked older, more serious. She pondered for a moment how much she had changed too.

Despite her weariness, she had more questions for Jarus. "Jarus, how many Ungoverned are there living at Shimwood? Do you know how many didn't make it all those years ago? My mother and father, I never knew what happened to them after I was taken. After Oyvassa fell, I don't know where they went...I don't know if they're alive."

Jarus cleared his throat and bit into a potato. "At Shimwood, we built a cemetery. The family names of those who have died are inscribed onto headstones. I don't know if Serazar is there, but you should check. I'm sorry, but I don't think I've ever met anyone in Shimwood with the last name Serazar."

Oyza sighed. The words sent a chill through her spine. A cloud of blue fireflies lit up a nearby palm tree. "Thank you, Jarus."

The conversation paused. Somewhere, an owl hooted. The campfire crackled.

"Well," Teresa said, breaking the silence. "You can join our new family, here, with the Ungoverned."

It wasn't the answer Oyza had hoped for, but it was better than nothing. "Thank you," she said after a few moments. She really meant it. Except for Yars, perhaps, Oyza had felt as if she had almost no one in the world anymore.

The night went on, with rangers eating and drinking by the fire until only embers burned.

Oyza talked with Yars and some of the other rangers, but they turned their heads when they heard Jarus raising his voice before being cut off by Quorig's deep tone. "We're not torturing the poor boy, Jarus. Did you see how young he was? Probably a new recruit, had no idea what he's gotten himself into. The Gods would frown on us."

Jarus squinted and punched the log he sat on. "He's not a boy; he's a knight. You saw the armor he wore. And how many of ours have they killed?" He finished a jar of ale.

Teresa placed her hand on her brother's shoulder. "Quorig is right. We're Ungoverned—we don't torture. Question and learn, but we don't torture."

Jarus frowned, flicking Teresa's hand from his shoulder. He unrolled a leaf and began to chew more netiss nut. "What do you think, Oyza?"

Me? Oyza perked up, caught off guard. *Torture? All those years, Mapa was tortured, and he never spoke up. It's wrong, right? But maybe...sometimes it's necessary? I guess... I'm not sure. But it can't be right in this case—that knight was barely a man.* "It would be wrong to torture him," she finally said. "And if you want to win the people to your side, you can't sink as low as your enemies."

Jarus rolled his eyes and shook his head. He spat. "They surely won't join us if we're not willing to fight. And we're not going to win if we don't do everything we can."

Teresa scrunched her lips. "It doesn't matter. Right now, the Assembly has voted against torturing prisoners. We have to respect the Assembly, or else our whole project falls apart."

There was another pause, when Yars spoke up. "You know, I had to work in the mines at Judge's Pass my whole life. And, sometimes, my friends would be tortured, if they ever messed up. Didn't seem to help anything." He glanced at Oyza, then picked up the lute again.

Jarus sighed again. "We'll see." He turned to Oyza and eyed the blade at her side. "Can you fight with that? It's a pretty sword—plain but looks well-balanced, clean."

"I can," she said, "but I'm not very good."

"No problem," Jarus said. "We'll train you at Shimwood. Everyone's gotta learn to fight. We have no army, only the rangers, so we're always ready in case the time comes."

"Yars here has been learning to blacksmith too." Jarus slapped Yars's shoulder.

Yars raised his eyes in a cheery grin, not interrupting the music he played.

"Oyza, we think you'll fit right in," Teresa said. "The Ungoverned are split into seven districts in Shimwood right now. You can join ours, if you wish. We can find a house for you and Yars to share if you want it."

Oyza peeked at Yars, who simply smiled and nodded. "That would be wonderful."

The lingering embers crackled as a thin string of smoke swirled into the air, greeting the blue fireflies flickering in the canopy. Oyza peered for a moment into the stars and gazed at the Sword of Creation.

"I think you'll see," Jarus said, lifting his eyes into the distance, "we are really building a new world. If we can just capture a city—a kingdom—we'll be unstoppable." He spoke slowly and seriously. "We can show the world that a better life is possible."

Oyza nodded. Something about the way Jarus spoke filled her with inspiration.

The fires died, and most of the dinner was gone. The rangers put out what was left of the fires. They seemed to work without too much direction. It was very different from the world Oyza had known growing up with the Parthassians. She and Yars helped to clean up some of the food scraps too. They crawled in their tent, and Yars wrapped himself in a blanket next to Oyza. He began to doze off.

Oyza draped her arms around Yars. "You look silly on a horse, you know."

Yars scoffed. "What? What do you mean?"

"I don't know. Just didn't think I'd see you like that: a sword, shield, sitting high on your mount."

Yars laughed. "Me neither, I guess."

"Thank you, Yars."

"For what?"

"For coming back. To the crypts. And for waiting."

"Of course."

"Are you excited to be initiated?"

"Definitely." Yars stroked Oyza's arm with his thumb. His fingers left tiny frissons of electricity on her skin.

Oyza yawned. "Whatever happened to running away to Talazar City? Thought you were gonna sell the schematics, get rich?" She twisted a strand of his curly hair between her fingers.

Yars laughed. "Ah, things change, you know? And with a little luck and the right people at your side, there's nothing you can't do." He gripped Oyza's smooth shoulder and buried his face in her tangled hair before kissing her forehead.

A few moments of silence passed, crickets chirping. Oyza fell fast asleep.

CHAPTER 24

"It's not an easy route." Teresa wore a bow and a quiver of arrows on her back. "But the swamp is the best protection we have. It's part of the reason we don't want to return to Oyvassa." She kept her notebook in her front pocket and a sword at her side.

Oyza guided her horse around a clouded puddle. She rode next to Yars, who slouched on his horse. "I remember my master talking about the Ungoverned here. He said they could never find you here. But he didn't care much to find you. But Liviana cared, he said." *Maybe I'll be safe here from her?*

She looked up at the labyrinth of creeping plants and leaves. There was a gloomy feeling in the bog, but also a kind of security. Blackbirds whistled and cawed. They were splashing through the mud when suddenly the air was brimming with the aroma of smoke, pepper, and roasting meat. Oyza's mouth watered.

"We're getting close." Teresa pulled a leaf off a low twig and stuffed it in her pocket.

Oyza beamed at Yars. All the years spent wondering what the Ungoverned were like was finally coming to an end. "I told you," she said. "They're not demon-worshippers."

He rolled his eyes and laughed, but jumped when his horse slipped on a slimy stone.

They crossed a stone bridge cloaked under a willow tree and were greeted by a cozy home on the other side. Its walls were made of brick, and on top was a thatched roof partially buried in moss that draped down to the ground. Smoke spiraled out of a chimney, and an elderly woman hunched outside in a garden full of mint plants. A large water wheel on the side of the house turned in the river's slow current. The woman hailed the line of riders as they went by with a joyous wave.

A little farther down the road, they came to a clearing. Goats meandered in a field, bells around their necks clanking. There were a few cows and pigs running around too.

Oyza turned to Jarus. "Fields?" She bobbed slightly on Olive as he trudged through the muck and swatted flies with his tail. "In the swamp?"

Jarus smirked. "We've been able to drain the waters here and there, which lets us grow some crops. Not much sun down here, so we've cleared the canopy too."

Warm light hit Oyza's cheeks as she made her way across. Farmers worked in teams on the pastures. They smiled and waved.

Wood, brick, and mud houses dotted the landscape as they rode toward Shimwood. They trekked through meadows growing all sorts of things: chestnuts, celery, rhubarb, spinach, blackberries, mint plants, wheat, and more. White cranes stalked the waters like quiet assassins. The rivers were lined with water mills, and more than a couple beavers played in the waters. Men, women, and children saluted them with warm smiles as they passed. A slight breeze blew wherever there was a clearing in the canopy, carrying the scent of fresh rain and sweet flowers.

They reached a road that was raised above the water, out of the sludge. The sky darkened as they left the fields behind. Small houses still dotted the landscape, some of them inhabiting the gnarled roots of trees bigger than Oyza had ever seen before. Some houses even sat perched in the branches, rope ladders dangling to the ground.

They came to an arch made of three giant pieces of wood. Two planks stood up straight and held a third sitting on top. Bundles of moss draped down, black butterflies fluttering among the knots. An ash-colored flag hung from the center, adorned with the same pattern of blue vines the rangers wore on their chests. Four sentries armed with pikes and longbows guarded the path. They waved to Jarus as he hollered back at them.

"This is it," Jarus said. "Shimwood."

"I still can't believe I'm here." Yars swatted a gnat. "Back in Goldfall, would have never guessed it. The guys would never believe I'm here either, not in a million years."

Oyza laughed. She could hardly believe it either. "Feels like just yesterday we were rotting in the dungeon." She glanced at Yars as they passed underneath, but the flag decorated with weaving blue ivy caught her eye. "Jarus, what does it mean?"

"That's a vine that grows all over Shimwood. If you cut off one end, three more grow back." He pulled aside his cloak, tapped his own patch, and winked.

Oyza eyed the emblem on his chest, already wishing she had her own.

"You'll get one when you are initiated," Jarus said.

The road fanned out in three directions. Each was lined with houses carved into the bottoms of enormous trees. Smoke billowed from chimneys, and the smell of burning wood, roasting meat, and a cinnamon fragrance Oyza recognized from her childhood drifted in the breeze. They made their way into the village when groups of men, women, and children clamored toward the arrivals. The residents waved and smiled at Jarus, Teresa, and the rest of the rangers. A group of young women blew kisses to Jarus, drawing eye rolls from Teresa. Jarus grinned. He lifted his arms in a triumphant flex, prompting more cheers from the congregation. Others whispered and murmured as they pointed at Oyza.

"Is that her?" some of them asked.

Oyza felt a little uneasy and shifted in her saddle.

"Yes, yes—she's the one, the one the Assembly said brought us guns," another said. One of the younger spectators began to cheer, while two more applauded. "Oyza!" a voice cried out.

Jarus raised his hand, and the gathering quieted a little. "Yes, yes—this is Oyza, the one who, with Yars, brought us the schematics."

The crowd cheered.

All Oyza could think to do was smile and nod. *Me? Some kind of hero?*

Yars rode up beside her. He hoisted his hand to the sky and bowed his head. His black curls tumbled over his eyes. "Thank you! Thank you!" he shouted. He leaned to Oyza and whispered, "Just take it in."

A shriveled woman with wrinkled hands handed Oyza a bouquet of violet flowers. Oyza accepted graciously, her heart stirring. *Gods, why not?* She took Yars's hand, and together they raised the bundle of flowers toward the clouds.

The clustered townspeople eventually dissipated. Quorig and most of the rangers departed with the wagon carrying Sir Plinn.

"We'll show you to the town square first," Teresa said, "and the communal storehouses nearby, where you can get everything you need. Then we'll take you to your house."

Oyza wrinkled her nose. "How do I...get what I need?"

"I'll show you how. You just take what you need. But don't take too much—you'll piss everyone off that way," Yars said.

Jarus nodded. "We have enough for everyone in Shimwood, but only that. Everyone who is able to work does so, and everyone takes freely whatever they need."

Oyza's eyes widened. It was a little unbelievable. *I wonder what stops them from stealing?*

They made their way down a broad road lined with houses, some surrounded by cloudy pools. Children splashed in the water, chasing each other through the streets as horses pulling wagons packed with apples, eggs, and oats crossed on the other side of the road. The town square buzzed with people crisscrossing in all directions, an orchestra of chatter and noise. At the center stood a statue of the Sword of Creation, their bodies pierced by an indigo sword. A trio of musicians sat on a carpet. Others gathered around them, listening and clapping along. There wasn't a beggar in sight.

This is not like Goldfall at all. Or anywhere else, for that matter.

They dismounted. On the opposite side of the plaza stood a large wooden structure. Jade petals clung to wooden columns.

"That's where the Assembly meets," Teresa said.

A group of men and women talked at the peak of the stairs.

"And that's Gaspar, our older brother," Jarus said with some hesitation. "And some of the men who follow him. The older man in the brown robes next to him—that's Rui."

Oyza strained to see over the whirring crowd. Gaspar looked of average height, clean-shaven, with short hair. He held a finger to his chin, huddled in conversation. He was taller than either Jarus or Teresa and had broader shoulders too.

Jarus perked up. He dashed off toward an approaching woman with her arms outstretched. She was plain-looking, with short black hair falling to her chin. A lustrous golden flower adorned her hair. Jarus wrapped his arms around her and kissed her neck. She flashed a brilliant smile.

Teresa sighed and turned to Oyza. "That's Lirali, my brother's new plaything. Says she's a refugee from Goldfall."

Oyza and Yars glanced at each other.

Frustration tinged Teresa's voice. "There were only a handful of refugees. They told us Liviana sent guards after anyone who ran."

Lirali giggled while Jarus lavished her neck with more kisses. They clasped hands and walked back.

"Oyza," Jarus said, "I want you to meet Lirali."

Oyza and Lirali traded slight bows. "Pleasure to meet you, Lirali." Oyza noticed Lirali's fingernails were painted a cerulean blue. *Wonder how she keeps them so nice if* everyone *takes turns working the fields?*

"As to you." Lirali spoke with a heavy lisp in her voice.

Jarus lobbed another wet kiss onto Lirali's cheek.

"We've heard much about you, Oyza," Lirali said, her voice delicate but keen, "and I'm sure there's much to learn." Her lips curled into a congenial smile.

"Yars," Jarus said, "why don't you take Oyza to where you've been staying now? We'll make sure to get you the accommodations you need. Rest up. I'll see you in the morning." With a nod farewell, he and Lirali turned away, his arm over her shoulders.

Teresa stood with her arms folded, watching Lirali as the couple disappeared down the road.

"You don't look...happy about her," Oyza said.

"I just... I don't know if I can trust her." Teresa frowned. "I told Jarus he needs to be careful, but he won't listen to me." She tightened her gloves. "But that's for another time. Don't tell Jarus I asked, but let me know if you notice any strange behavior about Lirali. Just between you and me."

"Of course," Oyza replied. *I guess things aren't perfect, not even here.*

Teresa adjusted her headband. "Anyway, I can't wait to learn more about you, Oyza. We'll get you started at the library with me soon. Yars said you were a Starfish and you'd trained as a scribe. Figured we could get you in at archives. How does that sound?"

An archive? Scribing? "That sounds great," Oyza said.

"Yars, show her the storehouses. I'll see you both later then." Teresa gave Oyza and Yars a hug, then turned to leave.

"I wonder what that was about," Oyza said.

Yars shrugged. "Yeah, Shimwood is a great place, but I guess you'll see they have problems here too." He nodded at Gaspar, who still stood atop the steps of the Assembly building with a handful of others. "Jarus and Teresa don't like their older brother, Gaspar, much either."

Oyza eyed him curiously. "Why not?"

"I guess they don't agree about strategy. Jarus and Teresa, Quorig and Syvre—you'll meet her later— they wanna send Ungoverned all over Vaaz.

194

Find people to join them in other kingdoms and all that. Gaspar says no—sending out Ungoverned is just asking for trouble."

Oyza had never considered something like that before. "But Jarus and Teresa have the right idea, right? To spread their message, they have to get out there?" *Curious.*

Yars ducked his head. "I heard Jarus one night when he was drunk. Said he thinks his brother is gonna make moves to get his crown back. Watch out for Gaspar. He comes off real nice at first, but Jarus and Teresa say he's a cold man with a soul like ice. I guess we shouldn't trust him either."

Oyza peered at Gaspar. Constant movement, constant growth—that's what Jarus had said was the lifeblood of revolutions. But what if Gaspar was right? Maybe they were just asking for kings and queens to quash them? "And the man next to him? Rui?"

"Stay away from him. I heard Teresa's got spies all over him—she thinks he's up to something...something dark."

Oyza instinctively reached for her sword's hilt. An oldest son of a fallen king lusting for a throne, a dangerous old man at his side, and Teresa had...spies? *Not what I expected Shimwood to be like.* "So you've learned a lot here in just a few weeks, haven't you?"

"Yeah, I guess. Jarus and Teresa, they've been really nice to me. Syvre too." He started walking. "Come on, I'll show you around."

Oyza took one last look at Gaspar and Rui, then followed Yars. A chill swept up her spine.

CHAPTER 25

Liviana scanned the blue horizon ahead from atop her black mare. *There they are. The Haf fleet.* She eyed the ships docked in the water. Behind her, Parthassian lancers rode in rows, clad in shining black-and-bronze plate mail, armed with long pikes pointing in the air like a wall of towers. Horses pulled a caravan of wagons between them.

A scout trotted up to Liviana from across an open field, but there was no need to deliver the message. Liviana could already see the Haf gathering on the other side, a motley army of half-starved crewmen and nervous officers. They carried a sea of Haf green and silver banners flapping in the gusts.

"We'll meet them here." Liviana motioned to a commander next to her. "Prepare the wagons." She dismounted her horse, then ordered the lancers to stand in a circle around them. She sent four lancers out to meet the Haf. "Bring them to me."

A couple of servants—none of them Moths—carried a long table out from a wagon. They draped the table in a black-and-bronze banner, then covered it with food and jugs of tea. The Moths brought out chairs. Liviana sat.

The lancers returned with two Haf officers: one was older and shorter, wearing heavy armor and carrying a pistol. He had white hair and pale skin. *But the other one... What is this? A Vaazian?* He was younger, with tan skin, black hair, and brown eyes. The officers stood, hands on pistols.

"Well, are you going to sit?" She gestured toward the chairs. "It's not a trap, I assure you." Liviana wasn't sure how well they understood Vaazian, but she hoped for the best.

The officers sat, hands still on pistols.

They look like they're starving. Liviana snapped her fingers, and a throng of servants came to place still more food on the table: plates of strawberries, almonds, pastries, and more. "Tell me, commanders, with whom do I have the pleasure of speaking? And you," she said, peering at the Vaazian officer, "where are you from then?"

The young Haf man reached for a glass of tea. "My name is Alden. I am Haf, or as you might know them, the Men without Gods," he said. "I am the admiral of this fleet."

His accent. There isn't one.

"And I am Svend, also of Hafrir," the other one said in Vaazian with a very thick Haf accent.

Alden seems to waver, unsure of himself. I can see it. Svend looks like he wants to kill me. Liviana scooped up a handful of berries. "No, where are you from?" She bit into a berry. "Where were you born?"

Alden fidgeted for a split second, then composed himself. "I was born in Oyvassa."

Curious. They must have captured him when Oyvassa fell. But he's an admiral? "Then why do you sit on the other side now, an admiral?" Liviana asked.

Alden took a sip of tea, shared a glance with Svend, then straightened.

He must be desperate. Trying so hard to look tough right now. Liviana wanted to look at their pistols but kept her face still and stoic. She knew they could kill her at any moment with them.

"Never mind that," Alden said. "Why do you come to us today, Commander Liviana Valador? What is it that you want?"

"You know what we want." She allowed her eyes to glance at his side where his gun rested.

"Of course," Alden said. "You want guns." And what's in it for us?"

Liviana felt more nervous than she dared show. But the deal was a good one. She snapped her fingers. Servants standing by the wagons lifted up the covers and revealed crates stuffed with food. There were apples, pears, heads of lettuce, loaves of bread, bundles of dried meats, wooden boxes filled with cheeses, and drums overflowing with plump grapes.

Liviana watched them closely, gauging the reactions she knew they suppressed. Svend was better at hiding it, but Alden wasn't as good. His eyes froze on the stacks of luminous gold bars. Liviana made sure they would sparkle. She knew the look in his eyes. *They came here for all the gold of Goldfall, only to watch it fall into the abyss. Gold it is, then. That's what they want. But will they want what else I offer?*

"I propose an alliance. A pact between the Empire of Parthas and Hafrir. Take these gifts as a token of our goodwill," she said. "We are the most powerful force in all of Vaaz. No other empire has soldiers as strong and disciplined as ours, nor as many lands. Our fields are productive and cover half the continent, and our Empire only grows larger each day. It would be beneficial for you to have allies here."

Alden translated to Svend. Liviana could tell he was desperately trying to pretend he didn't care.

"And I offer you slaves. Fifty thousand, to be exact." An assured smile filled Liviana's face.

Alden's brows narrowed. "Hafrir has no need of slaves. Do you have hundreds of barrels full of coins to offer or not?"

Liviana edged forward. "So you will return with nothing? How will your queen—the Dron, you call her—appreciate that?"

Alden leaned back, thinking; Svend scowled. "Even so, we have twenty vessels but not enough room for fifty thousand. We could take ten thousand at the very most. It's a long way to Hafrir."

"Fine. Take as many as you want, and let the rest drown. It doesn't matter." Liviana bit into a juicy strawberry. "Do you accept or not?"

"And where will these slaves come from?"

"South of here lies the Shimmering Woods. Inside the swamp are thousands of rebels. We need to deal with them, and we have an army. Here is where you come in. From Judge's Pass, our men will drive the rebels

197

south toward Oyvassa. They'll have no choice but to retreat back behind the walls of their empty city. There, your fleet will be waiting with your cannons. We have many warships at Groshe that can assist you. We'll drive them like cattle to a slaughter. You'll have as many as you like without doing any of the fighting."

Alden rubbed his neck, lines of worry creasing his face.

Take it. Take the offer, fool. Look at your men. Starving!

"And you want guns, then?" Alden asked.

Liviana sat her glass on the table. "Guns and ships." She stared directly into his eyes.

Alden scoffed. "Ships? No, we cannot."

"I want three of them. Two to sail into battle if needed and one to leave at Groshe, where our engineers can learn to build as you do. And I want pistols, muskets, cannons—and for your men to show us how they work."

Alden placed his hand on his gun, thinking.

Take it. Take the deal. She refused to show the heat of nerves rising inside her. *Think of your Dron. Take it!*

Alden glanced at Svend, whose angry eyes demanded a translation. "What will you do with the ones we cannot take?" he asked.

"We'll kill most but send some to work in our mines. You can have the first pick, of course."

Alden translated. Svend choked, his face turning red as he shouted expletives in Haf. Alden reached out to Liviana. "Deal."

Yes! Liviana wanted to jump out of her seat. Instead, she leaned forward to shake his hand. *Father would be proud. He was the negotiator, not me. And they all said I couldn't do it without him. The future of the Empire belongs to me now.*

Svend shouted something in Haf. Alden snapped at him back.

"I look forward to our alliance," Liviana said. "And I look forward to receiving your weapons we have coveted for so long. And of course, my Empire is here to aid. Take all of these gifts for you and your men."

Alden gave a grateful nod.

And now, the next part... Liviana reached for a berry. "Before we make preparations for our assault, I have one last proposal to make," she said. "When we have chased the Ungoverned south, men from our ships will assist you on the shore in rounding them up. You'll have to sail into the harbor to pick them up. But I have a very, very important request. I'm looking for someone in particular, someone who did terrible things to me and my family and perhaps knows an important secret, a secret I don't want anyone else in Vaaz to know."

Alden squinted his eyes. "Who?"

"Her name is Oyza Serazar."

Alden froze, his eyes turning to ice.

Oh? The name... Does he know her? Could he? He couldn't. But he's thinking something... What?

Alden cleared his throat.

"She's a Starfish girl," Liviana added. "Younger than either of us. I want her found—and kept alive. There's a good chance she's somewhere in the Shimmering Woods now. Before any slaves board your ships, my men will inspect every woman first." She took another sip of tea. "If you find her, I will let your people live alongside ours at Goldfall. I will give you land. We will rule the city forever, your permanent port and gateway to Vaaz. I imagine trade between our empires could be quite prosperous."

Alden tapped his fingers on the table. "Goldfall?"

"I know what Hafrir wants. I know you'll be back. Let it be a testament to our cooperation. You could try to eradicate us, but you would fail. It would be best if we found a way to live peacefully."

Alden's eyes grew wide. He relayed to Svend, then seemed to freeze again.

"This means we might need your help when rounding up the slaves. After the fighting has ended, we can let none escape. Not into the swamps, not into the sea. Your men must be careful not to kill them until we've inspected them all," Liviana added.

Alden took a quick breath and raised his chin.

Something in his eyes. This worries him. But why?

"Deal."

Liviana locked her hand with his. "Then it is done." A triumphant smile overtook her face. "Two worlds become one today." She rested her hand on the shining hilt of Xalos. "Two empires ruling over the whole world. May we forever know peace."

Chapter 26

Oyza stretched her arms as she woke the next morning. Birds chirped, and the odor of wet mud and damp logs hung in the air. She rolled over in bed, expecting to find Yars, but he was gone. *We are never ever going to wake at the same time, are we?* She rose and sat at the edge of the bed.

Their house—more of a mud hut—was small but cozy. Pots and pans dangled over the bed, and embers burned in a small hearth in the corner. An old rug filled with holes sprawled across the floor. A lute sat in one corner. Oyza felt an urge to rearrange and clean all of it, but suppressed it when she saw Yars through the front door. He stood at a grill, shirtless, with his back turned to her. Smoked coiled into the air.

For a moment, Oyza watched him quietly, thinking about Goldfall for some reason. *We really made it out. We did. And he looks so much healthier now.* She threw on her clothing and greeted Yars outside with a kiss on the back of his neck. The moss on the ground felt slimy beneath her bare feet.

"Good morning." Yars held a metal fork in his hand and poked at pieces of bacon. "Breakfast will be ready soon."

Oyza smiled and looked up at the top of a giant tree standing beside their house. Its trunk was wider than the whole house. Other houses sat nearby, all made of dried mud and wood. Pools of murky water occupied the spaces between them.

"Smells good." She took a seat on a soggy stump. "I love the house. But...we're going to have to do some cleaning. And some rearranging."

Yars grinned. "Sure thing." He nodded toward a building far across a field. "I've gotta make my way over there soon. Been learning how to work the forges with Jarus but also working in the fields." He turned over a few pieces of sizzling strips. "Oh, but before I go, I got something for you." He nodded at a bag. "Open it."

Oyza raised an eyebrow. She picked up the bag and untied the opening. She pulled out a toy—a small dragon—and smiled. "Yars, where did you find this?" It was painted a dark red, and two wings stretched out from its back.

"Saw it in the storehouses, and they said I could take it. I remembered you said you played princess, knight, and dragon with your brother and sister. You said you always wanted to be the dragon. Well, now you can!"

Oyza laughed. "I can't believe you found this. And it's just like the one my father bought." She turned the toy over in her hands, remembering the games she used to play. "Thank you, Yars."

"Ah, it's nothing," Yars said. "But glad you like it."

"So you said you're going to the farms after breakfast. Everyone here works on the farms?" Oyza asked, yawning. She sat the toy on her lap.

"Many, but not all. Some aren't cut out for it—so they do other work instead. Take care of the kids, helping the old, weaving and sewing, cleaning, you know."

Oyza wanted to laugh. Something was funny about watching him cook. "It's amazing how they run things here." She took a bite of bread that tasted sour.

"Yeah, and another Gathering is coming up too."

"Gathering?"

"Every now and then—I think Jarus said it was each time the Sword moves to a new Origin—the assembly and Guardians from all the districts gather to talk about who's making what, how they're gonna give it out to everyone, stuff like that." He sliced off a piece of white cheese and handed some to Oyza on the end of his knife. "Teresa told me if they need more of something, then they just get more people to do that work. If they need less of something, they have those people do other things instead." He shrugged. "I guess it all works out somehow."

Oyza leaned back. *Just like* The Frailty of Kings *said—we do all the work, why shouldn't we have all the power?* "No masters, no emperors, no kings...and somehow, it all works out." She bit into the slice of cheese. "I can't wait to see it all. Remember that book I showed you back in the dungeon—this was all in there!"

She chewed on a piece of bacon as Yars scarfed down a slice of bread. Something about him caught her gaze. Was it the muscles in his shoulders and chest? The way his curls kept falling in front of his eyes as he cooked? Or maybe just his smile, which seemed to glow so much brighter than that first day back in the dungeon?

Yars looked up at her. Oyza looked away. She gnawed into a crisp apple, then changed the subject. "I'm glad you didn't sell the schematics."

Yars rolled his eyes and laughed. He scooped another slice of bacon onto Oyza's plate.

"I was wondering, do you still have that dagger?"

Yars took a slow breath. "I'm sorry. I think I lost it on The *Chandelier*

Lover when I was knocked over." He pointed with his chin at her chest. "I see you've still got the necklace, though."

Oyza reached up and rubbed the seashell. She had worn it so much now, she had almost forgotten about it.

"Take it to Syvre. She'll know what it is." Yars leaned over a little. "But watch her too. They say she's a witch."

"A witch?" Oyza let the necklace fall.

"Don't worry, though; she's nice. She's like a grandmother to Jarus and Teresa."

Oyza nodded. She took a last sip of mint tea. *So much to keep track of.*

A loud bell rang from across the meadow.

Yars perked up. "I have to go!" He wiped flakes of bread from his chin, then threw on a ragged shirt. "Oyza, can you bring all this back in?"

Oyza nodded, her mouth full. "Of course."

Yars turned and ran, avoiding the muddy waters dotting the swamp. "One more thing—almost forgot. Someone came by earlier and told me Teresa wants to meet you at the library at the town square after you wake up. Bye!" Yars waved and ran.

Oyza finished her breakfast, cleaned up some, and headed to the plaza. She followed a long winding trail lined with wet trees and coiled vines. There were so many aromas in the air—stagnant water, crisp leaves, a slight hint of mint, mud and dirt—Oyza wasn't sure whether it smelled good or bad. She passed all kinds of buildings: stables where men and women fed and groomed horses, water mills turning gently but steadily in flowing streams, granaries and tanneries, and a school where young children were climbing trees and playing small instruments. Gray banners with patterns of weaving blue vines hung from windows. Farmers waved. She even went by a chapel. A statue of the Two Lovers pierced by a blue blade sat in a garden. Images of the Origins adorned the walls around the door.

Fascinating how no one here seems to care about Starmarks. I guess the Celesterium doesn't even know they're here.

When she arrived at the town square, it buzzed with life, people and beasts coming and going in all directions. Above the library's front door hung a sign with an image of an opened book.

Oyza knocked. No answer.

After waiting a few moments, she stepped in. It smelled much like she expected. The air was musty, and a slight scent of mold permeated the room. She passed a desk buried in torn scrolls and made her way through a narrow corridor. Paintings adorned the hallway done in tones of dull ambers, rich jades, and heavy browns that reminded her of the fallen tree limbs sinking into the swamp's cloudy waters. On one side was an image of Sorarlir. On another side was a depiction of Oyvassa, its wall stretching over the beach and into the sea. The Pearl Spire was at the end of the wall, gleaming in the sun as it rose from the depths.

The walls of the main room were buried from top to bottom with books and stacks of papers. A few openings in the ceiling let some light through, but candles also burned. The musty air reminded Oyza of both Minister Valador's personal study and the *Chandelier Lover*'s storage room. She leafed through some pieces of parchment. "Fifth Expedition to the Wastes in the Reign of King Liorus III," one read.

She heard a noise from beyond the hallway and quickly put the scroll back down.

"Ah, there you are. Sorry, I was out back, feeding my cats. They keep the rats out of the library." Teresa gave a loving stroke to the orange feline sitting on her shoulder.

After snuggling into Teresa's shoulder, the cat jumped and ran outside.

"They're remarkable creatures, cats. Smarter than most other animals, you know. I've been taking care of some of these since they were kittens." She carried a wooden crate stuffed with papers and empty bottles. Her hair was, as always, wrapped in a gray headband atop her head.

She smiled at Oyza. "It's all right—you can look at anything here. Just be careful." She lowered the box to the ground and gave Oyza a hug. "These are old scrolls we've collected from the palace at Oyvassa." She picked up the scroll Oyza held and blew away a layer of dust.

"From the palace?"

"Yes—we used to go back to salvage things. Some still go. Lots to find at the university also." Teresa set down the scroll and picked up a candlestick.

"Welcome, Oyza Serazar, to the great, wondrous archives of Shimwood," she announced ironically with arms outstretched.

Oyza chuckled. "I think it's great. There's so much here."

Teresa shook her head, a rueful expression on her face. "It's...much better than it used to be, actually. But nothing like the grand libraries in Mélor or Talazar."

She lifted the wooden container and led Oyza into the next room. An old tapestry depicting the Trident—sigil of the Liorus family—was draped on the wall. Oyza remembered Teresa was a princess—or ex-princess? It made her more nervous than she wanted to admit.

"You'll have to work in the fields too, but most of the time, you can help me out here—if you want to stay, of course. Jarus will want you to practice with your sword too. Anyway, a Starfish, right? And you've worked in archives before?" She set the crate of books in the middle of the floor, then stretched her back.

"Yes," Oyza said. "Back in Goldfall, actually, for Minister Valador."

"That's right," Teresa said, "you were close to the Valadors and the Empire. The Assembly will want to learn everything you know about Liviana."

"Of course. I'm more than happy to help. But I probably don't know as much as you would like." *Plus, Liviana is the last thing I want to think about.*

"Regardless," Teresa said, unfolding an especially ripped scroll, "the Assembly wants to meet you anyway. You and Yars brought us the coveted Haf firearms—you're quite famous now around here, you know."

Oyza still wasn't sure how that made her feel. *Famous?* But she was getting more used to it.

"After we finish here, there's a feast tonight. Why don't you and Yars come? Syvre and Quorig will be there. Jarus too, though he'll probably be off with Lirarli." Teresa rolled her eyes.

Oyza toyed with her sleeve. "Definitely. I'll be there." *Teresa really doesn't like Lirali, but she trusts me?*

Teresa sighed. "Anyway, Oyza, you can spend the day here with me. Tomorrow might be best to get you in the fields. We can initiate you the night of the Gathering. You won't be able to attend this one, but you can come to all the ones after it." She rested her hand on Oyza's shoulder. "And then you and Yars will be truly one of us."

Oyza gave a confident nod. "Thank you, Teresa. You've been really kind to us." She spun around to look at some of the books, then turned back to Teresa. "I have a question, though. If we finish up early today, could you show me where the cemetery is? I'd like to...to see if my parents are buried there."

Teresa paused, picking up a black-striped kitten that meowed incessantly. "I'm sorry, Oyza. I know this is all much too fast. Yes—we'll wrap up here soon."

Teresa showed her the rest of the library and explained how everything was organized. A few moments of quiet passed while Oyza scanned through the documents Teresa handed her. Some of them had been signed with the wax seal of King Liorus—a purple trident. Oyza could hardly believe she was holding them.

"What was it like?" Oyza finally asked. "Being the daughter of King Liorus? When all this happened?"

Teresa took a deep breath. Her gaze didn't leave the box she was sorting. "I was still just a young child when my father died and the kingdom was scattered. But as far as I am concerned, I am no longer Liorus." Teresa rose to her feet. She placed her hands on her hips again. "I am Ungoverned. I grew up this way my whole life. I don't think of myself as royalty."

Oyza wasn't quite sure how to respond.

"What about you? All those years in the Valador household? How do I know you aren't with the Parthassians?" Teresa winked. She knelt again and started to unload another crate of withered tomes.

A feeling of disgust sank in Oyza's stomach at the thought of Minister Valador. "I am not. In fact, I'll do whatever I can to stop them. Them and the Haf. They've taken everything from me." *And Liviana. I know she's out there, somewhere, hunting me still. I can feel her eyes on me...*

"The Men without Gods..." Teresa began. "You know, many here have suggested for years that we ought to return to Oyvassa. Seems to be sensible enough. But after Goldfall, I don't think we'll be returning any time soon."

They returned to their tasks. After a few moments, Teresa said, "Here, these are papers we collected from the Haf. Found them on a dead man's body in Oyvassa."

Oyza held one of the papers and inspected the letters closely. They were unlike any she had ever seen before. "Do we know what they say?"

"Not even a little." Teresa shook her head. "For years, we've tried to decipher them, but they don't seem to bear any relation to any languages in Vaaz. I checked every book on writing and language I could."

Oyza opened another scroll. After blowing away the dust, she saw that this one contained a map. It reminded her of the globe she saw on Alden's ship.

"What do you know about them? The Men without Gods?" Teresa asked. "Learn anything from the Parthassians about them?"

Oyza stared at the partial map. Oyza wanted to trust Teresa, but she figured it was too soon to bring up her brother. She remembered Hjan, the gap-toothed and kind old prisoner she had met on the ship. But how much could she trust Teresa? "I heard them say the world is round, like an orange," Oyza said. "Keep going in one direction, and eventually you end up back where you started."

Teresa lifted her finger to her chin. "But how..."

"Other than that, nothing more than you would know." Oyza rolled the scroll back up. *Not yet. I can't tell anyone about my brother yet.*

Teresa scrubbed away a layer of dust that had built up on her hands. She wiped more from her thighs. "Well, we know one thing. They've camped south of Goldfall for a while now. No one knows what they're doing. With the city abandoned, it's a wonder they haven't moved in," Teresa pondered.

Oyza nodded and began to finger through more papers. "I wonder what they're waiting for." *I know what my brother wants. Gold, just gold.* Oyza eyed a map of Western Vaaz on the wall, tracing the lines from Oyvassa in the south all the way to Mélor at the very top. "Are there Ungoverned in Mélor?"

"Yes," Teresa said with a slight hesitation in her voice, "but we've had little success. Really, Mélor and Judge's Pass are the only places we've got a foothold. But Judge's Pass slips away more each day. We've lost good people there. Liviana executed eight just a few months ago."

Oyza tapped her fingers on the table. "Yars told me about your brother, Gaspar. He says we shouldn't send Ungoverned...well, anywhere?"

Teresa twisted her lips and caressed a kitten. "Yes. Gaspar and I, we have our disagreements. His faction in the Assembly is powerful, though."

"But I don't see how his side makes sense. How can you spread the word about the Ungoverned if we never leave the swamp?"

"Well, Gaspar thinks we can form alliances with other kingdoms. But I disagree. We need to start uprisings, Oyza. Uprisings everywhere. We'll never defeat them in battle, but if we can get them from the inside, if we can convince people all across Vaaz to overthrow their masters and become Ungoverned, we might just have a chance. We have to spread the revolution. Even though there never really was a revolution, only a...a sad wandering into the swamp fifteen years ago."

Oyza raised her eyes to Teresa. "But what you've already done *is* revolutionary. No poverty, no hunger. If people on the outside knew," she trailed off, not sure what to say. "*The Frailty of Kings* was right."

"Ah! Yes." Teresa ran to a shelf and pulled off a copy of the book. "You know, the author was a friend of my father's. Gaspar says father should have hanged him for writing such a treasonous text." She flipped through the pages. "And his faction thinks it's a waste to try and spread the revolution. They say it will never happen, that a revolution across all of Vaaz is impossible."

Oyza didn't respond at first, waiting a moment to consider what Teresa had said. *I can see where Gaspar is coming from—it does seem like trying to spark revolution all over the world would be asking for kings and queens to snuff you out.* She remembered Mapa's words: *Rebellion is always right.* "Revolution, impossible? Certainly with that attitude," Oyza said.

Teresa sat down the purring kitty and wrapped her arms around Oyza. "Oyza, I think I'm going to like you." She pulled away. "You know what, I want to show you something. Follow me."

Oyza followed her through a hallway and into a large room below. Shelves overflowing with more books rose to the ceiling. Different colored feathers stuck out of the tomes. A table on one side of the room was buried in a mess of opened notebooks. The pages depicted tables, figures, and scribbles.

"What is all this?" Oyza asked, the wooden floor creaking beneath her boots.

Teresa fanned out her arms. "Welcome, Oyza, to my encyclopedia!"

Oyza gazed around the room. *Fascinating!*

"I'm compiling all kinds of knowledge here—history, people, families, plants and animals, everything I can. I'm focusing on collecting insects right now." She turned around to face one of the walls.

Oyza picked up a book and opened it. A gray feather marked a page about chocolate recipes from Chan-Chan-Tuul.

"You see, there's a color-coded system here. A gray feather means the book is not very interesting, but potentially helpful. The yellow, orange and red feathers mean I'm going to come back later. The ones marked with blue and green feathers are the ones I'm reading now," Teresa climbed atop a small step stool and pulled out a large tome. Inside it was a blue feather.

Oyza's eyes grew wide. She investigated another book. This one was about the history of Ten Orchards and all the magewares magic hunters had collected from the Wastes.

"I realized there are so many books we've recovered, but none of it is organized. So, over there, I'm cataloging as much as I can. You can take a look if you wish. I may not be as good a fighter as Jarus, but I'd rather spend my time here anyway." Teresa fingered through the pages of the book she held. "Don't tell Jarus, but I only joined the trip down to the crypts to see what bugs I could find. That's not to say I didn't want to help you, of course. But, truth be told, I wasn't sure if I believed Yars. He insisted we'd find you there. My brother trusted him, but he's pretty careless, if you ask me." She laughed and nodded at an assortment of jars and vials filled with insects, plants, and gemstones.

Oyza recognized the moth from the crypts. The small notebook Teresa had carried the night before was on the table too. Oyza's eyes drifted to a different pad of paper. Inside was a purple feather. She picked it up and began to read, "Hair like the sweetest honey, eyes like almonds, voice like a warm summer morning, she breathes the clouds of angelic—"

Teresa snatched the book away. "Um, not this one." She shut the book and set it on the shelf behind her. Her face was red.

Oyza smiled. "Poetry?"

"It's nothing."

Oyza nodded and looked away. She turned back to the table and pretended to examine a drawing of a beetle.

"Anyway, Oyza, feel free to come in here anytime. But please don't just let anyone in—everything in here is meticulously organized. I only ask that if you look at something, put it back where you found it. *Exactly* where you found it. And don't bother bringing Jarus—he thinks it's all a waste. Too busy with Lirali and playing vineball—a stupid sport they like to play here. Jarus is the captain of the team." She pursed her lips. "Anyway, whatever you do, don't move the feathers around."

"Of course," Oyza said. "I'd love to help organize your writings."

Teresa opened a book marked with a bright blue feather, then put it back down right away. "You know, now that I think about it, you must be dying to see them, right?"

"See what?"

"The schematics!"

Oyza's heart leaped. There was so much happening so fast, she had almost forgotten about them. "Of course. I'd love to see them."

Teresa led her to the corner and pulled out a locked box hidden under a loose piece of wood in the floor. "There's an engineer here named Broyva. He designed all the waterwheels and everything here. Dabbles in alchemy, machines, that sort of thing. He made copies of these right away, but we keep the originals hidden down here. Doesn't feel like it, but this is probably the safest place in Shimwood."

Teresa unlocked the box and delicately lifted out a stack of papers. She handed them to Oyza. "Yars found a lot of sheets down there. The top one details the materials needed and the process to make something Mapa called gunpowder. Unfortunately, Broyva says we don't have what we need here to make very many guns or gunpowder."

208

Oyza held the brittle paper close to her face. Her heart settled, knowing she had fulfilled Mapa's wish. *This is it, the schematics. Gods, I can't believe it. Thank you, Mapa.*

Teresa flipped to another set of sheets. "This is where Mapa drew up details of how to actually make the weapons."

The papers were frail and torn at the edges. Mapa had drawn lots of diagrams in thin black ink.

"They're fascinating." Oyza turned them over in her hands, poring over more pictures, before looking up again at Teresa. "Thank you."

"Of course."

They packed up the papers and made their way back upstairs.

"Let's get started, and then I can show you the cemetery. Oh, and after that, make sure to visit Broyva. He's dying to meet you but busy in his workshop. He said he has something for you."

For me? Oyza thought. *I wonder what it is.*

CHAPTER 27

Yars sat at one of the communal house's tables, his stomach growling and mouth watering. Before him sat a feast of roasted chickens and boars, trays of juicy strawberries and hearty cheeses, and baskets of warm breads. There were bottles of sweet wine and jugs brimming with ale. He looked up at a chandelier decorated in flickering candles and flowery vines. The room was loud, with a band playing music and people laughing and talking. He sat with Teresa, Quorig, and Lirali.

"Still hard to believe." Yars reached out for a slice of a meat pie. "All this food, all these people—if the guys back in the mines could see me now."

Jarus came to the table with arms full of mugs. He handed a cup of beer to everyone, though Teresa refused.

"I don't drink," she said to Yars.

Yars just about choked. "What? Not at all?"

Teresa shook her head.

"She doesn't eat meat either." Jarus laughed and rolled his eyes. "Turns her brain to bark." He gave his sister a teasing grin.

Teresa raised her chin. "It does not. The priests of Mezzer have been vegetarians for thousands of years, and they've mapped the stars better than anyone else."

"That's because there're no animals in the desert!" Jarus took a mug and toasted with Yars. "And you know what they say about those Mezzer priests: man-lovers, all of them. Not natural, I say. Against the gods. The Two Lovers were a man and woman."

Yars gulped his brew. *Dining with a prince and a princess! But they don't really act like highborns.* Still, he tried to sit a little straighter and eat a little more properly than he normally would have were it just him and Oyza.

Teresa looked down at her plate of beans, garlic potatoes, rye bread, and blueberries, then looked up at her brother. "That's not true. I see it all the time in nature."

Jarus snorted. "If I ever loved a man, the guys on the vineball team would have my head." He wrapped his arm around Lirali's shoulders.

Yars stole a glimpse of Lirali. The woman wore a string of flowers in her hair. While Yars watched, she ran her violet-painted nails through Jarus's hair, lips slightly pouted in a way that made Yars a little uncomfortable.

Teresa inched forward. "Oh please, brother, we're all aware what goes on during your so-called 'practice' retreats. You'd better watch out." Teresa winked at Lirali.

"Oh yes. I keep a close watch on this one—trust me," Lirali said, trying to conceal her lisp. She pretended to strangle Jarus with a leash.

He feigned a suffocation, then faked his death by burying his face in her chest.

Everyone erupted in laughter. More food trekked across the table, plates brimming with buttered biscuits, honey cakes, steamed sturgeon, sliced pears, and lumps of roasted quail moving between candles and vials of wine.

Yars looked around the room, raising his head to see above the tables. At the other end of the room, Gaspar sat with his friends and supporters. Something about the man put a sour feeling in Yars's stomach. And there was Rui, too, sitting next to him. "Teresa, where's Oyza? Wasn't she with you?"

"She was going to the cemetery and then to meet with Broyva. Probably still there."

Yars shrugged and returned to his supper. Melted cheese steamed amid onions, carrots, yams, and gravy. A few moments later, Oyza walked up to the table.

"There you are." Jarus rose to his feet to pat Oyza's shoulder. "Here, sit down."

210

"Thanks." Oyza set her bag down on the floor with a slight grunt. It looked heavy. She took a seat next to Yars.

Yars eyed her bag curiously. "Where you been? Food's getting cold." He passed her a bottle of wine.

"I spent more time at the cemetery than I would have liked, and then to visit Brovya." She scooped heaps of meats, cheeses, and bread onto her plate.

"Brovya? He's really out there, isn't he?" Yars hadn't visited the workshop, but he'd heard stories: explosions in the middle of the night, machines that could drain rivers, contraptions for lifting things high into the treetops.

"Yes," Oyza said, her mouth full. She looked around the room, her eyes stopping on Gaspar and someone next to him in a rolling chair. "Who is that sitting next to Gaspar?"

Yars pursed his lips. "That's his wife, Yala."

Yala sat in a chair with wooden wheels attached to the bottom. Her head dangled over her chest. Tangled black hair fell nearly to her waist.

"Why...why don't you tell her, Jarus?"

Jarus downed another mug of beer and wiped his mouth with his sleeve. "Years ago, Yala took off from Shimwood, ran for the Wastes. She was always so warm, full of life—but she came back like that. No one knows what happened to her."

Yars couldn't bear to look at the listless woman any longer. "Did they find any magewares?"

Jarus shook his head. "Not that we know of. But who knows. Gaspar might have something." Jarus passed a plate of roasted chicken spiced with basil and thyme to Yars.

"I heard stories in the mines about people like that. Said magic hunters see ghosts that frazzle their minds." He made twisting motions with his fingers around his head.

"I wonder what happened," Oyza asked.

"You know what I think?" Quorig asked, his voice deep. "She defied the gods. Yala was always defying the gods—I remember, I do."

Teresa's eyes fluttered in annoyance. "Quorig here is quite superstitious."

Quorig met Teresa's eyes solemnly, but the corners of his mouth twisted into a tiny smirk. "Not superstitious—it's respect. Respect for the gods."

Yars and Oyza exchanged smiles. His eyes flickered to the seashell necklace around her neck. He thought about asking her if she'd figured out what it was yet, but decided not to—no one else at the table knew it could be a mageware. He felt a little sad, realizing he'd probably never have the gold to buy Oyza jewelry as beautiful as that. *Guess I could steal one*, he thought before correcting himself. *No, no, Yars, not anymore. No more stealing.* He shoveled a spoonful of peas into his mouth.

A short older woman dressed in heavy brown robes approached the table. She walked slowly with a wooden cane and wore several bracelets on her wrists of all colors—dark purples, bright bronzes, peaceful greens. There were beads too and all kinds of clanking charms. Around her neck she wore a shining blue scarf. But as she approached, Yars remembered Syvre didn't wear a scarf. Rather, a blue fox sat on her shoulders. It lifted its head and skipped down the woman's side to the floor.

"Now, now, Yip—be careful," Syvre said in a cordial voice, the wrinkles in her face deepening as she smiled at her companion.

The furry critter jumped into the open seat and curled into a ball. Its radiant blue fur gleamed.

Oyza perked up. "A blue fox? I haven't seen one since I was a kid."

Yars said, "This is Syvre. And that's Yip."

The old woman lifted her cane and nudged the fox out of the seat. "Out, out, Yip!"

The fox sprang onto the floor to sit at Syvre's feet. He yawned, baring sharp teeth, and slept.

"Oyza, meet Syvre." Teresa helped the woman sit.

"Thank you, dear, thank you." Syvre placed a roll on her plate.

Quorig poured her a glass of wine as Jarus offered her some chicken.

"And you must be Oyza?" Her voice was tender, but there was a sharpness in her eyes.

Oyza smiled. "Yes. Pleasure to meet you, Syvre."

Yars eyed the jewelry around Syvre's wrists, remembering what he had heard about Syvre: she was some kind of witch.

Jarus touched Syvre's hand warmly. "Syvre here has been around since the beginning—she knew our father, watched over us all these years. We wouldn't be here if it weren't for her."

"Yes, yes." Syvre stretched for a lump of cheddar. She slouched toward Oyza, getting very close. "Oyza, we'll have plenty of time to get to know each other—first, I just want to say thank you. Thank you to both you and Yars." She grasped Oyza's hand.

"You're welcome, Syvre. I think we're just both glad we could help. And thank you too, for taking us in. You've all been so kind," Oyza said. "It's incredible, what you've done here."

"The weapons, they will certainly make a difference. But I want to hear about *you*, Oyza. How are you liking our little swamp village?" Syvre sipped her wine.

"It's... I don't even know what to say. You've all figured something out here, a world with no masters, no lords—it's remarkable."

Yars looked at all the delicious grub on the table. He could hardly believe he was eating like a king.

Syvre nodded and smiled. "Good, good. You can trust these ones here. Jarus is right—I've known them ever since they were kids, back when this all started. I was an advisor to King Liorus when we fled Oyvassa."

"I'd love to hear all about it sometime. I'm from Oyvassa too. Until...well," she said, looking down, "I don't know how much Yars told you about me already."

"He did tell us some, about Oyvassa and your family, and Liviana. I'm so sorry, dear." Syvre frowned not in anger, but with compassion. "What a life you've lived already—and so young still."

Oyza took a slow breath.

"You're in good hands now. And I hear you're to be initiated soon? Both of you?" Syvre gestured to Yars.

I can't wait. Me? A part of something like this? It was so far beyond what Yars had ever hoped for, had ever thought to attain in his life. And yet here he was, feasting with friends and freer than he'd ever thought possible. And different from hacking at rocks all day in the hot mines and eating bowls of stinking mush. *And I'll never have to steal again.*

"Yes," Quorig said. "I've offered to perform the initiation rites."

Syvre nodded in agreement. "Good, good—after you're initiated, you'll be able to vote at Gatherings and to vote for Assembly." Syvre continued to eat, apparently satisfied with Oyza and Yars's decision. "I think you'll both fit in wonderfully."

Yars took in the sounds of the band. The music was warm, permeated with melodic variations of Oyvassan songs. He thought about picking up a lute himself and joining the musicians. Some people danced—perhaps they had had too much to drink already.

Yip climbed back onto Syvre's shoulders. Syvre stroked his elongated body. "We're all very grateful for you, Oyza and Yars. Thrilled for your initiation. I want to welcome you to our family. A toast to Oyza and Yars." She raised her cup, careful not to knock Yip over.

"A toast to the Gods!" Quorig said.

"To the Ungoverned!" Teresa added.

"To the new world and all our friends in it!" Jarus exclaimed.

They hoisted their glasses. Yars and Oyza shared a joyous smile as they downed their mugs of beer. His eyes locked with Oyza's. His heart raced. Was it the ale? No. He reached out to grasp Oyza's hand under the table. Everything suddenly just felt...real.

Jarus finished yet another mug, slamming it onto the table. "What we're doing here has never been doing before." Yars tried not to laugh. Jarus was nearly drunk again. "No kings, no masters, no poor—we're building a new world."

Oyza and Yars shared another glance. He gave her a slight nod. *Building a new world with Oyza. Wouldn't have it any other way.* He took a drink of ale.

The conversation became a blur as he focused on Oyza. Their fingers intertwined beneath the table. He stole glances at her, peeking at the black hair pulled into a bun at the back of her head. He loved the way a few of the strands fell beside and behind her neck. *Her hand, it feels so soft.* Oyza gazed up at him, eyes twinkling with something Yars couldn't describe. He moved his hand to her thigh, her knee... *We should...we should marry. Would she? What is she going to do now that we've found the schematics? Maybe we could settle down, stay in our little mud home.* Home. The word still stung him. *A new home with Oyza...*

"I think you're right," Oyza said to Jarus. "We have to spread the revolution everywhere we can. Gaspar is wrong. We should send Ungoverned to the villages outside Judge's Pass. There's a famine there now, lots of unrest."

Yars's fantasies ended abruptly as Oyza's voice snapped him back into the conversation. *Revolution? Who am I kidding; Oyza is restless. It's all she thinks about. She won't want to stay here in Shimwood.* Where before his heart raced, now Yars felt only hollowness. It was foolish to think Oyza would ever be happy with someone like him.

Jarus rubbed his temples wearily. "Yes, yes—I'm glad you see our way, Oyza, not like our brother. We have a message to bring to the world, a message of hope, of message to uproot the entire order of the world."

Yars felt a little jealous of Jarus: his princely looks, his broad shoulders, his sharp jawline, his skill with just about every weapon there was. Yars had none of that. He slumped back, listening to Oyza and the others talk about sending Ungoverned all over Western Vaaz to start uprisings. *I guess home will have to wait.* He nibbled on a biscuit, not really participating in the conversation. Politics just wasn't his thing. *But I'll be here for Oyza no matter what.*

Suddenly, someone was shouting loud enough to drown out the din of conversation and music. A man ran between the tables with his arms flailing. "Jarus! Where is Jarus!"

Jarus flagged the man down. "Ah, Ulop, come! Sit down, have a drink!"

"No. Jarus, listen to me closely. You should step outside with me. I have news, news from Judge's Pass." Ulop was younger than anyone else there, and shorter too. He had messy brown hair and was out of breath.

The music came to halt as all eyes turned on Ulop.

Jarus set down his mug. "Tell me now, what is it?"

"I really think we should go outside." Ulop eyes darted to Gaspar's side of the hall.

Jarus's jaw tightened. Then he cast a look at Lirali. He stood up and folded his arms. "Just tell me."

"Jarus, it's about Vimoy," he said.

Jarus's eyes narrowed. Teresa's brows knit in concern.

"A rider just arrived and told us Vimoy was captured, some weeks ago—but we just learned. Jarus, I'm sorry—in the dungeons of Judge's Pass, they...they say Blacklance killed him." Ulop hid his face in his hands, overcome.

Jarus's face paled. Lirali sprang to her feet and clutched his arm, but he jerked away.

"I'm so sorry, Jarus," Ulop whispered.

Jarus paced back and forth, eyes fixed on the ground. He walked back to the table, picked up his mug of beer, finished it off, and slammed it back down. It echoed through the silent hall. "Stay here, Lirali." He donned his cloak and made for the door.

Lirali drove her nails into his arm. "Where are you going?"

"Nowhere that concerns you. Now let go of me!" He pulled away from her.

Teresa ran to him. "Brother, please, let's leave and talk about this together."

"No. No. Just stay here, Lirali. And you too, Teresa." Jarus fumed. "I'm gonna kill him. That fucking knight, down in our dungeon, I'm gonna fucking kill him. Every single last Parthassian I can get my hand on."

Lirali seized his wrists. "Jarus, stop, you don't need to do this. Listen, love, let's go home. Please, for me."

"I'm a prince, Lirali. I will do what I want."

Oyza tried to jump to her feet, but Yars stopped her. "No," he said. "We can't do anything."

Jarus stormed out of the building. Lirali chased after him, her dress swirling at her feet. Teresa started in their direction, then stopped.

"Let them go," Syvre said.

Teresa sat back down as chatter filled the room. "This is why I don't drink. My brother gets so drunk, he makes a fool of himself."

Oyza picked at her sleeve. "He won't kill him, will he? The knight?"

"No, he would never do that. The guards wouldn't let him."

"I suppose we should plan a ceremony for him." Sorrow suffused Syvre's face. "It's unfortunate, but some of us pay the ultimate price for the cause."

"For the darkness comes for every star..." Quorig said.

Yars and Oyza lowered their eyes. "Maybe we should go home," Yars said.

"Wait," Syvre said to Oyza. "Before you turn in for the night, I want you to come to my house."

꙳

Oyza stepped into Syvre's house. A fire burned in the hearth, and the fragrance of lavender hung in the air. The walls were adorned with all kinds of bizarre things: vials filled with colored liquids and powders, bones hanging from coarse ropes, rows of small statues, fragments of rocks and crystals, ornamented daggers, and more. A purple rug sprawled across the floor, and in the center of the room, candles burned on a low table. Yip sat curled on a pillow near the fire, his face buried in his blue fur.

Oyza eyed a crystal ball a little nervously. *It must be true. She's a witch.* "Yars said you're...a seer? Can you read people's futures?"

Syvre leaned on her wooden staff, her colored bracelets glimmering in the light of the fire. The top of the staff was carved into a wyvern, the frightening beasts who stalk the icy mountains of the north. "Ah, I dabble in a little magic from time to time. But read futures? No, no. I can only help you to see what's already inside your heart." Syvre walked to a closet in the corner and opened it. "And help you with whatever old things I can afford to give. Take this. A gift, for you." She handed Oyza a cloak.

For me? Oyza held it with both hands. Its exterior was made of thick linen, while the inside was smooth as silk, gleaming ever so slightly in the light of the fire. Oyza's eyes grew wide. Oyvassan thread? "Syvre, I can't take this." She shook her head. "This is priceless."

Syvre smiled. "Go on—try it on. I want you to have this, Oyza. For what you've done for us."

She hesitated a moment, then pulled the cloak over her shoulders. A large hood fell halfway down her back. She grabbed two straps hanging from the inside around the neck and attached them. The inside glowed a dim blue, illuminating her face and reflecting blue light into her hair. "It's wonderful," Oyza said.

She looked down at her hands. A few moments later, the cloak was so bright, it slightly lit up the walls of Syvre's house. "How long have you had this? It glows like it's still new." Oyza rubbed her fingers on the plush fabric.

"Never worn before," Syvre replied with a smile. "I've kept it for years in this trunk, waiting for someone to give it to. And Jarus and Teresa, they both already have one."

Oyza untied the strap, not wanting to waste the precious light stored in the thread. "Thank you, Syvre. I don't know what to say."

"What you've done for us is already enough. Excuse me while I sit down now. I'm old, if you can't tell. And us old folks can't stand like we used to."

Oyza folded the cloak on the table, then helped Syvre sit on her bed. Yip jumped beside them, gave Oyza a curious sniff, then lay down in a poof of blankets.

"Oyza, I suspect we'll get to know each other much, much more over the coming weeks. But I'm inspired by your story." She rattled her bracelets. "I was young once too, you know. Took my place at a Celesterium monastery, but I quit. Decided it wasn't for me. Went into law instead and quit that too. I took my place at my father's side—he was a friend of the king's—may he find peace with the Origins." She closed her eyes for a moment. "I guess what I'm trying to say is, life will take you through all kinds of twists and bumps. What matters is that we bounce back stronger each time. You seem strong, Oyza, someone we need now. You've brought us all hope."

Oyza sat down on the bed. Syvre reminded her of Mapa.

"But, Oyza, there are other things you should know. I'm often afraid our little experiment in the swamp is coming to an end, and I don't even know how much guns will truly help us."

"What do you mean?"

"I feel it, Oyza. I feel it in the waters, in the winds. In the way the children laugh. Change is coming. And I'm sure Jarus and Teresa have warned you about Gaspar and his faction. I fear dark clouds swirl above him and those close to him. Dark, dark things on the horizon..."

Rui, Oyza surmised.

There was another moment of quiet.

Syvre lifted her chin and looked into Oyza's eyes. "But Jarus is right—we've created a new world here. This is worth saving, Oyza. Right when you did. You and Yars both." Her eyes trailed off into the distance. "And I know the King would have supported this. He wasn't like other kings, you know. Always took care of the people."

Oyza nodded, not sure what to say.

"The Haf are still at our shores. And the Empire is only growing stronger. And I hear whispers of stirrings in the Wastes, visions of Soralir and what hides in the shadow. Dark times, Oyza, scary times. But every now and then, a ray of sunshine."

Oyza played with her sleeve. Syvre's gloomy words clashed with the hope she had felt since coming to Shimwood. She thought for a moment about her time in the cemetery earlier, her eyes flickering toward the crystal ball on the table.

"Ah, don't let me get you down, Oyza," Syvre said.

Oyza reached out to grip Syvre's hand. "You're not, Syvre. I believe in the Ungoverned. And I'll cherish the gift you gave me."

Syvre tapped her fingers on her bracelets. "I can feel them, you know."

Oyza wrinkled her nose. Feel what?

"The magewares on you, both of them."

Oyza blushed. "I don't... What do you mean?"

Syvre turned toward the fire. Her eyes seemed to shine like onyx. "The sword at your waist. I can feel...an energy radiating from it. They say spirits are attracted to magewares, Oyza. And I feel your necklace too."

Oyza reached for the seashell resting on her chest. If Syvre knew, there was no use in hiding it. Oyza unsheathed the sword. The pearl at the end of its hilt gleamed. "This blade belonged to my father. Would you believe it, he won it gambling in Oyvassa. It could turn into an ax and then back again." She waived it a few times in the air, but nothing happened.

But Syvre's eyes were fixed on the piece of jewelry. "And where did you find this?" She reached out to touch it.

Oyza swallowed. "I...we, Yars and I, we found it. In a wagon that must've belonged to a magic hunter."

"Hmm." Syvre squinted at the necklace. It shined. "Do you know what this is?" She let the shell fall back to Oyza's chest.

"No."

"Inside this is mermaid's blood."

Oyza froze. "Mermaid's blood?"

"This is priceless, Oyza. Don't worry, an enchanted treasure like this is indestructible, I'm sure. But it holds a liquid that kings would pay a fortune for. It is said mermaid's blood can reverse death."

Oyza stroked the necklace. Her throat tightened.

"Yes, yes, be careful with that, dear. I don't know for certain what it is, but you should be careful with it."

Oyza didn't know what to say. "Thank you, Syvre." Reverse death? Worth a fortune? *What am I going to do with it now? Do I tell Yars?*

Syvre coughed, then cleared her throat. "Oyza," she began, "I'm so sorry about your parents. I know how hard it is to lose those we love. I lost my own husband fifteen years ago."

Oyza lowered her eyes.

"But we can be your new family. The Ungoverned, all of us here. We're here for you, Oyza. If you ever need anything, you can reach out to me. My home is your home."

Oyza sheathed her sword. "Thank you, Syvre." She gave Syvre a long hug. "I should probably be going. Yars will be waiting for me."

She was about to open the door when Syvre stopped her. The old woman stood, wrapped her fingers around her wyvern staff, and came to Oyza. "Before you go, I've got a question for you. What do you want to do? Now that you are here?"

Oyza kept her eyes on the floor. In truth, she wasn't sure. For now, just surviving seemed hard enough. "Well," she began, "Teresa is showing me how to work at the library. Tomorrow I'm to work the fields with Yars. And Jarus wants me to improve my skill with my sword."

Syvre shook her head and thinned her wrinkled eyes. "No, no, dear. Think inside yourself. What do *you* want to do here?"

Oyza stared into the fire. She looked down at her hands for a brief moment. Memories of Goldfall and beyond flooded into her thoughts—Mapa, Nalus, Liviana. Alden and Hjan. Her sister, Rosina. There was so much to think about, to worry about, to wonder. What could cut at the heart of all of this? Oyza felt a strange urge to slice at the whole mess of the world with a cleaver.

"I want to go to Judge's Pass," she answered at last. "I want to help start a rebellion. Jarus is right—if we can win the heart of the Empire, we can win Western Vaaz and even fight off the Haf. And Yars knows the city well. We could go together. He even knows the mining districts."

Syvre grinned. "Well now, dear, that sounds like quite an ambitious plan. I can't say the Assembly will support you, but perhaps Jarus, Teresa and Quorig can sway them." She bowed and waved Oyza off. "But also, Oyza, don't forget to take care of yourself too. And Yars. He needs the support."

"Thank you," Oyza said. "I'm very grateful for Yars. We look out for each other." *I love him*, she wanted to say but, for some reason, didn't. She couldn't, not yet. There was so much else to do. She had plenty of time to sort things out with Yars later. She opened the door and turned to leave.

CHAPTER 28

Sir Plinn woke the next morning to a slap. "What the fuck?"

"Are you crazy?" Voy hissed, her lisp sharp as ever.

The captured knight rattled his chains to rub his bearded face but couldn't reach. His skin stung. Bruises still covered his head, neck, and arms where Jarus had struck him. Sir Plinn spat into the wall and turned back toward Voy with hard eyes. The air in the cold windowless dungeon was stagnant and dry.

"My name is Lirali now." Voy knelt next to him, holding a candle. "Don't forget it. You're lucky Jarus doesn't remember much of that night. You called me Voy *right in front him*."

Sir Plinn looked away. "Why have you come?" he asked, his voice hoarse.

"Jarus sent me. He wants to apologize. For hitting you when he was drunk."

"Why?"

"He thinks you'll reveal more information if they can 'win you over.'" Voy snorted with derision. "They're so stupid and naive, all of them."

Sir Plinn gave a reluctant huff.

"Well, not him, actually," Voy continued. "But his stupid sister, Teresa. Annoying, she is. She tried to make him apologize, but he refused, insisting I come for him instead. You're lucky, you know? If Jarus had his way, they'd be torturing you nightly."

Sir Plinn gulped. After seeing the way the prisoner had been tortured in Judge's Pass, he could hardly fathom what it would be like to feel so much pain. His stomach churned. *Still, when I'm out of here, I'll kill every single one of them.*

"Anyway, it's good Jarus sent me here. I've been meaning to speak to you in private." She turned to make sure the guards still waited at the door, then lowered her voice. "They said you tried to take Oyza's bag in the crypts?"

Plinn nodded. "I did. She said she had the schematics."

Voy sighed. "She didn't. She lied. Someone else had already found them. This drug-addicted thief, Yars. The one who escaped Goldfall with Oyza."

Sir Plinn closed his eyes. His stomach sank; then his hands balled into fists. *It was all a waste then?* He wanted to cry. "I'll kill them both the second I get the chance. Oyza—I'll strangle her with my bare hands. I am a *knight*."

Voy sneered. "I don't see a knight. I see an angry boy in chains."

Sir Plinn fumed, shaking. *How dare she talk to me like that?*

Voy laughed. "Calm down. You'll be a knight again soon enough."

Sir Plinn tried to cross his arms, but they wouldn't reach. "Well, what do we do now?"

Voy edged closer. "Listen to me closely. I can't give you the details because they may begin to torture you soon, for all I know. But you'll be free. I'll be sure they don't kill you before that."

A half smile leaped onto Sir Plinn's face. *Free? How?*

"Don't get too excited. It's for Liviana, not you. You're one of her knights now. Even if you failed, she'll want you back. She'll be happy I got you out of here."

Sir Plinn winced, but he was glad there was a plan at least.

"I need your help. Liviana's promised me a seat at court and more gold than I'll ever need. Help me to help her, Plinn, and I'll see to it you're rewarded."

Sir Plinn studied Voy, scarcely believing what he'd heard. There was *more*?

Voy brushed hair from Plinn's eyes with a look of pity. "The sister, Teresa. She's a threat, and I think she's got spies on me. Jarus will come to speak to you soon. Tell him his sister has been meeting with you privately. Tell him she told you not to tell anyone, that the meetings were secret, and she's been feeding you in exchange for your silence. Tell him she has been asking you about me, about if I'm a spy. Then, tell him his sister said she would free you if you told her information about me but withheld it from him."

Sir Plinn licked his dry lips.

"The more of a wedge we thrust between everyone here, the more Jarus will trust only me, the more he will tell me, and the more we can share with Liviana. The more information we bring her, the less likely she'll be angry with you. Do you understand?"

Sir Plinn gave a prompt nod.

"Good. And remember, I am Lirali now." Voy brushed dust from her knees, adjusted a bracelet of yellow beads, and turned toward the ladder. The candle flickered as she walked.

Sir Plinn tugged at his chains. "Wait. How are you going to get me out of here?"

Voy turned back around and knelt again, whispering, "The days of the Ungoverned are numbered, Plinn. And I can count them on both hands." She kissed his cheek and turned away.

Sir Plinn closed his eyes. His heart bounced. *I'll get out of here soon. And I'll get my revenge.*

Voy stopped just as she reached the ladder. "Plinn, what is it you want?" she asked without turning.

He gave a hesitant smile. "Whatever my commander wants, of course." Voy left.

There was silence in the room. Darkness. *Whatever my commander wants.* The phrase made his heart grow warm. He must have said it ten thousand times in his head now, repeating it over and over to pass the time. *That's what makes the Empire strong: duty, obligation, honor. Whatever my commanders wants, I want.*

But a sudden coldness sank into his stomach, like an icy needle that pierced somewhere deep inside his body. *But what does my commander want?*

CHAPTER 29

Sir Yirig stumbled into the town square at Judge's Pass, following hordes of people congregating around a stage. A beard covered his chin, and his armor was filthy. Clouds of dust hung in the air, coating his armor in gray. Only moments earlier, Celesterium priests and guards had poured out of the city on horseback right past him, chased by Parthassian lancers in a whir of blue, black, and bronze that shook the ground.

What's going on? Is Liviana all right? He squinted to get a look. There was a wagon, a handful of Parthassian soldiers, and was that Uriss? *It can't be.* The Archvicar knelt, golden robes flowing onto the floor, with his hands tied behind his back. Liviana took the stage, Xalos dangling at her side. She raised her hands to quiet the crowd. Minister Woss stood at her side.

"People of Judge's Pass! I, Commander Liviana of the Parthassian Empire, have ordered the arrest of all Celetsterium priests in Parthassian lands. I have ordered the confiscation of all Celesterium properties. For I bring to you today a traitor, a traitor of the Empire and an enemy of the great people of this city."

A chorus of boos. Sir Yirig looked around, nervous. *By the Gods...*

"Our brave soldiers intercepted this wagon leaving a Celesterium monastery." Liviana walked over to it and kicked over a chest. The chest popped open, spilling out a mountain of grain. "Do you see? Do you see what's in it?"

The crowd erupted in hisses.

She knocked over another chest. It, too, spilled grain and oats. Liviana lifted her arms. "The Celesterium has lied to you, lied to the great people of this city. They have starved you!"

The mob shouted curses. Nervous, Sir Yirig reached for his ax out of habit.

Liviana pulled Xalos from its sheath and placed the blade on Uriss' neck. He flinched.

"Tell them," she said. "About where the grain was going."

Uriss said nothing. He didn't move.

"Tell them, Archvicar, before I have your head!"

Silence. The hairs on Sir Yirig's arms stood up.

Liviana kicked the priest over. His body skidded on the wood. Liviana grabbed him and sat him up again. Blood trickled from his lip. She placed the sword on his neck, driving the blade deeper. It drew blood.

Uriss exploded into tears. "Commander, please, you must understand..."

"Understand what? That you starved this city and aided Mélor? Yes, yes, you did, Archvicar. Snuck food out of the city to starve all these people here." She raised her arm to the people. "And aid our enemies in the north! Why, Archvicar? Speak!"

Uriss quivered, tears flowing down his face. "Commander, I only ever meant..."

Liviana sneered. "You only ever meant to lie to everyone here."

The crowd roared.

"As commander of the Parthassian Empire and ruler of this city—"

"No, no," Uriss begged. "Please, just let me—"

"I sentence you to die. For the darkness comes for every star."

Gods! Has she gone mad? Sir Yirig held his breath.

"My brother will have your head, Liviana!" Uriss shrieked. "Mark my words. You're a *bitch* and a *harlot* and a filthy—"

The Archvicar's head tumbled onto the stage.

Shouts and roars. A triumphant Liviana. Xalos raised high, blood dripping from its gleaming blade.

Sir Yirig rushed toward her, trying to push through the tightly-packed bodies. "Out of my way! Out of my fucking way!"

"See what happens when you betray the Empire!" She picked up the priest's head by the hair, spat on its forehead, and tossed it to a cage of dogs. "People of Judge's Pass, know this: I am always on your side. I will forever be protector of this city, even from the Gods themselves. Make no mistake: Cerras and the priests are *not* on your side. But *I* am. *Only* I am. And soon, we make our next bold step. We crush the Ungoverned, the demon-worshippers and killers who threaten our Empire and our great city!"

The throngs of people cheered and clapped.

"Remember, they could be here, any of them, among us! Be vigilant! Be strong!"

Sir Yirig reached the stage but was stopped by Hawk and Tower shields. "Get out of my way, you idiots," he said. "It's me, Yirig."

The guards traded anxious looks. "Yirig? What happened to you?"

He scowled, and they let him pass. Liviana was already gone, but Minister Woss and a few servants stayed to clean up.

"Has she gone mad?" Sir Yirig clutched Minister Woss's shoulders. "Beheading the Archvicar? Like this? She means to anger the whole Celesterium?"

Minister Woss looked at him with wide eyes. "Yirig, you're...but what happened?"

Sir Yirig shoved past the old minister and stomped to the citadel, climbing the steps, with sweat pouring down his brow and trickling from his beard. His body ached, but he had to find Liviana first. In the citadel, the guards pointed him toward the basement. At the end of a long hallway, Liviana stood before a statue of Soralir.

Sir Yirig fell to his knees behind her. "Liviana, I'm sorry. I failed you. Plinn failed you. We were ambushed, right when we found her."

Liviana turned. "Yirig? You're back?" She gestured at the knight to rise. "What happened?"

Sir Yirig wiped away dust from his arms. "We chased her into the crypts, but Ungoverned followed us. They captured Plinn, killed the others. I made it out, just barely." He wanted to cry but managed to hold the tears in.

Liviana turned back to the statue. "I know about Plinn. A rider just came to me with a message from Voy."

Sir Yirig's throat grew tight. "And what's going on here? Are you crazy, Liviana? Executing Uriss like that? Now every priest in Vaaz will ally themselves with Cerras against you."

"Yirig, we don't need the Celesterium. And to hell with Cerras. I am preparing our armies to march south, into the Shimmering Woods. I've received information from Voy. And I struck a deal, a deal that will seal our future."

She is always scheming! Sir Yirig noticed that instead of stroking his beard as he normally did when trying to gather his thoughts, his fingers had entwined into the hair and tugged, hard. *Always something else, always something bigger! Gods, Liviana!*

"I just returned from Goldfall. I made a pact with the Haf. We have guns now, Yirig, and bigger, more powerful ships. Our army will march south, pushing the Ungoverned to the sea, where the Haf believe they will be collecting them as slaves. We'll take Oyvassa for the Empire."

An alliance with the Haf? But how? Why?

Liviana laughed, apparently enjoying the confusion Yirig knew she saw written on his face. "Hafrir believes we'll be aiding them with our fleet. But that's not what we'll be doing. Instead, after they've fired on the city and exhausted their ammunition, our ships will neutralize theirs. I want to capture all of their boats. Everything. Their guns, their cannons, their fleet. All of it will be ours."

Sir Yirig contemplated her plans, but his heart pounded. His head spun.

"I saw their men, Yirig. Scared, hungry, afraid, desperate to go home. They are not warriors, not any longer. We'd be fools not to do this." Liviana rubbed her chin, staring at the statue of Soralir. "Then, we'll throw them all to the bottom of the sea, for all I care. Except Oyza, of course, if we find her. I will personally execute her for what she did to my father. For what she's always done to me."

She has gone mad. "Why not just forget her, Liviana? And forget the Ungoverned—let them die in their swamp. You've just angered every priest in the world. And Cerras will not tolerate your—your insubordination for long. Do you think he'll stay in the North forever? Did you forget he has an army too?" The sweat trickling down Yirig's neck was cold with dread.

Liviana pursed her lips. "I *cannot* forget her, Yirig. She murdered my father. And she *tried* to murder me! Do you even care? Do you care that this—this servant, this whore, has mocked my family for so long? And I've lost both my parents now. Once because of *your* failure."

That stung. He looked at his muddy boots and took a long, slow breath. "I regret what happened to your mother—every day, Liviana, I regret that I failed to protect her. You know that." He ignored the gnawing feeling inside, the one that, if it had a voice, would sound like Yendra screaming, "Murderer!"

Liviana's eyes trailed off into the distance. She cleared her throat. Yirig wondered, fleetingly, if Liviana regretted her outburst. His hope was short-lived.

Liviana paced across the room. "I have to ask, though...what was Oyza like? When you saw her?"

Is that all you care about? Vengeance? No, of course not. She's always wanted power, always to be the best. And with Nalus gone, what's to stop her? "She looked...afraid, maybe. It was dark in the crypts, and I only saw her for a moment."

Liviana tightened her gloves. "It's you and me now, Yirig. You, me, Voy, Minister Woss, and our commanders. The army and our fleet. Our knights and our lancers. The only ones left to weather the coming storm." She stared at the sculpture of Soralir. The wizard's eyes were full of sorrow and angst.

226

"War is coming, Yirig. War unlike anyone in Vaaz has ever known. The men from Hafrir are not the only ones. Every shore in Vaaz will be swarming with men from the far side of the world. Who will stand up to them? Talazar? Chan-Chan-Tuul? The Celesterium? Cerras? No, only we have the might to do so."

Liviana stepped closer. "But even with better ships and guns, I worry it won't be enough." She placed her hand on the hilt of Xalos. "Our spies stationed in Ten Orchards share whispers with me. Whispers about the Wastes, about dark things stirring. Once we've taken care of the Ungoverned, I will go to the Wastes myself. I will finish what my mother set out to do."

Sir Yirig swallowed, not daring to take his eyes from the wizard before him. He remembered the Wastes, the way Liviana's mother had shrieked as she fell from their wagon. The Hellhounds, the dust storm, the scroll that was lost in the wind—every second of that day followed him like a ghost, no matter how hard he tried to forget, haunting his dreams.

May the Gods forgive me, he thought. *May the Gods forgive me.*

CHAPTER 30

"What are you thinking about?" Yars asked.

He and Oyza were lying on their backs at the top of a watchtower, watching the sunset. Oyza's head rested on Yars's arm. She loved feeling the muscles in his bicep.

Oyza tossed a twig into the wind. Black butterflies fluttered above their heads. "What am I thinking about? I can't believe we're missing the Gathering."

Yars smiled. "Sounds boring anyway. An all-day meeting to talk about farming and all that? No thanks."

"But that's how they get everything done. They decide who will do what, who will get what. It's a brilliant system, don't you think?" Oyza asked. "It's just like they said in the *Frailty of Kings*."

Yars tapped his fingers on her arm. As the sun melted behind the horizon, blue fireflies flickered in the leaves. The swamp hummed with the sounds of insects and frogs.

"What do you think about Teresa and Jarus?" Yars asked.

"Teresa's been really nice, and Jarus seems really dedicated. I love when he talks about revolution. It's inspiring."

"Inspiring? I dunno, I guess. You know, when he found me on the beach, I thought he was going to kill me." Yars rubbed her shoulder.

"I still feel bad about him, about his friend. He was really torn up," Oyza said.

"Yeah. It's not easy to lose a friend."

Oyza ripped at another twig, leaving the subject behind. "Syvre, too, she's been very kind. She reminds of me Mapa a little. And she gave me this cloak too. It's lined with Oyvassan thread."

"I was wondering where you got that. They didn't give *me* anything." He laughed.

Oyza threw the twig and sat up. She stared at Yars, her heart racing. *Should I? Can I?* "That's fine. I'll give you something." She leaned in and kissed Yars, her hands trembling.

Yars kissed her back, wrapping his arms around her shoulders.

Oyza loved the way he tasted, soft lips and sweet breath with a hint of metallic tang. And his hands, too, felt wonderful gripping her body, sending shivers out from every tip. "I'm glad you're here, Yars. I'm glad you didn't run to Talazar. And I want you to know, I'm proud you gave up witchdust too."

"Thanks Oyza. It's not easy, you know, giving that stuff up."

Oyza caressed his arm.

"And hey, what's in Talazar anyway? I like it here in Shimwood. Everything's free!" He leaned over to open his bag and pulled out a half-full bottle of sloshing red wine. "Like this." He took a sip and handed it to Oyza.

The wine was sweet with hints of blackberries. "I'm assuming you didn't steal this."

Yars grinned. "Course not. I don't steal anymore. No more witchdust either. I've been thinking, Oyza, and I feel like...like I found a home here."

They laced their fingers together as the sky turned a lustrous violet.

"But we don't even have to do this, you know? We could just run," Yars said. "Leave all this behind." He took a slow breath. "But it wouldn't be right, would it?"

"It wouldn't. I don't really know why, but it just wouldn't," Oyza said. A blue firefly flashed near her face. "I still haven't told anyone here about Séna, my brother. Only you know, Yars." She had told him—reluctantly—only a few days ago.

228

Yars nodded. "He sounds like a jerk, anyway." He paused for a long moment, his fingers gliding along Oyza's side. "Where do you think he is now?"

"I don't know. Last I heard, his fleet was still at Goldfall."

"I wish we were still on the *Chandelier Lover*. That was my first time on a ship," Yars said. "I never would have dreamed I'd be on a big boat like that someday. Most of my life, I never thought I'd get out of the mines. Not until the day we escaped. That was the best day of my life. Well, until I met you, Oyza."

Oyza's heart melted. She nuzzled her face into his neck. Leaves and vines rustled. "What do you want to do after we're initiated?" She pulled part of the cloak over herself and Yars.

"I'm not sure. Might just keep blacksmithing with Jarus, see what happens. What about you?"

Oyza paused for a moment before responding. She hadn't really thought of it, but Yars smelled like a blacksmith: an odor of metal, smoke, and rock clung to him just slightly. She stared at the clouds. "I want to go to Judge's Pass, help the Ungoverned to bring rebellion there and to every corner of Vaaz."

Yars crinkled his nose. "You really think that's possible?"

"Of course. Look what happened here. Why can't this happen everywhere?"

"Well, things are different, you know. I mean, not everywhere is like the Shimmering Woods."

"Well, I don't see why not. There are prisoners and peasants and poor soldiers and slaves all over the world. They all want freedom, equality, food, and peace. If only they knew about what has happened here..." She sat up, turning to Yars as her long hair splashed like a waterfall onto his chest. "Will you come with me?"

Yars raised his eyebrows. His mouth opened but he didn't say anything.

"You heard me. Will you come with me to Judge's Pass, with the Ungoverned?" Oyza asked again. "After we're initiated. Syvre thinks we could sway the Assembly to support a mission."

"Back to Judge's Pass?" he asked. "But why there? Oyza, that's the last place I want to go."

Oyza placed her hand on his shoulder. "For revolution. And for love." She kissed Yars on his cheek.

He closed his eyes again as a smile conquered his lips.

Oyza gripped his waist. "And because you know the city. I don't. I've never been there."

Yars sat up and wrapped his arms around her, kissing her neck. "Ah, there we have the truth," he said. "You just want my...expertise."

They laughed together. Below, fires burned in Shimwood's houses like a lake of tiny candles. Smoke billowed from chimneys.

"We should probably be going." Oyza helped Yars to his feet. "Quorig said to meet him just after sunset."

They climbed down the rope ladder and made their way into the swamp, hands clasped tightly together.

***

"It's the biggest one in the Shimmering Woods, we think." Quorig's bushy beard glowed in a mushroom's blue light. "And this is where you will be reborn as Ungoverned, where you will declare, forever, to never bow to a master or king or queen again." He pointed at the pool of water beneath the mushroom. The ground was damp, and a thousand stars twinkled overhead as flashes of blue light sparked.

Oyza and Yars stood next to the water as Quorig walked over to the other side and stood beneath the immense mushroom. It lit up the curves of his face, and his long cloak glistened. He smiled. "Now, take off your clothes."

Oyza and Yars stared at him, confused. "What?" Yars asked.

Quorig chuckled. "You are being born again in the most sacred waters of the Shimmering Woods. It's only fitting you become again as you were when you were born the first time, as the Gods made you and granted you your Starmark."

Oyza glanced at Yars. The thought of being ordered to take off her clothes reminded her of Minister Valador. It brought up painful memories, memories she had struggled to push away ever since fleeing Goldfall.

No, I can't let those memories hold me back. Still nervous, she saw something in Yars's eyes that gave her courage and strength. She began to remove her clothing.

Yars did the same.

As they undressed, Oyza stole glimpses at Yars's naked body. His muscular arms, jutting hip bones, and supple skin glistened in the blue light. Oyza saw the pickaxe mark branded into his skin. Yars plunged into the water. Oyza followed, sinking to her shoulders. The water was warmer than she expected.

Quorig straightened. "In order to become Ungoverned, you will repeat each line in the oath after me, together. Is that understood?"

Oyza and Yars nodded. *I wish Mapa were here*, Oyza thought.

"And you understand what this means, right? You will live with us in Shimwood and learn to participate in our ways. You will find your place here, working with us, as equals. You will have a voice at Gatherings and will be able to vote for Assembly Guardians. And you will swear to never bow or kneel before a lord, king, or queen, or anyone else in Vaaz, ever again. Or anyone from across the sea either." His eyes shined like sapphires underneath his hood.

Oyza and Yars lifted their chins a little.

Quorig raised his arms. "Repeat each line after I do. 'From this day forward, I am Ungoverned. I will take no lords. I will take no masters.'"

"From this day forward," Oyza and Yars said in unison, "I am Ungoverned. I will take no lords. I will take no masters."

Quorig continued, "I shall bow to no one, and none shall bow to me."

"I shall bow to no one, and none shall bow to me," Oyza and Yars repeated.

"As equals, we share in all. We share in labor and in wealth, in joy and in sorrow, in strength and in love." Quorig lifted his arms high.

"As equals, we share in all. We share in labor and in wealth, in joy and in sorrow, in strength and in love," they said back.

A smile crept up Yars's face as he snuck a glance at Oyza from the corner of his eye.

She returned a half grin. *This is it. We're really doing it.*

"Together, we shall live, and together, we shall die."

"Together, we shall live, and together, we shall die," they said.

The smile left Oyza's face as a deep feeling sank into her chest. There was a power in the words that reverberated in her body, as if a spirit were possessing her and filling her with strength.

"I pledge myself to the Ungoverned, now and for all time, and to all those who remain unfree, 'til the last chain is broken," Quorig said.

"I pledge myself to the Ungoverned, now and for all time, and to all those who remain unfree, 'til the last chain is broken," Oyza and Yars said in unison.

Oyza lifted her eyes to the endless night sky. *Nothing will be the same after this. Nothing.*

Quorig lowered his arms and waded into the swamp. He placed his hands atop their scalps. "Deep breath now." Oyza and Yars inhaled as

Quorig pushed them underneath the water. "Gods, watch over Oyza and Yars, and all the Ungoverned, for all time to come. May we be worthy of your blessing," he said.

Oyza could barely hear him under the water. He tapped on their heads. They rose, hair dripping with water, and hugged each other.

"We did it," Oyza whispered.

"We did," Yars said.

Quorig returned to the water's edge, boots slopping in the mud. "Welcome, friends, to the Ungoverned." He gave a warm smile.

Oyza took another moment to look up at the stars. *I am Ungoverned. I am free. 'Til the last chain is broken.*

They stepped out of the water and dressed themselves.

"We don't usually let people come to the Gatherings so soon, but why don't you come with me? The meeting is over, and I'm sure the festivities have begun," Quorig said.

Oyza and Yars shared surprised smiles.

"Of course." Oyza clasped her hand in Yars's. "We'd love to."

They trudged back through the swamp and made their way to the Gathering. The air was filled with a light smoke and the scent of roasting meat. Blue and gray streamers hung from soggy branches while a band played music under the sprawling limbs of a giant tree. Torches burned. People danced, young lovers with hearts burning and elderly couples with tender smiles on their faces. Oyza and Yars made their way to a table covered in barrels, and they were served two glasses of dark, foaming beer.

"Cheers to the Ungoverned!" Oyza raised her glass.

"And to us!" Yars added.

They tilted their heads back and gulped. It tasted just as dark as it looked, with a heaviness that reminded Oyza of the chocolates from Chan-Chan-Tuul.

"Not bad for demon-worshippers, eh?" She winked.

Yars laughed. "Fine, then. You were right." He took another drink, then smiled into Oyza's eyes. "Thank you, Oyza. For everything."

She gave a lighthearted shrug. "Thank you too, Yars. I wouldn't be here without you either." She wiped a line of froth from her lip when someone grabbed her shoulder.t

"There you two are!" Teresa gave Oyza a hug.

Jarus and Lirali stood near, holding mugs of ale. White flowers were woven into Lirali's hair. She smiled pleasantly at Oyza.

"How was the Gathering?" Oyza asked.

"It was boring." Jarus rolled his eyes and took a gulp of beer. "Boring as always. Drags on all day."

Teresa's eyes narrowed. "Boring, yes. But it's how we run things here. It's how we eat, how we make sure we have everything we need. And for *everyone*, not just for a few." She wasn't drinking anything.

"I'll take vineball over this any day," Jarus said. "But you're right, Teresa, this is important. This is what we fight for, after all." He reached out to give Oyza and Yars pats on their shoulders. "One of us then, eh?"

Oyza and Yars nodded.

"'Til the last chain is broken!" Jarus raised his glass.

They clanked their beers and laughed.

The music grew louder as the bonfires raged, lighting up the bottom of the canopy. The heat warmed Oyza's skin, and beads of sweat began to form on her forehead. Huge boars roasted and turned. The tables were brimming with piles of baked apples, pears, walnuts, figs, and bowls of white puddings. There were wheels of yellow cheeses and plates of cakes too. Red wine flowed. They ate together, laughing and talking late into the night.

Jarus leaned back from the table, finishing another mug of ale. "Come on, Lirali." He wrapped his arm around her shoulder, then took a last bite of a turkey leg. "Let's go dance!"

She planted a wet kiss on his cheek, then grabbed his hand and dashed to one of the bonfires, where they joined a ring of dancers circling the fire. The band played a tune Oyza recognized as Oyvassan in origin: faster and with more vivacity than the warlike Parthassian songs she had grown accustomed to over the years. Oyza and Yars finished their glasses and followed them to the ring of dancers surrounding a mountain of flames so large, it seemed it might catch the whole swamp on fire. Tonight, in a joyous chain of friendship and love, Oyza knew in her heart that a new kind of world was possible. *'Til the last chain is broken.*

❀❧

Oyza and Yars made their way home after the Gathering ended, stumbling back to their house while sharing a last bottle of rum.

"I told you, Yars, didn't I!" Oyza giggled.

They clasped hands.

"I know—I know, I told you! You were right, Oyza!"

They opened the door and fell into bed. Rays of moonlight poured through the windows.

"This is our home. Can you believe it?" Oyza asked.

Yars smiled. He rubbed his fingers against Oyza's side.

Oyza's heart began to pound. The way his hand glided up her side, her stomach, then her chest sent a thrill through her body. She took his hand and weaved their fingers together, then pushed his palm to her breast. She unlaced her shirt.

Yars trembled. A moment later, he tore off his clothing.

Oyza gave a slight moan, then plunged her nails into Yars's bicep. It felt hard and sturdy, and it filled her chest with fire. She dragged her fingertips from his knee up to his groin.

They stared deeply into each other's eyes, melting into one, as Oyza felt the beating of her heart merge with the rhythm of his. Somewhere inside, a wall came down, a barrier she had put up for as long as she had ever known, and in that moment, she knew that nothing would ever take from her the way that Yars made her feel now.

They slept that night in a ray of moonlight, in love, in freedom.

CHAPTER 31

"You've really never shot a bow before?" Jarus chewed on netiss nut.

The question irked Yars. He'd grown up working in the mines, an orphan. Of course he hadn't shot an arrow. "Never."

Jarus smiled. "Well, if you're to be a ranger with us, you've got to learn a bit of archery." He handed Yars a longbow.

"But we have guns now..."

Jarus laughed. "We'll have guns *soon*. Besides, you'll want to get good with a bow and arrow anyway. This is one of the most important skills to learn."

Yars nodded. His eyes darted around the wet leaves and moss-draped branches swirling around them.

Jarus picked up his bow and instructed Yars to watch: stand up straight and firm, aim with one eye as best as you can, and pull back forcefully but steadily. He nocked an arrow and drew it back as the wood tightened. He let go. The projectile whizzed through the air at a bale of hay on the other side. A direct hit. "Now you try." He spat out some netiss nut juice.

Yars did exactly as Jarus did. *I can do this. I can shoot.* Straight into the trees. *Damn.*

"Too high," Jarus said, "but not bad. Don't aim so high next time."

Yars prepared another try. The arrow whizzed just slightly above the hay.

"Not bad, not bad. You're pretty good for a beginner." Jarus patted Yars's shoulder.

Yars flicked his curls out of his eyes. "I liked practicing with the sword better."

Jarus smiled. "You're not bad at that either. Real street style, you've got—must come in handy."

Yars grimaced. *Street style? So be it. Street style's gotten me this far...street style, friends, and a bit of luck...* He nocked another arrow and let it loose. Still too high. "I never really had training with a sword either."

"I fought Commander Liviana with a sword, you know." Yars bent down for another arrow.

Jarus raised an eyebrow. "Really? When?" His arrow landed straight into the bale of hay with a thud.

"When Oyza and I ran from Goldfall. Liviana found us when we got out of the dungeon. Almost got killed 'til I threw sand in her eyes."

Jarus lowered his bow. "See, street style!"

Yars twisted his lips. *Maybe he is another prince after all...*

"What was she like? Blacklance?" Jarus asked.

Yars paused for a moment to think. "I don't know, she was strong. Didn't flinch. Like a tornado coming at you. I felt like she was going to kill me, like she just didn't care at all." He released another arrow. Finally, it hit the bale of hay, although far from center.

"Great shot!" Jarus launched another, landing it right next to the one Yars had fired, then turned and spat again. "We need to know about her. Everything we can. Really, we don't have *that* many rangers. Only a few thousand across seven districts, at best. It'd be hard to stop an army. Arrows don't do well against Parthassian lancers."

"Lancers? You think they'd send lancers through the swamp?" Yars picked up another from the quiver.

"It's passable enough." Jarus stopped to watch Yars, inspecting the other man's form. He gestured for Yars to straighten his spine and pull back his shoulders.

Yars cleared his throat and fired a shot. He missed. "You ever think maybe Gaspar is right, though? Your brother says if we stopped messing with them, maybe they'd stop messing with us?" Yars took time to aim before making another attempt. He couldn't quite figure out why he kept missing.

Jarus scoffed. "And then what? We die here, alone in the bog? We need allies, Yars, and Gaspar is crazy if he thinks kings or queens will go on and be our friends." His usually jovial voice was tinged with annoyance.

Yars aimed carefully.

"Besides, doesn't matter if we provoke them or not. The *idea* of the Ungoverned is what worries them. They want to kill the *idea*, not us. We're no threat to them, not like Mélor or the Haf are."

Yars barely heard Jarus, distracted by the bale of hay across the field. *Come on, Yars. You can do this.* He aimed, muscles tense, and released. A miss. *Fuck me!* It veered just slightly to the left.

Jarus fired. Direct hit, again. He smiled, lowered his bow and turned to Yars. "Speaking of the Parthassians, what do you think of Oyza's plan?"

The past few weeks with Oyza had been calm, but she was concocting a plan to infiltrate Judge's Pass and start an uprising there. Yars thought it was a terrible idea. He wanted nothing less than to return to Judge's Pass, but he also wanted Oyza to be happy. He thought for a moment about her before saying anything—about her persistence, her idealism, the glimmer in her eyes when she talked about her dreams. "I don't know." He rubbed his neck. "I like Oyza, but the plan sounds crazy to me. How do we even know if people there want an uprising? And Ungoverned have been caught there before." He didn't mention Vimoy by name—Jarus seemed to be over it by now.

Jarus smirked. "*Like* her? You mean you *love* her?"

Yars blushed and looked away.

"Everyone knows. You should just ask her to marry you."

A lump formed in Yars's throat. It wasn't that he was afraid to ask Oyza. He just knew she wasn't ready. And damn it, Jarus was right. He loved Oyza too much to make her choose between him and her dreams. "Marry?" He feigned a perplexed look to bely the truth they both knew. "I dunno. You really think she'll want to marry if a rebellion starts out and she's there?" He closed an eye and took aim. *One more. This time, for Oyza. What if she was here, watching? Come on Yars, get just one hit for Oyza. She doesn't need a dumb boy from the streets; she needs a warrior.* He wanted to add, "like Jarus."

"Not a question of *if*, Yars, but a question of *when*. It's a tough choice, but Oyza's right."

236

Yars's neck muscles tightened a little. *You're the son of royalty. What do you know about tough choices? Now, back to Oyza...* He thought about the night after the Gathering, how it felt like he could have lain with her in that moonbeam for an eternity, how all the years of torment he'd endured were worth it if it led to meeting Oyza in that filthy dungeon under the castle in Goldfall. He released the arrow. A direct hit.

"Well then, would you look at that!" Jarus slapped Yars's shoulder.

Yars grinned. *Whew. Maybe I'll be good enough for her after all.*

They stopped as they heard hooves splashing nearby. Ulop approached, scared and out of breath, on a small horse.

"What's going on?" Jarus asked.

"Jarus, you're needed. Emergency meeting of the rangers and the Assembly. Parthassian soldiers have poured out of Judge's Pass, heading south. Led by knights and lancers. Hurry! I have to find the others." Ulop thundered back into the swamp.

Jarus turned to Yars, his eyes wide. "Go find Oyza. I want you both there. Come to the Assembly building." He mounted his horse, waved goodbye to Yars, and disappeared between a thicket of trees.

Gods, can't we get a break? Yars ran to the library building, where he knew Oyza was working for the day.

❀❦❀

Oyza dashed toward the Assembly building with Teresa but stopped when she saw Yars. "Yars!"

They embraced.

"You heard the news?"

"Yeah," Yars said. "Come on. Jarus said we have to go to the Assembly building."

Oyza, Yars and Teresa ran as fast as they could, squeezing and slipping behind a flurry of carts filled with baskets of apples, jars of milk, barrels of oats, and more. There was chaos on the plaza.

"Looks like word has already gotten out," Oyza shouted. *Liviana, I know it. She won't let me go.*

They ran up the stairs of the enormous building. Guardians, or the acting members of the Assembly, and rangers were gathered, shouting at one another. Oyza expected the Guardians to resemble those in the courts back in Goldfall—highborns wearing opulent silk cloaks, golden rings, hats and sashes adorned with silver and rubies. Instead, they were dressed in gray leather jerkins or plain linen tunics. The men had shaggy beards, and none of the women were dressed in the usual markers of wealth. Their clothes were dull and plain, and while some wore flowers in their hair or brightly colored beads around their wrists, no gold or silver jewelry was anywhere to be seen.

Oyza found Jarus in the crowd. "Jarus, what's going on? Invasion?"

Jarus hugged her and was beginning to speak when Gaspar stood on a pillar, rising above the crowd. He lifted his arms to quiet them. A ruffled gray cape fell down his back. Rui and a handful of rangers stood at his side.

"Where's Syvre?" Oyza whispered to Teresa.

"I don't know. Haven't seen her."

Bile churned in Oyza's stomach.

Gaspar began to speak. "Brothers and sisters! The day has come! The day we all knew would be upon us! The day we warned you all about!"

About half the room erupted into cheers. Oyza glanced at Yars with anxious eyes and clutched his hand.

"The Parthassians march south to snuff us out! Brothers and sisters, we have no choice: we must return to Oyvassa! There, we can defend ourselves and drive every last lancer into the sea!" His voice was deep and hoarse. A broad silver sword hung from his side.

"Back to our home! Back to Oyvassa!" they shouted.

Rui stood up. His oak-colored robes fell down his sides. "Friends, Gaspar is right. We cannot defend the swamp. But at Oyvassa, we stand a chance."

Again, the room burst into cheers. Gaspar urged them to quiet down again.

A woman raised her hand. "But we have no ships. How will we stop the Parthassians if they send their fleet? We should stay and fight. We can lay traps, hide in the swamp."

Gaspar scoffed. "They can't attack by sea—the Haf are still at Goldfall. They won't be able to send their fleet south." He adjusted his leather gloves. "And staying in the swamp while an army approaches is suicide."

Another Guardian stood up. "We should send for aid. Chan-Chan-Tuul, Talazar. Why not Mélor..."

"No," Gaspar said. "No one wants war with the Parthassians now. We are on our own."

The crowd cheered and drowned out whatever others tried to say next.

Gaspar quieted them again. "Our scouts report ten thousand Parthassian soldiers and lancers approaching. But we have an advantage: they cannot bring siege weapons through the swamp. Brothers and sisters, we will defeat this force at Oyvassa, reclaim our ancestral home, and send a message the Empire will never forget!"

Oyza whispered to Jarus. "Back to Oyvassa? While the Haf are out there? While we have no fleet of our own? Jarus, this is insane!"

Jarus gave her a cautious nod but kept his eyes fixed on his brother. Rangers loyal to Jarus came and stood near them, while others clustered around Gaspar.

Oyza turned back to Yars. "I knew it. We should have left for Judge's Pass weeks ago. We could still incite a riot. Liviana would have to call back the army."

A Guardian stood and hushed the room. He was a large, muscular man with a scruffy black beard. "This settles it! We have to go to Oyvassa, and we have to go now! Each second we waste is a second the Parthassians move closer!"

More cheers and applause.

"And I want to propose something else. I propose we put a spear in the hand of every man and woman ready to fight! And we put Gaspar in charge to plan the defense of Oyvassa. Gaspar ought to lead us. Gaspar, the first born son of King Liorus and the true heir of the Oyvassan throne!"

Swords rang into the air amid howls. Jarus and Teresa began to shout about the importance of making this decision collectively, but their voices were overtaken by the fervor of the room.

Oyza's eyes widened at the mention of King Liorus. She had not wanted to believe that Gaspar really desired it. "Yars, we have to do something!"

Yars threw up his hands in desperation. "What am I supposed to do, Oyza?"

Jarus and Teresa continued to rally the Guardians and rangers on their side, to little avail.

Just then, a bell began to ring. A tinkle at first, but then louder. Oyza stood on her tiptoes, struggling to see where the sound came from. Heads turned toward the door. A silence swept over the room as all eyes fixed on Syvre, who tapped a small bell with a metal rod. She gripped the wooden wyvern on top of her staff, its long tail wrapping around the stick. Yip sat curled atop her shoulders, a sleepy smile on his blue face. Syvre's mess of colored bracelets and baubles coiled around her frail wrists.

"Thank you all for calling this meeting. I'm afraid, however, the power to plan all our defenses cannot be given solely to Gaspar without a proper vote from the Assembly." She inched toward the center of the room, her walking stick tapping against the floor.

Gaspar stayed on his pedestal. He crossed his arms. "Syvre, we don't have time for voting. Not anymore. Your games endanger us all!"

There was a smattering of applause from those around him.

Syvre smiled and shook her head. "I know one man cannot do it alone. And I know if being Ungoverned means anything, it means we share responsibilities like this. I propose we first take a vote."

"She's right," Jarus said. "We should vote."

Gaspar glared at his brother and sister, then again at Syvre. Oyza smiled. She admired Syvre's ability to command the crowd. Syvre had respect.

Gaspar consulted with Rui for a moment before speaking. "Fine then. I call a vote. All those in favor of defending the Ungoverned at the walls of Oyvassa, raise your hands!"

Oyza scanned the room. It was packed with farmers, mothers, bricklayers, fishers, and shepherds—faces scared and tired. A clear majority raised their hands. Oyza shared a nervous glance with Yars. Back to Oyvassa? *Maybe it is the best plan we've got?*

Jarus grabbed a wooden chair and stood on top of it. He kept his head held high and shoulders firm. "Then it is done! We need to all help prepare the defenses. We begin evacuating immediately and make for Oyvassa. Guardians should return to their districts. Make it known every able-bodied man and woman will be armed in Oyvassa. We will leave Shimwood by nightfall."

Murmurs and whispers swept through the crowd. Oyza felt a blow in her chest. Nightfall? She turned to Yars and reached for his hand. He gulped.

Teresa stepped forward, her hair snugly wrapped in her headband. "There's nothing left in Oyvassa. We'll need to bring as much food as we can. Weapons and armor too. Anything of significance."

Gaspar glared at Syvre with thin eyes. "I warned you. I warned you all—you meddled and meddled all over Vaaz, and now judgment day is upon us." He placed his hand on his sword's hilt. "But this is what the Assembly wills. We vacate the swamp by nightfall." He stormed out of the room, Rui and half the Assembly following him.

"Thanks, Syvre," Teresa said.

Syvre nodded. "Yes, yes, dear." She fidgeted with her staff. "But returning to Oyvassa has its dangers too. Mark my words, Gaspar will make his way to the throne room as soon as possible. We cannot let him. We'll use the palace to store our goods and as cover during the attack, if needed."

Oyza snorted in disgust. "Does he really have so much power? That the Ungoverned would set him back on the throne and bow to a king again?"

Jarus nodded reluctantly. "All those men and women who just left with him—they've all been promised positions of power if they support his claim to the throne. They've been poisoned to betray our revolution."

Oyza's stomach churned. Why would they put up with him? She and Yars shared uneasy glances. *I guess they've had no choice.*

"We should go now. Lirali will be in a panic," Jarus said.

Teresa barely muffled her groan of annoyance.

Syvre nodded. "I should go as well. Much to pack, much to do. If we get separated on the way, do not let your brother hole up in the palace. Do not let him sit on your father's throne."

"I'll find Lirali and pack up everything we can. But then I'm sending her without me. I'm going to ride with Quorig and the rangers. We need to keep our eyes on Gaspar and his men." Jarus gripped Teresa's shoulder.

Teresa's shoulders slumped. "Of course, brother."

Jarus turned to Oyza and Yars. "You two—I expect to see you at the palace. You can fight. We'll defend the walls together." He hugged them both and left.

"Can you come with me first?" Teresa's eyes implored them. "We have to pack some things from the library. I am not leaving my encyclopedia behind."

Oyza toyed with her seashell necklace, nervous. It felt like only yesterday they had arrived in Shimwood. "Do you think we can really bring all those books?"

Teresa shook her head. "No, but we can take the most important ones."

Oyza let out a tired sigh at the thought of leaving behind so many rare books.

Yars wrapped his arm around Oyza's waist and kissed her cheek. "I'll go start packing up our things. Don't leave without me, all right?"

"We'll meet you on the edge of town," Oyza said.

They split up, intent on their mission.

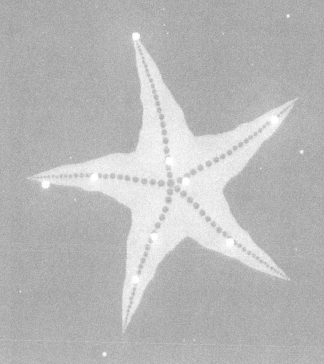

PART 4

OYVASSA

CHAPTER 32

Oyza's muscles ached from days of slow riding. She looked around at the faces of those in overstuffed wagons and on weary horses: desperate, tired, weak, scared. The air felt soggier than usual. She looked at Yars, who forced a desperate smile back at her. His curled hair was greasy, and his skin looked burnt. He slouched on his horse, lute still strapped to his back.

On the run again. Oyza reached out to pet Olive. *Always on the run.*

They began to climb a rolling hill. It seemed to ascend forever, rising above the marshes at a sluggish pace. After some time, they reached the peak and decided to pause for a rest. Oyza peered into the distance toward Oyvassa, scanning the horizon for any signs of the Indigo City. Nothing.

A woman cried out and pointed behind them. "Look!"

Oyza turned. They were high enough on the hill they could see above the top of the swamp. Black plumes of smoke spiraled into the cloudless sky.

"They're...burning Shimwood," Teresa said flatly. "Must be less than a week behind. Come on, let's go."

The wheels creaked against the bumps on the hillside. Sobs and cries suffused the air. "Our home! Shimwood!"

Oyza shared a sorrowful glance with Yars, then turned to follow Teresa toward Oyvassa. Nowhere to go but forward now. They pressed on as the sun trailed above, its warm rays beating down on their faces.

Oyza was stretching her arms and letting out of a heavy yawn when suddenly a man at the front of the column yelled. "The spire! I see the Pearl Spire!"

They froze at the top of the hill, a cool wind blowing into their faces. The Pearl Spire rose from the sea.

"We made it." Oyza inhaled the light breeze brushing past her face. She felt a warmth in her chest. She was home. "We can stay at my family's old house," Oyza said to Yars.

Yars flashed his beaming grin and nodded, his sweaty curls sticking to his forehead. He picked up his reins and followed Oyza down. They made their way toward the city in a single column that stretched for miles. Some fifty thousand people had fled Shimwood. Where Oyza once saw weary and scared eyes, she now saw signs of hope.

They reached the foot of a palm tree-dotted hill near the edge of the city's outer wall. Oyza looked up at the wall, a sandy wind stinging her face. A chill went up her spine. Jarus, who sat atop a tall sturdy horse, raised his hand as the caravan came to a halt. Hooves thudded onto the sand-spattered Coral Trail.

A squadron of rangers greeted him. "Jarus, good to see you. We've already begun fortifying the walls."

"Good," Jarus said. "Keep looking for weak areas, and fortify with whatever you can. I'll send more groups to scout the city as we get these people in. You, get up these walls and get started. We can't waste any time."

"Aye!" A contingent broke off and scaled the stairs, gray cloaks whirling behind them.

Jarus turned to Syvre, who sat in a large carriage stuffed with her belongings. Yip sat curled on her lap in a snug ball. "Syvre, take everyone you can to the palace. It will be the safest place to store our supplies. We'll need all the help we can get during the fighting. But if anyone wants to run to the crypts or elsewhere, let them. Gather the Assembly as fast as you can, and send out crews for anything they can find—I need you to find rocks, debris, boulders, whatever—and bring them here. We'll have to seal the entrance that way."

Syvre nodded, and the men driving her took off right away as the stream of refugees from Shimwood poured in. Horses and oxen pulled rickety wagons as farmers corralled goats and chickens. Children carried crates of apples, bread, cheeses, and salted meats. The elderly sat in carts, holding on to everything they could.

Gaspar showed up with more warriors on horseback, their hooves slamming into the sands below. "Jarus, what have you ordered?" Thick stubble grew on his chin, and a golden pendant hung over his chest. He adjusted his black leather gloves. His wide sword dangled at his side.

Jarus explained the plan.

Gaspar gave a hesitant nod. He dismounted his horse and paced in the sand. "No doors at all anymore," he grumbled, looking up.

"Someone must have taken them for scrap metal." Jarus's eyes also studied the top of the broken gate.

"You don't think they'd attack from the north?" Gaspar asked.

"No. It would be suicide for them. This is the city's only weak point, and they know it."

Gaspar stopped and stroked his chin, then lowered his eyes back to his brother. "Fine then. We'll fill in the hole as much as we can. I have some ideas in mind they won't expect, if Brovya is right." Gaspar turned away and climbed the steps to the wall, chasing away the birds nesting there. His boots slid on bits of sand sprinkled on the bricks. "My men and I will post up here." Gaspar scanned the beach beyond the wall. Waves crashed to his left, and to his right, skinny palm trees grew at the bottoms of the low hills. "Here, our arrows will rain on them, thin their numbers. We'll destroy their ladders. We'll pour hot oil on their lancers."

Oyza listened closely. She didn't know anything about defending a city, but learning about it was fascinating.

Yars exhaled loudly. "I don't know, Oyza. I don't feel good about this."

Oyza twisted her lips, still listening to Jarus and Gaspar. She looked around at the rangers gathered nearby as fatigued but hopeful souls streamed into the city. Their eyes were hard, and she could feel their determination. *Gods, we'll need your help.*

"Here, we'll make our last stand. In the land of our forefathers," Gaspar announced to cheers. "Here, we'll put the Hawk and Tower bastards out of their misery and send them a message that the Ungoverned will not be defeated!" His eyes were full of confidence.

But something about him still left a sour taste in Oyza's mouth. They marched through the abandoned city.

"Did you ever think you'd be here, stepping foot into the Palace of King Liorus?" Oyza looked up at the palace's vine-covered spires.

"Never. Never in my entire life. Gods, if the crew could see me now. Did you?"

Oyza shook her head. She had been close to the nobility for years as a servant. But the king's palace? This was something else.

They entered through immense rusty doors. The hall was so high, they could barely see the ceiling. Streaks of pale sunlight poured in the from windows filled with specks of dust. At the center stood a massive sculpture of a whale strewn with cobwebs. No water ran through the fountain. A brass chandelier that had hung above the statue lay in fragments scattered across the floor. A mildewy odor saturated the air.

"This room was full of mirrors." Syvre accepted the help of two rangers and got out of her carriage. Yip climbed down her side and hopped into the empty hall, chasing rats. "I haven't been back here in fifteen years...but I remember the way the sunlight lit up the room. I remember the flowers the Queen would lay out—it always smelled sweet in here, like lavender and honey. Yes, yes, I remember it." She walked around the floor, her fingers clasping the chiseled wyvern atop her staff. "And there—there used to hang a painting of the Starfish. Used to have the same painting in the Temple, though I suppose that one's gone too." She raised a frail arm and pointed, bracelets dangling about her wrists. "And above the staircase, a blue Trident banner the size of three houses hung." She sniffed, and Oyza wasn't sure if it was from the dust in the room or Syvre's way of hiding sorrow.

Syvre turned to address the crowds. "The Assembly can meet here in the entranceway. It should hold us all. Everyone else—make yourselves at home wherever you like. We all won't fit in here, but there is plenty of shelter in the city. But leave the throne room empty. No one should sit on the Liorus throne. We must respect the dead."

Oyza pulled at a thread in her sleeve, worried. At Yars's questioning look, she said, "We should stay here instead of my family's place. I think we should stay by Syvre if we can."

Yars agreed, taking his lute off of his back. "I...can't believe it. Oyza, we're really here."

Teresa caught up with Oyza and Yars. "It's magnificent." Her eyes traced the center fountain all the way up the staircase toward the murals painted on the ceiling. They depicted scenes of Oyvassan soldiers dressed in indigo armor and wielding Oyvassan glaives. "That one there" —she pointed— "depicts my great, great, great, great grandfather."

Oyza looked up. The mural was faded and blanketed with grime, but she could still see it clearly. It depicted an older man with a black beard, sitting on a white throne. He carried a golden trident in one hand and an unfurled edict in the other.

"Come on you two," Teresa said, "we've got lots of books to unload. There's a study somewhere on the third floor. We can store them there."

"Did you say...third floor?" The whites of Yars's eyes showed.

Oyza hid a laugh behind her hand. "Come on."

They made trips up and down the steps, arms full of books.

"I hope...I never...see books...again," Yars said.

Oyza gave a tired huff. "It *was* a lot." She reached out for Yars's hand. It was hot. She turned to him and inhaled that musky, metallic scent she thought she'd never get enough of. "I'm exhausted too. At least we get to sleep in the palace tonight."

Yars smiled. "A new home, again."

CHAPTER 33

Oyza crept into the ballroom, her steps echoing across its smooth floor and barren walls. The vaulted sides stretched to the sky, elegant curves reaching to the heavens. There were holes in the windows, but the glass shimmered with moonlight poking through to caress the floor. Fireflies hovered in the cool air, bursts of blue light near the splintered shards. Thorny vines invaded the hall, a coiling menace in the darkness.

She walked toward the center and looked up. A mural was painted on the ceiling, but Oyza struggled to see it. Scenes around Oyvassa, maybe? She was certain she could see clouds, water, and flowers around the edges. There was a trident in one corner, and on the other side, what looked like saints.

The ballroom. Oyza's heart fluttered. *I can't believe I'm standing here.* She imagined the magnificent dances that must have taken place here.

"Hey."

Startled, Oyza turned around and reached for her sword.

"It's just me." Yars walked up to her.

"Yars." She tucked away her blade, then kissed his cheek. He was warm and soft as always, and grabbing his hand sent a thrill up her spine.

"What're you doing here?" Yars looked up, studying the ceiling.

"I could ask you the same question." *But I don't care, really. I'm just glad that you're here with me.* She gave his fingers a squeeze.

Yars smiled. "I was looking for you. Syvre said you might be here."

Oyza eyed the mural. The Two Lovers stood atop a mountain, blood pouring down the sides to the constellations below. "She says the palace is haunted, you know."

Yars crossed his arms. "I believe it."

"But isn't it beautiful?"

Yars scratched his neck. "I guess. I never thought I'd be *here* someday."

"Me neither." She wandered, her toes tracing the weaving circular patterns on the floor. "I remember watching the noblewomen dance in Goldfall, watching their dresses whirl and flutter. I hated watching them dance, you know. And Nalus with his constant 'Oyza, more wine. Oyza, where are the chocolates?' And now look at me." She curtsied.

Yars laughed and bowed. "Here we are, about to die in a castle with 'revolutionaries' we only just met."

"We know them. Jarus, Teresa, Syvre—they're our new family, Yars. Quorig too. And we're not going to die here."

Yars kicked a pebble. "You're optimistic."

Oyza stared at Yars with a daring twinkle in her eyes. "Dance with me." She extended her hand.

Yars shook his head. "Oyza, I've never—I don't know how—"

"So? Me neither."

Yars stammered, but Oyza cut him off. She grabbed his hands and placed one on her hip and held another in her hand. "Just do what I do. Pretend there's music playing." She bent her legs rhythmically and rocked her waist back and forth. "You're good at music. So you can dance too."

Yars gave a nervous grin but tried to follow. They swayed in and out of pearly moonbeams, playfully mocking the ways they imagined highborns danced. Oyza tripped more than once, as did Yars, their ankles occasionally butting into each other.

"You know you have to twirl me, right? That's what all the fancy princes in Goldfall did."

"As you say, Your Majesty." Yars extended his arm as Oyza spun on one foot with an imagined dress swirling around her. "Like that?"

Oyza beamed. *Gods, he really is adorable.* The way his eyes crinkled at the edges whenever he smiled warmed her heart. "Now you."

Yars chuckled, cheeks reddening. He ducked to spin under Oyza's hand. They floated in the room amid flashing fireflies, hands clasped and hearts pounding.

"It's funny, you know. When we first met, I thought you acted so much like a noble that maybe you were one," Yars said.

"What do you mean?"

"I dunno. You could read. You knew all this history."

Oyza gave a playful jerk. "Well, I'm not, Yars. I never was. And I'm a revolutionary now."

Yars snickered. "Me too, I guess." He swung Oyza to the side.

"No. Not 'I guess.' We're in this forever now, Yars. We swore an oath." She pulled him close, her eyes glancing at the patch on his chest. "Did you forget?"

"Not too late to run, you know? Before the Empire gets here. We could still run."

Oyza shook her head. "''Til the last chain is broken.' I spent my life a captive, Yars. Never knowing where I belonged, never knowing what I should be doing. Always dreaming, always wanting something else. There's no going back now. I think this is what I want to do—to liberate the world. I can't run—not when so many people are in chains like I was." She gripped his shoulder. "My family is dead, Yars. I have no one." *No one? What about Séna...*

Yars looked away for a moment, deep thought behind his eyes. "You have me."

Oyza leaned forward to bury her face in his neck, breathing deeply. It felt right, more right than anything she had ever felt before. *Gods, he's right. I have you, Yars. I have you.* "That day we fled Goldfall—I won't lie, I was skeptical about you. Didn't know if I could trust you. But I'm glad, Yars—glad we have each other."

They took a final whirl. Yars placed his hands on Oyza's hips, breathing heavily and staring into her eyes.

"I love you, Yars." Oyza peered into his eyes. She stroked his neck.

Yars looked at her lips. "I love you too, Oyza. If I die here, I want it to be by your side." His hands trembled.

"We won't die here. I know it," Oyza said. *Gods, help us. It can't all end. Not now. Not now that I have you.* "Have faith. It's all we've got now. Faith in each other." She pressed his lips against hers and buried her fingers in the soft curly hair that so entranced her. They embraced, then made their way back to their beds in the library, where they fell asleep, wrapped in each other's arms.

"Wake up! A rider is here from Groshe. Assembly meeting now. Hafrir fleet—they're coming our way!" Teresa raced in from around the corner. She wrapped her headband around her head.

Yars yawned. "What? What's going on?"

Oyza sprang from bed. "Come on." She and Yars threw on clothing and dashed into the hallway, tearing cobwebs out of their eyes. *Séna, Brother. Why?*

They descended the stairs to a packed room as a rainbow of morning light burst through stained-glass windows. The messenger stood in the middle, surrounded by Guardians, rangers, and refugees. Their faces were full of dread. Gaspar and Jarus stood near the door, flanked by rows of rangers. A musty odor mixed with the scent of damp leather.

"Seventeen ships," the rider said, out of breath, "hugging the coast, heading straight for us."

Cries and whispers swept the room. Oyza's heart jumped. She reached for the seashell necklace and rubbed it. Yars clutched her other hand.

Jarus stepped forward. "We don't know they're hostile toward us. Let's send an envoy."

Gaspar scoffed. "Brother, are you mad? Of course they're coming for us. They must have struck a deal with the Empire."

"A deal? But how? You think Liviana would do that?" Jarus said.

"Their fleet moves for us right when her army pours out of Judge's Pass? Don't be a fool," Gaspar shot back.

"Then we'll have to abandon the walls," Teresa said. "We should go deeper inside the city. We can't be in range of their cannons."

"Not defend the walls? And just let the Parthassians march in? We're damned—all of us. I *told* you not to go prying all over Vaaz and asking for trouble. And now look!"

"We should abandon the city!" someone else screamed.

"And go where?" another said.

The room fell to chaos. "What if they come to attack the Parthassians, not us?" one Guardian said. "The Gods have abandoned us!"

"No, no—that makes no sense!" Jarus waved his arms.

Oh no. Oyza gripped Yars's hand. *Brother, why?*

Syvre stood up and lifted her feeble arms, colored bracelets dangling halfway to her elbows. The room grew quiet. Yip sat on her shoulders. "Listen! Listen to me. Teresa is right—to stay on the walls and fight at the shore is suicide. Look at what happened to Goldfall." Her voice was dry and cracked.

Brother, why? Why, Séna?

Gaspar shook his head. He placed himself at the center of the room, boots thudding against the stone floor. "I say we fight everywhere we can—on the walls, the streets, in the palace, fight to the death in the lands of our forefathers!"

The room erupted into cheers. The rangers standing behind him hoisted their blades. "King Liorus!" some shouted. "The true King of Oyvassa!"

Jarus tried to interrupt him but was drowned out.

Oyza's heart raced. *Gods, is this what I must do? Is this truly what you ask of me?* She pushed her way onto the floor, squeezing between bodies. "No! We can't stay here!" The room fell silent as all eyes fixed on her. "Yars and I were there in Goldfall when the attack happened. The city was *destroyed.* These ships—they'll go straight for the harbor and turn this place to ashes. We have to leave!"

Gaspar puffed up his chest. "And go where? There is nowhere else to run. Are we to run into the mountains and die there? Hide in the crypts and have them starve us out? Oyza, we have to stay and fight!"

More cheers, cries, sobs. Oyza cast a desperate glance at Jarus. His eyes fell toward the floor. Dark bags hung under his eyes.

Gods, listen to me!

Syvre stood up and raised a hand to calm the room. "We have no other choice. Those who cannot fight will hide in the crypts. The rangers will fight in the city as they see best. May the Gods have mercy on our souls." The fatalism in her voice made Oyza's stomach churn.

"To war!" Gaspar pulled his sword from its sheath and lifted it high above his head.

Blades and fists rose all around the room. "The King of Oyvassa! The King of Oyvassa!" some chanted.

"Wait!" Oyza cried. "Wait! Wait! I have an idea!" But nobody heard her. "My brother—on their boats..."

Jarus, Teresa and Quorig yelled at Gaspar. Yars shrank.

Oyza looked around the room, desperate for someone to hear her. *Fine then, if this is what it takes.* She took off her bag and pulled out a pistol. After loading gunpowder and a bullet, she fired it in the air.

Silence. Bitter smoke spiraled toward the ceiling. All eyes again on her.

Gaspar pushed his way to her. "Where did you get that?"

Oyza lowered the gun. "Broyva gave it to me. The engineer." She looked around to see if he was in the room, but he was nowhere to be found. She raised her chin. "Just listen to me for a moment. Before you found me in the crypts, I was aboard the Haf ships. My brother is commander of their fleet."

Whispers echoed against the walls. Friend of the Haf? Spy? Traitor?

Oyza turned to Yars and mouthed, "I'm sorry." She cleared her throat. "I will go to him. It might be our only chance."

Gaspar scoffed. "You speak nonsense. Any man from across the sea who attacked Vaaz is no friend of ours—brother of yours or not. And to think, you befriended the Haf? And you didn't tell us? I wouldn't be surprised if it was you who told them we were here!"

Applause, howls, and moans echoed.

Oyza shook her head. "Listen to me! No, I'm not a spy or on their side or anything like that. I know it sounds crazy, but...he won't—he won't

THE SPIRIT OF A RISING SUN

attack if I can just talk to him. Jarus, Teresa, Syvre—you have to listen to me!"

"No more of this!" Gaspar said, his voice echoing through the room. "You will not go to him. I forbid it. He will capture you, torture you—you'll give away our secrets!"

Syvre came forward. "You cannot make that decision yourself, Gaspar. No one can—not you, not the Assembly. Oyza is free to do as she pleases."

Gaspar stroked his chin. "She is Ungoverned now. She has sworn the oath. I say we hold a vote."

Oyza narrowed her eyes at Gaspar. "Fine then. Let us vote. I know my brother—I spoke to him. If I can reach him, I can persuade him to turn around. Oyvassa is our home. He would never attack us, not here."

Gaspar raised his hand as Guardians gathered. "All in favor of sending Oyza to negotiate with the Haf on behalf of the Ungoverned, raise your hand."

Oyza scanned the room, her heart pounding. Almost no hands were lifted—not even Jarus or Teresa. That stung. She lowered her eyes. Only Syvre raised a hand. *Yars, not even you?*

He looked away. Knives stabbed her gut.

"Then it is done," Gaspar said.

"I'm sorry, dear," Syvre said.

As people scattered about the room, hurrying to collect their possessions and make for the crypts, Jarus and Teresa ran up to Oyza. Yars stood behind them, arms folded.

"Oyza." Jarus hugged her. "Why...why didn't you tell us this before?"

"I believe you." Teresa threw her arms around Oyza too. "But do you really think the Haf would help us?"

Oyza pulled away, tears forming in her eyes. "I have to go anyway. This is the only chance we have."

Yars glared at her. "But they're right, Oyza. What if you get captured? They'd just torture you. Oyza, this is crazy! You know it." He reached out to rub her shoulder.

Oyza jerked back. "I'm sorry, Yars."

"He's right, Oyza. This isn't a smart choice." Teresa looked away. "Maybe you should take some time to think about this."

Oyza frowned. "Jarus, what do you think? What other choice could we possibly have?"

Jarus scratched his neck. "Oyza, how long have you really known your brother?"

Oyza looked toward the windows. "I...well, we grew up together, and..."

Jarus placed both his hands on her shoulders. "Look at me, Oyza. What chance do you *really* think you have in swaying them?"

Oyza choked. "I have to do this." Did they not get it? She had the answer. She turned to Yars. "You were there, Yars. You know we have no chance against those cannons. You know they'll burn the city down. You have to let me go."

Yars stared at her with solemn eyes. Syvre gave a heavy nod.

Oyza stumbled backward, shaking her head with tears in her eyes. "I have to go. I'm sorry. I just have to go." She ran.

❦❧

Oyza left the palace and hopped on Olive, grabbing anything she could fit in her bag. A strong wind blew, tousling the few strands of hair falling over her shoulders.

I have to do this. I know it's right. Revolution is always *right.*

She galloped toward the edge of the city, refugees and buildings swirling around her, but decided to stop at the Temple of the Starfish. Something called her there. She ran to the Starfish fresco adorning the abandoned temple's wall. It was faded, and large chunks had fallen off. The air smelled dry and stale, and dusty rays of light illuminated white marble columns.

Just as she reached the door, it opened.

"Syvre?"

"Yes. Hopped in my little wagon as fast as I could."

Oyza didn't know what to say.

"I came to talk to you, Oyza." She sat down on a soggy bench. "Come, sit."

Reluctantly, Oyza sat down.

"I liked what you did what Brovya's gun. You know, he's made very few. You have one of the only ones."

Oyza nodded. She fidgeted with her sleeve.

Syvre rubbed her chin. "I am sorry, Oyza, that the vote failed. It is always important we respect whatever outcome the Assembly reaches." She looked up at a hole in the roof. Gray clouds lumbered across the sky. "And yet, sometimes, we know even the majority can be wrong. Sometimes, there are truths only we know, deep in our hearts."

Oyza kicked a pebble with her foot. "What should I do?" *Gods, is it all lost?*

Syvre smiled. "I cannot make that decision for you, Oyza."

"Will they...will they expel me if I go?"

Syvre shrugged. "Perhaps." Yip jumped from her shoulders and scurried toward a mouse. "But we might not make it through the night either." She looked up again. "You know, my old master once told me the world always changes—behind our backs, the Gods direct the flow of time, playing tricks on us, taking us in places we never predicted. And only after it's all said and done does it all make sense."

Syvre coughed, then continued. "And there are certain people, Oyza, certain people who are ahead of all the others. People who drag the new world behind them against all those who cling to the old. My master said these people are like the rising sun. Yes, yes, they have the spirit of a rising sun. The light, bursting forth through the night, obeying nothing and no one but the truths in their own heart."

Oyza took a slow breath, her hand dropping away from the fraying sleeve.

"You're not like the clouds, Oyza, wandering aimlessly, following anyone and everything with no purpose or rhythm. No, dear, you're not."

Oyza wiped away tears from her eyes. "So you're saying I should go?"

"I am only saying what I feel. Only you can make that decision. But do so with no illusions—where you go, you go alone. There are no guarantees in this world, Oyza." Syvre looked up at a statue of the Two Lovers, their bodies pierced by a crumbling sword. "Even Gods can die."

"Do you think we are going to die here?"

"I can't say."

It was not the answer Oyza wanted. She couldn't remember a time when she felt so low. Last night with Yars had been perfect, and now this? She thought about Mapa for a moment, remembering all the years of whispers they'd shared. *Rebellion is always right. I'm never going to get the answer I want.* She stood up. *Never. No more questions, no more wondering. I have to go. I will make my own answers.* "Thank you, Syvre. I...I have to go now." She ran from the temple, climbed atop Olive and stormed through the crowds.

Bands of rangers galloped past her, quivers full of arrows and pikes rising high above them, the hooves of their horses thumping like earthquakes against the ground. Oyza came to the city gates, gray clouds blanketing the sky. She gave Olive a light kick and hurried down the Coral Trail, her cloak flapping in the wind. She didn't look back.

CHAPTER 34

Sandy winds tore through Oyza's hair. Black clouds spread over the sea. She had passed another empty fishing town when she found them: huge white sails on the horizon.

Séna, I've got you.

The ships were close to shore. She approached another abandoned town sitting on a high ridge, then made her way toward the piers. Fishing nets and barrels lay strewn across them. She dismounted Olive and ran to a small rowboat on the beach. Next to it lay two oars covered in dried barnacles. She dragged the boat toward the ocean, waves crashing at her ankles. Her hair whipped in all directions around her face.

"Oyza!"

Oyza lifted her head and looked up at the grassy steps.

Yars sat atop a brown horse. He dismounted and scrambled down the steps to her. "Oyza! What are you doing here?" He threw his arms around her.

Why? Why did you come? "Go back, Yars." She dragged the boat over a pile of kelp. The storm closed in as the winds blew harder.

"No." Yars dug his heels into the sand and pulled on the other end of the boat.

"You shouldn't have followed me. Go back to Oyvassa." It hurt. It hurt deep down in her bones to say that, but she had to stay focused on the mission.

Yars pulled even harder. The boat slipped from Oyza's hands. She stumbled backward into a wave.

"Stop, Oyza. This is crazy! What are you doing?" His black curls fluttered.

Oyza tugged the rowboat, but Yars didn't budge. *I love you Yars, I do, but you don't understand. You just don't understand that I have to do this. There is no one else who can, only me. If it has to come to this, then so be it...* She drew her father's sword and aimed its tip at Yars. "Don't make me, Yars. Please, don't make me. I have to go." Her eyes welled with tears. *Gods, how has it come to this? Please just turn and go, Yars, don't make this harder for me than it already is.*

Yars let go and raised his hands.

Oyza kept the blade aimed at him. "I'm sorry, Yars. Just go back. Go back with Jarus and Teresa." She pulled the boat back as waves crashed at her waist. Thunder echoed across the ocean. *Please. Please just listen to me.*

Yars ran after her. He wrapped his arms around Oyza and exploded into tears. "Oyza, this is crazy. Come back to Oyvassa with me. Remember the night after the Gathering, when we slept in the moonbeam in each other's arms? We can have that forever, Oyza, but not if you go and die."

Oyza pulled away from him. "I can't—you don't understand. I have to talk to my brother, I can convince him—"

"No, Oyza, you *can't*. He attacked Goldfall! What makes you think he won't attack us too? Come back, come home—come back and fight with us!"

Oyza clenched her jaw and shook her head. She dragged the boat out more, trying to stay focused. *I'm sorry, Yars. But there's nothing else I can do.* "Go back, Yars. Please, just go. I'm begging you. I am going to find my brother."

"What if he says no? What will you do? Oyza, I know you feel bad about your brother and sister, about losing them when you were young—but this isn't going to bring them back!"

Oyza glared at him. "Don't you dare talk about that to me." *I'm not going to think about the moonbeams. I'm not going to think about this.*

Yars wept. "I'm sorry, Oyza. I'm so sorry. I just don't want to lose you. Not now. I love you, Oyza. Please come home."

Oyza broke down and cried. The ocean's fury crashed into them both. They embraced, her lips pressing against his as the sea rose up around them.

She pulled back. "I love you Yars, but I have to do this. I have to. Even if my brother throws me in his brig again—I met the prisoners on the ship, I can convince them, I know it. I can convince them they can do it—"

"Oyza, please! You *don't* know them. You don't know *anything* about them. These are people from all the way on the other side of the world. You don't know what they want!" Yars gripped the boat again.

A crack of lighting lit up the sky.

"But *I* know what *I* want!" She ripped his hands from the boat and climbed in. "They can follow me if they wish, or they can die in their brig." She picked up the oars. "I'm sorry—but I have to do this. Go back to Oyvassa. Just go back and fight." *Please, gods, just go, Yars!*

Tears fell down Yars's cheeks.

"Please, Yars. Please just go back. I love you. Just go back—for me."

Yars stood in the water, arms flat at his sides. Oyza said goodbye one last time, then rowed toward the fleet of ships.

❦

Oyza landed with a thud against the deck, soaking wet. Rain fell. Haf sailors stood around her in a half circle with jaws gaping open, blond hair and pale skin dripping.

"Alden!" she said. "Where is Alden? Where is my brother?"

Alden stomped onto the deck, flanked by officers wearing green coats over chain mail. Silver capes flapped in the wind. Each wore a pistol at his side. "Why have you come here?" Alden said in Vaazian.

More sailors gathered around, whispering and murmuring.

Oyza hated seeing her brother wearing Haf clothing. The silver crown on his chest, the green diamonds on his sleeves: it all made her sick.

Alden snapped his fingers and gave an angry command in Haf. The sailors and officers dispersed, leaving only Oyza and Alden behind.

Alden kept his distance from her. "Oyza, I'll ask you one more time. Why have you come here?" He glared at her with thin eyes. The wind howled.

Oyza climbed to her feet. "Stop this, Séna! We know you're headed for Oyvassa. You and the Parthassians. Just stop, please—go back to Hafrir, go anywhere—you don't have to do this." She straightened and fought back tears.

Alden scoffed. "And do what? Go back with nothing? Oyza, I can't do that. Oyvassa will burn to the ground, and you'll all be enslaved or thrown into the sea. This is the reality now, Oyza."

"It's not, Séna. You can turn around and go. Tell your queen you won't slaughter your own people. Or you can stay—come back to your home, join us—help us fight the Parthassians."

Raindrops drenched Alden's hair and ran down his neck.

Oyza removed her bag, pulled out the toy dragon Yars had given her, and tossed it to Alden. "Do you remember, Brother? What would Mother, Father, Rosina say about you now?" Tears gushed down her cheeks. "And look, Father's mageware sword." She slid it across the wood.

Alden examined the figurine. He shook his head. "I told my men we killed you. Do you know how hard it is to be a Vaazian leading a mission like this? Do you not understand—or care—how serious this is? Do you care that I have a wife and children to care for in Hafrir?" He picked up the blade and inspected it. After a long moment, he turned around and called two men from inside. "I'm sorry, Oyza, but you should not have come here. The mission has to proceed."

"Brother, please!"

"Oyza, I can't. I'm sorry. You just don't understand." He said something to the guards in Haf.

The officers unsheathed their swords and approached Oyza.

She ran to him and spat on him. "How could you! You betrayed all of us! Mother, Father, your whole family."

Alden hit Oyza across her face. She fell onto the deck and slid against the rough wood. A trickle of blood mixed with rainwater. Heavy thunder boomed in the distance.

"I'm not betraying you, Oyza. I made a deal with Parthassian heathens to get what I need: gold. And I won't betray them, not really. Because I am Haf now. I can't betray anyone in Vaaz. Just like you can't betray that mule I put you on when you left the last time. It's not betrayal to break a promise to an animal." Alden wiped rainwater from his face, dismissing Oyza.

The officers grabbed Oyza's arms and dragged her into the cabin.

She was a prisoner again.

CHAPTER 35

"Teresa!" Yars dashed through a light rain. His boots and pants were drenched in water and mud. "We have to talk. You, me, Jarus. It's about Oyza." He climbed down from his horse and put his hands on Teresa's shoulders. His eyes were red.

"Yars, where were you? Were you out in the storm this whole time?" Water trickled through the streets.

"Not here—let's go inside."

They made their way through the palace gates and up the winding steps back to the library.

He sat down at a table, exhausted. "Listen. They have her—I saw, I watched from a ridge over the sea. I saw him—her brother, he hit her. They took her. I saw all of it!"

Teresa lowered her eyes. "And what are we supposed to do about it?"

Jarus walked into the room, soaking wet. He ran to Yars and slapped his shoulder. "I thought I saw you come in! I knew you'd come back. Where's Oyza? What happened?"

"We have to save her. They have her—I saw it from shore, they took her below the ship."

Jarus's brow furrowed. Teresa tapped her fingers on the table.

"Listen—guys I knew in the mines—pirates, old pirates, they told me about climbing on ships at night, said you could stab blades into the cracks in the hull, slit captain's throats, steal gold. We can do it. I'm not letting her die there," Yars said.

Teresa shook her head in disbelief. Jarus sighed.

"We just need a rowboat, some rope with hooks..." He knew his eyes were bloodshot. They felt like sand every time he blinked.

Teresa and Jarus exchanged skeptical glances. "Listen, Yars...I'm sorry she's gone, but it won't work. All those ships? Even if you did manage to get out there, someone would see you. You'd just be captured," Teresa said. "You should get some rest."

Yars's hands tightened into fists. "Not if we go at night. I heard Quorig say the moons will be gone tonight—it'll be completely dark at sea."

Teresa ran her fingers through her hair. One of her cats jumped onto her lap and nuzzled its face against her chest. "I don't know, Yars. We need to stay here and help with the defenses."

Jarus stroked his chin and narrowed his eyes. "Well, wait a minute. I think I have an idea."

Yars perked up.

"Teresa, what if we gave Yars...well, father's old mageware..."

"Gaspar would never."

"We'd have to steal it. It could help. No guarantee, but it could get you through a window so at least you wouldn't have to get on deck," Jarus said.

Teresa slumped in her chair. "Do you think it even works? Hasn't the enchantment worn off?"

Jarus shrugged. "I don't know. Gaspar hasn't used it for anything, didn't want to drain it. He keeps it wrapped up in a metal box."

What? "Mageware? Breaking windows?" Yars interjected.

Jarus smiled. "Our father had an old mageware. Syvre took it from the palace when she fled, but Gaspar's held onto it since. It's a dagger. Leave your hand on it long enough, and it starts glowing red hot."

Teresa stroked her cat's fur. "It cuts through metal. I've read about other magewares like it. But we don't even know if it works or not. I don't even remember the last time he talked about that dagger."

Yars stood up and paced.

"And he would never give it to you. Never even gave it to us—said he's the oldest so it's his," Jarus said.

Yars cracked his knuckles. "No, this can work. I'll swipe the dagger. I have some lock picks I kept from Groshe. We'll climb up the side of the ship at night, break into a window, and then Oyza and I can swim to safety..." *Swim?* He gulped.

"And how will you know where she is?" Teresa sat her cat on the floor, but two more hopped to take its place.

"I remember the ship. It was the biggest one of them all and right out front. She's on that one. We'll just have to climb until we find the right window. Break it open, free Oyza, then jump into the water and make our escape." *We broke out of prison once, and we can do it again. I won't let them torture you, Oyza.*

"I don't know, Yars. They'll probably see you. You'll both just be killed," Teresa said.

"No. Nobody is dying—not us and not Oyza. Look, I wouldn't be here if it weren't for Oyza. I'm not letting them take her again."

Jarus smiled at Teresa. "Love makes us all crazy, I suppose." He winked.

Teresa huffed.

Yars stopped pacing and grinned. "Will you come with me?"

Jarus and Teresa froze.

"I, well, I don't think..." Jarus shrugged.

Teresa frowned. "Yars, I support you, but I don't know about this."

"I can't leave the rangers, Yars." Jarus wouldn't meet Yars's eyes. "Gaspar and I are in charge of the defenses. My men would think I abandoned them."

Yars turned to Teresa with desperate eyes.

"I'm sorry, Yars," Teresa said.

Yars frowned and looked at the floor.

"But," Teresa added, "I can help you steal the dagger."

"Yeah?"

"Gaspar has been staying on the floor just underneath the throne room," Jarus said. "He and I will be outside all day today. The storm made a mess of things, but it might work in our favor. You should be able to go then."

"I can help to keep a watch in the hallway. But the stealing—that's all you," Teresa cautioned.

Yars smiled and clasped his hands together. "Then it's done. We can do this! We won't leave Oyza to die. Not today."

❦❧

Yars and Teresa stood in the hallway.

"I'll wait here," Teresa whispered. "No one should be in there now. If someone comes, I'll say I was just looking for Gaspar. You, on the other hand—you'll have to hide or jump out of the window. I don't know. But if you're caught snooping around there, Gaspar will have you locked up. Or worse."

Yars nodded. In truth, he felt he didn't even need her there—he had stolen a million things in his lifetime, and surely stealing from an opened room at a time like this shouldn't be difficult. Right?

"And one more thing," Teresa said. "Don't take *anything* else but the mageware, got that?"

Yars agreed. But he made no promises. Teresa kissed his cheek and left. Yars crept to the room and peeked inside. Empty. A window on the far side was open, and a white curtain waved in a light breeze. Yars squeezed his body through the partially open door. It creaked, sending echoes down the hall.

Fuck me! Are you serious? Not a good start. His heart pounded. *All right, Yars. You've done this a thousand times. Now stay calm. If were I a secret mageware dagger, where would I be?*

The room was packed with all sorts of things, and none of it appeared to be organized. To make matters worse, there was another room off to the side. He started with the first room, digging through a stack of books and trinkets sitting beside a mound of burlap bags. He found old papers and some clothing. Next, he pried open a chest and sifted through it. There was no dagger or metal box. He found an old flute, stacks of faded paper bound together with yellow string, an old book on swordfighting, and a bag of golden rings. His eyes grew wide as he held the rings.

No, no, don't get carried away. He closed the chest and moved on to the next one. It was locked.

Ah-hah. He pulled out a lock pick and got to work. The chest opened. *Easy.* It smelled stale and musty. Yars found random things inside: more old books with pages fraying at the ends, a set of half-rusted keys, empty glass vials, a pair of silver candlesticks, and... *A smaller tin? This looks promising.* He opened it.

There it is! Inside was a small dagger and a piece of old folded paper. The dagger was no bigger than the length of his hand. Its handle had a scorpion carved into it. *This has to be the one!*

He heard a noise from the hallway. *Fuck! Fuck, fuck fuck...!*

Teresa opened the door just slightly. "Someone is coming up the stairs! I'm leaving. Go, Yars, now!"

Loud footsteps echoed through the hall, closer, closer, closer. With no time to think, Yars threw both the dagger and the folded paper into his bag and ran into the other room. There was a closet with an old wooden door—*thank the Gods!*—and a huge mound of straw with sheets and a couple pillows tossed on top. He ran into the closet and pulled the creaky door as shut as he could get it. It was dark behind the door, save for a few beams of light pouring through slits.

The footsteps thudded in the main room.

Yars's heart pounded so hard, it might leap out of his chest. Sweat trickled from his forehead, dripping down his nose and cheeks.

From the slit in the closet door, he saw who it was: a woman with purple flowers in her hair. *Lirali? Why?*

Lirali walked into the room and tumbled facedown on the straw, burying her face in her arms. A thin linen cloak dangled around her body.

Lirali in Gaspar's room? But why? Yars took slow and quiet breaths. He waited for a few minutes, watching her to see what she might do. Her body hardly even moved. *Is she asleep?*

Yars closed his eyes and gulped. *Gods, I know I've lived a terrible life. I know I'm not deserving. I know I've done horrible things. I've killed, I've lied, I've stolen, there was that one time with the pearl necklace on that blind old—you get the idea. But if there's ever a time for you to watch over me, let it be now, Gods, for me and Oyza.*

He crept out of the closet, his feet barely lifting from the floor.

Lirali coughed and shuffled around on the bed. Her face was still buried in her arms.

Fuck! Fuck, fuck...! Yars tiptoed as fast as he could from the room, his nerves strung tight. The door to the main room was open. He slipped out.

In the hall, a rush of relief fell over him. He looked to the sky and thanked the Gods, then climbed up the steps.

Teresa waited at the top around a corner. "Did you get it?"

Yars beamed.

Teresa threw her arms around him and kissed his cheek. "Come on then, let's go!"

Yars gripped the dagger. Its blade turned glowing red with heat. *Don't worry, Oyza. I'm coming for you.*

CHAPTER 36

Oyza woke in a cell, exhausted. Her face stung where her brother had hit her. The rain had finally stopped, and a pale light poured from the window. *Behind bars, again. Gods, why?*

"Hello...you..." a hoarse voice whispered.

Oyza lifted her head and rolled over to the edge of the chamber.

"Oyza." Hjan smiled, showing the same gap in his teeth Oyza remembered.

"Hjan, you're still here." She wrapped her hands around the cold rusted bars. A flea jumped on her ankle.

There were more prisoners this time. They spoke to Oyza in both Haf and a broken Vaazian, but she could hardly understand them. Only Hjan seemed to know enough of the language to hold a partial conversation.

"We think, uh, we think you...are kill?" Hjan scratched his blond beard with black fingernails.

Oyza shook her head.

Hjan laughed. Her gestures for "no" at least seemed to be understood well enough.

"I'm alive," she said. "Alden kept me alive."

One of the other captives, a skinny and pale man with chipped teeth and greasy white hair, asked Hjan a question. His body was covered in scars and faded tattoos, and bags hung under his eyes. Hjan tried to relay the question to Oyza. "He ask, uh, why? Why you here?" He pointed with his bony hands first at Oyza, then to the floor.

Oyza swallowed, fighting back tears. Had she failed? Failed to persuade her brother? Or was there still a chance?

No matter how torn up she was, no matter how terrible things were, the opportunity to meet a man from the far side of the world raised her spirits a little. And who knew—maybe she could help him believe a mutiny was possible? It was her only chance now, she figured. She looked at the window. *We'll be at Oyvassa by nightfall*, she guessed. The muscles in her neck tightened.

"I...I don't know." She was unsure if Hjan would understand. She tried her best to signal with her hands and her face what she failed to communicate with words. "Alden...he's my brother. We are...brother and sister?"

Hjan tucked his hair behind his ears and frowned. He certainly did not understand the words.

"Friends?" she asked. "Alden and me...we are friends..." she said, pointing to herself. Then she pointed to her face, trying to signify that she looked like Alden.

"Ah!" Hjan replied. "Friends."

The other men in the cells started to ask questions. Hjan translated.

Suddenly, the door creaked open. The prisoners scrambled back and slouched against the walls. Oyza did the same.

A guard wearing chain mail under a torn coat entered the room. A faded green diamond was emblazoned on his chest. He carried a jug of water and a plate of crusty bread. Without saying a word, he sat them down on the floor outside the first cell, then left the brig, locking the door behind him.

One of the prisoners grabbed the jug. He took a sip of water and passed it. The next guy took a bite of bread and handed it off. The others shouted and jeered at him for taking too big of a bite. Oyza drank from the jug and ate a few crumbs of bread when it was her turn.

One spoke to Oyza. "How...Vaaz..." He made gestures and shapes with his hands.

Oyza raised her eyebrows, confused.

Hjan smiled. "He...uh, want to know...how is...uh, like...here, in Vaaz?"

Oyza tried her best to answer in simple terms. "It's...well..." Suddenly, it hit her. "No kings." She formed the shape of a crown with her hands on her head, then threw it to the floor. "No queens. I am Ungoverned. We live as equals. No dron."

Hjan tried his best to translate. Some of the men smiled, a sign Oyza understood to mean the translation was at least a little successful.

"Alden...he wants to attack, to fight us, to fight Ungoverned, people with no king." She tried her best to signal.

Hjan translated. The men laughed at her.

"No, really! No king, no queen—no dron. Living in peace, no fighting. But Alden, he wants to take it all away."

One of the other inmates, a shirtless man so thin you could see his ribs, asked Hjan a question. "He wants to know...how, uh, how we come to Vaaz? How we...too, no king, no queen? No...dron?"

Oyza smiled. "Join us, me." She pointed to herself. "You can live in Vaaz with me. You can have a house, land, a place to stay."

The men nodded. They seemed to understand the pantomime she'd given with her words. But they also snickered.

"But we...like you..." He aimed a bony finger at the prison bars.

I wish I had an answer. If only I could talk to Séna again... She scanned the room, her eyes locking with the eyes of the prisoners.

One of them leaned forward and pressed his face into the barrier. "Knutr." He gestured to himself. He pointed toward Oyza. "Oyza."

Oyza nodded. "Knutr."

He was much older than the others, bald and sagging skin. Hjan told Oyza Knutr used to be a farmer back in Hafrir.

Oyza turned to face the next prisoner. "Fjorn." Long bright hair draped past his shoulders, the blond mixed with gray streaks. Hjan explained that Fjorn was a fisherman.

Next, Oyza turned to the last man. His name was Kunnusta. He had a cheerful smile but lips so chapped, they bled. His skin was paler than any Oyza had ever seen before. Oyza shuddered when he turned and showed her the scars covering his back from lashings. Hjan explained he was a servant back in Hafrir, and he had also tried to run before Alden caught him.

Fascinating just how similar our struggles are.

The five of them spent the rest of the day talking and learning about one another. Oyza tried her best to explain how the Ungoverned lived. Hjan, Knutr, Fjorn, and Kunnusta all wanted to know what her Starfish tattoo meant and tried to learn Vaazian words. The day flew by. Oyza stared at the window and watched the light disappear. At sunset, another guard opened the door and brought them another round of water and stale bread. At nightfall, they slept. Only Hjan was still awake, but he and Oyza couldn't see each other. She reclined on the pile of itchy straw.

Suddenly, she had an idea. She pulled her cloak close to her body and connected the straps of Oyvassan thread around her neck. The inside of the cloak began to glow. The room filled with dim blue light.

Knutr, Fjorn, and Kunnusta woke and crawled to the edge of their cell bars. The cloak didn't give off much light, but it was enough to light their faces and the walls around them. Oyza tried her best to explain, but translating something like this was hopelessly complex. The prisoners were impressed, and that was what mattered. She looked around at their faces in the blue light: they were scared and tired, sickly. But she saw something else too. She saw a spark for liberation, a yearning for freedom, and a willingness to fight for a better world—even die or it. It was a look she had seen for years. Now if she could just convince the guards to free them...

CHAPTER 37

What was that? Oyza sprang up. It sounded like glass had shattered. The room still glowed blue. *My cloak—I fell asleep!*

In the blue light, she saw someone lying on the floor. They climbed to their feet, brushed shards out of their curly hair, then ran to her cell. Oyza's heart sank.

"Oyza." Yars grinned and pressed a molten dagger into the lock. "We're getting you out of here." Smoke coiled into the air.

"Yars! How did you get here? What are you doing here?" She ran to the edge of her cell and kissed him through the bars. Suddenly, she felt safe again, like she wasn't even in a jail. But getting out of here? What about the plan?

"Not too many windows glowing with blue light, you know." He winked. "And mageware." He nodded at the dagger in his hand. "Long story. Come on. We're gonna get you out of here."

Gods! Freed again. But she was going to persuade the guards or break out somehow or talk to her brother one last time or something. Something *had* to work.

"You are...Ungoverned?" Hjan crept to the edge of his cell. "Oyza? Vaazian?"

As Yars continued melting the dagger through the lock, Oyza looked around the room at the prisoners' faces. Her gut tightened. *We have an opportunity here...and I can't leave them behind.* "Yars, I can't leave. I've been talking with the prisoners here and—"

The muscles in Yars's shoulders tightened. "There's no time, Oyza. We could be caught any second."

"No, listen to me. From inside the ship we could—"

The door at the end of the room opened. A guard walked in. In one hand he held a candle, and in the other, a short sword. He was beginning to shout in Haf when Teresa fell through the window and knocked him over. The sentry turned and flung his sword. In a flash, Yars leaped behind him and smashed his hand into the guard's mouth as Teresa ran to grab the sword. The guard tried to break free, wrestling with Yars. Both men fell to the ground, grasping at each other desperately.

Teresa grabbed a rope and wrapped it around the guard's hands. "I got him." She held the guard down and gagged him. "Good to see you, Oyza."

Yars ran back to Oyza and opened the lock. The door swung open. She ran into Yars's waiting arms.

Yars buried his face in Oyza's neck, kissing her over and over. "Let's go home."

Oyza jerked back. "Wait."

Yars lifted his eyebrows. "What do you mean, wait? We have to go now, Oyza. We have to go while it's still dark and before they catch us. I don't want to lose you. Let's go back to Oyvassa, to our home." He kissed her forehead and tugged at her hand to follow.

Oyza lowered her eyes and pulled back from his embrace. *I would love to, Yars, and I love you more than anything. But now that I'm free, this changes things. We can do this. We have to do this, for everyone. This is bigger than you and me.* "Yars, wait. If we leave, these ships will still fire on Oyvassa. But look," —she gestured to the prisoners around her— "I've gotten to know them. Hjan, Knutr, Kunnusta, and Fjorn."

They smiled and waved at Yars.

She took a step backward, removing her hand from his. *I'm so sorry Yars, but we can't throw this chance, the one chance we have.* "This ship is ready to mutiny. These people, the prisoners, they're just like us. If we could promise them land, a home, they'd join us. They even tried to run and find us. They deserted. That's why my brother imprisoned them."

Yars's mouth gaped open. Teresa froze, arms folded.

"They told me Alden plans to attack at dawn." She stopped short at the sound of footsteps and movement through the ceiling. "The guards always come at dawn." Oyza eyed the tied-up man on the floor.

Yars ran his fingers through his hair. "Oyza, this is crazy. You don't know that they'll start a mutiny. Listen to me, *please*." He placed his hands on her shoulders. "I know you think you can do anything, but you can't.

You don't know these people, Oyza." He wrapped his arms around her and hugged her.

But Oyza pulled away again. *No. This is our last chance. Our only chance.* "I'm sorry, Yars, but I'm staying. We can do more here than on shore." She grabbed the ring of keys from the guard's belt. "We can free these men. They can stop the attack. If enough join a mutiny, I bet all the other ships will too. These men don't want to fight, Yars. You have to trust me."

Yars looked at Teresa with sad eyes.

"Oyza, I'm not sure this is a good idea. The sun will be up soon, and we should leave," Teresa said.

They won't believe I can turn my brother. But maybe I can help them to see that a mutiny is possible? I have to show them. I know it sounds crazy, but what else can we do? The Gods gave us a chance, and I'd be a fool not to seize it. She stole glances at Yars and Teresa. *They don't believe me, I can see it. But I have to try. There is* nothing *else we can do.*

"Think about Jarus and Gaspar. Syvre. All the rangers on the walls right now. Do you think they can withstand these cannons? You both have to understand, we have to take a chance. We at least have to try." She walked to Hjan's cell. "Here, this is Hjan."

Hjan waved. "Hello, friends."

"He was a farmer back in Hafrir. We talked about farming, about land. He tried to run, to live in Vaaz before he was captured by my brother's men," Oyza said.

Teresa cautiously smiled at Hjan.

Yars sighed. "And my name is Yars." Yars smiled hesitantly.

Oyza explained the plan to Hjan as best as she could as she made her way around the room, unlocking the cells.

"Yes, yes!" Hjan explained the plan to Knutr, Kunnusta, and Fjorn. They filled the room with eager grins.

Oyza gestured at the wall near the door. "Over there, there's a hatch on the floor that leads to storage. You two and the guard—hide down there. When the time is right, we'll burst out of this room and grab as many weapons as we can. Hjan can stop the men from firing the cannons. We can take the deck, then signal to the other ships." Oyza took a few steps back into the cell. She hid the keys in her cloak.

Teresa and Yars nodded. "Oyza, I hope you're right," Yars said with reluctance. "Because this is madness."

Oyza leaned in and kissed him as they embraced. *I love you Yars, but I'm glad you understand. This is bigger than us, bigger than any home in Oyvassa. This is about saving all of our lives, saving the rebellion.*

Yars stepped back as Oyza closed the cell door. He ran to open the hatch and threw the guard into it as Teresa grabbed the short sword and followed him. Oyza closed her eyes and took a slow, deep breath, listening closely to the sounds of footsteps above. Dawn approached. She heard rumbles. Sailors were moving the cannons into place.

Oyvassa, where this all started. Somewhere on the deck, she knew Séna shouted orders. *He rejected her, threw her in the brig, but still...I can't accept it. Mother, Father, Rosina—my whole family, gone. He's the only family I have now. My older brother, the dragon, the dragon I always wanted to be. For all my life, I wanted my family back. I wanted my childhood back, the childhood I was robbed of. These Haf took everything from me. I won't let them take him too. Not my brother. Maybe if we win the day, he'll see the light. Séna, maybe there's one last chance to redeem you...*

❦

Oyza crouched under a window, heart pounding and pistol in her hand. It hadn't taken long for Yars and Teresa to pilfer some weapons from the store room. Oyza looked out of the window. An orange glow lined the horizon, broken by the mountains and the palace spires of Oyvassa.

Gods, this is it. She pressed her shoulder against a door.

"Men of Hafrir!" Alden yelled above, "today, we end our journey! Today, we begin our trip home! Before you lies the city of Oyvassa, where fifty thousand slaves are gathered for our taking—slaves we will take back to Hafrir. When the Dron sees we've brought her something even better than twenty ships of gold, you'll all be rich beyond your wildest dreams! It has been a hard journey, but you—brave men of Hafrir, brave men who have stuck with me to the end—you'll soon be drowning in the Dron's gold! Men of Hafrir, are you with me?"

Oyza shared a nervous glance with Yars.

Sailors cheered and raised their fists into the air.

"Men of Hafrir...fire!"

Oyza turned to Hjan and smirked. He gave a toothless grin back.

There was silence, save for the sound of gulls cawing and waves lapping against the hull.

"Fire!" Alden shouted louder.

Officers again called out orders to the floors beneath the deck.

"Out of my way." Alden stomped toward the door.

"Now!" Oyza knocked the door open. She aimed a pistol at Alden's throat. "Sorry, Brother."

Yars and Teresa leaped behind, weapons drawn. Hjan, Knutr, Fjorn, Kunnusta, and the rest of the prisoners on board burst onto the deck, armed with pistols, pikes, swords, and crossbows. Their cries filled the dawn as they dashed all directions.

Alden put his hands up, mouth gaping open.

Oyza smiled at him, her pistol still aimed at his throat. She grabbed the mageware sword hanging at his waist. "I think this is mine." She twirled the sword.

An officer cursed in Haf and fired a shot at Knutr, nearly striking Knutr's arm. Others grabbed swords from their waists and fought back, slashing at the horde of prisoners ambushing them. More sailors joined in the mutiny, wielding whatever weapons they could find. Some lobbed punches at officers, knocking their bodies off the ship and sending them tumbling into the sea.

"Hjan!" Teresa pointed. "Tell the other ships, before they fire—this is a mutiny!" Hjan nodded, then ran to the side of the ship and signaled to the others, his arms flailing. The sailors plunged their swords and pikes into the remaining officers and threw their bodies into the water. Cheers and shouts rang through the air.

Alden stood with his hands up. "Sister, please…"

"Keep quiet. I won't kill you, Brother." Oyza kept her pistol aimed at him.

Yars and Kunnusta ran up to Alden and tied his wrists with rope behind his back.

"Don't hurt him," Oyza insisted as she walked to the boat's edge.

Sailors hollered around her as Yars carried Alden into the ship. Oyza scanned the fleet as Hjan, Knutr, and Fjorn shouted at them. The mutiny spread. Oyza looked down at her chest, eyeing the patch of blue vines she had sewn onto it. Her heart raced.

The sailors lifted their blades and pistols high into the air, drunk on the high of liberation. They hugged. They cried. They rejoiced. Oyza felt a surge in her chest like she had never felt before.

She scanned the horizon as Teresa ran up to her. "Look. Those are Parthassian warships. They're right outside the harbor. The attack must have begun."

Oyza squinted at the shore. She called for Hjan. He ran up beside her.

"Hjan, translate as best as you can." Oyza hoisted her sword into the air. "Men of Hafrir! We have brought you liberation! We have brought you freedom! Those ships there—the Parthassians, we have to destroy them, or else they will destroy us!" She thrust her sword at the enemy. "Raise our sails, and take us in! Fight for us today, and I offer land! I offer food! I offer homes! No lords, no kings, no queens! We are Ungovered! Fight for us, so we may both live in freedom! Fight for us, 'til the last chain is broken!"

The sailors cheered. Sailors lifted anchors from the depths and raised sails.

Yars emerged on the deck and ran to Oyza. He threw his arms around her and kissed her neck. "Your brother's downstairs. And you're mad, Oyza, you're completely mad! I can't believe this worked!"

Oyza grinned. She could hardly believe it either.

"Look, the other ships," Teresa said.

All around them, sailors tossed their officers overboard as the air rang with cries of liberation. Sails raised.

"If we can go around the Pearl Spire and break through their fleet, then we can fire on the shore with the cannons. It's the only way we'll survive this attack." Oyza crossed her arms, refusing to pull at her sleeve and show her fear.

Yars and Teresa nodded.

Oyza gripped the hilt of her sword, her hair whipping in the morning gusts. The sun crested the horizon, the end of dawn.

CHAPTER 38

"Why haven't they attacked yet?" Liviana stood at the bow of her ship.

Behind her was the rest of the Parthassian fleet. Sir Yirig, her Iron Towers, and legions of soldiers and lancers stood gathered on the beach, ready to launch their assault as soon as Hafrir finished their assault on the city walls.

Liviana scanned the armada just beyond the Pearl Spire one more time. Her eyes narrowed. "They've raised their sails. Why? Svend, what's going on?"

Svend shrugged.

Liviana clasped her hands behind her back, her black cape tugging in the wind. "They're coming this way," she hissed. "They should have already been in the harbor by the time we got here. They're not going to the harbor, are they?" *Is everyone but me completely incompetent?* Liviana unsheathed Xalos and aimed the colossal sword at Svend. "Tell me what's going on, Svend. Tell me now before I slice open your throat!"

Svend lifted up his hands in confusion, then implored Liviana to calm down as best as he could with his limited grasp of the Vaazian language. He pulled out a small bronze tube from his pocket and pressed his eye to it. He cursed in Haf.

"What is that?" Liviana lowered her sword.

Svend handed her the device. "Telescope."

Liviana looked in the telescope and scanned the boats on the horizon. They were swarming with sailors as they approached, and... *Is that...Oyza? It can't be. How did she get there? Gods!* She handed the trinket back to Svend, fuming. "It's a mutiny," she said coldly. "And Oyza." She walked to the other side of the ship and looked at the army gathered on the beach. "Signal to Sir Yirig he is to begin the assault immediately. There will be no bombardment of the city, but we have enough men."

A commander nodded and dashed away.

Liviana waited for a moment, gauging the situation. She turned to one of her officers. "Prepare our ships in defensive formation. We will ram and sink them before they get too close to the shore. I want oars, and I want them now. Don't let anything through. Prepare our archers." Liviana walked back to the center of the deck, surrounded by sailors awaiting orders. She lifted Xalos high above her head. Its ruby-tipped hilt gleamed in the morning sun. "Men of the Empire, prepare for battle!"

❧❦❧

"Here they come!" Jarus shouted from atop the wall.

Legions of Parthassian soldiers charged across the sand. They wore heavy black and bronze plate mail and carried long spears and halberds.

"Arrows!"

Behind him, rows of rangers, soldiers, and anyone who could fire an arrow stood ready with long bows.

"Get ready!"

They lit the ends of their arrows.

"Fire!"

A torrent of flaming shots sailed over the wall, landing in the ranks of soldiers. Fires shot in all directions as smoke billowed in the air.

"It's working," Jarus said to his brother.

Gaspar wore shining blue mail emblazoned with the Trident on the front. Earlier that day, they had soaked parts of the sand with flammable oils. The enemy soldiers panicked as flames shot up around them. They scattered toward the entrance as fast as they could.

Gaspar stroked his chin. "These are not lancers, not even soldiers. Just squires sent to die, to test our defenses."

Men and women atop the wall shot arrows while Parthassian soldiers ran through the opened gate.

"Now!" Jarus said.

A moment later, an explosion ricocheted across the beach, so strong it nearly knocked Jarus to his feet. The top of the gate crumbled to pieces, crashing down on the Parthassian soldiers crammed underneath. They wailed as rock crushed flesh and bones.

"It worked! Broyva did it!" He patted his brother's shoulder. "It worked!"

Gaspar smiled cautiously.

"Rangers, to me!" Jarus ran down the staircase.

Parthassian soldiers were trapped between a wall of glaives and a mountain of smoking rubble. They clashed at the gate, blades ringing as men and women screamed. A moment later, Jarus lifted his glaive high, and with one strike, the last Parthassian soldier fell to the ground amid a stack of bodies covered in blood. Flies already buzzed about their soon-to-be-rotting corpses. The scent of blood and burning flesh mixed with the salty breeze from the sea.

The Ungoverned cheered, raising their weapons high in the sky. Jarus lifted his glaive in triumph. "Too easy!" He wiped a splash of blood from his chin. He smiled, exuberant from the high of an early victory. *But Gaspar is right. They're only testing us.*

"Fleeing, Jarus, they've all fled!" a woman yelled from atop the wall. She was armed with a long bow and surrounded by rangers wearing studded leather jerkins. "But they'll be back. They didn't send very many that time."

Jarus shifted his attention toward the sea. *Still no firing from the fleet.* Clouds of gray smoke hung in the air. The way into the city was sealed by piles of jagged rocks and crumbled bricks.

Someone atop the wall pointed at the sea. "They're leaving!"

"What's going on?" Jarus asked, climbing a flight of steps.

"The Parthassian warships!" one of them replied. "And...the fleet from Hafrir, they're coming right for them!"

Jarus's eyes grew wide. *Maybe they pulled it off? Fuck me, did they really do it?* He smirked at Gaspar and patted his shoulder. "Oyza, eh? Maybe she really did it, Brother?"

Gaspar raised his chin. His clean armor sparkled in the morning sun. "I'll believe it when I see it. For now, let's not get distracted. Rangers, get in formation! To your posts! Today, we fight until the last man, until the last woman, until every single one of those Parthassian scum lays dead in the sand!"

Jarus ascended to the peak and hoisted his glaive. "Ungoverned, this is our day! For I shall bow to no one!"

"And none shall bow to me!" the rangers shouted in unison.

Jarus gazed out over the sea at the Haf boats beyond the Pearl Spire. A breeze tugged at the hair falling beside his face and carried the odor of smoke, salt, and dried seaweed. *Oyza, Teresa, Yars...may the Gods watch over you.*

❧❦❧

Liviana stood on the side of her ship, watching the battle, muttering invectives under her breath. She watched helplessly as her men were crushed under stone and burned alive. She sent a scowl in Svend's direction as a strong wind gusted at her face. "Do I have to do everything?" She made her way to the center of the deck. "Stop our ship from turning. I want you to fire all of our cannons at that pile of rubble. Make a clearing for our men to breach. The catapults won't be enough. Waste no shots in the city. Fire everything we've got at the wall. Understood?"

The commander looked away. "We don't have much ammunition. We might need it for our attack—"

Liviana glared at him. The man nodded and ran.

A messenger ran up to Liviana and knelt before her. "Commander, I have urgent news from Sir Yirig. He says you must fire on the gate now—"

"Good. He and I always think alike. Come with me." She walked past the man. "Watch."

Beneath the deck, men shouted orders. Cannons sent booms reverberating across the beach. Explosions pounded at the pile of debris, huge chunks of rock scattering onto the beach.

Liviana raised her chin, an endless ensemble of blasts echoing over the sand. "You see. *This* is power."

The messenger's mouth gaped open.

"Look," Liviana said a few minutes later, pointing to the left side of the beach where the Parthassians were camped. Lines of catapults began to fire in succession, sending flaming rocks across the sky to land at the gate. Red streaks arced across the battlefield.

"Tell our flag men to signal to Sir Yirig to begin the full assault now," Liviana said, a half-smug expression on her face. "We will snuff them out quickly."

The messenger nodded and ran off.

Liviana pulled out the telescope Svend had given her and pressed her eye up against it. The Haf ships were closing in, their sails raised, pushed by the morning winds. Liviana looked to her left and then to her right. On each side, rows of Parthassian warships lined up for battle.

"You knew the whole time, didn't you, Svend?" She refused to so much as glance at him. *Gods, I should have known.* She unsheathed Xalos.

"Liviana, no—Alden, I cannot tell him—" he began.

Liviana lopped off his head.

"Fool. I should have never trusted you." She pushed Svend's body into the ocean but left his head rolling on the deck. "Admiral, come here."

An older man with hardy eyes walked up beside her, nervously pretending not to notice the conspicuously severed cranium. Liviana handed him the telescope. He pressed his eyes up against it.

"They'll be here any minute. The wind works against us. Can we build enough strength to ram?" Liviana asked.

"Absolutely," the admiral said. "We outnumber them two to one, but they have cannons on each ship, while we've only got them on three. We'll need to ram them head-on to avoid exposing our sides to their cannons, though they have some forward-facing guns too."

Liviana clasped her hands behind her back. "I wouldn't worry about their cannons, Admiral. They'll want to save them to fire on the shore. If we can keep them far away, they won't have a good shot. And they haven't got much ammunition left anyway, if Svend told the truth. Their men are weak and tired. This should be an easy victory."

"Indeed." The admiral's eyes flickered to the blood-squirting and unhinged skull.

"And one more thing. Aim our ship straight at their flagship. I wish to board it personally," Liviana added.

"Of course, Commander." With a bow, the admiral turned and left.

Liviana eyed the approaching fleet, squinting as a cool breeze tugged at her hair. She placed her hand on the hilt of Xalos. *I will avenge you, Father, if it's the last thing I do. And I will kill Oyza Serazar.*

🐉

"The firing stopped." Jarus still covered the back of his neck with his hands. He rubbed away a layer of dust that had fallen from the ceiling of the old house where he and the rangers had sought cover from the blasts. "Come on, let's go." He sprang to his feet and ran outside, kicking open a creaky door on rusted hinges.

They gathered by the entrance, black smoke stinging their eyes and burning their lungs. There was hardly anything left, only craters in the sand where the mound of rubble once lay.

"It's over," one of them said. "We can't defend this now. There's nothing to hold them in..."

"No, no—it's not. We'll move to the backup plan," Jarus said.

Gaspar nodded. "Carts, wagons! Get the barricade up, now!"

"Come on!" Jarus grabbed a barrel and rolled it in one of the blast holes. Others did the same, pulling crates, boxes, barrels, and all sorts of junk from wagons and throwing it at the gate.

"Incoming!" one of the archers on the wall warned. "Take cover!"

Jarus looked up as a flaming stone streaked across the sky and landed on a house and exploded. "Catapults!" Jarus grimaced and detached a wagon from a horse. He and three others pushed it toward the rubble. "Come on! Just a little more." Beads of sweat dripped from his forehead.

"Cover! Incoming!" an archer on the wall cried.

Jarus plummeted to the ground, his face digging into the sand and dust. Three fiery rocks landed farther in the city, two of them crashing into houses, while a third landed near Gaspar, crushing two nearby rangers and igniting their bodies. They screamed as booms resounded through the empty city.

Fuck! Jarus jumped to his feet. He cleaned dust from his eyes.

"We have to pull back to the palace!" one of the Ungoverned said. "We can't defend the walls!"

"No!" Gaspar shouted. "Not all of us. We need archers on the walls. We'll have to leave them, try and keep a lookout for the catapults as best as possible."

Another flaming projectile landed in the city, blasting into an abandoned home and exploding it to bits. Plumes of smoke billowed into the sky.

"Army approaching!" the archers howled. "Ladders too!"

Jarus took a moment to calm himself. He climbed up the stairs to the top of the wall and picked up a longbow. "Prepare for battle, rangers!" he said amid deafening cheers and applause. "We fight for the Ungoverned! We fight to the end, until the last ranger!"

And we fight for Oyza. He glanced at the sea one last time.

❧❦

Oyza stood on the deck as sailors scrambled around her to load their muskets and pistols. They were low on ammunition, Hjan had told her, so many of them armed themselves with whatever they had left: crossbows, pikes, swords, and shields. Oyza loaded her pistol and clutched her father's mageware sword at her side. She looked up at the unfurled sails as strong winds propelled them toward the enemy fleet. The ships tore into the waters and sprayed cool mists of sea salt into the air.

"We're getting close." Yars's curly hair blew in the breeze. He fidgeted with a curved cutlass in his right hand and a round buckler in his left. The buckler was decorated with an intricate pattern of interlacing emeralds. He kept Gaspar's mageware dagger tucked behind his belt.

"Look, behind the ships, smoke rises from the city." Teresa gestured.

"I wonder what's going on." Oyza gazed into the distance, unable to see the coast clearly behind the wall of Parthassian warships.

"There are so many," Teresa said, her voice shaky. She was armed with a long Haf rapier and iron shield.

Oyza clutched her pistol tighter as knots formed in her stomach.

"But we've got cannons," Yars said.

Oyza shook her head. "We have to save our shots for the armies on the beach. It's the only way any of us will survive."

"Do you feel ready to fight?" Teresa asked them both.

The question made Oyza more nervous than she wanted to admit. "Yars and I have been training with Jarus..."

"Doesn't matter anyway." Yars's mouth twisted into an uneasy grin. "No choice now."

Hjan pointed at the Parthassian fleet as Knutr, Kunnusta, and Fjorn walked up behind him, each armed with a long musket. "A lot," he said. "So many...so many ships..."

"They'll try to ram us." Teresa explained to Hjan with her hands as best she could. "We have to try and avoid them head-on."

Hjan nodded, then translated for the crew.

Oyza yanked at a loose thread on her sleeve. "At least these will be sailors, not lancers or soldiers." Her heart thumped as the boats came closer. She could see Parthassian sailors scrambling on board. Rows of oars lifted from the sea and crashed back down, pushing the line forward.

"We're close now." Yars licked his dry lips. "Any minute..."

Oyza peered at the oncoming ships. They were in such a tight formation, there was no space to navigate between them. They would have to take them head-on and try to avoid being rammed as best they could.

"We should take up our positions now," Teresa said.

Yars nodded.

"Let's go." Oyza ran to the back of the ship, where one of the mutineering sailors turned a steering wheel.

He smiled a large toothless grin full of delight.

"Take us between their ships as best as you can!" Oyza said.

The sailor nodded. "*Herif skirra hund*!" He beat his chest twice, then lifted his fist in the air.

"*Herif skirra hund*!" the rest of the sailors called out with raised fists.

Oyza cast Yars a confused glance.

"I think it means we're gonna win, Oyza. It means we're gonna fight and win!"

Hjan turned toward Oyza. "It means...we ready to...be killed."

Oyza gulped.

Teresa climbed atop a barrel and scanned the oncoming fleet. "We have to take cover, now!" She jumped down from the barrel.

"Hjan, can we fire these?" Oyza pointed at two cannons sitting atop the deck.

Hjan nodded. He gestured to Knutr, Kunnusta, and Fjorn, and the group descended to the floors underneath to grab cannonballs.

"Come on, over here." Teresa pointed her sword at crates and barrels near the middle of the deck.

Sailors had ducked behind them for cover, aiming muskets and crossbows outward. Others wielded long pikes or short swords and wooden bucklers inscribed with the sigil of Hafrir.

Oyza looked ahead at the Parthassian warships one last time as they crept closer, the rising sun eking above the mountains behind the city.

"Teresa, Yars, look—their ships are shorter than ours. Will they even be able to board?"

"They'll have ropes and ladders. One ship will try to ram in the front, while other ships on the sides will try to swarm our deck," Teresa said.

"Right." Oyza stood up one more time to get a look at the oncoming fleet.

Teresa was right: three boats approached theirs, while others fanned out, heading directly for the others. The ship heading straight for them veered off to the side.

"Look, that one—it's changed direction," Oyza said.

"But why?" Yars said.

Teresa scrunched her lips. "It's a Haf ship flying the Empire's sails."

They crouched behind a stack of barrels held together with coarse ropes. The wood felt scratchy and dry. It was the best protection they could find. Oyza sat with her back against one of the barrels, preparing her pistol. Yars sat next to her.

"Remember the last time we were on a ship?" Oyza clasped her seashell necklace.

Yars's lips curled into a half smile. "Captain Seralus."

Oyza reached out and grabbed his hand. "We're gonna make it through this time, Yars."

Yars nodded and smiled, leaning in to kiss the top of her head. "I know."

There was a moment of silence as the sails fluttered in the wind. Not even the gulls squawked anymore. Oyza's heart pounded as she tried to calm herself, closing her eyes and taking slow breaths. The Parthassian warships were only a moment away. She gazed down at her pistol, gripping its cold metal handle, then looked up at Yars.

"*Herif skirra hund?*" She tapped her chest twice.

Yars and Teresa gave nervous smiles. "*Herif skirra hund!*"

CHAPTER 39

"Ready...aim!" Jarus said to the rows of archers standing behind him atop the wall. He held his breath for a moment, the scent of smoke, salt, and metal filling his nostrils.

Lines of Parthassians approached, boots kicking up sand. Black and bronze armor sparkled in the warm light of the dawn. They were protected by huge rectangular boards of wood that blocked arrows.

"Incoming!" a ranger screamed as a streaking flame landed in the city, crashing through the cracked roof of an old forge and exploding the building to bits.

Jarus ducked to take cover. A whole row of houses burned as streams of black smoke spiraled into the sky. He turned again to face the beach and the oncoming soldiers. "Ready, again! Aim!" Jarus said as archers prepared their longbows. Jarus took a deep breath and slowed his heartbeat, assessing the distance as best as he could. "Fire!"

A torrent of arrows flew from the wall and arced across the sky, landing into the rows of oncoming fighters. They dropped as screams rang against the walls and blood soaked the sandy hills, but many arrows landed into the wooden boards.

"Again!" Jarus raised his glaive into the air. "Fire!"

Another cascade flew from the walls, gliding through the air and piercing the soldiers below. More cries echoed through the air, punctuated by the blaring of Parthassian warhorns.

"Keep firing!" Jarus yelled, his voice hoarse.

He scanned the battlefield. A column of soldiers approached the pile of debris filling the gate. They marched with large round shields held over their heads along the Coral Trail.

Gaspar walked up beside Jarus, chin high. "Ten ladders. No siege towers though."

Jarus eyed the approaching sea of black and bronze. Arrows continued to soar through the air around him. He turned to look back at the city, black smoke stinging his eyes. He stroked his jaw. "I have an idea."

Gaspar tightened his gloves and leaned in. "We're not going to be able to defend the wall very long. They have ladders, and our gate is already gone. I say we fire everything we can, then get out of here and pull back toward the palace like we originally planned. And with all the smoke and fire from the catapults, the traps we laid may be more effective anyway." Gaspar straightened his back, eyeing the approaching army as arrows zipped through the air. The ladders would be at the wall in less than a minute.

"Fine," Gaspar said. "I'll pull my men back to the palace. We'll get the riders ready for our attack when their lancers arrive. Fire everything you can, and get the hell out of here." He dashed down the steps.

Jarus went back to the edge of the wall as a Parthassian arrow ricocheted off the edge and nearly struck the side of his face. The ladders were close. "Rangers, listen to me! Pull back!" Jarus shouted. "Rangers, pull back!"

One of them turned to him with raised eyebrows. "Pull back? Already?"

"Yes! Finish your arrows then pull off the wall, and take up positions in the city as originally planned!"

Another arrow brushed up against Jarus's cheek and drew a trickle of blood. It stung. He wiped the blood with his sleeve and spat. The Parthassian soldiers below were raising their ladders to the walls as others made for the entrance.

"Come on! Pull back! Into the city! To your positions in the city!" He rallied his fighters and hopped down the stairs, running back and winding through streets permeated with hellfire and smoke. They had packed certain roads with debris and wreckage to try and funnel the Parthassians toward the palace where those on horseback armed with pistols and lances awaited orders to charge.

"This way!" Jarus ran as fast as he could down a smoldering alleyway past the Temple of the Starfish. They found protection inside an empty house.

"Upstairs—those of you with arrows left, take positions upstairs. On my signal, we'll set off our trap. Don't fire until after," Jarus ordered. He hunched and took his longbow off his back and nocked an arrow.

The others sat with him underneath a row of broken windows. The musty air was filled with specks of dust suspended in the morning sunbeams.

"They won't be long," Jarus said. "They'll break through the gate shortly. At least the catapults have stopped firing." His heart pounded. *Gods, if you're listening, we need your help now.*

The rangers nodded and nocked their arrows. Jarus wiped sweat from his forehead. Distant shouts rang through the streets. He peeked outside the window and looked at the upper stories of the house across the street. Rangers crouched in the windows and on the roof, their gray cloaks blending in with the solemn colors of the empty city. Thorny vines crawled up the broken walls as sturdy roots tore apart the cobblestone roads. Thin palm trees lined the edges. The approaching fighters howled war cries that echoed through the abandoned streets. Black pikes and halberds glimmered in the sun.

"Ready, everyone!" He gripped his bow with tense hands and aimed out the window. "Now!"

Outside, two rangers sat atop horses with long ropes attached to them. They kicked the horses' sides and flew down the street. The other ends of the ropes were attached to pillars underneath two empty buildings on opposite sides of the street. The ropes tightened and pulled the bottoms from the pillars. Stacks of stone collapsed into a cloud of dust.

Jarus held his breath. The buildings began to lean over the street. A moment later, they toppled over completely, burying the Empire's men in stone and dust. The buildings attached to them fell too, and within an instant, the entire street was little more than a lane of wreckage, ripped flesh, and blood.

The rangers cheered. Below, shrieks echoed as dust spewed into the air. Some began to dig themselves out of the rubble, while the soldiers standing behind froze.

"Fire!" Jarus released his arrow. It flew through the window and pierced a soldier's neck. A flurry of arrows zipped past him as more shots rained from the rooftops. "Now!" Jarus lifted his glaive and charged into the streets.

The rangers roared as they dashed into the roads. Jarus charged and thrust one side of his glaive into a soldier's waist as it sliced through his armor. A fountain of blood poured as the soldier wailed in terror. He dropped his pike and reached for the short sword hanging from his waist. Jarus pulled the glaive out and, in a frenzy of flashing metal, sliced the enemy's neck. Blood splattered all over Jarus.

More rangers dashed into the narrow streets and fought atop the mountain of rubble. Jarus sliced his glaive into another soldier's face as an arrow from above pierced the back of another. A Parthassian pike stabbed a ranger's side as the man screamed and reached for the wound, blood leaking between his fingers. The soldier aimed his pike at Jarus and stabbed repeatedly. Jarus deflected with his glaive before another ranger dove forward and plunged his sword into the soldier's knee. The man keeled over and dropped his pike. An arrow from above sprouted from the enemy soldier's shoulder.

"Great shot!" Jarus said to the ranger, smiling and wiping blood from his cheek.

The air stunk of dust, metal, sweat, and blood. Jarus surged forward with his glaive in a whirlwind of flashes and glimmers that struck down the

Parthassians before they even had a chance to respond, struggling to maneuver their pikes against the nimble rangers. Some of them dropped their spears and charged with swords. Metal clashed against metal, and cries of anguish filled the air as limbs were cut loose and bodies were gutted on both sides.

"Drive them into the sea!" Jarus led a column of rangers forward, slicing through Parthassians as arrows fell from above. He turned into an alleyway to catch his breath.

Above, rangers hopped across the rooftops, cloaks fluttering in the wind.

Jarus grinned, sweat and dust mixing into his blood-stained teeth. "Onward, Ungoverned! Onward until we win the day!"

<hr />

Booms rocked the hull as cannons fired into the warships just beside them. The blasts tore through the side of the boat, sending bits of wood and metal flying into the air as sailors shrieked and fell into the sea. Oyza felt a mist of water cool her skin. A torrent of flaming arrows landed on the deck.

"Fuck." Yars covered his head. "Fire!"

More fire arrows tore into the folds of the sails.

"Look!" Teresa pointed to the edge.

Three ladders fell onto the sides of the ship as Parthassian sailors headed for the deck. Oyza shared a nervous glance with Yars as the harsh scent of smoke infused the air.

Haf sailors let out a ferocious battle cry. They sprang to their feet and ran to the edge, weapons drawn and gleaming in the bright morning sunlight. "*Herif skirra hund!*"

A Haf sailor leaned forward and aimed his musket at an approaching Parthassian sailor. He fired. The sailor tumbled into the sea. A flaming arrow shot into his face, igniting his clothing as the man screamed. Flurries of arrows soared as everyone took cover. One of the sails already smoked.

"This ship's going to burn!" Teresa yelled as a sailor shot a musket at a charging Parthassian. "Come on!" She leaped to her feet and dashed toward an oncoming sailor with her rapier drawn.

"Let's do it!" Yars said to Oyza.

They jumped and ran to the deck, swords drawn, howling as they charged the Parthassian sailors. Teresa clashed with a sailor —a strong one with fierce dark eyes bent on death—her sword crashing into his black shield. The sailor took a swipe at Teresa, the edge of his blade barely missing her neck. Teresa plunged her sword into the sailor's stomach as he wailed. His blood spilled like a waterfall onto the deck.

Yars ran up behind her, eyes wide. "Are you all right?" He raised his shield and watched the sky for arrows.

An arrow whizzed past Teresa's arm and landed in a barrel. She lifted her sword, preparing to strike another Parthassian sailor diving onto the boat. The sailor charged at her, but Yars darted forward, swinging his sword as it banged into a shield. Teresa was turning to thrust her sword into another sailor when a shot from a musket tore through the man's armor and knocked his body into the sea.

Oyza ran to Yars, who struggled with a Parthassian sailor. She jabbed her sword at the sailor over and over. Her thrusts were deflected one after the other. Yars leaned in, thrusting the tip of his sword into the man's belly in a surprise attack. The sailor keeled over as blood trickled out of his wound. He launched one last desperate swipe at Oyza before she kicked him. He fell over the edge and crashed into the waves.

"Great job!" Yars shouted with a grin.

Oyza nodded, clasping her sword and muscles tense. *Gods, I should have practiced more with Jarus.* She wiped away a trickle of sweat from her forehead with the back of her hand, then coughed from the black smoke spewing from the flaming sails. "Watch out! More are coming!" she said.

"What do we do if the ship catches fire?" Yars asked.

"I don't know." Oyza gnashed her teeth and looked up at the sails. Fire devoured them. Haf sailors scrambled for buckets of water. Two more Parthassian sailors climbed the ladders and rushed toward Oyza and Yars. Two shouting Haf sailors with long pikes ran past them. The Parthassian sailors knocked the ends of the pikes out of their way and aimed their swords at Oyza and Yars, shouting war cries as a torrent of flaming arrows glided in the air behind them. Booms shook the floor beneath them.

"Watch out!" Oyza cried.

Yars lifted his shield as the two Haf sailors dropped their long pikes and reached for short swords at their waists. One of them was too slow—the Parthassian sailor drove his sword into the man's flesh once, twice, a third time, as blood leaked onto the deck and the man fell over, screaming and reaching for his gaping wounds. Oyza and Yars rushed the Parthassian fighters as the second Haf sailor lifted his sword high over his head and prepared to swing it. A bolt from a crossbow landed in the center of the

Haf's chest with a loud thud, sending him stumbling. More Parthassian sailors climbed the ladders.

Oyza glimpsed over the boat's edge. The Haf fleet was burning everywhere. Flames leaped as black clouds buried their decks. Parthassian warships rammed into others as sailors jumped in the water. The sounds of cracking wood and booming cannons rang across the surface of the sea. She felt her muscles tighten when she saw a Parthassian sailor aiming a crossbow at Teresa. Without thinking, she reached for her gun and fired at the sailor from across the deck.

Teresa turned and saw the man drop. "Great shot!" she said, out of breath.

Hjan called out to her. He pointed at a ship across from them. It was sinking. Water gushed into its cracked hull where two Parthassian warships had rammed it. Fire arrows caught its sails on fire. Haf sailors leaped into the water, some firing crossbows and muskets at the Parthassians in a last-ditch effort to kill as many as they could. They thrashed in the foamy water, grabbing at barrels and fragments of wood.

A blast rocked their vessel. Oyza and Yars fell to their feet, skin scraping against rough wood. Teresa and Hjan screamed as they stumbled, reaching for anything they could, and toppled over the edge.

Oyza lifted her head and shook dust from her hair. "Where did that come from?"

"Over there!" He pointed to a massive ship approaching theirs.

"Wait, where is Teresa? Hjan?" Oyza ducked to avoid two Hawk and Tower sailors fighting with Haf mutineers next to her.

"I don't know." Yars frantically looked around the deck.

Haf sailors cheered as they chased away the last of the Parthassians. "*Herif skirra hund!*"

"I think we held them off for now," Yars said.

"For now." Oyza eyed the colossal boat remaining.

They kicked away the ladders, then scanned the waters for Teresa and Hjan. Bloodied corpses littered the bay as sailors thrashed in the water. Smoldering pieces of wood dotted the waves.

Yars's eyes grew wide. "Look! That looks like Teresa and Hjan."

Oyza squinted. "They're headed for that other Haf ship." She indicated one not yet in battle with any Parthassians.

"They'll be all right then."

"I hope so." She looked up at the burning sails, then paused to examine the giant ship heading straight for them.

Yars gulped. Haf sailors reloaded their muskets and crossbows and prepared for the next assault, hiding behind whatever they could find on the blood-drenched deck.

Oyza's hands quivered a little as the Parthassian monster inched closer. *I have a bad feeling about this one.*

"Take cover!" Jarus dove into an alleyway.

Another projectile fell into the city, landing in a gap between two houses and sending shrapnel in all directions. Another soared above him and crashed into a two-story house as those on top plummeted into an inferno.

"Watch for the catapults!" Jarus shouted to the archers above. "Ungoverned!" He rallied his troops and charged the Parthassians.

They clashed, banging iron swords against wooden shields, slicing limbs and drenching the dusty road with blood. Their screams resounded off the walls and through the narrow streets as more artillery flung into the city, burning houses and buildings everywhere.

"Lancers!" one of the archers standing atop a roof shouted to Jarus. "Up ahead, they said lancers are coming! Jarus, take cover!"

Three Parthassian soldiers appeared behind the archer as one of them drove a black sword through the ranger's heart. His body twitched and fell from the roof onto the brawl underneath.

Jarus dashed into a narrow alleyway, a blaze burning his skin. "Call our riders! Now! Get my brother and his men out here!"

A contingent of rangers ran toward the palace. Jarus slowed to catch his breath, leaning over his knees to breathe as much fresh air as he could. He ran back to the bout only to find black and bronze swords carving through Ungoverned and heading straight toward him. The ground began to shake. He heard a distant rumble.

"Rooftops! Get on the rooftops!"

The rangers funneled into empty houses, gray cloaks flapping behind them as they ran up steps to the roofs. Jarus climbed a winding staircase in a house caked with cobwebs and rotted wood before crawling through a hole to the ceiling. A strong gust blew atop the roof and tugged at his hair. He turned his gaze to the streets below. Fires engulfed the city. Parthassians hung their flags from the walls, and throngs of crossbowmen stood guard atop. At sea, smoke and fire shrouded ships with broken hulls sinking into the water.

Jarus ducked behind a crumbled chimney and readied his bow to fire on the lancers. But from the opposite side, Gaspar and his men swept through the streets on horseback, their blue armor sparkling in the sun. Their blades sliced through ranks of Parthassian men. Jarus cheered as he and his fighters began to leap from rooftop to rooftop, cloaks flying in the wind. They watched as the Ungoverned horsemen rushed through the narrow roads, slashing Parthassians down as they made their way toward the wall.

"Come on!" Jarus shouted to the rangers on the rooftops, his hair fluttering. "To the walls!"

They hopped across rooftops back to the wall. A monstrous column of Parthassian lancers stampeded through the gate.

Jarus felt his lip tremble. He lifted his arm to aim his bow, then turned his head toward the sea. *Come on, Oyza...*

CHAPTER 40

Oyza clutched her sword as the Parthassian ship approached. Black smoke burned her lungs. She looked up and saw their sails were little more than smoldering embers.

Yars gulped and grabbed her hand. He twisted his neck and peeked above the barrels. "This is it." Yars grabbed a coil of rope. "It's about to collide with us!"

They braced themselves as the ships slammed into each other. A loud crash rocked through the air as wood crunched beneath them. Oyza held her breath. Shouts rang across the deck. Sailors leaped aboard. Haf mutineers charged at them, swords and shields held high. Knutr and Fjorn sat near Oyza and Yars, armed with long muskets. They each took aim and fired. Two Parthassian sailors fell, bullets piercing their chests and knocking their bodies over the edge. Swords banged into bucklers and pikes tore through flesh as sailors cried out.

Oyza swallowed. "Ready?"

Yars gave a nervous nod.

Oyza gazed at a lone gull circling in the sky. "For the Ungoverned?" she asked, raising her sword.

"For the Ungoverned!" Yars shouted, his black curls dripping with sweat.

They leaped from behind the barrels and dove into the brawl, hacking and slashing at the Parthassian sailors leaping onto their ship. An arrow grazed Oyza's arm and left a trail of blood. She wiped the stinging wound with her sleeve, then blocked a blow with her sword. Another sailor swung his blade high.

"Gotcha!" Yars plunged his sword into the sailor's stomach.

A stream of blood fell onto the deck. Another sailor charged at Oyza with two gleaming black swords.

"Watch out!" Yars tried to make his way to Oyza.

The sailor launched a flurry of strikes at Oyza—up, down, across her face, then right at her heart. She sidestepped at the last moment, the blade swiping just past her cheek. The sailor hurled his elbow into Oyza's face as she stumbled, boots thumping against the deck. She caught herself against the railing, coughing in the bitter smoke. The sailor launched again, swords raised high above his head. He let out a howl that sent chills up Oyza's spine. She fumbled for her pistol with sweaty fingers and shaking arms. She dropped it.

"Damn!" She watched the pistol splash into the water. She turned back to the sailor and readied her sword.

The sailor froze as a bullet ripped into his neck and a stream of blood sprayed in all directions. His swords rattled onto the deck as he clutched at his neck.

Oyza looked across the deck and saw Knutr smiling at her, musket still aimed at the dying sailor. Knutr was beginning to load another shot when a bolt popped through a plume of smoke and slammed into his face, knocking him back.

Oyza ran across the deck to the sailor who fired the shot. Oyza jabbed her sword and struck a blow at his arm. She pierced his gut as the man writhed.

Yars placed his hands on his knees to catch his breath. He ran his fingers through his hair and coughed.

"Come on." Oyza ran behind a stack of crates.

She and Yars huddled next to Knutr. His face was white.

"He's dead." Yars said.

Oyza closed Knutr's eyes and covered his face with a rag, then picked up his musket. It was heavier than her pistol, but its metal handle felt just as smooth and cool. "Bullets. Where are the bullets?"

Yars frantically searched the deck for bullets on his hands and knees. "I can't find any!"

Oyza sat the musket back down and helped him search but couldn't find bullets either. She wiped sweat from her stinging eyes, then peeked above the crates. She saw Kunnusta, Fjorn, and other Haf sailors trading blows across the deck. She scanned the Parthassian boat next to theirs. A knot formed in her throat. *It can't be. It just can't be.* A sparkle of red light caught her eye.

"She's here." Oyza said.

Yars's eyebrows rose. "Who?" He peeked his eyes above the crates and squinted through a heavy plume of smoke.

Oyza clutched the musket. "Liviana. She's here."

❦

Jarus aimed his last arrow. *Slow, steady, stay calm.*

A droplet of sweat fell from his forehead. The ground rumbled with Parthassian lancers charging toward the Ungoverned riders.

Steady now... Jarus glanced below as the horsemen surged through the narrow streets.

Parthassians in chain mail on the wall loaded crossbows and prepared to fire.

Deep breath... He glanced to his sides across the rooftops, nodding at the rangers who squatted with longbows pointed and arrows nocked.

The lancers tore through the wreckage in the way, their lances gleaming. Jarus could see the Hawk and Tower sigil painted in gold on their shields.

"Now!" he shouted.

A flurry of arrows soared toward the Parthassian lancers. Nothing seemed to happen. Jarus frowned and loaded another arrow. The lancers charged into the city and pummeled into rows of Ungoverned cavalry as lances banged into shields, swords pierced through metal, and gunshots echoed against the walls. Parthassian crossbowmen fired on the Ungoverned from atop the wall.

Jarus gritted his teeth. "Fire what you've got left, then come with me! We've got to clear the walls of those crossbowmen!"

They let loose another torrent of arrows as Jarus ran from the rooftop and headed back down the steps. Gunshots burst from both sides. The streets were drenched with blood. Horses whinnied.

Jarus signaled to those behind him to follow. They took off running through the narrow lanes, weaving in and out of abandoned alleyways buried in smoke.

"Almost there," Jarus said as they darted into another alleyway. "Here." He crouched behind an old wagon and peered out at the skirmish, pausing for a moment to catch his breath. His lungs burned. "There, on the other side, we can find a way up to the wall."

The rangers nodded.

"But we'll have to make it across the battle. Waste no time engaging. Get past the horses as fast as we can, and get up the wall. Got it?"

"Got it," one of them replied.

Jarus took another breath and waited a long moment, the noise of the fight seeming louder and louder. "Now!" he shouted.

They rushed into the streets. He lowered his head and dashed through the clashing lancers and horsemen, swords and axes thrusting into shields above him and bursting to pieces. He almost gagged at the scent of blood, horses, and burning flesh. A spiked mace fell in his direction and nearly lopped off his ear before he ducked.

Blood leaked from the wounds of a panicked horse. It reared, the Parthassian soldier on top struggling to keep his balance, slashing his sword against an Ungoverned shield. Jarus tumbled to his feet to dodge the blow, then rolled over on his other side before the horse's hooves could crush him.

Another ranger was hurrying to help him up when a bullet burst through her shoulder.

"Come on!" Jarus helped the ranger to her feet.

The end of a lance flew at him. An Ungoverned horseman blocked the blow with his wooden shield. The shield exploded, the force of the lance too much for it. Fractured wood and metal showered into Jarus's hair.

"Go!" The horseman thrust his blade at the Parthassian lancer.

The sword rattled against bronze armor, slicing through a weak spot around the neck. Droplets of blood sprayed onto Jarus.

He wiped the blood from his eyes and gestured to the rangers behind him to follow. "Come on! We're almost there!"

They ran across the cobblestone street, careful to avoid roots between the stones. They had reached the steps when three Parthassians lancers barreled toward them, riding like boulders tumbling down the side of a mountain. The ground shook.

"Watch out!" Jarus evaded one of the lances, jumping toward the wall and sliding his body against the ground.

A ranger shrieked as a lance pierced his chest and lifted his body from the ground. His feet dragged against the ground as his guts spilled out and his torso shredded. Two Ungoverned horsemen smashed into the Parthassian lancers and flung their swords into them.

Jarus jumped up the stairs. He paused just before reaching the top and crouched with the rest. "We go in fast. We go in hard. Throw them from the wall. Got it?"

The rangers drew their swords and glaives.

"Let's go! For the Ungoverned!"

A crouching Parthassian soldier with a round helmet aimed a crossbow. Jarus pushed him off the wall. The man squealed as his body tumbled into the brawl.

Jarus ran down the wall and pushed crossbowmen from the wall or sliced them down with his glaive. "Keep going!" he shouted as the rangers took off in both directions.

They knocked down ladders as they passed, cracking open throats and plunging bodies to the ground on the way. They ran almost to the end of the wall and stood near where the gate had once been. Heavily-armored soldiers with broadswords stood in formation. They carried huge shields emblazoned with bronze towers.

These aren't ordinary soldiers... Those shields... Is this Liviana's guard? Jarus looked around, then stared straight ahead at one guard who stood taller than the rest. A large ax sat at the man's side. *Is that Sir Yirig? Does this mean Liviana is here too?*

The towering knight smiled and pulled his ax from his belt. In the other hand, he held a round shield emblazoned with a golden tower.

Jarus narrowed his eyes and clutched his glaive. He scanned for weak points in the armor. His heart pounded. *Under the arm, perhaps? Or maybe just above the waist. No, the neck—that's the only place I'll get him.*

He glanced at the battle beneath the wall. Parthassian lancers had pushed far into the city as the Ungoverned riders withdrew. He gazed out at sea. The bay was filled with sinking ships, fire and black smoke. *Come on, Oyza...*

Sir Yirig stepped forward and grinned. He threw his shield from the wall and lifted his ax. "Don't need it," he said in a cool voice. "Not for you."

Steady... Jarus wiped a trickle of sweat from his chin, never taking his eyes off the knight. He held his glaive with tired arms. "Ungoverned! Are you ready?"

The Ungoverned hoisted their weapons.

Sir Yirig took another step forward, ready with his giant ax. He lunged, slashing at Jarus over and over. Jarus ducked and deflected, the sun glinting off his constantly-moving glaive.

The rangers charged at the Iron Towers, swords drawn as battle cries echoed across the wall.

Jarus lifted his glaive high and swiped at Sir Yirig three times, missing every time as the knight evaded. Yirig flew forward, hacking at Jarus with his ax. Jarus blocked the blows. A ranger next to him fell with a shriek as one of the knights pierced his blade straight through her chest, sending the woman toppling over the wall.

Jarus clenched his jaw. He came at Sir Yirig in a wild flurry of jabs, aiming at the throat. Sir Yirig blocked the assault with his ax, deflecting the blows one after the other as Jarus fumed. He turned red and lunged, jabbing and hacking with his glaive in a frenzy.

Sir Yirig dodged the attacks, but one swipe went right against his cheek, drawing blood. "You stupid fuck," he hissed. He swung in retaliation with his ax.

Jarus stumbled. When Sir Yirig let his guard down, he sliced his glaive upward and hit the knight's jaw, drawing more blood.

Sir Yirig cursed, hacking with his ax again in a frenzy.

Jarus slipped, catching his balance right at the edge of the wall.

Sir Yirig lifted his ax, slamming into Jarus's glaive.

After three blows, the glaive split in half. Jarus stumbled and held a side of his glaive in each hand. He lunged at Yirig with both blades, crashing in a crazed fury as Sir Yirig wavered. Jarus stepped back. He took a moment to catch his breath as rangers clashed with the Iron Towers around him.

Sir Yirig grinned and spat. "So the brat of Liorus knows how to fight?"

Jarus's eyes grew wide. He bit his tongue. *How does he...?*

"Yeah, I know who you are. We've got spies everywhere, kid. We know you're going to die here. *You* know you're going to die here," Sir Yirig said.

Spies? Jarus froze and wiped more sweat from his forehead. "You won't win. The Ungoverned, we fight for something higher, something you can't understand." He spat.

Sir Yirig scoffed and readied his ax. "We'll see about that, boy."

Fear gripped Jarus, fear like he'd never known before. He couldn't look, couldn't take his eyes of the mountain of a man bearing down on him. But his heart was out at sea, past the legions of Parthassians amassed on the beach. *Come on, Oyza, Teresa, Yars...we need you...*

❀❦❀

Teresa and Hjan grabbed dangling ropes and climbed up the side of the Haf ship, water dripping from their soaked cloaks. Mutineering sailors cheered as they reached the deck.

"We did it!" Teresa kissed Hjan on the cheek.

They both shook their bodies to remove water. Hjan spoke to the armed sailors in Haf as Teresa assessed the situation around them. They had not yet engaged the Parthassians. Two Parthassian ships had rammed a Haf boat near them. Water poured through giant holes as the hull lifted into the air. The cracking of muskets ricocheted off the surface of the ocean. Sailors plunged into the sea.

Haf sailors handed Hjan and Teresa swords and shields as Teresa called Hjan toward the edge. "If we can turn that way," —she indicated a wisp of smoke between two ships— "we can get close to the shore."

Hjan stroked his blond beard and nodded.

Teresa turned toward him. "Do you understand me?"

Hjan smiled. "Yes."

A strong wind blew away the smoke between the ships. Teresa's stomach sank. Beyond the opening, three, colossal Parthassian warships blocked the path to the beach. They sat just at the base of the Pearl Spire.

Teresa frowned as her hair fluttered in the gust. Hjan lowered his eyes. Their white sails roared as a flock of gulls struggled in the wind. Teresa looked again at the gigantic vessels between them and victory, then up at the Pearl Spire.

"Wait." She pulled her headband tight. "I have an idea."

❀❦❀

White gulls pecked on the deck at burning dead bodies.

"She's here for me, I know it." Oyza slouched behind the stack of crates.

"How could you know that?" Yars asked.

Oyza turned to peek above the crates. She saw Liviana step onto the deck.

Yars grabbed her hand. "We beat her before—we'll do it again." He flicked sweat-soaked curls from his eyes.

Oyza's eyes stung. "You're right, we can do this."

Yars sprang to his feet and raised his sword in the air. He and Oyza charged onto the deck, boots thudding through a cloud of acrid smoke. Their swords clashed with the blades wielded by Parthassian sailors as blasts rocked the hull, shaking the floorboards and sending more fire into the air.

Oyza wiped her eyes and tried to see beyond the smoke to find where Liviana was. "She's gone." Oyza parried a swift jab, then saw more sailors climbing aboard the ship, pushing back Haf mutineers. Her eyes grew wide. "Run!" she screamed. "We can't hold them here any longer." A bolt whipped past her arm and slammed into a barrel.

Yars ducked and slashed a man's knee. He turned to Oyza and nodded.

They ran through the smoke and entered the doorway to the cabin. Kunnusta, Fjorn, and more Haf sailors followed.

Oyza ran to the cannons, hands covering her ears to block the deafening booms. "We should fire everything we've got left at them!" she shouted to the sailors.

They loaded another round of shots as the Parthassians just next to them did the same.

Oyza's heart pounded as the heat from fires burned her skin. "Hurry!" She lifted a cannonball and carried it to a sailor.

She looked out the window and saw the Parthassians preparing to fire. A Haf sailor shouted a command, his voice harsh and bitter.

A blast tore into their hull as explosions fired in the opposite direction. It knocked over Oyza and Yars. They tumbled into shards of wood and metal. Oyza's ears rang. Her face scraped against the wood. She crawled to her knees, wiping dust from her face as more blasts exploded from both boats. Bloodcurdling screams pierced the smoke.

"We gotta get outta here," Yars said as flames engulfed the floor.

Bodies lay strewn about spattered with blood and scrapes. Oyza peered through one of the openings and saw the Parthassian warship burning as bodies fell into the sea.

Oyza's heart raced as she heard footsteps above. She clenched her jaw.

"Oyza!" Fjorn shouted, wiping dust and wood from his hair. Kunnusta stood next to him, a nervous sweat drenching his forehead.

"Let's go!" Oyza grabbed Yars's hand and pulled him deeper into the ship.

The surviving Haf sailers followed. Kunnusta jumped in front and led them to a room with a small hearth at one end. Pots and pans hung from the ceiling. Crates packed with apples and bags of flour sat on one side of the room. On the other end was another door. Kunnusta shut the door behind them, locked it, and threw a frightened glance in Oyza's direction.

Parthassian sailors pounded on the door.

"We have to run." Yars's eyes were so wide, Oyza could see the whites all around them.

They ran to the next door as three Parthassian soldiers burst in. Fjorn and another Haf sailor let out grisly cries and dashed toward the Parthassians, swords flying as they clashed against Parthassian shields. Fjorn lifted his sword high, knocking off a row of pots and pans toward the sailors. He aimed for a sailor's throat, then screamed as the end of a long pike struck his side. His sword fell from his hand as the pike pierced through his body. The terror of death seized his eyes. He gripped the pike with both hands, then fell over.

Kunnusta let out a bitter howl, gnashed his teeth, and bolted at the Parthassian sailors with another Haf sailor at his side. He thrust his sword in swift blows, jabbing straight at the Parthassian sailors as his strikes were deflected one after the other. The sounds of clashing steel rang through the room. His blade pierced a sailor's stomach. Another Parthassian sailor landed a kick at Kunnusta's stomach and sent him crashing into a barrel of flour in the corner. The two remaining Haf sailors clashed with the Parthassians, pots and pans and knives rattling throughout the cramped kitchen.

Oyza gripped her blade.

"No," Yars said. "We have to keep going."

Oyza followed reluctantly, her heart pounding and throat tight.

They ran deeper into the boat, passing through a narrow hallway then up a small staircase. They found themselves in a large room. A table ran down the middle. Stacks of maps and scrolls, silver candlesticks, and a small globe sat on top. Paintings hung from the walls, and in the corner sat a small rack holding bottles of alcohol. Large windows lined the wall.

"Looks like a captain's room." Oyza stepped onto a green rug decorated with a pattern of diamonds and crowns.

Yars nodded.

They looked up and noticed the ceiling caving in. Fires burning above must have been weakening the wood.

Oyza walked up to the table and picked up a sheet of paper. She couldn't understand any of it. She sat it back down, then looked up at the door. Her heart sank. "We're trapped here." She peered outside a window.

Fires leaped from sinking boats. Sailors thrashed in the waves. Oyza looked toward the shore and saw the city blanketed in smoke.

"Do you think any ships made it to the beach?" Yars wiped sweat from his brow.

"I don't know." The muscles in her body tensed as she heard footsteps approaching. She turned to face the door. "This is it," she said to Yars.

He raised his cutlass and buckler. Oyza stared into his eyes for a brief moment and leaned in for a kiss. His lips tasted like salt and blood, no trace of his familiar metallic scent.

"Yars..." she began, her eyes turning back toward the window, "if we don't make it, I just want you to know...that first morning we spent together in Shimwood, in our little home, when you were out there cooking breakfast under that big tree—that was the happiest moment of my life. I knew that you were everything I ever wanted, right then and there."

Yars wrapped his arms around her, tears in his eyes.

They heard a crash.

The sound sent a chill through Oyza's spine. "Here she comes." Oyza gritted her teeth.

Yars shook his head. "Let's just jump out of the window. We can swim away."

Oyza stepped forward, sword drawn. "No. No, Yars. We fight. We end this. Both of us—we can take Liviana."

Embers from the ceiling fell onto a chair. Smoke began to swirl. A fire spread from the hull and leaped through a window. Sweat dripped from Oyza's forehead as burning moist air warmed her skin. More holes began to burn in the ceiling as fire ate away at the wood.

This is it. Oyza's heart pounded as she dug her heel into the rug. *Today, we end this.*

CHAPTER 41

Jarus lunged at Sir Yirig in a flurry of sloppy blows with both ends of his broken glaive. The muscles in his arms ached as the hot sun beat down on his neck. The towering knight stumbled and barely dodged the blades jabbing at his neck. He lifted his ax high above his head and swung a bone-cracking blow at Jarus with a grunt. Jarus fell as the huge blade swiped just past his nose.

Jarus caught a glimpse at the battle below. Rangers around him had retaken the wall, but the Empire's men swarmed the steps. Lancers had pushed even farther into the city. He searched in vain for Gaspar. *Have we lost?*

Jarus turned back to Sir Yirig as Ungoverned appeared at his side, glaives drawn and ready. Bodies littered the wall. Jarus coughed and spat, bloody streaks lining his arms.

Sir Yirig wiped blood with his thumb from the gray stubble on his chin. He raised his ax. Jarus and the rangers howled and lunged forward, glaives flying at Sir Yirig in a torrent of slashes and swipes.

Jarus pulled his head back, barely dodging an attack before thrusting forward again, the ends of his blades flying at Sir Yirig like a viper's bites.

"Ha!" Sir Yirig laughed, blocking the assault with his ax. He cleaved the blade at Jarus in an upward direction.

Jarus shrieked as the blade sliced his arm. Blood seeped through his leather jerkin. Distracted, he stumbled as the giant knight advanced, lashing out at him in a frenzy. Lumps formed in his dry throat. *I'm going to die. We're all going to die here. Gods!*

✤❦✤

"Yes, take us closer! As close as you can get!" Teresa shouted. "Look—there." She pointed to the base of the Pearl Spire. Giant chunks had eroded away and fallen off. Underneath, three Parthassian ships blocked the path to the shore. "We can fire there. The tower could fall and land on the ships."

Hjan was translating as best as he could when the Parthassian fleet fired on them. Blasts cracked into their hull as mists of sea salt sprayed into the air. They heard screams from underneath as the floor shook.

The sailors nodded at Hjan and Teresa. They seemed to understand. Teresa helped them turn the cannons. The Parthassians fired again. Streams of water flew into the air as a shot ripped across the deck and sent shrapnel in all directions.

The sailors lit the fuses and covered their ears. Teresa ducked and covered her neck. *Gods, I hope this works.*

Four blasts smashed into the base of the Pearl Spire. Chunks of stone and brick tumbled into the sea. Bitter smoke coiled in the air.

"Again!" Teresa crouched to pick up a heavy cannonball.

The sailors loaded the guns and prepared another round. They covered

THE SPIRIT OF A RISING SUN

their ears and stood back. More blasts slammed into the base of the tower as brick disintegrated and fell into the water.

The Parthassian ships launched more shots. Teresa, Hjan, and the sailors went flying in the air as a blast erupted close to where they stood. Their bodies scraped against the rough wooden deck. Teresa's skin burned as streaks of blood fell down her arms. Flames billowed. The cannons were destroyed. The steering wheel was ripped to shreds.

Teresa crawled to her feet, wiping dust from her hair. Her ears rang. *What happened? What's going on?*

"Look!" Hjan shouted.

The Pearl Spire toppled over. Its base crumbled in a cloud of dust as the tower fell onto the Empire's ships. A deluge of brick and rock collapsed onto their decks. They bent, warped, cracked, started to sink, then suddenly exploded in bright fiery flames as bodies went flying. The explosions were so loud, it nearly knocked Teresa and Hjan to their feet. They cheered.

"Fire on the shore! And take us forward!" She ran back to the steering wheel, but it was gone, engulfed in a blaze.

The base of the Pearl Tower sat just ahead, a smoldering ruin. Strong winds pounded into their sails.

"Brace yourselves!" Teresa yelled. "We're going to crash!"

❀❦❀

Liviana stood on the other side of the room, a wall of flames roaring at her back and Xalos in her hand. The ruby on its hilt glowed. "I finally found you, Oyza."

Oyza gripped her sword, muscles tight.

Yars stood at her side. He stared at Liviana, clutching his sword and shield with slippery fingers.

Liviana took a slow step forward. "I should have killed you when I had the chance. You killed—murdered—my father. My father who groveled at the emperor's feet to save your worthless life."

Oyza held her jaw firm.

A piece of burning wood fell from the ceiling and crashed into a rack of empty glass bottles in the corner, shattering it to pieces.

Oyza took a careful step back as Liviana approached. "We don't have to fight, Liviana. We're all going to die here if we don't run." Oyza's eyes darted to the fire behind Liviana.

Liviana stepped forward again, raising her enormous sword in the air. "Don't have to fight? You still don't it get." Liviana's face twisted in a

300

dismissive smile. "If you don't fight—day after day, after day, you die. It's a constant struggle, never ending...until there is only one left standing."

Oyza squinted, coughing in the thick smoke.

"Will you be left standing? When Hafrir returns to our shores, burning our coasts and pillaging our people—will you be the one left standing?" Liviana continued her advance. Her reflection shone in a brass jug on the table. "And what about you?" Liviana aimed Xalos at Yars. "Will you be left standing?"

Yars stared at her with thin eyes.

"No, *little jewel*, neither of you will be left standing. But I will be. Because you are weak, and I am strong, and only the strong stand at the end of the day." Liviana's eyes glowed a bright red in the red-hot inferno swirling around her.

Oyza stepped back again, glancing over her shoulder for a moment through the windows beside her. She dug her heels into the rug again. *Not now, not anymore, not ever again. I am done running.* She looked down at the blue vines on her chest, then raised her chin. "I rotted in the dungeons for years. I wasted away. But I learned something there. For every person like you in the world, there are a thousand who rise up."

Yars gulped, his face and hands dripping in sweat. He wiped a dribble of blood from his lips, never taking his eyes off of Liviana.

Liviana laughed. She wrapped both hands around Xalos. Her frenzied eyes burned. "We'll see about that. The Ungoverned are dead. Your ships are burning. Let's end this." She lifted her sword and charged straight for Oyza, going for the kill in one massive slash.

Oyza deflected the attack, their swords crashing against each other and ringing through the air.

Liviana shrieked as Xalos scraped against the floor and gashed the rug.

Yars lunged at Liviana, shouting as he jabbed his sword at her throat. Liviana dodged his assault, rebounded, and swung Xalos again in a torrent of rage. The sword slammed into Yars's buckler as it shattered into a hundred splinters. The impact sent him tumbling. He fell and dropped his sword.

Oyza gritted her teeth and flung herself at Liviana, thrusting her sword in a whirlwind. Liviana fell backward. She struck Oyza's sword so hard it nearly flew from her hand as Oyza recoiled and lost her balance.

Yars climbed back to his feet and grabbed his sword. He hopped on the table and lunged at Liviana. Embers fell from the ceiling above his head. Liviana lifted her sword and deflected his attacks one after the other, then made a sweep at his legs. Yars jumped as the sword swept under his feet, sending papers, glasses and candlesticks flying. Liviana swiped again as Yars hopped one more time, landing onto a stack of papers. He slipped, tumbling forward and falling onto the floor.

Liviana shouted, lifting Xalos high above her head and slashing toward Yars. He rolled to one side as the sword smashed into the floor beside him. Liviana lifted her sword a second time and was preparing to strike when she heard Oyza running behind her. She turned and swung at Oyza, hacking in mighty blows.

Oyza ducked, dodging a blow that would have chopped off her head when Liviana kicked, landing a blow on her shoulder and knocking her back. Oyza leaped to her feet as Liviana turned to deflect a blow from Yars. Oyza gnashed her teeth and was moving in for the kill—her blade flying like lightning—when Liviana turned again and hurled Xalos, blocking the attack. Oyza was knocked to one side, and before she caught her balance, Liviana roared with fury and plunged the sword downward.

Oyza ducked as the sword slashed at the skin of her arm, leaving a long stinging streak. She tried to regain her balance but was too slow. With the end of her blade stuck in the cracked floor, Liviana kicked Oyza with all her might.

Oyza tumbled, the wind knocked from her chest. She crashed through a wall as a wooden plank and flaming debris fell onto her body. She frantically tried to push the beam away.

Liviana turned back toward Yars, who had climbed back to his feet and charged at her with his sword.

Oyza struggled to breathe as she panicked. Her vision turned dark as thick burning smoke invaded her lungs. *I can't move! I can't move!* The heavy beam crushed her body. Her sword was just out of reach, lying on the rug. It gleamed in the fires. *Gods!* she thought, stretching out her fingertips toward her blade as the scorching flames soared around her. *Please...*

❀☙❧

Jarus dug in his heel. Sir Yirig grinned, delighted with his all-but-certain kill. The knight moved in, ax raised high above his head, ready to strike. Jarus lost his footing, slamming into a ranger behind him. Jarus's jerkin was soaked in blood and covered in dust. The taste of bitter smoke hung in his mouth. He lifted his shattered blades in both hands and parried Sir Yirig's blows in a whirlwind.

The edge of Sir Yirig's ax sliced into his left arm. Blood spurted. Jarus fell back again.

Sir Yirig smiled, a lust for death in his eyes.

Jarus squinted. *What's...? The Spire?*

All around him, soldiers pointed and shouted.

Sir Yirig turned.

Jarus climbed to his feet, his eyes fixed on the top of the Pearl Tower. It fell over in a cloud of fires and explosions. Jarus felt his heart flutter. *Gods!*

Sir Yirig turned to face the battlefield, then back to Jarus. "Doesn't matter. It's already over."

His arm burned where the ax had struck him.

Suddenly, blasts exploded onto the Parthassian hordes amassed outside the wall. Bodies flailed into the air amid explosions of sand. Screams echoed against the walls as soldiers began to run.

Sir Yirig turned again. He let out a nervous grumble. More blasts rocked into the beach. The lancers and soldiers scrambled toward the palm trees on the hills. Haf boats funneled toward the shore between smoldering Parthassian warships. Sir Yirig lifted his ax and turned back to Jarus. He raised his chin and spat.

Jarus was lifting his blades to defend an attack when a blast landed into the wall right underneath them. The ground shook as he and Sir Yirig fell over. A thick cloud of dust filled the air.

Jarus crawled to his feet, coughing and gripping his arm where the ax had struck. Sir Yirig was preparing to lunge at him again when they heard shouting from the other side of the wall. Jarus thought he recognized a voice.

Teresa and Hjan charged onto the wall with swords, shields, and pistols. A column of Haf sailors followed. Their cries rang across the wall as they clashed with Parthassians.

Teresa! Jarus beamed. His heart leaped.

The smoke settled, and Sir Yirig was gone.

Jarus ran down the stairs, climbing a hill of wreckage and rushing toward his sister. Parthassian lancers fled as Ungoverned knights chased them out.

"Brother!" Teresa threw her arms around Jarus.

They cried and embraced underneath tall palm trees swaying in the smoky wind. Cheers of "Ungoverned! Ungoverned!" and fists soared into the air.

303

Jarus erupted into tears and hugged Hjan. He stopped for a moment, then pulled back, a serious look overtaking his face. "What about Oyza?"

Teresa scrubbed dust from her eyes and looked away. "I don't know. We...we were separated, and I..."

Jarus, Teresa, and Hjan turned toward the sea, leaves rustling in the breeze above them. Distant booms rang across the sands.

🐎🦂

Oyza struggled on the other side of the room, trapped by a burning plank of wood and a heap of debris crushing her body. Her sword lay just beyond reach as she stretched her arm to reach it. *Just a little more...*

She looked up again at Yars, who flailed and stumbled around the scorching room as Liviana vaulted over a fiery beam and swung at him. He tumbled and fell onto the table. Liviana swung again. He rolled to his side as the sword cracked the table in half. A flurry of papers flew into the air.

Yars swiped a silver candlestick and threw it at Liviana.

She dodged. "Not this time, boy," she hissed, charging at him again and slashing at his torso.

Yars lifted his sword to deflect the blows as he slipped, his back to a wall of fire.

A flaming beam fell from the wall and crashed between him and Liviana.

Oyza grunted and pushed with all her might. The beam didn't budge. *Fuck!* Flames leaped near her face. The weight crushed her stomach.

Liviana landed a blow.

Yars went flying toward the windows. He lost his balance, then glanced at Oyza underneath the wood. Before Liviana could reach him, he grabbed the mageware dagger from his belt and threw it at Oyza. "Take this!"

Liviana turned toward Oyza. Yars ran between them, his blade flailing at her. Oyza grabbed the dagger, her sweaty fingers gripping its scorpion handle as tightly as she could. The blade began to glow red.

Yes, yes! She pressed it into the beam. Smoke hissed into the air as it melted the wood. "Come on..."

Liviana tried to smash through Yars and get to Oyza. "Out of my way!" She hacked her sword at Yars in a frenzy.

He parried and dodged, the blade nipping at the skin on his arms and drawing blood.

Gods! Oyza broke the wood in two and sprang to her feet. She picked up her sword in her other hand and ran to Liviana.

Liviana grunted and pulled her sword high. It crashed down on Yars in a sundering blow. He blocked at the last moment but tripped and fell through a wall of fire.

Liviana turned as she heard Oyza running toward her. The room sat at a tilt as the ship sank. Oyza charged at her with her father's sword in one hand and a glowing red dagger in the other. Liviana swung at Oyza, the blow deflected by Oyza's sword. She swung a third time, and then a fourth, the clash of metal ringing. Liviana smirked. She surprised Oyza with a swift jab.

Oyza blocked, but her sword was thrown out of her hand. Liviana moved in for the kill but tripped on the sloping floor and fell into Oyza. They wrestled on the ground. Then Liviana dragged Xalos to Oyza's throat.

Oyza stopped the blade with her glowing dagger. Sparks exploded in the air as their blades clashed. Oyza grunted, pressing her dagger into Liviana's sword as hard as she could.

"Give it up, Oyza!" Liviana snarled through gritted teeth, sweat and blood trickling down her forehead. Hellfire burned in her eyes.

Oyza stared into Liviana's eyes. "You are *not* fit to rule Vaaz. The people will rule themselves." She pulled away in a burst of sparks and jumped to her feet.

Liviana slashed her sword in a fury, screaming and cursing. A fiery beam fell from the ceiling as searing embers erupted into the air. Oyza covered her face, then picked up her sword and charged at Liviana. Liviana lost her balance. She raised Xalos and made a desperate thrust at Oyza. Their blades clanged. Oyza was thrown to the floor. Her sword and dagger went flying. Liviana's blade splintered the wood. She screamed.

"Just like that day in the courtyard, huh?" Oyza said.

Liviana cursed, stumbling to catch her balance. Oyza lifted her leg and tripped Liviana. Liviana tumbled back and fell through a burning window, eyes frantic and hands gripping Xalos. She fell into the sea.

Oyza breathed a sigh of relief. She crawled to Yars, who had just risen to his feet again. They embraced and kissed, flames engulfing the room around them.

"We have to go, now."

Yars grinned, his curls dripping with sweat. "We did it, Oyza. We did it." He hugged her again, burying his face in her hair and rubbing her shoulders with his thumbs.

Oyza looked up into his eyes. *Gods. It's over.* "Let's go."

They made for the stairs.

A shot fired. Yars choked. His eyes opened wide. Blood leaked from his throat. Oyza caught him, falling to her knees.

Alden rolled on his side down the slanting floor and tumbled into the burning room. A shard of wood tore through his body as a pool of blood formed on the ground. Water began to rush into the other side of the room. Alden laughed, his teeth stained with blood.

"You..." Oyza cradled Yars's head in her lap. His face was white. "No. No, Gods, no..."

Alden let out a bitter laugh and spat blood. "You...you took everything from me..." He pulled the dragon figurine from a pocket and rolled it toward his sister.

Tears fell from Oyza's cheek as she searched Yars's lifeless eyes. Her seashell necklace dangled from her neck, shimmering in the light of the fires. She remembered. She took off her necklace and unscrewed the wooden cap. "Yars...take this. Syvre said...she said it could reverse death." Tears poured from her eyes and splashed onto his face. *Gods, no, please no...*

Alden laughed, thick blood spewing onto the floor. "No... Save me, sister... Save me..." He reached into a pocket on his chest and pulled out a small bronze locket and threw it at Oyza. It rattled against the floor and gleamed in the fire.

"Why would I save *you*?" Oyza spat. She didn't pick up the locket.

Alden pushed his hand into his side, trying to stop the blood from pouring out. "Our sister," he began, coughing up more blood, "she lives. Rosina lives. Look, there, two little sons, she has. Look just like you..." He coughed again.

Oyza opened the locket. Inside were two paintings of twin boys that looked just like her and Alden. They had her eyes and her little sister's big smile.

"Save me, Oyza, or you'll never see our sister again... I can take you...take you to Hafrir..." His body slid toward the water. "Help me, sister..."

Oyza clenched her jaw. She had come here in desperation, needing Séna to save her, to come home. He'd imprisoned her. *I thought after all this, he'd change his mind. And now he actually is... And Rosina? She lives? Or is this just another lie?*

A curl of Yars's hair fell onto her nearby hand. She looked at him, the first man she'd ever loved, the first person to love her as herself. Who sacrificed everything for what she wanted—even his own life. *I have everything because of him, all because of him. I wouldn't be here without him.*

And now, she had to choose. Choose between her past and what she realized now was her future. As water swirled around her ankles, Oyza knew what she had to do, though it broke her heart to do it. *Forgive me, sister...but Séna abandoned us. He abandoned us years ago. Mother, Father, his homeland, all of us... I won't let him take this from me too.* "You are *not* my brother. Not anymore. You are a *monster.*"

A beam fell and crashed into a burst of sparks.

Alden coughed again, blood spewing. "Sister..."

Oyza turned away from her brother and poured the blue liquid from the seashell into Yars's mouth. *Please...* She cradled Yars's head in her arms and ruffled his curls in her fingers. *Please...*

Sea water rushed onto the sinking boat as Yars's body began to float. Oyza struggled to keep her balance, knees sliding. The table fell past her, candlesticks and papers swallowed by the water.

Please... Tears dripped from her eyes. *Please...* Oyza prayed to the Gods with every ounce of energy left in her body. Knots formed in her throat.

Yars sank into the abyssal grave, darkness devouring him. Oyza's muscles wouldn't move. Alden groaned a final time as water consumed his body.

"Oyza!" a voice called from behind. A Haf sailor ran into the room.

Oyza watched Yars's body fade into the rising sea. The sailor pulled her from the room. Oyza looked back at Yars one last time. *Gods, please...*

The sailor dragged her away. And the ship sank beneath them.

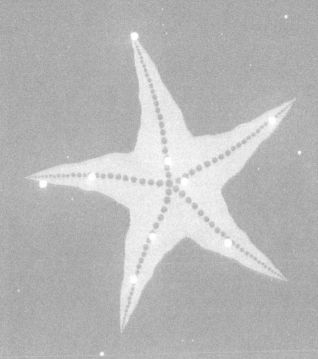

EPILOGUE

"You're sure? This is your last chance." Syvre held the ink-soaked blade with care, trinkets on her bracelet jangling.

Hjan nodded. He was certain he wanted the Frostpetal tattooed on his neck. Teresa had told him what the Frostpetal Starmark meant to Vaazians: medicine, healing, and peace.

"Well hold tight then, dear," Syvre said. Yip yawned.

Hjan squirmed as the blade dug into his skin. Teresa had also told him once his grasp of the Vaazian language was better, he could learn to serve as an apothecary, finding roots and herbs and mixing them into powerful tonics and ointments. Healing was what Hjan needed. It was what everyone needed. He had cut his blonde hair short, hoping to wear the new Starmark with pride. He was a Vaazian now. He was Ungoverned. And he was free.

With his new tattoo, Hjan made his way back into the city. Scaffolding covered the buildings as Oyvassa buzzed with new life. Children played in the streets. Musicians filled the town squares with music. Artists repainted the Temple of the Starfish. Cannons lined the walls and the harbor. Hjan stood before the university, where Teresa had been teaching the Haf sailors how to read, speak, and write in Vaazian. The warm sun crawled across the sky as he filled his lungs with the salty winds of the sea. Thin palm trees bristled in the wind. As he climbed the polished steps up, a voice called out to him from behind.

"Hjan! How have you been?" Jarus smiled and stretched out his arms to hug the former marauder. Lirali stood next to him, a necklace of yellow summer petals dangling over her neck.

"Good, good! I am good," Hjan replied with his thick Haf accent. He turned and showed his new tattoo to Jarus.

"Fantastic! What do you think, Lirali? Looks good, no?" Jarus put his arm around Lirali's shoulder.

"It looks lovely, Hjan," she said, trying to hide her lisp as always. She smiled.

"Hey Hjan, we've been looking for Oyza. Didn't show up to the fields this morning. Teresa hasn't seen her either. Know where she is? Riders came just now, news from the north. Rebellion has broken out in Mélor. Can't wait to tell Oyza. We're preparing a ship to head there as soon as possible. I want to invite her."

Hjan shook his head. "No, no. I no see Oyza." He scratched the blond hairs on his chin. "Wait. Oyza goes to docks. Harbor."

"Right." Jarus patted Hjan on his back. "Take care."

Hjan ascended the steps to the university then froze. *Rebellion? What is…rebellion? I will ask Teresa, first thing.*

❧❦❧

Sir Plinn paced about his cell in the dungeon. He walked up to the window and stared out. The sunlight felt good on his skin. He sighed and sat back down on the bed. *Blacklance is dead. Cerras Edras on the throne.* His mind raced. *The Empire. Liviana. Sir Yirig. Whatever my commander wants…*

He pulled the patch Oyza had given him from his pocket, eyeing the blue vines that crisscrossed it.

He shook his head and plunged it back into his pocket. *I am a knight! A knight of the Parthassian Empire!* He balled his fists and punched into the bed. *I will never join them. I will kill them! I will kill Oyza Serazar! I will watch her bleed in a slow, miserable death!*

He tore chunks of his hair out. Taking a deep breath, he leaned back and gazed out of the window. How long was he going to feel this way? *But what if they're right…? Maybe I should just join them…*

No! What are you thinking? He closed his eyes and shook his head.

There was a knock on his door. Someone opened the lock.

"Voy." His face turned red with embarrassment.

"How are you?" She removed a circle of beads from her head.

Sir Plinn opened his fist. Strands of hair fell out.

Voy gave a pitiful smile. She shook her head and leaned in. "Listen close, Plinn. Things have happened. Things you need to know about. Things that are coming," she whispered.

Sir Plinn stared at her with empty eyes.

"Plinn, what would you do for your freedom?"

Sir Plinn leaned back, puzzled. "Anything. I would do anything to get out of here. I would do anything to kill Oyza." He imagined strangling her, watching her skin turn purple as her eyes burst out of her skull. It made him feel good.

Voy smirked. "Plinn, what do you *want*?"

Sir Plinn's eyebrows knit in concentration. "I want whatever my…commander…" He stopped midway. Tears welled in his eyes.

Voy smirked again. "You have no commander, Plinn."

He choked.

"But there is the emperor. Cerras sits on the throne at Goldfall. He has the backing of the Celesterium and an army of mercenaries. Guns now too.

He raises more armies in Judge's Pass and in Parthas. Tell me Plinn, would you pledge yourself to Cerras? For your freedom? To be a knight again?"

Is this a trick question? What if Liviana lives? I am so sick of being played with! He balled his fist. His throat tightened.

A devilish grin consumed Voy's face. "Plinn, the poor and the weak follow the law against their will and against all their yearnings for freedom. But who writes the law, Plinn?"

Sir Plinn waited for a moment, remembering his first conversation with Liviana. "Whoever has the most swords," he replied through gritted teeth.

"And who has the most swords now, Plinn?"

He lowered his eyes. What other choice did he have? He reached his hand in his pocket and stroked the Ungoverned patch. *No!* He pulled his hand back out.

Voy snapped her fingers. The door creaked open. Gaspar stepped in.

Voy grinned and kissed Gaspar on his cheek. "We found something to offer our new emperor. And you're coming with us. A captured Parthassian knight returned to sweeten the deal. You didn't think I'd leave you here forever, did you?"

Gaspar smiled.

"Deal...what deal?" Tears streamed down Sir Plinn's cheeks.

Voy smirked again. "A deal with Cerras, Plinn. A deal that helps us all."

Plinn gazed up at Gaspar. "But you...what do you get out of this?" His stomach churned. His muscles felt weak. *Whatever...my commander wants...*

Gaspar locked eyes with Voy for a brief moment before turning back to Sir Plinn. "My crown, boy," he said coolly, putting his arms around Voy's shoulders.

☙❧

Oyza sat on the dock bathed in warm sunlight. Her feet dangled over clear water. Its surface sparkled, reflecting the white puffy clouds strolling across a calm sky. A lone gull squawked overhead. She stared at the pictures of her nephews in the locket. Footsteps approached from behind. She tucked it away.

"Oyza," Jarus called out. He walked the length of the dock as Oyza rose to her feet. Jarus greeted her with a hug. "There you are. We've been looking for you. I have news."

"Sorry. I couldn't make it to the fields this morning. Too much on my mind..."

Jarus lowered his eyes. A breeze pulled at his hair. "I'm sorry, Oyza, about Yars. We're all sorry. We loved him. And...I'm sorry about your brother too."

Oyza turned to face the sea. "My brother... I still can't believe what he did."

"I can," Jarus said. "Your brother died a long time ago, Oyza. When he joined the other side."

"I know. I just thought there might still be some good in him somewhere."

"I'm sorry, Oyza."

"Thanks, Jarus," she said. "I guess...it's easy to see in some people what you want to see. To think you can change them. But some people are truly lost..."

Jarus raised his chin a little, eyes on the blue sky. "But for everyone like your brother, there is someone genuinely good—someone like Yars. I miss him dearly."

Oyza felt a piercing in her chest. "I miss him too. I'll always miss him." She wanted to break down and cry, to wrap her arms Yars one last time, to feel again what she felt that night after the Gathering, suspended in a moonbeam with him forever and ever until every last star in the universe burned out. Sometimes, she thought she could hear him, his voice whispering when the waves crashed on the sand and the salty mists cooled her cheeks. She clutched at the seashell necklace around her neck. "But I know he died for a higher cause."

Waves lapped onto the barnacle-covered beams below.

"Some of us, Oyza, make the greatest sacrifice. But we don't do it in vain. Yars gave everything so we might know a better world. But he's here with us now. He's with us always. And we have to keep going. We have to keep going every day, every night, to save our children and our children's children and their children after that. And it is the only way the ghosts of those before us can rest."

His eyes traced the drifting clouds. He placed his hand on Oyza's shoulder. "Well, I have some good news, at least. A rider arrived from Mélor. Says rebellion has broken out in the Stonewoods. Ungoverned are there. And they've requested aid. I've told Lirali to stay behind, but I'm going. Teresa wants to stay here and keep working to restore the university. Oyza, I'd really like it if you came. The rangers trust you. They believe in you. We're already preparing ships. Remember what I said about constant change, constant growth?"

Oyza peered at the sea, thinking about the patch of blue vines on her chest. She took a slow breath, lungs swelling with salty air. She lowered her eyes to her hands, remembering the way she used to stare at them in the dungeons of Goldfall. *Someday, these hands will set us all free.* She looked up again at the ocean, the clouds, the sky. The horizon tugged at her.

"Let's go, Jarus." She placed her hand on the hilt of her sword. "The revolution won't win itself, will it?"

About the Author

Kyle Galindez lives in Santa Cruz, California, where he is pursuing a PhD at the University of California, Santa Cruz. He enjoys reading and writing epic fantasy. On the rare days and nights he's not writing his dissertation or the next book in his series, he's exploring beaches, playing video games (especially RPGs), or stargazing.

Follow him online:

Twitter @KR_galindez
Instagram @kr_galindez
KRGalindez.com

Authors 4 Authors Publishing

A publishing company for authors, run by authors, blending the best of traditional and independent publishing

We specialize in escapist fiction: science fiction, fantasy, paranormal, romance, and historical fiction. Get lost in another time or another world!

Check out our collection at https://books2read.com/rl/a4a or visit Authors4AuthorsPublishing.com/books

For updates, scan the QR code or visit our website to join our semi-monthly newsletter!

Want more epic fantasy? We recommend:

Exile
by Melion Traverse

After killing a paladin in revenge for her family, Squire Bryn is cast out by order of the god Avgorath himself. Now she seeks atonement with the father of the dead paladin. But machinations far greater than a disgraced squire are at play. Unicorn riders—believed to be only legend—ride through the land. A young sorcerer needs help in finding his father, and a mystery brews that could hold the fate of two worlds.

books2read.com/exile

CPSIA information can be obtained
at www.ICGtesting.com
Printed in the USA
FSHW010505020921
84458FS